Debo Kotun

ÀBÍKÚ

DEBO KOTUN

ÀBÍKÚ

A Novel

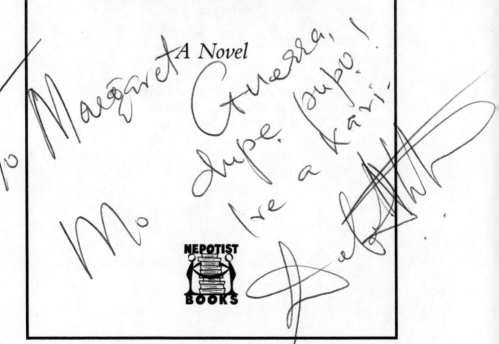

NEPOTIST
BOOKS

Published by
NEPOTIST BOOKS
P.O. BOX 94759
Pasadena, California 91109-9475
(626) 294-0090, (626) 294-0626 Fax
Copyright ©1998 by Debo Kotun

Publisher's Cataloging-in-Publication

Kotun, Debo, 1948-
    Abiku : a novel / Debo Kotun. -- 2nd ed.
    p. cm.
    LCCN: 98-68288
    ISBN: 0-9668772-8-4

    1. Yoruba (African people)--Nigeria--Fiction.
2. Nigeria--Fiction. 3. Mythology, Yoruba--
Fiction. 4. Dictatorship--Nigeria--Fiction.
I. Title

PS3561.O874A25 1999   813'.54
                        QBI99-1650

Printed in the United States of America

To the memory of:

Ken Saro-Wiwa
'What sort of nation is this?'
Doowo Inua!
(Goodbye. We shall meet again.)

and
Taslim Ishola Kotun
Sun re o

ÀBÍKÚ:

meaning A child that was born to die,
is a work of fiction. But …

In 1995 the military government of Nigeria under the leadership of General Sani Abacha hanged the world-renowned writer Ken Saro-Wiwa, along with eight other MOSOP (Movement for the Survival of Ogoni People) officials, in what the Nobel Laureate, Wole Soyinka, described as "a travesty of justice." Chinua Achebe, another notable Nigerian-born novelist and essayist, went a step further by declaring that "Ken Saro-Wiwa was not killed on the date announced by Sani Abacha's regime, but on June 23, 1993, the day the nation's democratic elections were annulled."

These were punctuation marks in a chapter in the history of a continent awash in its own blood.

Abiku is a work of fiction. But …

Somalia, Rwanda, Burundi, Ethiopia, Eritrea, Liberia, Angola, Zaire, Uganda, Biafra, Sudan, Egypt, Libya, Algeria, Tunisia, Ghana, Sierra Leone, Morocco and yes, Nigeria are real—all bloodied, "anesthetized, comatosed, indeed idiotized" (in the words of Wole Soyinka) by the ubiquitous power-chasing, money-idolizing "proven idiots" in their olive-colored uniforms.

Traditional rulers, kings, *obis* and sultans wholesale their subjects into slavery. Military dictators have gone one giant step better—they have embarked on a genocidal destruction of the continent. But a child that promises his mother a sleepless night will not blink an eye either.

Abiku is a work of fiction. But ...

The words on the pages of any volume that purport to represent the imagination of the author are real. Fiction is reality sublimated.

Abiku is a work of fiction. But...

The twenty-five million Yoruba-speaking people of Nigeria and Benin, together with their countless descendants in Brazil, the Caribbean, and the United States, envision the universe as consisting of two dissimilar yet inseparable spheres—the perceptible, corporeal world of the Living, and the shrouded, spiritual kingdom of the ancestors, gods, and spirits. *Abikus* inhabit the other sphere; they depend on the survival of humans in our world. It is therefore imperative for them to journey to the world of the Living to share their wisdom with humans, but they must return to the land of their nativity before the age of two. Over the millennia, however, the Yorubas have developed means to prevent most *Abiku* children from dying...

Abiku is a work of fiction filled with imaginary persons and places and no reference to any individual or group that was, or is, part of Abeokuta, Lagos, or the Nigerian army is intended. But...

Maps of Africa and Nigeria

PROLOGUE

Predawn mist enveloped the black rock that loomed over the village of Arinota. The fading choir of nocturnal animals announced their readiness to call it a night. Fifteen-year-old Segun Sakara was kicked awake by his father, a middle-aged man with the probing eyes of a fox. "Are you going to spend the rest of your life sleeping like a donkey?" he demanded in his native Yoruba.

"N—no, Papa," Sakara stuttered. Cuddled up in a fetal position on the raffia mat on the floor, he felt a draft enveloping his body, making him shiver with cold and terror.

"Get up! Slumbering nonentities never glimpse the brilliance of morning sun."

Sakara rose, and was up and about, a good two hours before other children his age. He wept as he had done several times in the past, lamenting the distance between him and his father. By dawn, he had fed the ten hens and four cocks, fetched water from the stream, chopped wood, prepared a breakfast of boiled yams and palm oil for himself and his father, and was ready to tend his family's cocoa farm right after breakfast.

"Do not leave the farm. I'm going hunting." His father swallowed a ball of yam.

Sakara shut his eyes, lips trembling.

"What is it?"

"Th—the—the sch—school—"

"Stop stuttering, you cross-eyed yellowbelly, I will let you know of my decision tonight." His father finished his meal and left the hut, an old *danegun* hanging from a rope over his shoulder.

Sakara went to the farm, knelt in front of the graves of his mother and twin sister, both of whom had died minutes after he was born. He shut his eyes and pretended that his mother was there, sitting on the grave, her face radiating like the moon: the picture he had created in his mind. He stayed there for the better part of the morning.

Suddenly, there was stirring behind the trees. Then two boys of the same age appeared.

"Has your mother given her permission?"

Ayo Crowder's words lanced Sakara's heart. "Leave me alone." His voice lacked conviction. Sakara envied the chubby and rascally Crowder mostly because of the closeness between the boy and his father.

"Is he coming with us?" Ola Ademola, the boy wonder that every adult in the village believed to be the brightest child ever born, was tall and skinny. Sakara harbored an open jealousy toward Ademola.

"I don't think so, he's not brave enough to ask for permission from his wicked father." Crowder rounded a cocoa tree filled with ripe fruit.

"This is an opportunity of a lifetime, don't throw it away. You must go with us. Education is the path out of this village," Ademola said.

"My—father say I—" Sakara began in English.

"Stop stuttering, and you shouldn't listen to that wicked old man all the time." Crowder jumped to grab a fruit from the tree.

"Don't do that. My father knows how many pods are up there." He completed a sentence without stuttering.

"Yeah, right!" Crowder broke the pod with a stone the

size of his fist. "Your father is the village fool. He thinks he knows everything, doesn't he?" Crowder taunted.

"Leave him alone," Ademola said.

"But it's true," Crowder snapped.

"Not!" Sakara whimpered, knowing Crowder said what everyone in the village believed.

"I bet your father doesn't know you are here visiting your mother's grave at this moment!"

"So?"

"Why don't you come to the park with us then? Everyone but your father will be there. And he won't know."

"Don't force him," Ademola said to Crowder.

"After all, the whole village is celebrating our achievements. It will be the height of ungratefulness." Crowder shook his head in mock regret. "You were right, this is a waste of time. Let's go." The two boys left.

Sakara waited for a few minutes before proceeding along the footpath to follow them at a safe distance.

The three boys had gained admission to a high school located in Abeokuta, on the other side of the hills which surrounded Arinota; Mayfield was one of the most reputable schools in the country. Founded by a visionary yet pragmatic educator, the school had gained towering academic prestige by the time the boys applied for admission in 1962 at the age of fourteen.

Sakara, Ademola, and Crowder represented the highest hope of the elders of Arinota: to produce a university graduate from among the sons-of-the-soil. It now looked attainable. Sending not one but three boys from the village to a high school was a giant stride on the right path and a source of pride to the people of Arinota.

Today was the day before the boys' departure, and Sakara was grateful to his two friends for forcing him to come along. He was enthralled by the air of festivity that permeated the entire village. Young girls swept the housefronts of

every dwelling, mostly mud huts, while their male counter-
parts carried neck-breaking loads of foodstuffs from the
farms to the village square. The air was thick with the smell
and sound of cooking as the women chopped, cut, boiled,
pounded, fried, stewed, and baked all types of mouth-water-
ing dishes. There were huge pots of *fufu*, *moinmoin*, pounded
yam, steamed rice, *eba*, peppered corn, stewed and fried fish,
and roasted goat meat. The men sat under the shade of *akee*
trees that hedged a nearby triangular playground, drinking
palm-wine, playing checkers, and swapping village gossip at
the top of their voices.

Shortly before the sun got red in the face and surrendered to the darkness of the night, the playground was lined
on all sides by crowds of people, all yelping and gazing,
shouting and pointing in different directions, their faces
creased with happiness and pride. Suddenly, the hot air
darkened with a cloud of red dust and the sounds of ceremonial drums vibrated as a throng of gyrating, jubilant, half-
naked, muscular young men, holding long thin branches in
their hands, burst into view. With the branches, they lashed
each others' torsos savagely. The crowd swelled as a masquerader came into view, rocking back and forth as he approached the center of the triangle.

The upper portion of the masker's frame was shrouded
in a box-shaped headdress with insets of brocaded textile
which covered the masquerader's head on three sides. The
face was concealed by a piece of indigo-dyed netting material framed on the sides by cowrie shells. The body was covered by a layer of indigo-dyed cloth of homespun cotton
beneath another panel of blue velvet and gold brocade. The
masker, whose last public appearance had been at the coronation ceremony of the king of Arinota half a century
before, whirled at the heightened pitch of the drums. The
multiple layers of cloth spread out in all directions, revealing
more colorful layers beneath. He stopped and bowed in salu-

tation, first to his left where the village elders sat, then to his right where stood the three boys whose common achievement was the source of the festivity.

The pitch of the drums changed suddenly, the human barricade parted, and Sakara's father charged in. He grabbed his son's arm and commenced to pull him away. The crowd gasped. The drumming stopped. Nobody moved.

"Lazy bastard, you dare to disobey my order!"

Sakara felt as though a jagged shard of ice pierced his heart when he looked into his father's cold stare. His fear metamorphosed into embarrassment which then lodged in his pulsating heart and turned to hatred. He wished the gods would open up the red earth to swallow him. He suppressed his fright and followed his father away from the village square to the family farm, just as the black shadow of the jungle swallowed the sun.

Upon entering the round mud hut, Sakara's father lit an *atupa*, a clay bowl with a strip of cloth dipped in palm oil. The yellow flame of the lamp nibbled at the darkness creating jagged shadows on the wall. "Sit down!" The voice sounded as though the spirit of the masquerader lurked nearby.

Sakara obeyed, squatting down on a straw mat.

His father got on his knees and said, "All that nonsensical commotion just because you and those two rascals gained admission to a secondary school, eh?" He didn't wait for an answer. "The sheep stays in the household of the man who feeds it but does it know his intentions?"

"No," Sakara whimpered and turned away so as not to see his father's petrifying gaze.

"Our people's foresight is clouded with laziness. That's why they are so backward. Education has its place, so does our traditional way of life. Both of which are means to a bigger end. Since the death of your mother minutes after you came into this world, with my aid you were wrenched from the claws of death, unlike other unprotected children who are born to die. I never tired in my obligation. My gift to you is making sure you don't become like most of our people, lazy and helpless as toads in a cage. The world belongs to you, but you can't own it with self-adulation by celebrating small achievement." He took a deep breath. "Fire kills water and *Sango* rides fire like a horse! Do you know what that means, eh?"

"No, sir."

"Power! And the determination to use it. Soon, the country will be in the grip of those who are not afraid to use brute force. The gun will gain its old power and vanquish the pen again. Learn hard but keep your knowledge to yourself. Don't be like the rest of the people who are as noisy and plentiful as the rain. Be like the coconut which stores its nutrient within a hard shell. Learn to protect yourself against everybody. The world is full of sycophants. Don't be one of them. If you are wronged by anyone, don't get angry, get even. Remember, one does not get so red in the eyes that one can light a cigarette with the fire!" He opened a clay pot from which he extracted an old wire ring, grabbed his son's right hand, and adorned the middle finger with it. He then got to his feet and commenced to leave the hut. At the door he glanced back and said, "You have my permission to go to school, but don't come back a failure. The world is tired of failures with mouths full of excuses." He exited and was swallowed by the famished darkness.

Sakara was barely an average pupil in his first year at Mayfield. No matter how hard he tried, he could not compete with the other two boys from his village. He envied Ademola, who seemed to succeed at every task with astounding effortlessness. Dormitory rumor had it that he was imbued with supernatural intelligence. Or, at the very least, his success emanated from a limitless supply of *juju* from his *Sango*-worshipping father.

Sakara liked and admired the other pupil from Arinota. Ayo Crowder had everything. First, Crowder was the only son of one of the most revered men in Arinota. Canon Crowder had been the first man from the village to shake hands in public with two mustachioed, jungle-helmeted, sweat-drenched white men who had come to represent the Queen of England at the opening of the first church in Arinota, long before Sakara was born. It was rumored that Canon Crowder's grandfather was a repatriated slave from America. The canon had the audacity to implore the white men to bring the biblical words of enlightenment from across the big river to a superstitious people who hitherto believed in the power of the dark. Canon Crowder never tired in reminding his fellow villagers of his accomplishments. He was well-liked for his joviality, respected for his home-grown intellect, and admired for his free spirit. His only son was just like him.

Crowder was a practical joker. He was generous to a fault with the assortment of canned food which filled his provision cupboard. Ademola, on the other hand, earned his popularity through academic excellence and sports. And he was shy and reserved.

It was only natural that Sakara did his best to befriend the duo from his village. Crowder was more receptive than Ademola, who seemed only to tolerate Sakara.

Nearing the end of the year, it was Crowder who Sakara approached with what seemed a simple problem.

"I barely pass last term exam, and I am very worry about the upcoming finals next week. If I don't get fifty percent I will not be promoted to form two," Sakara said in fractured English.

"It's not difficult to see why you didn't do well. Your

grammar is terrible." Crowder poked at him.

"I am weak in English language and literature. If I can manage to pass those two then I will be promoted. Can you help me?" he begged in Yoruba, his embarrassment cresting.

"I don't see how I can. But maybe you should do what Ola does." Crowder sat on the grassy part of the football field. He asked Sakara to sit next to him. The noise of other students playing soccer filled the air as they argued over a penalty kick.

"What does he do?" Sakara's voice was barely audible.

"You don't know? And speak a little louder, nobody can hear us," Crowder said with magnified importance.

"Know what?"

"Isn't your father a *babalawo* like Ademola's father?"

"He is, but—"

A white soccer ball rolled to where Sakara sat. He got on his feet and kicked it back to the center of the field.

"Didn't he give you any charm before you left Arinota?"

"He—he d—did—" Sakara stuttered.

There was applause as one of the players kicked the ball into the net.

"Why haven't you used it?" Crowder enquired.

"How?"

"Come on! What is it?"

"A ring."

"That's what Ademola has." Crowder's voice was conspiratorial. "He uses his. Please, don't tell anybody this because I use it too. You must do the following: Pick any subject you wish—in your case, it should be English language and literature. I know for a fact the tests for the two subjects are taking place on the same day. From now on, do not study. The night before the exam, put all the textbooks and notes under your pillow on top of the ring. You will wake up the next morning bursting with knowledge. Don't get too excited. Bring the ring to the hall with you. As soon as you receive the exam sheet, place it over the ring and forget about it. Don't be the first to leave the room, otherwise the proctor will be suspicious. Hand in your blank answer sheet and you will be pleasantly surprised. You can use it only once, though. Trust me, it's magic," Crowder said with the innocence and spontaneity of a young preacher.

Sakara believed his friend and did as he was told. While he waited for the result, he imagined how happy and proud his father would be. He prayed that his success would soften his father's heart, endearing him to the old man. He showed his appreciation to Crowder by running errands for him, his anxiety elevating daily.

When the results were finally announced, he got zero in both subjects, missing the aggregate passing mark by five points. Ademola was at the top of his class, scoring one hundred percent in all subjects. The principal gave him a double promotion to form three. Crowder passed, going on to form two. Sakara had to stay behind to repeat form one. Outraged, he confronted Crowder, "Why?"

"It's nobody's fault that you were so gullible. It was a joke!" Crowder laughed at him.

He believed that Crowder had deliberately misled him. He suspected that Ademola also participated in the malicious deception. "I don't find it funny at all. You've ruined my life." It was a lesson he never forgot. A mistake he would never repeat. A transgression he never forgave. But most importantly, it was a debt he would collect. A head for an eye!

⤳

Sakara went home for the end-of-year holiday with apprehension, knowing full well his father would not spare the cane. Approaching his father's hut, he wrapped his arms around his body, a futile attempt to fight off the cold and the encroaching darkness. It was a moonless damp night and the sound of crickets and other night creatures heightened his fear of the dark. Just as he was about to knock on the door, he heard footsteps and held his breath, crouching, realizing they were not his father's but lighter and faster, more hurried. He dashed around the hut, flattened himself against the mud wall, eyes shut as the footsteps became louder. The moonless night gave cover as he crept into the space between the wall of the hut and his father's *ibeji* shrine, made of ten pairs of carved human figures, representing the deaths of twins over several generations.

Then he heard voices coming from the hut. One belonged to his father and the other was that of a woman. He peered through a hole in the wall and saw his father squatted on a raffia mat, facing the newcomer, a woman, who looked ghoulish in the dimly lit hut.

"… Your son came back from school today with his report card. The charm you gave him helped a lot," the woman said in a hushed voice.

"Did you ever doubt it would work?"

"Oh, no, please, forgive me if I gave that impression."

Sakara froze.

The woman facing his father was the one who had always acted in public as though his father was the reincarnation of abomination. "What was she doing with him, alone?" he thought as his confused mind raced around like a rabid dog furiously chasing its own tail.

The answer hit him like a rock falling from the sky, infusing his essence with glacial hatred. He swore absolute revenge.

⌢

BOOK ONE

1

LAGOS

August, 1985—Twenty-two years later:

Lagos—LAH gus—a word coined by Portuguese explorers, the first Europeans to arrive in the area in the late 1400s, was a leading slave market until the mid-1800s, before it became a British protectorate in 1851 and a crown colony in 1862. It became the capital of Nigeria in 1914.

For a moment the afternoon promised a day of vision with the sky looking as though it had been prepared for a wedding. It wore a blue suit perfect for a gentleman with a white carnation, in this case the gathering cloud on high, on its lapel. The golden sun blazed.

Major Segun Sakara sat to the right of his driver in the back seat of a black Peugeot 505 sedan. As the car neared the end of the bridge which connected the island of Lagos to the rest of the most populous black nation in the world, Sakara turned to the driver. "You told Lieutenant Achibong to expect us, didn't you?"

The driver nodded. "I did, sir."

Sakara heard a din and turned back to the windshield. There was rumbling, the sound of a tin drum rolling on a bed of pebbles. A lone bright thread lacerated the sky and its

3

head split to become a mouth with the jagged teeth of a silver flying crocodile. It roared as it crashed through the sky. Then it started to drizzle. Rain drops splattered the hood of the car. It rained harder, each drop the size of a coffee bean, faster. It turned torrential. The sun yawned; its wind lent force to the thunder crackling across the sky. The traffic slowed to a crawl. Sakara rubbed his temples as he felt a cyclone of irritation throbbing inside his head. His mind became filled with riddles as an inner voice said to him, "The battle between the scorching sun and the thirst-quenching rain has erupted. A lioness is giving birth. But why now?" demanded the voice before it lapsed into silence.

Sakara took a deep breath and rolled down the window. The dank, rancid stench of swamp mud mixed with rotten fish assaulted his nose. Then the car was invaded by the foul odor of chemicals that failed to neutralize the smell of tons of human waste dumped nightly into the lagoon. He quickly rolled the window back up. His nose twitched as though he was about to let out a copious sneeze. He didn't, however, though the sensation remained. Furrows of annoyance creased his forehead as he said to the driver, "One does not ask, 'Do you see something?' when an elephant charges by." Then becoming silent for a while, he focused on the task ahead. There was fury, not pity, in his eyes. He took another deep breath as the rain ceased and the car surged forward, gathering speed.

The driver turned off the main road to a side street and stopped in front of a school building. As Sakara turned sideways, he looked as though he was inspecting the tip of his nose. He wasn't. His crossed eyes were gawking at the street and its pockets of potholes. Outside, a man stood astride an open gutter, urinating, his male organ dangling obscenely in his hand, the steaming liquid mixed with the earth and emitting a putrid smell into the air. Barefooted young girls in sun–bleached clothes balanced trays loaded with guavas and peeled oranges on their heads, their necks struggling for balance, their smiles exposing rows of pearly teeth. Sweating black faces of the men were set in anguish and frustration, speaking of hunger and sleepless nights of battle with the ever-present, malaria-infected mosquitoes.

Sakara looked away, but his view was blocked by equally depressing rows of houses with broken windows, and doors with multiple locks which failed to protect them from armed robbers. The overwhelming poverty contrasted with the palatial homes of the rich and infamous government contractors.

The city of Lagos, once a happy and prosperous place, had lost its dignity. Its proud people had been turned into street mendicants by institutionalized laziness and official corruption. Sakara felt anger flaring in him as though an ember had been fanned. But he calmed himself, remembering his father's favorite words, "One does not get so red in the eye with anger that one is able to light a cigarette with it." He sighed his resignation.

Two men emerged from the house next to the school. They looked like soldiers, despite their apparent effort to disguise themselves as civilians. They sprinted toward the Peugeot, one holding a package the size of a shoe box under his arm. The one with the package tapped the window as though afraid to offend the man inside.

Sakara had grown into a man who elicited fear from most people; they usually would look away on meeting him. The thirty-seven-year-old Sakara looked much different from his fellow Nigerians, or anybody else for that matter. His five-foot-eleven muscular physique looked as though it had been carved out of the black rocks surrounding his village of Arinota. But his most peculiar feature—a small head, out of proportion to his thick neck and broad shoulders, a nose that looked like a pair of water hoses, and the two hypnotic crossed eyes gave him the appearance of a graceful but

5

deadly black mamba.

The two soldiers stepped backward and became rigid when the back window rolled down. They saluted in unison.

"Is the package ready?" Sakara asked without preamble.

"Yes, sir!"

"When is it timed to detonate?"

"1400 hours, sir."

Sakara looked at his watch, nodded, and said, "Good. You know the drill. Let's go!"

The soldier handed the package to him and snapped a salute as Sakara rolled up the window, dismissing them with a wave of his hand. He watched as they ran to a black minivan parked a few yards across the street.

"Follow them," Sakara ordered his driver, who engaged gear and drove off toward the Government Reservation Area in Ikeja, a suburb of Lagos.

↬

A day-old boy began to cry as the strong hand of the diviner caressed his wrinkled face. The baby's shrill voice deafened the silence inside the cave as four full-grown fetuses, their umbilical cords held firmly in their tiny hands, hurried away, levitating toward the sky. A glacial draft drifted over the baby's body as the diviner incised his face with a razor blade. The baby shivered with terror.

Then a naked boy stood on an oil drum, arms raised in the air, begging the gods to bring down the sky and break the necks of all his enemies. The sky descended in fury and broke the necks of every resident of the town, including that of the boy. The boy's identity remained unknown.

Dr. Ola Ademola woke from his sleep with a frown. The dream had wafted through his mind, churning itself like a fugue as it had done several times in the past: Same subject, different variations. He opened his eyes and lay on his back as the door to his unconscious clamped shut. He tried in vain to recall the dream, to glean its meaning, to decipher the message. None came. "If only I can recall it when awake, I will be forewarned, prepared," he thought just before a familiar sound pierced the darkness of predawn:

Allahahu Akbar. Allahahu Akbar. Ashhadu—

"It's time to pray," his mother said from the other side of his bedroom door, drowning out the voice of the muezzin of a nearby mosque. He got out of bed, stripped off his pajamas and headed to the bathroom. "I will come out shortly, mother," he said in Yoruba.

"Yes, *oko mi.*" She called him *husband,* a Yoruba term of endearment reserved for loved ones. "Your brother and I will be in the parlor."

He shaved, took a shower, rubbed a piece of alum crystal on his face and armpits, and emerged dressed in white cotton brocade dashiki and trousers. He was slim, looking much younger than thirty-seven; a good-looking physician who, on several occasions had been told that but for the two fading scars on each side of his oval face, he looked like Sidney Poitier. On each occasion he had felt honored to be compared to someone he also admired. But it was Ademola's manner which marked him most. Regardless of where he was or what he was doing, he conveyed a sense of self-control, offset by his accessibility. The patients and staff at the hospital in Ikeja liked and respected him.

Ademola found Tunde, his younger brother, seated on a goat skin a few feet in front of his mother in the parlor. He bowed in greeting to his mother, who responded with a smile, then to Tunde, who prostrated himself first, got up and embraced him. Ademola commenced to lead the prayer. Midway into his Quranic recitation, the rhythmical voice of *bata,* the drum of choice used by the worshippers of *Sango,* the Yoruba god of thunder, floated into the parlor through

7

the window:

Ko-nkolo-nko-ko-nko-lo. Kolo-nko-kon-ko-lo...

The power of the drum abated and Ademola concluded the prayer just as the drumming stopped, and was replaced by a barrage of chanting:

"*Sango, Oba Koso.* I wish you well, o-o-o.
I hope you awakened happily o-o-o-o.
My lord, save me from trouble o-o-o-o.
Did you awaken happily?
You have fire in your mouth,
Fire in your eyes,
And scorch the metal rooftops—"

The voice belonged to his father who, upon arrival the previous night from Arinota, a farming village sandwiched between two historically warring townships of Abeokuta and Ijebu, had propped a makeshift shrine against the lone palm tree in the middle of Ademola's backyard.

The chanting changed pitch and became throaty and solemn:

"—*Sango* is as tough as a dried yam.
When he enters the forest,
He strikes with his thunderbolts.
He strikes a tree and shatters it.
He plunges a hot iron into the eyes of
Mischievous children—"

The chanting infused Ademola's prayer, distracting him. He turned round to face his mother, who said patiently, "One can not serve two masters equally, my son. The choice of God is simple. There is only One. Your father has chosen *Sango.* I chose Allah. It is with mutual respect and suspicion that we coexist."

"*Sango* is not God," Ademola said simply.

"But many of our people worship *it* nonetheless," she sighed. "There's no ladder one can climb to heaven in the morning and descend back to earth in the evening to correct worldly mistakes. We are granted only one chance to do the right thing in this life."

Ademola nodded: "With such wisdom, why hasn't she converted my father after so many years?" he thought.

As though reading his mind, she said, "Your father was much older than me when we married. He was already set in his ways. Besides, it wasn't a woman's place." Then, without raising her head, she untied the top of her beige tie-dyed cotton wrapper, extracted a long strip of black cotton fabric from her midriff, re-tied the wrapper, and extricated several currency notes from the fabric. She separated the money into three piles on the floor in front of her. And in a silky voice she said, "This one is the money you sent me for your brother's school fee. On Monday, I will escort him to register at your old school so that he can continue with his education. We pray to Allah for his success, and hope that he follows in your footsteps. This one—" She pointed to the second pile and took a deep breath. "This is your last contribution for the construction of the infirmary in our village. Of all the sons and daughters of Arinota, you have been the most generous. You made your father and me proud indeed, and I thank you from the depth of my soul. The clinic will be of great service to our people, especially pregnant women who must travel long distances to Abeokuta for basic medical attention."

"It is my duty, mother. Besides, you know how I feel about the infirmary. And I hope to come and serve there as soon as it is completed."

"God willing." She closed her eyes, and Ademola was touched by the depth of his mother's emotions. His love for her overwhelmed him as he remembered that she had suffered the deaths of six of her eight children before they were two years old. All were Abikus, spirit-children from the domain of the Unborn, whose survival in the sphere of their nativity depended on the continued existence of humans in the world of the Living. Upon arrival here as newborns, Abiku children were endowed with distinguishing characteristics—superior intelligence, captivating beauty, specific purpose, and the ability to will their own deaths without any explicable cause. Some, like Ademola and his brother, were forced against their will to linger in this world by *babalawos*, native diviners, who scarred the flesh of the children with razor incisions, and performed sacrificial rituals. Their fates remained enigmatic since half of their beings were always in the spirit world, always ready to return wholly and join their companions in the land of happiness and ecstasy.

Ademola snapped back to the present but remained silent, giving his mother time to regain her composure.

She did. "This last pile, a generous amount, is a bit worrisome. If I had done as you suggested, Arinota would have become a ghost town as we speak. Most of the people would have come here to express their appreciation. And your household would have become as tumultuous as a village marketplace."

"But it's only a token gift for a few surviving Abiku children like my brother and me."

"Every household in Arinota has had some experience with an Abiku child. Most died as expected, but were never forgotten by their mothers. Your generous offer will touch the heart of every citizen, but there are a few who will not appreciate your offer. They have become very whimsical; it is difficult to know how they would receive the gift."

"What is your wish then?"

"Leave the matter in my hands as you've always done. Upon my return to the village, I will offer the gift in keeping with our tradition. Timing is everything." She smiled, exposing a glistening set of white teeth, and Ademola felt as though the parlor had brightened.

"As always, you're right." He got up.

"How is Eniola? I like her. It's time someone else called you husband." There was delight in her eyes.

"She'll be here soon. I like her too. And I intend to ask her to marry me. She is a fine woman, isn't she?"

"You chose right, my son. But is it true you like her because she reminds you of me in my younger years?" She teased him with affection.

"Who told you that?" He hid a small smile.

Indeed, Eniola reminded many people of Ademola's mother in both appearance and character. Both women's skin had the velvety smoothness of predawn blackness. And their essence was laden with suppressed energy. But for the tribal marks on Eniola's high-cheeked face, identifying her as a native of Abeokuta, the more prosperous town west of Arinota, the two women could have been sisters.

"Don't wait too long. Time runs faster than a cheetah, my son."

"Don't you always say timing is everything?" Ademola smiled before exiting the house to join his father under the palm tree within the high brick walls of his bungalow.

Ademola's mother waited for him to shut the door. She turned to her younger son. "I wish to pray alone."

Tunde bowed and left the parlor.

She looked around the room to make sure she was alone. Satisfied, she untied her wrapper again and pulled out the long strip of black cotton fabric from which she extracted a wooden charm, twice the size of a matchbox, the shape of a double-headed axe, symbol of *Sango*. She got on her knees and bent forward, her head almost touching the floor.

She pressed the charm to her chest, between her breasts, close to her heart, and touched the floor with her forehead eight times, once for each of her children. She thanked the god of thunder for having spared two of the eight, especially Ola. As she had done for many years, she prayed and begged *Sango* to help keep her secret.

It had been forty years since it happened, but the fruit remained forever: She had been young, beautiful, and ignorant of the complex world she lived in. She had gone to fetch water from the stream. Halfway back to her father's farm in the forest, she heard a strange sound. A chill ran down her spine, causing her to stiffen, as her eyes darted toward a monstrous *iroko* tree.

"Who goes there!" The voice sounded nasal. Then it changed, becoming the throaty voice of an *egungun*, a masquerader. "Glimpse the face of the spirit and dry up like the spittle in the hot desert sand."

She opened her mouth to scream but her voice failed to respond. Her knees started to shake before the rest of her body. The clay pot on her head fell and broke into pieces, splashing the footpath with water, muddying it. She heard the ruffled sound of feet on dried leaves and what looked like the phantom of a jungle stalker pierced through the morning mist, a huge double-headed axe held above its head. "Drop your wrapper," ordered the phantom, wearing the mask of a vulture through which she saw its cunning eyes.

She untied her wrapper, revealing skin that glistened like polished ebony. But for a string of red coral beads adorning her slim waist she was naked from the navel down. The masker dropped the axe, and with a gentleness which betrayed his aggression, he pulled her to the wet ground and commenced to caress her. His hands were clever, knowing. So was his body as he took her, deflowering her, amidst the softness of the morning mist, on the ground muddied by the

12

sweet water from the village stream. After the initial shock and sharp pain, his body maddened her with pleasure, making her scream. It seemed to last forever, and yet it was over quickly. He got up, put on his masker's garment and before he disappeared behind the tree, he said, "I know you crave power and success. That is the food of the gods. Now, you have tasted it. If what you experienced was good, come back again." And he was gone.

It wasn't until three years later that she saw him again. She had since married Ademola's father and had her first daughter, an Abiku who died a year after she was born. After the mourning period, she went back to the forest, but not before thinking guiltily of her husband. She always thought of him with guilt. Her husband was kind, though strong in his beliefs. He had the heart of an angel. She did not love him at first, and he suspected but never mentioned it. But he never suspected that she—

She had gone back to meet the masker and the seed of her secret was planted right there in the middle of the forest under the *iroko* tree. Nine months later, Ademola was born with that crooked smile on his face, looking as though he held her secret in his tiny heart. "It has been forty years. Please, *Sango*, keep my secret atop the highest *iroko* tree in the jungle," she prayed.

As soon as the morning prayer ended, the people had commenced to go up and down the streets like apparitions of soot-black hobgoblins, spreading dark rumors. And in accord with their culture, they created excitement heightened by anxiety. Their noise vaulted over the walls surrounding the house in the middle of the affluent Government Reservation Area in Ikeja. Ademola was reminded that the eight million inhabitants of the city were ready to endure again the soul-sapping assault of the sun.

But today was different. It was Tunde's fifteenth birthday, the reason Ademola's parents and brother had come to the city his father called the den of predators in olive-colored uniforms. "I see you prayed to your mother's foreign god before joining me," his father said.

Ademola knelt in supplication before the shrine. "*E kaaro o.*"

His father did not return the greeting.

Ademola's eyes narrowed, and the corners of his mouth twitched despite his effort to conceal his discomfort with a forced smile. He glanced over his shoulder.

"Ever since you were delivered into this world and compelled to stay among the living, you've always had trouble deceiving people with your face. Don't start now!" There was the beginning of a smile in his father's eyes.

"It is never my intention to deceive you," he said in Egba, a dialect of Yoruba language.

"You speak our vernacular well."

"I learned from the best teacher." Ademola smiled.

"I am happy."

"You are troubled." Ademola frowned.

"You notice, eh?"

"Is it deep?"

"Depends on the meaning of the prophecy."

"What did it say?" Ademola asked.

"The cloud is pregnant! A calamity is soon to be visited upon the land."

"The country is—"

"This is not about the country. The spirits of our ancestors spoke about you. One who does not wish his eye pricked by a stick must observe it from a safe distance. I consulted the master diviner before I left Arinota and he perceived the rumbling of ocean waves surging toward us. He prescribed specific sacrifice for your protection."

"It is deep then," Ademola said, troubled.

"Of course it is! Deeper than the length of a raindrop from the sky. Though the prophecy seemed nebulous, the warning was ominous. Many will die. Tonight, there will be merrymaking. But—" He looked up, mouth half-opened, as the black sky belched and then sneezed.

Ademola felt water particles smaller than rain but larger than predawn mist. Suddenly, an ominous silence filled the air as the spirit of the palm tree loomed in the background. The sky sneezed again and lent its force to the air, which turned windy. The wind swayed the fronds of the palm tree. The harder the wind blew, the firmer the tree remained, though some of its unbending leaves fractured and fell, only to be blown away before touching the ground.

"We must proceed quickly with the sacrifice to appease the gods, my son. The gates of the hell that is the future are wide open," his father said between clenched teeth, rubbing his bald head as though a school of fish from heaven had suddenly landed there.

As the black Peugeot sped toward its destination Sakara expertly opened the box on his lap, checked the timing device, and felt satisfied his assistants had not disappointed him. "One can never be too careful. Always respect and suspect everybody," he thought. He closed his eyes, as he often did whenever he was about to inflict his venom on a foe. He felt a flaring emotion, like acid churning inside him. He shelved his anger and forced his thoughts, wings fluttering like those of a butterfly caught in a bush of thorns, to go back to the interrogation which had taken place earlier.

While the rest of the more privileged residents of the city had been indulging in slumber, and their less fortunate countrymen were in battle with the indomitable mosquitoes, Sakara had been at the Directorate Military Intelligence headquarter, DMI, interrogating a journalist who proved to be less formidable.

"Do you mean to deny that you plan to publish a scandalous story on the National Oil Corporation; hold talks with certain elements which dream of a communist Nigeria; conspire with junior military officers to import arms?" Sakara whispered into the ear of the young journalist, named Lade Ogawa, as though he were sharing adolescent gossip with a friend.

"Wh—" Ogawa looked flabbergasted, his breathing labored. "Why would anyone concoct such a ridiculous story? I am neither a communist nor do I sympathize with or befriend any; I am certainly not a gun runner. You have to believe me. Please, tell me this is a joke, Major." The journalist began to shake.

Sakara's eyes centered at the tip of his nose, glaring at Ogawa, expecting him to refute the first allegation. But it didn't happen. "My boys must have mistaken you for someone else," he said, but thought, "I know you have the document which implicates the head of state, General Bukha, in the disappearance of two point eight billion *nairas* from the account of the National Oil Corporation. That document belongs to no one but me." He got up as though his bladder would suddenly overflow, both hands massaging the sides of his head as he exited the room.

"Let him go!" he told a sergeant stationed at the entrance to the interrogation room.

"Has he confessed?"

"Now!" Like a boomerang, he returned to the room.

Ogawa looked into Sakara's black eyes and he cringed as though he had stepped on the tail of a snake. "What can I do to prove my innocence?" His lips quivered.

"Nothing! You can go home now. But there's something

I wish to show you after the *Jum'at* prayer. Meet me at your house at two." He turned and exited yet again. He hurried to the end of the corridor, opened a steel door, and entered what looked like a photographer's dark room. The only source of illumination was the red glow from a naked bulb hanging from the ceiling. The room was long and narrow. He picked up the earphone, strapped it over his head, and sat at a table pushed against the wall. Through a tinted glass window, he saw two soldiers interrogating a man seated in a chair. He watched as one of the soldiers smoked a cigarette, and anxiously looked at his watch. The other soldier snapped in an officious tone of voice: "You will confess to the allegation against you!"

Sakara adjusted the volume knob of his earphone, lowering it.

"I will not confess to a trumped-up charge. Who do you take me for?" the man burst out. "I am Dr. Ayo Crowder, Senior Editor of the *Daily Telegraph*, not some plebeian journalist you can push around. I do not wish to answer any more of your silly questions until I see Major Sakara. He is a friend of mine!" Crowder looked out of place in his blue Oxford shirt, faded khaki pants, tasseled loafers, and round tortoise-shell eyeglasses. He sounded more like a college professor than a journalist as he said, "Where is the Major? I wish to speak with him!"

"Major Sakara is out of the country on assignment," the officer with the cigarette lied.

Sakara whispered to himself, "Crowder, you should know a fire that warms the body also scorches the fingers."

Sakara watched the driver of the black minivan as he exited the expressway at the Airport Road off ramp, turned left, and pulled to the curb. The Peugeot sped past and continued for another mile before stopping. Sakara pulled out a walkie-talkie and adjusted the knob to reduce the crackling. "Choirboy, do you read me, over?"

"*Roger, sir, I read you loud and clear, over!*"

"What is the code, over?"

"*The sparrow has landed, over!*"

"Ten-four, choirboy!" Sakara switched off the instrument and ordered his driver to move on. The driver did so as Sakara glanced at the clock on the dashboard. It was one-forty. The sun looked angry, its heat lapping up the moisture in the air, and threatening to incinerate everything on the baked earth. Sakara took a deep breath, eyes closed, as he tenderly ran his fingers over the lid of the box on his lap. The flame of crimson fury licked his spirit, filling him with unfathomable energy, fueling his resolve. "A leper that cannot milk the cow is capable of kicking the bucket," he thought as the car pulled over and parked in front of a white brick wall concealing a bungalow. He peered through the car window, surveying the empty tree-lined street, and nodded. The driver reached into the glove compartment, extracted a gun fitted with a silencer, left the car, and went to the black wrought-iron gate fronting the house. He tapped the gate with the butt of his gun, and the sound of metal-on-metal filled the air. He picked the lock and commenced to open the gate just as Sakara opened the door of the Peugeot. Suddenly, there was the sound of running feet on gravel and the barking of a German shepherd as the dog rounded the edge of the house and charged toward the gate. The driver took aim and fired three rapid shots in succession. A red dot appeared between the eyes of the dog, and the barking turned into a groan as the second bullet lodged in the dog's throat. The third bullet pierced the fur between the dog's forelegs, killing it instantly.

Sakara entered the gate, stepped over the animal. "Get rid of it!" He walked into the house with the box cradled

against his chest. As he entered the study, he recited the
lyrics of his favorite Yoruba poem:

> *Ileke Awo-o-o maa fi s'eke.*
> *Ileke Awo-o-o maa fi s'eke.*
> *L'ojo t'omode-e-e d'ale*
> *Oti dagun,*
> *Ileke Awo-o-o maa fi s'eke o-o-o.*

> (One does not tattle,
> Tattle on the secrets of spirits.
> The day a child so tattles
> Is the day he loses his spirit.)

2

Sakara had been in the house for seven minutes, enough time to find the document, plant the bomb, and get out. "Self-veneration is the mother of failure." He admonished himself for expecting the task to be as routine as the others he had carried out in the past. He commenced the search again as though he had just entered the journalist's study. Midway into his inspection of the desk, he found a file jacket beneath a manual typewriter. He extracted a manila envelope marked *Oil Corp. Document*, and was about to open it when a crackle filled the air. He spun round to face the door, and realized the sound was a signal from his walkie-talkie. He unhooked the instrument from his hip, and snapped, "What's the matter, over?"

"The sparrow has landed, sir. But it's moving faster than a squirrel! Two minutes to your position—plus the family, over."

"Stay in place, ten-four!" He replaced the file jacket and left the room with the envelope. He was fuming by the time he entered the car. "What are you waiting for? Go!"

The driver engaged gear and accelerated. Four houses away, he swerved to avoid a head-on collision with a white Mercedes Benz 200 sedan. The journalist was driving, his wife next to him, and their two children, a boy and a girl, in the back. The sedan sped toward the bungalow.

"Turn around and park there," Sakara snapped.

Ogawa slammed on the brake, ran out to unlock the gate, hurried back to the car, and drove in. He went into the house with his family. Moments later, his wife came out. And as she began to shut the gate, an explosion rocked the bungalow. Its impact reverberated through neighboring houses. Shattered glass and chunks of human flesh hailed on the street. Mrs. Ogawa was knocked against the fence. The air seemed like a centrifugal oven, making the woman look as though seared by an invisible conflagration. She sprung to her feet and looked like a centaur kicking a monster with her hind hoofs. A small crowd had gathered, and they watched in dread as she sprinted to the house, screaming.

At the entrance to the study, she took off her wrapper to cover her shrieking four-year-old son whose shirt was on fire. As she put out the fire, she saw her daughter's mangled body next to her husband; lying in a pool of blood on the floor. "Holy Jesus!" Her heart missed a beat. The journalist looked as though a prehistoric cannibal had used a crude weapon to hack at the left side of his chest and arm. His clothes were on fire. She rushed to him and tore off his burning trousers.

He groaned, "They have killed me!" Then, his body started to roll, curl, gyrate, turning darker at every stage before it finally stilled, and puffs of smoke ascended from it. For a brief moment Mrs. Ogawa looked as though she saw the smoke coalesce into the form of a man who turned to stare at her with pleading eyes before merging with the rest of the smoke in the room.

Her head pulsated as she recalled her husband's words just before they arrived at the house: "My life is in danger! If anything happens to me, please don't let me die in vain. Right here, under the driver's seat, there's an envelope containing the evidence needed to implicate General Bukha in the oil scandal. Someone at DMI does not want it published. And there's more damaging information in the envelope.

My informer at DMI Headquarters gave me the document yesterday. And I intend to publish it. These people must be exposed. But if anything happens to me, don't let anyone know you have the document unless you find the right person to give it to. Do you understand?"

She had nodded understanding, alarmed.

Now this. She looked at the dead bodies of her husband and daughter, and a blind fury engulfed her. With the agility of a gazelle, she vaulted to her feet, arms thrashing, a beastly rasping, primeval caterwaul erupting from her. She picked up her son and carried him out of the house. Two men came to help her place the boy in the car. "My husband and daughter have been murdered! Please, call an ambulance," she implored the men before driving off toward Ikeja General Hospital.

Sakara watched the unfolding spectacle with equanimity. His heart swelled with dark potency as he leafed through the papers in his hand a second time since leaving the journalist's house. "Without a doubt, the document is somewhere in that house," he thought, throwing the blank papers from the envelope to the floor of the car. He signalled his driver to move.

Sakara's mind was filled with a sense of failure as the Peugeot cruised past the crowd in front of the bungalow. His eyes focused on the tip of his nose as he gazed into space with malevolence, comprehending the futility of going back into the house right away.

"Soon as those idiots leave, I want that house burned to the ground!" he ordered with glacial fury.

"Yes, sir," the driver responded.

"Don't mess it up!" He shifted his bulk sideways, extracted the walkie-talkie, and in a voice that suddenly broke, said,

"Choirboy, are you there, over?"

"Here and ready at your command, sir, over."

"The sparrow's car is approaching your position. Follow it, over!"

"Will do, sir, over."

"Search and terminate the occupants, ten-four!"

Tunde's birthday party started well. Immediately after breakfast, several women and their children arrived from Arinota to help Ademola's mother in her laborious but gratifying chore of cooking and preparing for the happy occasion. The celebration commenced after *Jumat* prayer. There was laughter in the air. Happy voices greeted and praised and lectured and admonished in friendly jests. The birthday cake Eniola brought was displayed on a table beside the makeshift shrine at the foot of the palm tree. Eniola came out of the house holding a candle and a box of matches. She placed the candle in the center of the cake and was about to light it when Ademola's mother said from behind the tree, "*Iyawo mi*, is Ola coming out soon?" she asked Eniola, calling her "my wife."

Eniola rounded the table to face Ademola's mother and her eyes sparkled as she returned the older woman's smile. "He'll be finished in a few minutes, mama."

"Please, go and ask him to hurry up. Tunde says he will not cut the cake without him."

"Yes, ma. By the way, my junior brother brought more minerals. We ran out of Fanta—Tunde's favorite."

"No wonder his mouth is yellow. He probably drank at least six bottles of the orange mineral all by himself." The older woman shook her head, and they both laughed. Eniola turned to leave.

Ademola's mother thought, "Her voice is silky and

sunny, like peppermint. I wonder what her secret is." Then she smiled with her eyes and heart. "My son is lucky indeed to pick such a fine woman for a wife. Or is he? But then, so is she. Ola is the most sought-after bachelor in town. Just like his father when we were both young. Will they be as troubled with Abiku children as we have been?" she wondered. "Please God, don't revisit my pain on her," she prayed silently.

⤸

Ademola walked over to his desk in the parlor and, hoping against all odds that a miracle might be in the offing, picked up the telephone and dialed the hospital number. He stared at the black rotary telephone which looked more like a decorative relic than a communication instrument. Unintimidated, the phone did what it had always done. It responded with a busy signal. He hung up and tried again. Same response. He gave up and smiled, and was about to replace the receiver to its cradle when Eniola walked into the parlor.

"Ola, mama asked me to—" Her almond-shaped eyes enlarged, giving her face the expression of one who expected a pleasant surprise. "Is that thing finally working?"

Ademola shook his head and grimaced.

She smiled.

He felt a sudden warmth as though a door eased open, letting in a shaft of sunlight. The type that endeared men and women to each other. He smiled back, and making light of his frustration, said, "I need to reach the hospital to check on the status of some patients. All I get from the silly thing is a busy signal. And I know there isn't anyone at the other end."

"Of course not. Anything I can do to help?"

Ademola shook his head again. "Is there anybody else I

need to see before I—" He looked at his watch and winced. It was already three in the afternoon.

"My brother—he can wait for later. Mama asked me to tell you Tunde refuses to cut his cake until you are present. She wants you to come out for the celebration."

"We will join them soon. Let me take care of your brother first." He remembered why the young man wanted to see him. "Where is he?" he asked, sitting down at his desk.

"In the guest room. I'll go get him," Eniola said, and hastily left the parlor.

Ademola smiled, staring after her as she rounded the corner. "What a gem," he mused. "She's not just a woman of action but a beautiful one too."

At five feet two inches, Eniola radiated the ambience of a much taller woman, self-assured and purposeful. Her shapely legs looked as though sculptured by a master carver. The white lace fabric wrapped around her small waist rustled gently, adding beauty to her generous buttocks which bounced sensuously without being vulgar. "What a jewel, what vitality for one so young," Ademola mused with a pleasant untoward yearning. "And what a wonderful wife and partner she will make. Together we will be the source of envy to lots of people. She's certainly worth the wait." He nodded self-congratulation, filled with his love for her.

He opened a drawer, pulled out a sheet and an envelope, and commenced to write a note:

Dear Segun,

The bearer, Femi Adenekan, is the junior brother of my fiancée. He has just graduated from the London School of Economics with first class honors in the subject dearest to your heart—Agric/ Econometrics. The young fellow is desirous of following your giant footstep with a career in the military, albeit lacking your legendary bravery. He hopes, however, to work in the civilian section. I believe

*he will be an asset to you personally. He is terrific with numbers
and plants—a rather odd combination, don't you think? (Laugh).*

Please help him to land a good position.

*By the way, Ayo and I wish to share some serious palm-wine
from Arinota with you soon.*

Cheers, and thanks.

Ademola signed, folded, and stuck the note in the envelope which he moistened with the tip of his tongue before
sealing it. In a bold, sweeping cursive that had become his
trademark, he addressed the envelope to:

MAJOR SEGUN SAKARA, *Deputy Director*
DIRECTORATE OF MILITARY INTELLIGENCE
DEFENCE HEADQUARTERS
VICTORIA ISLAND, LAGOS.

As he started to get off the chair, he remembered that he
did not date the note. He slit open the envelope, extracted
the note, and wrote the date on the lower left side, below his
signature. "Sakara will know this is an afterthought," he
reflected before putting the note in another envelope which
he addressed.

Eniola came back to the parlor with her brother.

"*E k'ason*, sir." The young man bowed in greetings.
"Good afternoon, Femi. How's Lagos treating you since
your arrival back from London?" Ademola smiled warmly.
"What a remarkable resemblance to your sister."

"Thanks for the compliment." Eniola nodded. She
looked at Ademola's hand as he ran his finger over the edge
of the envelope on his desk, his eyes riveted to her face. She
felt her cheeks burn. "Thank God my blushing doesn't show
easily," she thought. "Thanks for being the only man that's

been able to bring out the very best in me. You have my total love for eternity, darling," she promised silently and then smiled.

Eniola had not been like other girls her age. She was exuberant without being reckless. Her father was a successful building contractor at a time when the government embarked on a grandiose plan to house every citizen in the country. It was a sham. The generals and a few civilian contractors got rich while the people waited for the houses that were never built. She was pampered without being spoiled. She was a bright student who did not believe in sleeping with her professors in exchange for good grades. What attracted her the most was power. And the soldiers had that in abundance. She gave up her innocence at the end of her first year at the university to a lieutenant. That was before meeting the General Officer Commanding, GOC, of the garrison in her university town. He was a general. The lieutenant was a very ambitious soldier. He introduced her to his boss, assuring her there was much more power at the top. She agreed. Anything less was unacceptable. But she did it discreetly. She was contemptuous of the girls who flaunted their escapades with captains and those of lower ranks. Power resided at the top. She tasted it and went on with her life. She graduated with honors and kept her secret.

Now at twenty-six, she had become attracted to a different type of power, the one Ademola wielded at the hospital, limited in scope, but potent and lasting, the type that saved lives. She loved him. She would be happy to spend the rest of her life with him and their children. She admonished herself for being so careless the previous night. "What if I get pregnant? God, please, don't let that happen. Not yet," she prayed silently.

Ademola's voice snatched her from her reverie when he said, "Why in the world would a bright fellow like you want to join the military? With first-class honors, you qualify for a

Ph.D. program."

"Well, affirmative to the statement and no to your question, Dr. Ademola. I'm not joining the military. My employment with DMI, the bloodline of the albatross that is the Nigerian Army, is merely to gain access to the wealth of data I need for my doctoral thesis." Femi spoke plainly, meeting Ademola's stare.

"So you want to spy on The Spy, eh?"

"That is true if you can call researching the machination of the Nigerian military oligarchy spying."

"What does that mean in simple English? You have to remember, I am only a physician, a baby doctor, if you will," Ademola teased. The men laughed.

"I simply mean to say—"

"I know what you mean. I was only *serious*, young man!" Ademola laughed some more.

Femi became quiet.

So did Eniola. But only for a brief moment. "Seriously, Ola, isn't it time somebody looked into how the army boys are able to keep their heavy feet on the necks of the people?" Eniola sounded slightly irritable.

"That's right. It's been thirty-five years since the country won independence from Britain. Look at how long the soldiers have been in power, not to mention the mess they have made running the country." Femi smiled stiffly.

"We did not win independence. It was given to us." Eniola corrected her brother, a gentle I–love-you-still smile in her eyes as she continued. "There was no revolution to force the Brits to relinquish power. Our so-called independence was granted by the colonial master so easily we should have looked into the gift horse's mouth before accepting it. But instead, our people took to the streets, celebrating. The Brits left the country in the hands of carefully selected neocolonialists. What is left of Nigeria, like the rest of the continent, is still being exploited, albeit by remote control. *B'oyinbo ba kuro lori aga a su s'aga.* (The English do not vacate a chair without soiling it). Indirect Rule worked during colonization. The only difference now is that there are fewer white faces on the continent. And the boys in uniform have replaced the *Obas* and Emirs."

Ademola shook his head and smiled. He turned toward Femi and asked, "What would you have done differently?"

"First thing is to send the soldiers back to the barracks where they belong. Then I would put an end to the fake war against Bribery and Corruption. It is a national disgrace. The most guilty are those in uniform."

"You didn't answer my question, young man."

"Which is?"

"I asked for the solution, not the symptoms."

"Dr. Ademola, I just gave you solutions. My point though, is, how can we govern ourselves with just a few holding all the cards? A segment of society believes it has a monopoly on wisdom."

"Let me share something with you, Femi. Remember when you were schooling here in Nigeria?"

"Yes?"

"There were always two parties in the classroom. The pupils and the teachers. Each had a role to play. The teachers, who were all Nigerians, gave their students just enough information they deemed appropriate at the time. They knew more than the students then and still know more now. Some have become advisers to the soldiers, giving them information about all the causes, the symptoms, and especially the solutions to our problems."

Femi shook his head. "What's your point?"

"Don't assume that because you have studied overseas you have all the answers. You don't!"

"Come on, Ola, you don't mean that, do you?" Eniola asked, but thought, "Does he sound like my dad or what?"

Femi's eyes darted back and forth, he looked like he was

aiming at a moving object. Then he said, "By the way, Eniola, I have a bone to pick with you on your paradigm about the Brits, as you called them earlier."

"Do you?" Eniola asked, challenged.

"Yes! I am tired of our people blaming Europeans for all our miseries. Thirty-five years is enough time for us to govern ourselves properly," Femi said.

"Of course not. Look at America, it has taken them two hundred years to get to where they are today," Ademola offered patiently.

"But America did not start with kleptocracy, *coup d'etat*, and military dictatorship. And besides, as my sister rightly said, they fought for their independence. That is a huge difference," Femi said.

"So our people should have revolted? Let me remind you that the African landscape is replete with stories of freedom fighters who have died and continue to die by the millions. There is Angola, Ethiopia, Liberia, Sudan, not to mention South Africa, Mozambique, Zaire, Morocco, Libya. The list is endless. Do we want Nigeria to join the club? Don't forget there are more than eighty million people in this country. Can you imagine having five or even ten million Nigerians in refugee camps in neighboring Cameroon, Togo or Ghana?" Ademola asked.

"Why not? I don't believe the plight of the people can be worse than it is." Femi had a glint of stubbornness in his eyes.

"Oh, yes, it certainly can. We are not talking about the silly inconvenience of power failures or water shortages. You are speaking of bullets, bombs, land mines, unimaginable human misery, and lots of dead people. Someone among them might even be your relative."

Eniola looked surprised. "What is he talking about—is Ola playing the devil's advocate, or is he a hopeless pacifist?" she wondered silently. Then, with the cool appearance everyone around her had become accustomed to, she said, "Instead of having our brains blown to pieces with a shotgun, we seem to have been injected with the syphilis virus which is slowly destroying our brains. The end result is the same. Our people are dying daily by the thousands already. The only difference is they're dying in silence, enabling the generals and the rest of the world to go on with their business."

"Well put!" Femi looked at his sister with admiration.

Looking burdened, Ademola got up, and as he handed the envelope to Femi, he said solemnly, "Be careful what you say in public. The country is not what it used to be."

"Thank you. I hope you are not offended."

"Not at all. Be careful, eh?"

"He will," Eniola responded before her brother could. "Power," she screamed silently. "The generals are using theirs to fight against goodness. And you two, like the rest of the intellectuals in the country, are using big grammar to fight against evil. You are both doomed to failure. But I love you and your adversary as you lock horns in the new game of survival of the weakest."

Back in the observation room at DMI, Sakara set the telephone receiver onto its cradle and cracked his knuckles. A wave of irritation surged through him. He looked at the telephone as though the man he just spoke with was there in the room. "What is it about Dikko that infuriates me so much? It must be because he was one of those born with a silver pacifier stuck between his buttocks," he thought.

The call had come from the office of the Director of DMI, Brigadier Aminu Dikko, who was thirty-eight, a year older than Sakara. The short man with premature balding at the temples was three ranks Sakara's senior. The director was brought from obscurity to head the newly-created intelligence-gathering division of the joint military services. His only qualification was being a graduate of the Military Defence Academy where Sakara had worked hard to finish among the top twenty in his class. But the unofficial reason was that Dikko hailed from a zebu-herding nomadic clan whose family were now village-dwelling Fulani from the northwest. Happenstance had become the norm in the country. Dikko was introduced to the nation as a computer expert by the head of state immediately after a preemptive coup by generals as corrupt as the civilian government they overthrew. Though rumor had it the man did not know the difference between a megabyte and a megaphone, he was promoted over better-qualified candidates from the south.

"Who do they think they are fooling?" Sakara asked the glowing red bulb dangling from the ceiling. Expecting no answer, he continued, "The military has its own culture. Salute, obey, and ask no questions. Zombies! But I am first and foremost a Yoruba before I am a soldier. And that supersedes everything else." He took his time to check every piece of paper in each file. He double-checked to make sure not a single piece was missing. Satisfied, he put the folders back in the cabinet, walked out of the observation room, locked the door, and strode to the director's office quietly singing his favorite Yoruba poem, "*Ileke Awo maa fi s'eke...*"

He strode into the director's office with the last letter of the poem on his lips. The room was large and tastefully furnished with an overstuffed L-shaped sectional sofa on one side and a conference table with twelve chairs on the other. Dikko sat behind a half-moon-shaped French hunting desk. There was a well-stocked wet bar to his right, next to a mahogany coffee table atop which were two silver kettles. The smell of freshly-brewed Kenyan coffee filled the room. "Good afternoon, sir," Sakara saluted.

"I am glad you are here at such short notice. Would you like a cup of coffee or a drink?" Dikko asked.

Sakara declined both with a shake of the head.

"Have a seat." Dikko pointed to one of the two Louis XIV replica chairs facing him.

"What seems to be the problem, sir? You sounded troubled on the telephone." Sakara sat down.

"How did it go with the operation?"

"Which operation, sir?" Sakara feigned ignorance.

"Weren't you working on the case of the journalist with the missing files?" the director snapped, unable to control the sudden tic on his left cheek.

"You are nervous and scared. So this is bigger than I imagined," Sakara wanted to say. He smiled instead, his gaze focused at the tip of his nose, studying his boss, enjoying the anxiety in the director's eyes. He leaned back, partially covering his mouth with his left palm, the thumb caressing his chin.

Dikko asked again, "Are you not working on the journalist?"

"I was, sir."

"What happened?"

"Nothing! It was a goose chase, sir."

"What do you mean goose chase? The man is in possession of documents which *can*, I mean could, embarrass the head of state."

"What document, sir? I didn't know exactly what to look for. Do you?" Sakara glanced coldly at the light-complexioned man seated across the desk.

"Yes, I mean, no, I don't know exactly what it is. But our intelligence indicated it could be very compromising." Dikko walked away from his desk like a diver who decided the diving-board was too high to jump from. He stopped at the window, and without turning around, said, "Listen, there is something I'm instructed to share with you. Something that could affect the lives of lots of people, including mine—and yours."

Sakara approached the window and stood next to Dikko. The two men faced each other. Dikko had to look up to meet Sakara's confident and condescending stare. Sakara took full advantage of the knowledge that his boss, like everyone else, found him unnerving. But he needed to be careful. He always sensed a trace of diabolical essence in his boss whenever they were alone together. "There is more to this man," he thought.

With a somber voice, a shade louder than a whisper, the director said, "When I was very young, I used to go cow-herding with my cousins across the northern plains during *harmattan* season. It was always cold at night. So we used to gather around a bonfire. Have you ever experienced a bonfire under a full moon, major?"

"Never."

"There's nothing like being on the plains, surrounded by hundreds of cows, on a cold night lit by a full moon. The expansiveness of the black sky with glittering stars, the plains, the silence, the cold wind blowing fine sand from the Sahara desert, and the perfect roundness of the moon, radiating like the face of a virgin, forced us to think about nature and human existence."

Sakara crinkled his nose as though a bushel of cowdung was suddenly dumped in the room. He longed to be back in his office to find out what had happened to the journalist's wife, real people condemned to die under his command. He wished he could tell his boss to go feed his nature story to the cows, and eat a piece of dung while he was at it.

Dikko looked at him as though he sensed his impatience. "Bear with me, major," he said. "On one of those nights, it occurred to me the whole human experience on this earth is reduced to a pair of eggs."

"Eggs?" Sakara asked with scornful impatience.

"Yes, major, eggs. Every child is born with a pair of eggs. Some break their pair, make the most delicious omelette and eat their fill. Life is sweet while they eat, but not for long. Like their parents, these children face a long-suffering life of hunger, frustration and poverty. There are more of them in this world than any other group.

"Next are those who eat one of their pair. And as they get ready to crack the other, their parents stop them, advising their children that their only salvation is to find another egg to pair with the one they still have in order to survive. Some of them get lucky. They incubate their pair, hatch them, mate the cocks and hens and repeat the cycle over and over. These are those in the middle class." He smiled. The contempt on Sakara's face had softened a bit.

"The third are those who do not have to touch their eggs. Their parents have enough to care for them, even pamper them. With their parents' help, they employ members of the first two groups to work on their farms, churning out innumerable eggs and chickens daily."

Sakara rolled his eyes as if he wanted to ask, "Everybody knows that, what's your point?" He didn't.

"The fourth group is the reason I am sharing my thoughts with you. The children in this group are those whose eggs are snatched away before they could do anything with them. Frustrated and angry, they have stopped wondering what they might have done with the eggs. They are busy looking for the eggsnatchers. The most dangerous people in this world are among this group. And in our business, they are the most useful. Show them who snatched their eggs, and bingo, there is another funeral service." Dikko looked at Sakara as though challenging him to ask the inevitable.

"How do you know who the real eggsnatchers are?"

Dikko left the window and headed to the bar where he poured himself a double shot of Johnny Walker Black Label, took a sip, and walked slowly back. He stopped halfway and resumed the conversation as though there had been no interruption. "You don't. But perception is reality, isn't it? So we create one to suit our purpose. It never fails. It is the stuff assassins are made of. Everybody is vulnerable. Take the Murtala Muhammed assassination as an example. People are still buzzing at each other like bees, trying to untangle the mystery of who was the mastermind behind Dimka."

"Do you know who it was?" Sakara's interest blossomed.

"That does not matter. The fact still remains that whoever told Dimka that Murtala was his eggsnatcher will never be known. That is how the game—" The telephone rang. Dikko strode back to his desk, picked up the receiver and his eyes looked like black marbles as he listened. "Will do, sir!" He replaced the receiver and swirled around, a frozen frown masking his face. "That was General Bukha." The nervous tic returned to his left cheek as he stared back at the telephone as though it was the head of state. He swallowed the rest of the scotch in one gulp, wiped his mouth with the back of his hand, and locked eyes with Sakara. "There's going to be a *coup d'etat*. If we don't recover those documents in time, it will fail and many good officers will be executed. History is about to repeat itself." He dropped the bombshell in a whisper.

Sakara reacted as if the ground trembled. "What are you talking about?" He jerked his head to the right, and then left. A warning bell went off in his head. "Am I being set up?" he thought. He scanned the room, looking for some sign of a hidden microphone. "Let's go outside," he whispered.

⤺

"Where's Ola?" Crowder shouted at the woman who was bent over picking a paper plate of partially eaten stewed rice from the floor. The woman looked over her shoulder and her eyes enlarged. "*Omo mi*, is anything the matter?" she asked, calling Crowder, "my son."

Crowder ran past the woman he had known most of his life without acknowledging her. She saw him yank open the front door so hard it slammed against the wall with a thud. Ademola's mother felt her heart lurch. "Something terrible has happened." She dropped the plate and ran after him into the house, screaming Crowder's name.

Crowder did not so much as look back as he ran into the parlor, bumping into Eniola, who lost her balance and staggered backward.

Ademola emerged from the bedroom and took in all the commotion in a glance. "What's going on?" he asked.

"Ogawa's house has been bombed. He's dead." He held his breath in an attempt to stop shaking. "I need to sit down."

Ademola nodded to Femi who hastily brought a chair to the middle of the living room. Crowder sat down and grasped Ademola's wrist. He looked into his friend's eyes and whimpered, "They killed his little girl too." His lips quivered as he asked, "Why?"

"Calm down. Which Ogawa?" Ademola's question was drowned by the voices of the guests who had followed Crowder into the parlor, all asking questions at the same time. Questions overlaid each other, giving Crowder no time to answer. The commotion added to his agony, his chest heaved. Ademola's father came in, took one quick look and threw his hands up in the air like a pair of striking cymbals. The sound deadened the voices, and everyone turned in his direction. "Now, all of you, leave my son alone. Tell me what happened?" He laid his hand on Crowder's chest.

"I am next," was all that came out of Crowder's mouth.

"What is he talking—will somebody get me a bowl of water?" Ademola's mother shouted.

Eniola ran to the kitchen and came back with a glass of

water. She handed it to the older woman.

"Here, son, drink. It will calm you down," she coaxed.

Crowder shook his head. "I don't need the water, mama. Thank you." He looked as though he just woke from a nightmare, making an effort to collect himself.

Ademola's father patted Crowder's shoulder like a child, to calm him, to assure him as he always did whenever any of his sons was distressed. "Don't worry, you're safe now. Take your time—Eniola, get me a wet towel. Now, tell me, what happened?"

Crowder ran a palm over his face, took a deep breath again and relayed his experience at the hands of the inter-rogators at DMI. "I swear it was Ogawa's Mercedes Benz I saw this morning at DMI. If he was there at the same time, there is no doubt someone followed him home and planted the bomb. You should see his house. The whole place was burnt to the ground. Eyewitnesses told me the bomb exploded about two o'clock. And an hour later, the house went up in smoke like fireworks." He took a gulp from the glass of water. "Ogawa's family came home with him. He must have picked up his wife from work and the children from school. His daughter died with him on the spot. I was told his wife carried their little boy to Ikeja General Hospital. The boy didn't look good at all. I was there at DMI at the same time. I know I am next. Those bastards killed—"

There was a knock on the front door. Femi hurried to open it and a man with a solemn look on his face stood there. "Is *oga* in, sir?" he asked nervously.

"Who are you?" Femi shot back.

"I am the ambulance driver from Ikeja Hospital. I come to fetch Dr. Ademola for emergency," the man said in Yoruba-accented pidgin English.

"Wait there." Femi turned around.

Ademola's mother admonished with her eyes. Femi turned again and commenced to shut the door when

Ademola said, "That will not be necessary. I know him." To the man at the door, he said, "I'll be with you, Taju." He went into his bedroom. And moments later he emerged, carrying a doctor's black bag. "Ayo, come with me, please."

Standing at the door, his mother said, "Be careful, my *husband*!" Her voice sounded far away. "Eniola, don't just stand there, pack some food and take it to the hospital."

Tunde came charging like a bull and screeched to a stop barely a foot away from the ambulance. Ademola waited for him to catch his breath. Tunde handed him a piece of his birthday cake wrapped in aluminum foil and then took a step backward, their eyes locked in silent conversation.

Their mother saw the unspoken, parting words, a farewell. She felt a sharp pain in her bosom, the same pain she had felt eight times in her life, the type only a mother could feel, proclamation of the imminence of birth. Then the pain was gone, like the exit of an Abiku child from the world of the Living, leaving a void half-filled with tears and sorrow behind. She looked up to the sky and a groan emerged from the depth of her soul: "Please!"

The two soldiers in mufti sat on the beach. The waves were massive and ferocious, readying to devour the sun which looked like a luscious orange over the horizon. Behind them, Eko Hotel stood arrogantly on a land that was once a river. It reminded Sakara of the times, only a century or so ago, according to his high school history book, when slave ships anchored at that same spot. Anger pounded his heart as he realized that those who sold his people into slavery then and the ones presently at the hotel, negotiating nefarious deals, were one and the same. He picked up a seashell and threw it into the water. It landed without a sound. He looked at his watch. It was already 1645 hours.

He did not remember ever spending nearly as much time with Dikko before. But the enormity of what the director had shared with him surpassed anything he had ever heard before. Comprehending the magnitude of the brewing carnage was mind-boggling. History was about to repeat itself indeed—

Nigerians traced their history back some 2,500 years to the Nok civilization which flourished from 500 BC to 200 AD. In the centuries that followed, Mali and Oyo empires significantly influenced the shaping of the country into what it is today.

The *Imales*, an adulterated Yoruba word, were Muslims whose predecessors came from Mali. Upon arrival on the northern plains, they declared a holy war against the local residents, converting most to Islam. Prisoners-of-war and those who refused the new religion were carted away and sold as slaves at various bazaars north of the Sahara desert. One of the converts, a Fulani named Othman Dan Fodio, carried the Quran-quoting, sword-wielding, Arabic-speaking mission further south. At Oyo he met an equally expansionistic, well armed, and better organized army of Yorubas led by the legendary Afonja. The jihadists were decimated, setting the stage for future schism between the Muslim north and the Christian south.

The dynasty of Kings at Ife, for example, regarded by the Yorubas as the place of origin of life itself and of human civilization, remained unbroken. Their urbanism was legendary. They had established trading ties with Europeans, and over the next three centuries their kingdoms flourished. Then the Europeans' interest shifted from gold and palm-oil to human labor, thus setting the stage for the shipment of the most able-bodied people of the kingdoms to the New World. The devastating effects of the slave trade and internecine warfare of the nineteenth century took its toll, making it possible for European colonization.

The political entity known as Nigeria, named after the great River Niger which runs through Guinea, Mali and Niger across the Nigerian border in the northwest to the coast in the south, came into existence in 1914 when 400 separate, often hostile, ethnic nations were amalgamated into one interest of the British Empire. Right in the middle of the country, the raging waters of River Niger locked horns with a south-westerly river from Lake Chad. Benue, a Batta word meaning Mother of Waters, and the River Niger formed a lake-like confluence before heading south together to form the largest delta in Africa. The two rivers looked like the letter Y in a square box, naturally dividing Nigeria into three distinct political, religious and tribal regions.

North of the two rivers is the Hausa-speaking Muslim enclave. The Christian, mostly Catholic, Ibo-speaking Nigerians occupied the south-east, while the Yorubas of mixed religions dwelled in the south-west. Lagos, a confluence of small islands in the south-west, was the capital and the seat of the Federal government—

"History is about to repeat itself indeed," Sakara thought again as he stood up, heart thundering. "I can't do it. The answer is no," he said.

"It was not a request. You are ordered to join us. You don't have a choice in the matter." Dikko laughed.

Sakara took a few steps away from his boss, who remained seated. He stopped and bent forward to pick up a black rock the size of a lemon. He fired the rock into the surf with such violence he lost his balance and broke the fall with his hands buried in the sand.

"You should learn to control your emotion. That's your weakness," Dikko said in Fula, a language spoken by a few people in the north, a language which Sakara understood, but which he believed no one ever suspected that he did.

Sakara did not respond. But his fingernails burrowed into his palm. He straightened and walked back.

"You should learn to control your emotion," Dikko repeated in Fula.

"Stupid indeed to suppose I will nibble at such a moronic bait," Sakara thought as he continued to stare at the tip of his nose while the rest of his face remained expressionless. "What is that?" he asked.

"Fula," Dikko said it simply.

"I don't understand the language," he lied.

"Is that a fact?" Dikko asked in crisp Yoruba, forcing Sakara to frown in surprise.

"You speak—" he started in Yoruba but completed the question in Fula. "—You speak my language? How long have you known I speak Fula?"

"Does it matter? After all, we are spies. Now that we know each other's little secret let's stop playing games. Much is at stake as we speak."

"But I am of no use to you."

"Don't underestimate yourself, major. And furthermore, don't insult my intelligence. If I did not believe you are important to us, do you think I would have risked telling you what I did?"

Sakara did not answer him.

"Sit down, major. My neck is beginning to hurt," Dikko said, his voice friendly. "Remember that joke of yours while you were at the Academy?"

"Which one?" Sakara asked, sitting down.

"The one about the three Nigerians and the orange tree. Let me see if I can tell it the way you often did: A Hausa found a tree full of ripe oranges. He pulled out his praying mat and commenced to beg Allah to bring down the oranges. A Yoruba came along and saw what was going on. He rushed to town and brought back an Ibo who agreed to climb the tree and shake down all the oranges for a fee of ten percent of the sales. The Yoruba bagged the oranges, sold some to the Hausa and took the rest to the market where he sold everything. He gave the Ibo his share. And everyone went their different ways with happiness in their hearts. Isn't that the story?"

"Very good, sir. What's the point?"

"Commerce! Free enterprise that flourishes if there is stability. General Bukha and his stupid advisers have decided to nationalize some foreign-owned corporations in the country. The last time that happened was during the Murtala/Obasanjo regime. Coincidentally, General Bukha was part of that administration. Remember British Petroleum, Barclays Bank, Bank of America? They were all nationalized and their assets turned over to the thieves in government. All because we wanted to play big brother— the giant of Africa protecting the interest of black freedom fighters in Rhodesia. Now that we got Zimbabwe, what did we gain from it?" Dikko wiped a film of sweat off his forehead with a white handkerchief.

"I have always believed the government's action was reckless at best," Sakara said in Yoruba.

"Reckless? It was stupid and dangerous!" Dikko spat. "Do you think the British and the Americans left happily and forgot the whole thing? Of course not! They left angry, swearing to get even. And they did. Look at the state of our economy. While we are on our knees, begging them to lend us money for some sham projects, Bukha wants to nationalize the assets of Shell and Agip. It's time for a change. Your name came from the lips of the leader of our group. He wants you to be part of the next administration." He paused. "Find the documents and you will know who he is. That journalist is in possession of a damaging document. Its contents partly implicate Bukha in the oil scandal. It also reveals the names of the *coup* plotters."

Sakara's lips rounded into a whistle. "Is your name on the list?" The two soldiers sat on the beach staring at the crimson horizon as the waves gobbled the sun.

3

The Emergency Ward at Ikeja General Hospital looked sicker than the patients. All around were the resigned faces of those who had waited in line up to twenty hours for the treatment of their broken bones, migraine headaches, sore throats, malaria fever, sleeping sickness. The lucky ones sat on the cold concrete floor, others leaned against the walls of the hallway, hoping in vain for a doctor or a nurse's aide to look at their ailment. The stench of antiseptic added to the agony. Its nauseating smell reminded both patients and the three-member staff, an intern and two nurses inside the operating room, that the only medication available in the hospital was already spent, its potency lingering.

Rumor had preceded the arrival of the next patient. Word spread among the sick and injured that war had broken out, several houses had been bombed by a battalion of soldiers, and mutilated bodies from the battlefield were on their way and would receive priority treatment upon arrival. Anger and incredulity appeared on the sullen and resigned faces of those patients whose pains had not yet numbed their minds. "This life is not fair *o*," whispered a man with goiter, whose neck looked as though he'd swallowed a cantaloupe which remained stuck in the base of his throat.

"Why?" snapped an ill-tempered patient who had been on the receiving end of a blunt object, his nose broken and face bloodied.

"Why should soldiers commandeer our own hospital, eh?" asked a pregnant woman with an Ibo accent.

"Because they are *patrioticians*. They give their life for the country. I was a soldier my very self," Broken-Nose said proudly.

"Go and fight in the front then," one of the patients said, stirring laughter among the others. There was upheaval as everybody took sides, their tolerance stretched to the limit. They swore at each other. The antiseptic smell seemed to have changed into anesthetic, deadening their pain.

The pregnant woman hissed, "*Shhhioh*! All soldiers are coward bastards."

"You call me coward, you *asewo* who get pickin without a father." Broken-Nose readied to pounce on the woman.

"Who do you call *asewo*? Your mother is a prostitute."

Into the midst of the chaos came Mrs. Ogawa, carrying the unconscious body of her fifteen-month-old son on her shoulder, her blouse soaked in blood. "Please, help me! Where is the doctor? My son is dying. They have bombed my house. They killed my husband and my daughter."

The appearance of the human face of war rearranged the symmetry in the air, replacing the confusion with order, and an infusion of humanitarianism. "This way, Madam. The *dokito dey* inside." A skinny young boy with a pair of large almond-shaped angelic eyes limped toward a door.

"Let me help you carry your baby inside," another patient leaning against the wall offered.

Mrs. Ogawa ignored her and charged toward the door. The boy grabbed the knob and pushed open the door. He waited for Mrs. Ogawa to enter first. Several patients rushed inside, crowding the operating room.

"What are you all doing in here?" snapped the older of

the two nurses, a bosomy, middle-aged woman. "Get out!"

"Please, help me. My son is dying."

"What's the matter—I said get out—You, what are you waiting for?" The nurse pointed at the boy who shook his head no and said, "I am here to help, Madam." He smiled, exposing overlapping front teeth.

"What are you, a doctor? Out," she screamed.

He did, but not before saying, "If you want my help, Madam, I will be outside."

The younger nurse and the doctor helped Ogawa put her son on a bed and he commenced to examine him. He shook his head as he asked, "What happened?"

She told him about the bomb, overwhelmed with grief, unable to fight the tears that ran down her cheeks.

"He's lost a lot of blood. There might be internal hemorrhaging. I need additional help. Tell the ambulance driver to go to Dr. Ademola's residence and bring him here quickly." The doctor wiped perspiration from his forehead.

When Ademola entered, the mood in the operating room changed. He took one look at the face of the little boy who lay unconscious on the bed and his heart started to race. The bed was soaked in blood. There were lacerations. But the ones that caught his attention were the two old scars on each cheek of the boy's face. Ademola took the boy's limp wrist in his hand, and as the two bodies connected a mild electric shock coursed through Ademola's body. He dropped the boy's hand, strained his ears for echoes, but nothing knocked on the doors of those organs. He stood still and held his breath. Momentarily something struck his ears; it came like a rumbling sound, ominous and full of sighs, laden with groans and lamentations. It sounded like what his father had once described to him as the presence of Death itself, cloaked in the garment of deep sorrow, stalking. He turned to the mother and asked, "What's your son's name?"

"J—Jaiyesimi," Ogawa answered.

"He's an Abiku." Ademola turned to the young physician and said the obvious, "This boy has lost a lot of blood. The worst bleeding is coming from the deep gash on his left thigh. Let's get that and the others sutured right away. Meanwhile, we need to give him a blood transfusion."

"We can't, Dr. Ademola," the older nurse offered before the intern could speak.

"Why not?" Ademola's eyes narrowed.

"There's not a drop of blood in this hospital. All our patients know they have to bring their own supply of blood and antibiotics," she said.

"Even in an emergency?" Ademola was aghast.

"Why do you always ask me that question? You know we don't have anything in this hospital, not even drinking water for the patients!" The nurse sounded frustrated.

"Did you ask what his blood type is?"

"It's Type O negative, doctor," Mrs. Ogawa offered.

"We need a donor with a matching type. What's yours?"

Ogawa shook her head in anguish. Her lips quivered as she said, "I am not Type O."

Ademola felt the grief that seemed to well up in her from that bottomless reservoir that ran back to the beginning of human existence. "But you're sure his is?" Ademola locked eyes onto Ogawa's, sympathizing with her.

She nodded yes several times.

Ademola turned to the younger nurse who was suturing the boy's wound, "Please, help me draw some blood, will you? I happen to be Type O negative also."

The nurse did not move.

"Now!" Ademola's voice was fraught with urgency and he commenced to roll up the sleeve of his shirt.

47

The nurse dashed out the room and the older one took over. Moments later, she came back with a tourniquet, a hypodermic syringe and plastic envelopes. Ademola took the tourniquet from her and strapped it around his arm, using his teeth and the free hand. He flexed his fingers, looked at the nurse and smiled as she tapped the inside of his arm, looking for a vein. She smiled back as she pressed the tip of the syringe against his skin, puncturing it. Ademola's bright red life-sustaining liquid spurted into the plastic tube, filling it eagerly.

After the IV was in place and Ademola's blood transfused into the boy's body, his little fingers twitched as though attempting to beckon someone toward him. Everybody stood still, watching him. He opened his eyes, left one first, then the other, and a faint smile appeared on his face. Ademola reached a hand out and touched his leg. The smile faded and the boy flinched. Ademola checked to make sure the boy was not bleeding internally. Satisfied, he commenced to assist the nurse in suturing and cleansing the wounds which had ceased to bleed as profusely as before. "Did you get an X-ray?" he asked.

"No," the nurse answered.

"Why not?"

"Dr. Ademola, please, don't give me a hard time. We haven't had electricity since yesterday."

"Is the technician around?"

"What difference will that make? There's no power."

"What about the generator?"

"There's no petrol, doctor."

"What are you talking about?"

"There's a jerrycan in the room next to the generator shed." The intern stepped forward.

"I see trouble o!" The nurse crossed herself.

"Why can't we use the petrol?" Ademola asked, enraged.

"It's reserved for VIPs," the younger nurse said.

"No, not just VIP *o*. It's reserved for Very Very Important Personalities! The Military Governor and members of his family," the older nurse corrected.

Heartless as the nurse sounded, Ademola knew she was speaking the truth, which irked him. "Nonsense! Are you telling me we can't use the petrol to save a dying child because a member of the governor's family might get sick?"

"That's right, doctor. And don't ask me to do it *o*. Last time a nurse used that petrol, a bunch of useless men in army uniform came here to beat her so much she was sick for six months. I will not do anything that will make those nonentities lay their foolish hands on me *o*."

"I'll get it myself then." Ademola stormed out.

Darkness raced after dusk into the operating room. Mrs. Ogawa saw the silhouette of a nurse against the window, then a flash as she struck a match and guided the flame with the cup of her hand to a hurricane lantern on the table. She lit a green mosquito coil which sizzled as it emitted a rancid smell that merged with the stench of antiseptics. The combination was unable to vanquish the mosquitoes that continued to suck the blood of everyone in the room.

"Thank you for everything, nurse," Ogawa said.

"I am only doing my job. Dr. Ademola is the one to thank. If anybody can save your little boy, he is the one. Do you know any other doctor who would give his own blood to a stranger? I am just tired of seeing him sacrifice so much for everybody. Did you know him before?"

Ogawa whispered no. Then she clasped her palms together, head raised upward, and commenced to pray. "Dear Lord, forgive my sins. Please, save my son and grant my husband and daughter entrance to your kingdom in heaven."

Tears rolled down her cheeks. She wiped her face with the back of her hand. "I thank you for Dr. Ademola who—" She looked around as though someone else just entered the room. Someone that should be there but couldn't. A void opened up inside her, making her feel alone, vulnerable. Then her heart started to race, as though her husband's ghost were in the room reminding her of his last words: "Please, don't let me die in vain. Find someone you can trust to give the document to—"

"Mrs. Ogawa, are you okay?"

She jumped. "Where is Dr. Ademola?"

"In the generator room on the other side of the parking lot," the nurse replied.

"Oh, my God, the document. Dr. Ademola is the one!" She dashed out of the room and ran to her car. She opened the driver's door and bent over, her hand rummaging under the seat. She was too preoccupied to see the black minivan parked across the untarred parking lot. A man eased open the front passenger door, got out and stretched, a lit cigarette clasped between his teeth.

As her fingertips touched the edge of what appeared to be an envelope, she felt her head grow bigger, hatred darker than the depths of the Dead Sea engulfed her. "This damn envelope is why my daughter and husband were murdered. And my son might die from his wounds," she said into the darkness. "What can be so damaging that people will kill innocent children?" She grabbed the envelope with such force a piece of it was ripped by a protruding metal. She stood up and as she commenced to open the envelope, she heard footsteps. She turned around and her heart froze when she saw a soldier running straight toward her.

Ademola emerged from the generator room holding a jerrycan of petrol. As he was about to replace the cap, he saw the dark figure of a man running toward a woman who stood beside a Mercedes Benz. Instinctively, he squinted his eyes, focusing on the woman, recognizing her. "It's Mrs. Ogawa!" He took off and reached her at the same time the soldier did. Ogawa stood beside her car, transfixed, the envelope held against her breast. "Are you okay?" He turned to face the soldier whose hand had reached out to grab the envelope. "What are you doing?" He dropped the jerrycan which landed on its side, spilling the petrol which snaked toward the soldier, soaking his shoes.

"Who are you?" the soldier snapped, spitting out the cigarette which landed on the pool of petrol.

The conflagration was instant. The can exploded, spewing its contents, spraying the soldier. The blue and yellow fingers of the fire reached upward, grabbing the polyester fabric of the soldier's trousers. He became a human torch, arms stretching out to grab Ademola whose healing instincts made him reach out a helping hand.

"Oh, my God!" Ogawa grunted. "Run, doctor, run," she screamed, and bolted.

Dikko picked up the red receiver on the first ring. The skin on the knuckles of his hand which held the telephone looked over-stretched. "Are you sure?" He held his breath for a moment. "Call the major and give him the same report. Get a replacement... Good. Bring them in... Send a team to search the doctor's house... Passport. Yes, and that of his friend too... Yes." He hung up, strode to the bar, poured himself a double shot of scotch, gulped it down in a swallow, walked back to his desk, and grabbed a black telephone. He dialed, and while waiting for an answer, his fingertips started to tap the surface of the desk, making the sound of a horse galloping on asphalt.

A voice snapped in Hausa, "*What is it?*"

"Trouble, my friend. We found the document. But it's with a doctor at Ikeja General Hospital." He wiped sweat off his brow.

"*Is the major with us or not?*" the voice enquired.

"He's being cautious but—"

Click.

Dikko picked up a yellow phone that did not have a dialing feature from his desk.

"*Dodan Barracks.*"

"Is the head of state available?"

"*Yes, Brigadier Dikko. One moment, please.*"

Dikko pulled the phone away from his ear when a voice boomed, "*Hallo.*"

"*Rankadede,*" he started in Hausa and immediately switched to Fula. "We found the document, sir."

"*Good, bring it here right away!*"

Click.

Eniola had just placed a tray of food on the coffee table when Ademola hurried into the doctors' lounge with Crowder and Mrs. Ogawa.

"Can you excuse us for a few minutes, please?" Crowder asked her.

"That's a good idea. Honey, please, just for a second, eh?" Ademola said.

Eniola smiled and exited.

"Mrs. Ogawa, your son has been stabilized, at least for now. Most of his cuts are superficial. The prognosis is good. But I'm concerned about you. Is there anywhere you can take him right away—a safe place, not your house?" Ademola pulled a chair to sit on.

"Dr. Ademola, I have to go back home and make arrangements for the burial of my daughter and husband. They—" She covered her face with her palm and began to sob. The air in the lounge thickened with grief, infusing Ademola with a sense of futility.

"I don't think going to your house is a good idea right now," Crowder said.

"Why not? They might as well kill me too."

"They will!"

Ademola's eyes bored into Crowder's, chastising him.

Crowder nodded understandingly, softening his voice: "Your husband was a colleague and I am sorry about what has happened. The people that killed him and your daughter are not finished yet. They will not stop until they get what they are looking for. I saw your husband's car at DMI this morning. One of the men that interrogated me was the one that came to the rescue of the fellow that was accidentally set on fire moments ago. I know them. They're not very nice people. I saw your house after it—"

"Let me handle this," Ademola snapped. For a split second he looked upset. Then he smiled as he turned to Ogawa. "Have you read what is in this envelope?"

She shook her head.

"It seems to me this is what it's all about. Do you mind if I open it?"

Ogawa shook her head again.

Ademola stared at her for a moment. "If we know what they're after, we might be better prepared." He slit open the envelope, extracted three pieces of legal-sized paper, and began to read. Half-way down the first page, his eyes looked as though they would pop out of their sockets.

"What is it?" Crowder jumped off his seat. He rounded the chair to stand behind Ademola and read over his shoulder. "Hey, not so fast," he snapped, stopping Ademola from turning the page. They read the second page and shook their heads in unison. Ademola's reaction when he read the third page was as though someone kicked him in the stomach. Crowder's mouth rounded before the words came out in slowmotion, "Oh, my God!" Goose bumps appeared on his arms.

"What is it?" Mrs. Ogawa asked, getting off her chair.

"You don't want to read this. The less you know the better off you are." Ademola stuffed the papers into the envelope. As he got on his feet, fright clouded his eyes. "We all have to get away right now—"

There was a knock on the door.

Ademola felt his heart diving toward a jagged cliff as the door creaked open. He shoved the envelope under the tray just as the older nurse stormed in, her body shaking. The ambulance driver was right behind her. "There's going to be big trouble *o*," she said.

"What is it?" Ademola asked, his inside churning.

"I was going for emergency when I see many army vehicle on the fly-over by the airport. I ask myself, where are they going? And my head tell me, They are coming to the hospital. I turn around and use the siren to get here quickly to warn you. The go-slow is preventing them from moving very very fast. But they will be here soon *o*." The driver's essence was as broken as his English.

"Well done, Taju. Where is the ambulance?"

"I park it in front, sir."

"Nurse, get the boy ready to be transferred." Ademola turned to the driver. "Help the nurse put the little boy in the ambulance. The mother will join you. Take her anywhere she asks." He reached a hand into his pocket, extracted a wad of notes, peeled off five twenty-*naira* notes, and handed the money to the driver. "Go!"

Ogawa followed the driver out of the room.

Ademola saw Eniola leaning against the wall opposite

the room. He beckoned her to come in. He shut the door and bolted it. "Listen, darling, there's a convoy of army vehicles on their way here. I want you to leave right away. Take this with you." He handed her the envelope.

She looked at him, curiosity masking her face.

"Don't, I repeat, don't read it! And don't let anyone know you have this document."

Eniola folded the envelope in half. She untied her wrapper, reached a hand behind and stuffed the envelope between her skin and undergarment. She retied the wrapper and asked, "Why don't you come with me?"

"We shouldn't leave together. Go with Taju in the ambulance. Don't go to my house or yours. If you do not hear from me soon, find someone you can trust to give it to. By then, my life and possibly everyone else's will depend on the document." He moved closer and held her in a tight embrace. He kissed her.

"I love you," she said before hurrying out.

Sakara stared at the phone, trying to comprehend the implication of the command he just received from his boss: "The head of state expects us at Dodan Barracks in ten minutes. Drop everything and come to my office now!"

Dikko had sounded troubled, alarmed.

"But I need to—" Sakara's voice was pinched off by a shrill order: "Right now!"

Sakara looked at the pile of classified folders on the table in the observation room and shook his head. He continued to read, taking notes. Then, the telephone rang again. He let it ring, knowing the caller was his boss.

Momentarily, he picked up a pile of folders, and as he walked toward the cabinet, he heard banging at the door. He hesitated. Nobody else but his boss dared come to the observation room. The banging got harder. He placed the folders on top of the cabinet and dashed to the door, yanking it open with such force that it slammed against the wall. A current of air rushed in as though sucked into an alien ship with the red glow of the lamp hanging from the ceiling. Sakara's aura bristled with inexplicable force as he stared at his boss whose right fist remained suspended in midair. The cold hatred in Sakara's crossed eyes betrayed the gentleness in his voice. "I was on my way."

"I—I—" Dikko stammered.

He slammed the door. "Let's go, sir!"

⸎

The croak of a giant African frog boomed nearby, punctuating a strange silence made more menacing by the moonless night. Then everything became still as the dark night mimicked the serenity.

"Without a doubt, this is the calm before the storm," Crowder said, breaking the tranquility.

Disconcerted by his friend's attempt at oracular prophecy, Ademola remained silent, his eyes trained between the two black posts at the entrance to the hospital. He felt the fingers of fear squeezing the base of his heart, forcing it to skip a beat. But his stern face refused to mirror his anxiety.

"What are we going to do?" Crowder asked.

"One to whom a bride is brought does not stretch his neck. We wait!" Ademola said with fractured confidence.

"Is that a joke? You don't sound convincing."

"What's that supposed to mean?"

"It means—oh, look, they are here," Crowder grunted.

Ademola saw a pair of yellow phosphorescent lights flashing in the dark like the eyes of a scavenger charging toward its prey in the jungle. Five more pairs appeared, and the pack approached like hyenas after a wounded cub. His heart pounded and then seemed to stop with such abruptness he thought he just had a cardiac arrest. He reached a hand to his chest and squeezed.

"Are you okay?" Crowder asked.

"Look over there, by the gate!"

The ambulance loomed across the parking lot like a black mausoleum. The six approaching vehicles appeared like pallbearers as they drove past it and stopped a few yards from the steps leading up to the Emergency Ward.

"Why hasn't Taju driven away? I pray to God that he is not still inside talking his head off. I should have—" He heard the slamming of a door. With the corner of his eye, he saw a soldier step out of one of the Land Rovers. Ademola recognized him as the same soldier who rescued the one that was set ablaze.

"Let me handle this," Crowder whispered. "I have dealt with these boys many times in the past."

The soldier from DMI approached them, holding a revolver in his right hand. A pair of dark glasses covered his eyes.

Ademola stared at him with nervousness and contempt: Nervousness because the soldier held a gun in his hand, contempt because his breath reeked of alcohol when he said, "Hand over the document!"

"What document?" Ademola asked.

The soldier took off his glasses, revealing a pair of cruel eyes, darker than the night. He pointed the revolver at Ademola's head. "I want the papers."

Ademola felt the nauseating stench of alcohol all over his face, and was about to step backward when the soldier grabbed his neck and pressed the muzzle of the gun to his temple. "Now!"

"I will—" He choked as the grip tightened.

"What the hell are you doing?" Crowder rushed to his friend's aid.

"Back off!"

"Yo—" Crowder swallowed the rest of the word as the soldier slammed the butt of his revolver against the side of his head, spinning him around before crashing to the ground.

"You will do exactly as I command. Get up! You two don't know who you are dealing with." The soldier sounded like one who finally was able to give orders to those superior to him. He turned around and waved his hand in the direction of the vehicles.

Several armed soldiers in combat uniform jumped out and marched toward the building.

"You." The leader pointed to two soldiers. "Go to the nearest police station and commandeer three Black Marias. I want everyone inside this building arrested. Every man, woman, or child, no matter how sick. Go!" He turned to face Ademola. "Let's go get the papers. You will smell pepper tonight."

As soon as the last guest left, Ademola's mother went into the bathroom and performed an ablutionary rite in readiness for the evening *Magrib* and *Isha* prayers. She asked Tunde to do likewise. Mother and son left the house for the nearest mosque.

Ademola's father stood in front of the makeshift shrine propped against the palm tree in the backyard. An immense space of uneasiness seemed to open inside him when he sensed the soft sound of the wind in his ears. He sat cross-legged on the dirt floor, looking like the statue of a starved Buddha, a bald, emaciated man with watery eyes. A vein above his right eye looked like a worm struggling to escape. As required by tradition, he wore a piece of white cotton from the waist down, exposing a glistening lemon-sized navel that reflected the flame from an *atupa* at the base of the shrine.

A gourd of palmwine, a bottle of palm oil, a white rooster immobilized by a string tied around its legs, two snails, and a metal bowl containing a three-lobed kolanut and a clove of alligator pepper were arranged on the floor. He shut his eyes and cleared his throat as he bent forward, touching the ground with his forehead three times. He straightened, picked up the gourd of palm wine, took a sip and spat, spraying the base of the shrine. He broke the kolanut, placed a lobe on the shrine, put another one in his mouth, and began to chew.

He looked up to the sky and sighed as a gentle wind swayed the fronds of the tree. His eyes dimmed and then shut, lips trembling as he started a nasal incantation in Egba dialect:

> *Sango*, god of thunder, I greet you o-o-o
>> My lord, hear my supplication o-o-o.
>>> I was advised to appease you,
>>>> Ritual sacrifice is the remedy.
>>>>> Accept my humble offering o-o-o.
>>>>>> They say one does not so fear death
>>>>>>> That one wishes one's child
>>>>>>>> To die before one o-o-o.
>> I offer myself as a sacrifice,
>>> Take me instead of my son o-o-o.
>>>> Dance will claim my feet as I come
>>>>> To you in death with happiness o-o-o.

He stopped to catch his breath, his face and neck drenched with perspiration. He took another sip of the palm wine, got on his knees, head to the ground, and continued the incantation, unaware of the screeching of tires outside. Six gun-toting soldiers, their faces ugly with hatred, jumped out of two Land Rovers. Their leader said in Hausa-accented pidgin English, "Search the house for *goberment passiporti.*" They broke the front door and marched into the house, turning furniture upside down, breaking tumblers and plates in the kitchen. One of them urinated on Ademola's bed after shredding the pillows. Another one shouted, "I got it!"

Ademola's father did not hear footsteps as two soldiers approached him in the backyard. He did not hear one of them, snap, "*Danduruwa,*" calling him a bastard in Hausa, "Superstitious old fool!" He did not see the man as he raised his gun and charged toward him. But he felt the excruciating pain on his back. He felt himself falling and heard the voice of the soldier who spoke with a Yoruba accent admonish his partner, "That was uncalled for, sergeant." He heard the other voice that said, "So what, let's get back in the house and search some more."

Ademola's father got on his feet and commenced to chant, his back throbbing with pain. As he picked up the rooster, his chanting became gloomy. He bent forward with both hands clasping the rooster in front of him, then swirled full-circle counter-clockwise. He stood straight, his right hand gripping the head of the rooster while the left held the body, exposing the long thin neck. He guided the pulsating neck to his mouth. He bit into the cock's outstretched neck, decapitating it. Warm blood spurted from the twitching stump. The bird's eyes looked stunned in death. Then, he stood on his toes, arms stretched out, back arched, like a dancer. He drifted backward a few feet and danced in a circle, gliding around the palm tree. He stopped to touch the shrine with the stump of the bird's neck, smearing it with blood.

His body began to shake. He dropped the bird and sat down, cross-legged, facing the shrine. He extracted a single alligator pepper from the clove on the ground, placed it on his tongue. As he swallowed the pepper, he felt energy swirling around him and he erupted into a torrent of guttural incantation.

The sultry night became infused with the choir of forest animals and insects. The diviner's eyes shone with brilliance in the darkness as he felt his spirit emerge from his body, elevating toward the top of the tree. Stillness all around. Suddenly, there was a presence. Ademola's father heard a whisper as the palm tree expanded and constricted, its breath shaking the fronds violently. As his spirit merged with that of the palm tree, his body spasmed and became still.

The soldiers marched out of the house. One of them handed Ademola's passport to the sergeant who sat behind the steering wheel of the lead vehicle. The soldier saluted his superior and then slammed the door. Instantly, the sergeant's agonized scream shattered the silence in the neighborhood as his left hand was wedged between the door and the edge of the roof of the vehicle. The other soldier yanked open the door, exposing four broken fingers. The soldier sitting next to the sergeant shook his head and murmured, "You shouldn't have assaulted that *Sango*-worshipping old man."

Darkness strangled Lagos into obedient silence. The smiling, yelping and jubilant throngs that usually lined the streets had disappeared. Doors and windows were shut tight, all household lights killed. Frightened inhabitants huddled on straw mats on the floor or crouched against the walls for protection. Nursing mothers covered the mouths of their babies with cupped palms, stifling their cries.

The curfew enforcers cruised the streets in Land Rovers and Black Marias like evil spirits masquerading as men in green uniform, armed with Kalashnikovs and whips. The government-controlled radio and television made the announcement right after dusk:

THIS IS A SPECIAL BULLETIN!
THE SUPREME MILITARY COUNCIL HAS DECREED
A STATE OF EMERGENCY IN LAGOS ISLAND.
ALL LAW ABIDING CITIZEN ARE ORDERED
TO STAY INDOORS FROM DUSK TO DAWN.
ANY UNAUTHORIZED PERSON FOUND ON
THE STREETS WILL BE SUMMARILY EXECUTED.
THIS HAS BEEN A SPECIAL BULLETIN!

Immediately after dusk, the curfew enforcers had taken to the streets. Screams of grief had accompanied sporadic gunfire. The unsuspecting victims had been those whose radios and televisions had been silenced by NEPA which had stopped supplying the neighborhoods with electricity.

"I'll drive," Brigadier Dikko told his driver, dismissing him and his *aide-de-camp*. Major Sakara sat next to him in a green Peugeot 505 sedan.

As soon as the car exited DMI headquarter, Sakara turned to his boss. "I assume you chose to drive in order to further our discussion."

Dikko shook his head and remained quiet.

Sakara seized the opportunity to think things over. He let his mind roam. He remained astonished at Dikko's ignorance. Granted, they were all pawns in this game of chess, but some had to be more important than others. An invitation to be part of a *coup d'etat* was an opportunity not to be missed as long as it was successful. Otherwise, Aaaeee! Dangerous to accept such an offer from an eel like this one before having all the facts. Now he had some, thanks to that story about the eggs. It was revealing indeed. Dikko had tested him. Soon, it would be his turn to be tested. Until then, Sakara's answer would be like the words of a mute.

Dikko whistled as he brought the car to a stop at a roadblock. "Something weird is going on. It looks like a whole battalion guarding the bridge."

Sakara recognized the officer that approached holding a sub-machine gun, his index finger curled around the trigger.

"What's the problem, captain?" Dikko demanded.

"Nothing, sir," the officer replied.

"Nonsense! This is nothing?" Dikko asked in Hausa.

"It's just routine exercise, sir. You can go now," the officer said in English.

Dikko engaged gears and sped off. "That captain will be demoted for insubordination!"

Sakara smiled to himself as the car neared their destination. In deep darkness a detachment of armed soldiers emerged from the gate of Dodan Barracks. They took position along both sides of the road leading out to the intersection. A soldier waved a revolver, signalling Dikko to stop. He snapped a military salute before stepping aside to let Dikko drive into the grounds of the barracks.

Once inside, Sakara saw several soldiers crouched behind military vehicles, combat-ready. Others were marching toward the main building. "Those soldiers don't look like regulars," he offered, testing his boss.

"Is that so?" Dikko sounded non-committal.

"Ordinarily it would seem to be a changing of the guard time. But those are not members of the Elite Unit."

Dikko slammed on the brake, stepped out of the vehicle and walked up a flight of stairs. Sakara followed at a safe distance. At the door, they met two corporals who saluted and remained still, like carved stones. Dikko nodded in response before marching into the official residence of the military head of state of Nigeria.

A double door at the end of the reception area was held open by a major who saluted. "Welcome, Brigadier Dikko. His Excellency and the members of the Supreme Council are waiting for you, sir." He stepped aside to let Dikko and Sakara march into the conference room.

General Bukha, six-foot-five-inches tall, was on his feet,

looking like a giant lost in the kingdom of hostile dwarfs. "Let me see the document," he barked.

"We don't have it yet, sir," Dikko said, his right hand an inch from his forehead in salutation.

"What do you mean, you don't have it?" an agitated officer yelled from the other side of the room.

Sakara stepped forward. "General Idi Amo, we have the envelope in a safe place, sir. But Brigadier Dikko and I believe it is best not to open it," Sakara lied, his eyes glued to the tip of his nose, glaring at the second-in-command of the Supreme Military Council.

"Where is it?" Idi Amo thundered.

"In a safe place, sir."

"Is it true?" the head of state asked Dikko in Fula.

Sakara's facial muscles stiffened.

"Yes, sir," Dikko responded in Fula.

Sakara scanned the faces of the ten members of the Council assembled in the room. The only ones known to speak Fula are Dikko and the head of state. "Let's see how the game is played out," he mused and a diabolical thought tickled his mind.

"I want that document in my hand before the night is over! The original and all available copies. I don't trust this assistant of yours. He's Yoruba. You know how cunning they are," General Bukha said in Fula.

"I don't trust him either. But you don't have to worry about him. He's an idiot, cunning, but an idiot nonetheless, like all Yorubas," Dikko responded in Fula with a straight face. "May I ask a question in confidence, sir?"

"Yes, what is it?"

"Why the sudden change in security, and the declaration of a state of emergency?" Dikko asked.

The head of state extracted a white linen handkerchief from his pocket and wiped a film of sweat off his face. "What sort of question is that, especially in view of what has happened so far? Besides, is this the right place to ask me that?"

"Pardon my impertinence, sir."

"Is there anything else you wish to share with me?"

"Excellent trap. Was he making a statement or perhaps questioning our loyalty?" Sakara asked silently as he held his breath, awaiting Dikko's response.

"N—not re—really, sir."

"Why are you nervous?" Bukha demanded.

"Please excuse my uncharacteristic behavior, it's been a hectic day. But there's nothing to worry about, sir."

"Is that a fact?" General Bukha snapped.

"Yes, sir. Maybe you and I should discuss this matter further in private. Even though our language is the most difficult one in the world, one never knows who is listening with their eyes," Dikko said.

"Good idea, but it doesn't matter."

"Very well then, Your Excellency. But you haven't answered my question." Dikko's smile appeared forced.

Bukha looked as though he did not hear Dikko. He lit another cigarette, took a swig. "I want you to transfer your assistant to another division and replace him with someone from the north, preferably a Fulani. I am going to make you the governor of Central Bank. With you gone as head of DMI, I don't want a southerner in that post."

"Thank you very much, sir. But you haven't answered my question," Dikko insisted in Fula.

"What is the question?"

"Why the change of security?"

"Brigadier Babasa uncovered a plot to overthrow my government. I have put him and his men in charge of the Elite Unit guarding Dodan Barracks."

"Is it possible that the fox is now guarding the chicken coop?" Sakara's mind went into overdrive in search of answers. Such knowledge would let him determine how bloody the *coup* Dikko talked about would be. "If Babasa is the leader, then I better find that envelope fast."

4

"**G**od have mercy on me *o*!" The nurse crossed herself.

"Stop your nonsense. I will rub pepper in your eyes if you don't tell me the truth," the officer snapped.

"It's the truth I—"

"Shut your mouth! You will wish you're dead many times over, all of you," he promised.

"Officer, soldier to soldier, I have told you the true story as I see it." Broken Nose shoved the nurse aside.

"Don't push me, you nonentity!" she cursed.

They were thirty in all, patients and staff, brought to DMI headquarters from the Emergency ward of Ikeja General Hospital. They stood bare-footed on the floor of the interrogation room. The body odor of so many people packed like sardines in a room measuring twelve paces long and ten wide was suffocating. Crowder and Ademola leaned against the wall by the door, staring at the officer who seemed ready to explode. He did, smashing his fist into the nurse's face. "Tell me how they left the hospital!"

"*Ye'paa! Mo ti ku o.*" The nurse spat blood, and two of her front teeth hit the floor. "Lord Jesus, have mercy on me. I warned you, Dr. Ademola. If it wasn't for you I'd be home by now, safe!" she groaned, covering her mouth as blood dripped through her fingers.

Ademola flew at the officer, who spun around, grabbed his head in both hands and slammed it against the wall. It sounded as though Ademola's cranium or the wall cracked.

"You are going to die here." Sweat dripped down the officer's cheek. He wiped some away with his shoulder.

"I want the docu—who is it?" He glared at the door.

"It's me, sir." A Yoruba-accented voice drifted through the crack in the door before the soldier came in.

"What are you doing here? Where is the sergeant?" The officer took off his sunglasses to reveal a pair of blood-shot eyes.

"He's at Creek Hospital, sir."

"What is he doing there?"

"Four of his fingers are broken, sir." The soldier stepped backward as the officer glared at him.

"What happened?"

"The door of the Land Rover was accidentally shut while his hand was in the way, sir. But I have the evidence." He handed over two passports.

Ademola shut his eyes and gritted his teeth to shut out the pain that ricocheted through his head.

"Get someone to replace the sergeant. Ask the corporal down the hall to go back with you to this one's house." He pointed to Crowder. "Bring every document you find there."

"Shall I take some of the men on guard duty with me?"

"Yes!"

"But the building will be without security, sir."

"Go!"

The soldier saluted and exited.

Ademola stole a quick glance at his friend who pursed his lips and nodded as though he understood whatever lurked in Crowder's mind.

"All of you, I am going to give you one last chance to tell me where the woman with the little boy is. If when I come back none of you has had the sense to be patriotic, let me assure you that you will suffer the penalty. Punishment for treasonable felony is death by firing squad!" he said before exiting.

"I *don* die before I die *o*. Dr. Ademola, is this not the thing I warned you about, *eh*? You and your Good Samaritan behavior. See what you've done. If you don't tell that evil man about your fiancée I will." The nurse began to sob.

"Which kind doctor you be?" the ex-soldier asked, his English as broken as his nose.

Ademola felt a tug at his trousers. He looked down and saw the boy with the limp bidding him to come closer. He tried to bend over but there wasn't enough space, so he got on his knees. The boy grabbed his head and pressed his lips to Ademola's ear. "Don't look, but up there where the black window is, there is a room behind it. The wicked soldier just entered there," he said in Yoruba.

"Where?" Ademola whispered.

"Over there—don't look!" He grabbed Ademola's arm, preventing him from getting up. "I will help you, *dokito*," he said with confidence.

"How?" Ademola asked, impressed.

"Don't worry."

"What's your name?"

"Ali."

"How old are you?"

"Seven. But I can help you."

"Thank you. How—"

"Sshh!" He released Ademola's arm.

Ademola stole a glance over his shoulder. His heart knocked on his chest when he saw what seemed the shadows of two men which looked darker than the tinted glass, gesticulating behind the fake window.

ᔦ

Sakara took the passports from the officer and snapped his fingers, signalling him to leave the room.

"Take that fat nurse to the other interrogation room at the end of the hallway. Torture her if you have to. She knows more than she is telling. But she will not say anything in the presence of her boss."

"Yes, sir!" He saluted.

"After that, take Ademola and his friend away for further interrogation."

"Will do, sir."

"And, captain, don't ever come into this room again," Sakara said, his voice weighted with threat as the officer turned toward the door.

"I—I am sorry about—"

"Get out!" Sakara turned to the glass and stared into the interrogation room. His anger rose in proportion to his frustration. "By this time tomorrow, you will all be dead," he said into the semi-darkness. He waited for the captain to enter the interrogation room before he strapped the earphone over his head. He raised the volume. His frustration fueled his anger when he could not hear what Ademola whispered into Crowder's ear. But the voice of the captain deafened him as he snapped, "What did you tell him?"

Sakara saw Ademola shake his head. He heard the captain order the nurse to follow him out the room. The woman started to protest. Just as the captain grabbed the front of the nurse's uniform and commenced to drag her out, the telephone shrilled. He picked it up, pulled the earphone off his head and snapped, "Yes, brigadier." He listened for a moment and banged on the table. "Are you sure? Right away." He put down the receiver and ran out, down the hallway, up a flight of stairs to Dikko's office.

"Sit down, major." Dikko was on his feet, holding a half-empty glass of whiskey. "Want a drink?"

"No." Sakara's stomach churned with contempt and

hatred for the man in front of him. "This fool is drunk," he thought, but said, "Are you sure the shooting is from inside the Barracks, sir?"

"Yes. We have to go there right away." Dikko gulped down the rest of the scotch and started for the door.

"I have to lock the observation room," Sakara said.

"We don't have time for that, major. Nobody but you goes in there anyway. Let's go!"

⌒

The nurse cringed, arms crossed against her chest.

"Take off that uniform!" The captain towered over her.

"Please don't touch me. I will tell you everything."

"Where did the doctor hide the document?"

"What document?" Her voice cracked.

"The one the journalist's wife brought to the hospital."

"God is my witness, I did not see anything *o*."

"I thought you want to cooperate."

"I do, *oga*, please believe me."

"How can I when I know you're lying."

"I take God beg you. It's the truth I speak."

"You are wasting my time. Take off your clothes, all of it." He reached out a hand to catch the front of the nurse's uniform. He yanked it so hard the buttons popped, revealing a lace corset stretched to its limit by a pair of voluptuous breasts. He stepped back and asked, "Do you want me to rip off everything?"

"Please! I did not see anything. The woman and her son left with Dr. Ademola's fiancée in the ambulance. That's all I know, please, believe me. I just had a baby two months ago. Please don't hurt me."

"Did you say the doctor's fiancée was at the hospital?"

"Yes, and she left with the other woman."

"In the ambulance? What's the driver's address?"

"Everybody calls him Taju. I don't know where he lives. But you can find out from the records department."

"Put on your clothes!"

The nurse clutched the front of her uniform and waited until the captain left the room before she moved, sitting on the floor, her body shaking as she sobbed.

The captain stormed into the interrogation room where Ademola and the others were. "You, doctor, and you too." He pointed to Crowder. "Come with me."

"Where?" Ademola asked.

The captain pulled out his revolver and pressed it against Ademola's nose. "From now on, you answer my questions. You do not ask any, understand?"

Ademola nodded and followed Crowder, who was right behind the captain, out the door. Midway down the hallway, Ademola looked back and to his amazement saw Ali limping behind them. The boy stopped right where the fire alarm activator hung on the wall. Ademola hastened his steps and prayed that the captain would not look back. In the interrogation room, Ademola saw the nurse sitting on the floor, crying.

"Did you think you could fool me? Before I call in my boys to start torturing this woman, I want your fiancée's address. I know she has the document."

The pain at the back of Ademola's head throbbed unbearably, reminding him that the madman in the room was capable of inflicting unimaginable pain on everyone. He also remembered warning Eniola not to go to either his or her house. He decided to take a chance that she did as he directed. "Give me a piece of paper and I'll write it down for you." With the corner of his eye he saw Crowder flinch.

As the captain reached a hand into his pocket to extract a pen, a sudden shrilling shattered the silence. The captain spun around, covering his ears with both palms as did Ademola and Crowder. The fire alarm had gone off. Ademola heard Ali screaming, "Fire! Fire! Fire!"

Then there was the sound of running feet. The captain ran to the door, yanked it open, and dashed out. Ademola looked out the door and saw the young intern and several of the patients running out of the interrogation room.

The captain bumped into the man with the goiter, raised his revolver and fired in the air. The sound filled the hallway. The man with the goiter fell on his knees, and as he did, the captain tried to jump over him, tripping, and hitting his head against the wall, dazed. The revolver hit the floor, sliding a couple of feet to where the boy stood. Ali picked it up and ran the other way. More people came out of the room pressing the boy against the wall. Some ran down the flight of stairs, others went upstairs.

Ademola saw Ali push open a steel door and enter. Then reappeared waving his hand, motioning Ademola and Crowder toward him. They ran to the door, stepping over the captain who stirred and began to get up just as they entered the observation room. Ademola slammed the door shut, bolted it and turned around. He squinted to adjust to the darkness.

&

Sakara insisted on driving when he and Dikko got to the parking lot.

"Do you think I've had too much to drink?" Dikko's speech was slurred.

"Yes," Sakara responded with uncharacteristic honesty.

"Is that a fact?"

"Also because you're my boss." Sakara flashed a contrived smile. As they neared the bridge that connected Victoria Island to Ikoyi, a sensation of foreboding overtook him. "Why do I feel so apprehensive?" he asked himself, ignoring Dikko's insistence that he should agree to join the *coup* plotters before they reached Dodan Barracks. He stopped the car at the roadblock, rolled down the window and asked a soldier who approached the car with a gun dangling from a strap over his shoulder, "What's the word?"

"The moon is on vacation, sir," the soldier replied, a conspiratorial grin on his face.

Sakara smiled back, fuming inside as he deciphered the hidden message. He rolled the window back up, made a sudden U-turn and raced back toward DMI headquarters.

"Why are we going back?" Dikko asked.

"There are files on the table in the observation room that need to be processed right away," he snapped, risking insubordination. "I did not lock the steel door? There's no telling what that bumbling captain would do."

Sakara stopped the car at the gate. A soldier on guard came out, saluted perfunctorily, and waved him in. As he drove into the grounds of DMI headquarters, his crossed eyes became clouded as though peering through an inferno. Ahead, several people poured out of the building, some limping, others running, all of them heading toward the gate. "What the hell is going on?" He turned to his boss who shrugged.

As if to add to the confusion, the captain came out, waving his hand, yelling words which Sakara could not hear. He quickly rolled down the window and the captain's voice became audible, though infuriating: "Don't let anyone escape! Lock the gate."

Sakara stepped on the brake pedal, opened the door and was on his feet, blocking the captain's path, just as the people reached the gate. He grabbed the captain whose breath reeked of alcohol. He slammed his fist against the captain's temple. The soldier's eyes rolled like the hands of a watch gone wild, and he began to fall backward, stunned. Sakara grabbed the captain's neck and began to shake him.

"Stop, major!" Dikko got out of the car.

Sakara looked over his shoulder and instead of seeing his boss, he saw the guard at the gate engaged in a hopeless battle with the people determined to get out. The guard looked helpless without his rifle which was propped against the wall in the guards' room a few feet away.

Sakara slapped the captain once more. "Where is the doctor?" Getting no answer, he released his grip, and dashed toward the building, risking being seen by Ademola and Crowder, not caring.

⤳

"*D*okito, we can hide behind that cabinet and shoot anyone who comes in to arrest us." Ali waved the revolver which Crowder snatched from his hand and stuck in his pocket.

"Hide? No, we have to get out of here!" Ademola grabbed a manila envelope containing the two passports and several sheets of paper from the table. He unbuttoned his shirt, pulled open the neck of his T-shirt, shoving the envelope between his chest and the fabric.

Crowder and the boy reached the cabinet when Ademola pressed the side of his head against the steel door. He held his breath as he listened for sounds from outside, hoping for free passage. His heart began to race as he heard approaching footsteps, faster, nearer. "Someone's coming," he whispered. He ran to where Crowder and the boy stood beside the cabinet. All three began to pull and shove the heavy metal.

"Look, there's a window behind it." Crowder pushed harder.

The boy crawled into the space and stood on his toes, grabbing the window latch, manipulating it while Ademola and Crowder pulled the cabinet, creating space.

Click! The latch gave. "I got it," Ali shouted.

"Sshh!" Ademola silenced the boy.

Crowder grabbed the window and yanked it open. He squeezed into the space and looked out. "Oh my God, the ground is at least fifteen feet down."

Ademola froze as he heard footsteps stopping on the other side of the steel door. "We have to jump!"

"What about the boy?" Crowder whispered, alarmed.

"He jumps too. Can you?" he asked the boy.

Ali started to climb.

"No! You go first, Ayo, someone has to catch him."

"Are you crazy? It's dark down there."

"Now!" Ademola hissed, hearing the jingling of keys outside. "Go!" He helped Crowder climb onto the windowsill.

Crowder crawled out, feet first, and jumped.

Ademola thrust his neck out the window and saw Crowder waving at him. He carried Ali, who seemed eager to jump on his own, seemingly enjoying the escapade. He saw the boy's arms and legs flailing in the air like a parachutist before Crowder caught him and the two fell to the ground.

As Ademola got on the windowsill, he felt a sudden blast of air against his face and heard the steel door bang against the wall. He twisted his body, feet dangling, fingers burrowing into the windowsill, getting ready to jump. His heart felt like a piece of rock when a strong hand seized his wrist. He looked but did not see the face of the man clutching him. He only saw the twinkling stars against the black sky, beckoning him to the other world.

Sakara stood in the observation room looking like a cobra bitten by a mongoose, his neck swelling with defeat and outrage: Ademola had slipped through his fingers to freedom. Sakara had entered the room as Ademola climbed the windowsill, preparing to jump out. He had grabbed Ademola's wrist. But Ademola had mustered all his strength, and with the shamelessness of a street fighter sank his teeth into Sakara's hand, biting so hard he had to let go. He was angry at both his boss and his subordinate whose drunkenness turned a routine investigation into a disaster.

"Dikko started the madness," Sakara fumed. "How could he have let somebody get into his office to steal the document which ended up in the hands of the journalist? That alcoholic Fulani is worse than the captain. Both of them are buffoons," he steamed as he checked the top of the table to assess what was missing. His outrage crested at the realization that Ademola and Crowder had stolen a file in addition to the two passports.

He checked again. "In the name of the god of evil, how could this happen? They have stolen the most classified document of all, the one bearing the names and secret Swiss Bank accounts of the twenty richest Nigerians, all of them generals. The loot totalling ten billion dollars," he fumed. "And who is that little boy? The one who kept staring in my direction from the interrogation room as though he knew someone was behind the tinted window. Who is he? And where will they go from here?"

Something shifted in his mind, an anomaly, a change. His mouth curved into a diabolic smile. He looked out the window one more time, staring at the dark night, knowing that Ademola and Crowder were on their way out of the grounds of DMI. "Ola Sakara, a.k.a. Ademola, you have just become Public Enemy Number One. There isn't a place for you to hide in this country. Since you've always assumed you have monopoly on wisdom, this is your chance to prove it. Whatever you do, rest assured I will outsmart you in the end," he said to the night before walking out of the room. He double-locked the door and headed upstairs to his office next to Dikko's. He picked up the telephone and dialed.

"*Hello?*"

Sakara recognized the voice that answered on the second ring as that of his most loyal and resourceful assistant, Ben Achibong. "Lieutenant, I want all roads leading in and out of Embassy Row sealed. Station Special Units in front of both the American Embassy and the British High Commission."

"*Who are we looking for, sir?*"

"Two men and a boy of about eight."

"*Any name, sir?*"

"Yes, Dr. Ademola. He's holding a Nigerian passport. And Dr. Crowder who is a naturalized American citizen. The name of the boy is unknown."

"*If there's resistance shall we terminate on sight?*"

"No! But don't let them near any Embassy building. They just stole classified government documents from here. If you have to, visit bodily harm on them, but I want them alive. National security is at stake. Get them!"

"*Will do, sir,*" Achibong replied with confidence.

"He's got a gun," Ademola whispered. Using Crowder's shoulder for support, he shifted his bulk to his better foot and hobbled as quietly as he could, keeping close to the wall fencing the grounds.

"So do I."

"Stop kidding!"

"I'm serious. Look." Crowder pulled the revolver he got from Ali out of his pocket.

"Put that thing away, please. You don't even know how to use it."

"But the guard doesn't know that."

"What's that supposed to mean?"

"Surprise. Can you walk to the gate alone?"

"Let me try." He let go of Crowder's shoulder, not thinking, and turned too quickly; pain ripped through his ankle and up to the rest of his body. He gritted his teeth and quickly grabbed Crowder's shoulder, his body trembling as the pain lanced his brain. He held on for a moment and sighed as he felt the pain ebbing. "I hope my ankle is not broken from the jump."

"You mean you can't walk at all?" Crowder frowned.

"I'll try."

"While you and our young partner-in-crime distract the guard, I'll come from behind, stick the gun to his head and force him to open the gate."

"The gate is open already."

"I'll be damned. I wonder why that is. Is it a trap?"

"Why don't we just ask him?" Ademola tried to free his arm from Crowder's shoulder again. The pain returned. "My ankle feels like it's broken. It hurts terribly."

"Hold on to Ali for support."

Ademola grabbed Ali's hand, careful not to move too suddenly. He shut his eyes and stilled himself for a while. There was no pain. He took a deep breath and held on. They inched toward the guard whose back faced them. "Hey, where is the toilet?" Ademola waved his free hand in the air.

The guard jerked his head like a lizard sensing danger. Ademola saw the man's finger curled around the trigger, his nervousness more threatening than the rifle. "Who goes there?" the soldier snapped. He bent forward and his upper body turned right and then left, looking like a child playing the game of cops and robbers.

Ademola saw Crowder stealing toward the soldier from behind, his revolver held high in readiness to strike. Then he heard the butt of the revolver landing on the soldier's neck. The sound of gunfire erupted as the soldier pressed the trigger on his way down, disoriented.

"Let's go!" Crowder stepped over the soldier who stirred and began to get up. Crowder left-footed him in the stomach with such force, the body rose a couple of inches from the ground and then collapsed, immobilized.

"Let me hang on to you, Ayo." Ademola gently let go of Ali's hand. The boy bent down to pick up the rifle.

"What is he doing? Do you know this boy?" Crowder helped Ademola get a grip on his shoulder.

"No, but I've seen him around the hospital before. Hey, Ali, leave that gun alone and come with us."

The boy obeyed and limped to the men, reached out a hand to hold Ademola's wrist.

"Who are you?" Ademola asked, a comforting sense of kinship filling him as their hands touched.

"I told you before. I am Ali."

"Where is your mother and—"

Ali let go of Ademola's hand abruptly. With a contained violence that creased his young face, he said, "That's none of anybody's business!" He then limped away without a backward glance.

"What's that all about?" Ademola turned sideways to look at his friend, perplexed.

Crowder shrugged. "That's strange. It's dangerous to keep him around anyway. I think we better let him go."

"We can't do that."

"Why not?"

"He's only seven years old. Victoria Island is a long way from his house in Ikeja."

"How do you plan to get him back there? We are not going in that direction."

"Where are we heading?"

"Our best bet is—what's that?" Crowder turned his head sharply and looked behind.

Ademola followed his friend's gaze to the road and ducked instinctively, pulling Crowder down with him. He saw a pair of headlights approaching from the DMI building, slashing the darkness like the torch of a welder. An army vehicle cruised past, unhurried. Ademola pressed his face against the leaves of the hibiscus plant that formed part of a shrubbery in front of a mansion, one of many in the area.

"Do you think he saw us?" Crowder stared at the red tail-lights of the Land Rover.

"I don't think so. Look over there." Ademola pointed to the other side of the road.

"It's Ali. How did he get over there? And why is he walking back toward DMI?" Crowder asked.

Ademola grunted, puzzled. He grabbed Crowder's wrist and with a voice infused with the discovery he said, "That's it! Ali is a genius, and maybe our savior. Believe me, he's going in the right direction."

"What?" Crowder's mouth hung half-opened.

"We should be going that way also," Ademola said, excited at the idea forming in his mind. "Listen, the only way out of this island is to cross either of the two bridges that connect VI to Lagos, right?"

"Right. But we are not crossing the bridge. Our destination is the American Embassy which is only about a mile from here. My passport is blue, not green. I am an American citizen," Crowder said proudly.

"They already know that and that's the more reason we shouldn't go near the Embassy just now. Later maybe. I bet you that Land Rover is on its way there."

"What are you talking about? How do we get out of the island?" Crowder challenged.

"I don't know. But let's think for a second. What if I'm right, and the entrance to Embassy Row is blocked before we get there? Our best chance is to go back toward Eko Hotel, find a place to hide. Then we can figure a way out."

"Are you talking about checking into the hotel?"

"No."

"Do you have a rich friend here who would let us hide in his million-dollar home?"

"No."

"Then where do you intend to hide?"

"Come on, let's think. You have a Ph.D. and I am an M.D. Are you going to tell me we can't think of a way to outsmart a bunch of idiots in army uniform?"

"Don't be naive, we're not dealing with ordinary soldiers. These boys at DMI are the very best and the worst, if you will, the joint military services have to protect their interests. They are not stupid at all."

They walked to the edge of the road and were about to cross when Ademola saw a flash and then darkness. He yanked at the sleeve of Crowder's shirt, pulling him back. They both turned and ran past several houses to take cover under a bush of banana trees in front of a huge building.

Ademola heard the sound of an engine sneaking toward them like a burglar readying to steal into a house. A spotlight beam shot from the vehicle and landed over the front lawn of the house next to the banana trees. Like a luminous protozoa, it split into two and spread to cover the base of the trees. Ademola crouched down lower and his ankle signalled discomfort at such a sudden move, sending a painful message throughout his body. He gritted his teeth to stifle a groan. Then a dog started to bark behind the wrought-iron gate of the mansion. The flashlight darted from the trees to the gate, remained there for a moment and then shot back, landing directly over Ademola's face, blinding him. He held his breath, ignoring the pain in his leg. The light lingered. The dog growled. The gate became illuminated again. And there was silence. And darkness.

Ademola sighed as the sound of the engine began to fade. He opened his eyes in time to see the dark shadow of the Land Rover negotiating a curve in the road as it disappeared like a burial palanquin into a graveyard.

Sakara looked at his watch and grabbed the telephone. He dialed and spoke rapidly, "Give me the editor... Get him!" His crossed eyes looked like a pair of black olives as he waited. "This is the office of the head of state... Stop press immediately. An officer is on his way with two photographs and an emergency message... What do you mean you can't... Do that! Replace the cover page... Yes, both front and back. Put the pictures side by side covering half of the front and back covers... Yes, WANTED, in red above the pictures... Dr. Ola Ademola and Dr. Ayo Crowder... Yes, the same one. Don't interrupt me again! The two men are wanted for a treasonable felony charge. They are known to be armed and dangerous. Any law-abiding citizen that helps in their apprehension will receive a reward of one hundred thousand *naira*. Anyone found guilty of assisting them will be executed. Did you get that? ... I know it's already three in the morning. Just do it. This is a matter of national security. The head of state will address the nation... You will have a copy." Click. Sakara spun around in his swivel chair to face General Bukha who sat at the head of the conference table, his countenance darker than the ebony statue on a stand to his left. A cigarette glowed between his fingers, half its length waiting to drop on the polished surface of the mahogany table. "Your Excellency, it's time to ask the Minister of Foreign Affairs to give the American Ambassador and the British High Commissioner a call. The two diplomats should be told to instruct their immigration officers not to grant Ademola political asylum status. The two should not be allowed into the premises of the embassies."

"Why do you think they will go there?" the head of state asked.

"Dr. Crowder is a naturalized American citizen. He studied both political science and journalism in America, sir. He knows his rights. But those rights do not supersede our desire to protect Nigeria's national sovereignty. America and

Great Britain are our allies, sir. They will not compromise their interest to save the lives of two troublesome black men. Oil, sir, our crude oil is your leverage." Sakara felt superior to both his boss and the hollow giant whose time as head of state, he reasoned, was about to run out. "I need you to help me catch those two, then you are history," he thought.

"Well said," the head of state approved, just as more ashes dropped onto the table. He took a long drag on the cigarette, blew out the smoke, fouling the air with the smell of tobacco. "What else have you planned?"

"I will not bore you with the details, sir, but in a nutshell, I have already alerted the Director of CID, the Inspector General of Police, both Directors of Custom and Immigration. All border posts in the southern part of the country are on the look out. The airport at Ikeja is being watched. Every house in Victoria Island will be searched. We will catch them before noon, sir."

"Good, major! I need to speak with Brigadier Dikko in private. You can leave now." Bukha dismissed Sakara with such nonchalance, Dikko looked uncomfortable.

Sakara saluted and marched out the room.

Ademola and Crowder came out of hiding behind the banana trees and ran across the road. Crowder led as they walked toward the beach, their movement slowed by the sand. The sound of the waves pounding the beach deafened the moonless night. The breeze was wet and salty.

"I wish I could just jump in and swim until I reach Coney Island," Crowder said, as they approached the beach.

"That would be quite a swim." Ademola stopped to catch his breath. He bent forward to inspect his ankle, moving his toes up and down. "I don't think I broke any bones."

"Good, maybe we both should swim out. America is on

the other side of the Atlantic ocean. If only we could swim, or make a raft."

"I don't see why not. It'll probably take us about two years to get there. Assuming the sharks have gone to visit their cousins in South Africa to help enforce apartheid," Ademola joked, needing to relax.

"I'm glad you see the light on the other side of the ocean," Crowder said. They both laughed. "In all seriousness, what if you're right about the embassy being sealed? It's also safe to assume that the bridges are not going to be left wide open for our easy passage to Lagos. And since we cannot hide here on the beach indefinitely, our only option is to get to the lagoon side of Victoria Island as quickly as we can. Do you get my drift?" Crowder said.

"And swim across? No, how about catching a canoe ride with a fisherman?"

"Brilliant, my friend. You're a genius like that boy. Where did he disappear to anyway?" Crowder looked around.

"I hope they haven't caught him," Ademola said, concerned.

"I hope not. I was beginning to like the little fella. Now, back to our problem, what do we do after crossing the lagoon, assuming we manage to do that?"

"That's one bridge we'll have to cross when we get there. Right now, we need to get going. It will be daylight soon," Ademola said.

They trudged along the sand for several minutes. Ademola started to limp around what looked like a mound of sand when it shifted. He peered down and was amazed to realize it was Ali. He dragged him up and they hugged each other.

"What on earth were you doing lying like that?"

"Hiding from the wicked soldiers," Ali replied.

"Do you want to come with us?"

The boy nodded yes. Crowder shook his head and continued to lead the way onward to the beach, staying under the cover of the palm trees scattered about.

Suddenly a voice, masculine and authoritative, interrupted the sound of the waves, "Who goes there?"

Ademola ducked behind a palm tree, dragging Ali with him. Crowder stopped midstride.

"Identify yourself," the voice ordered.

Ademola saw Crowder shrug and continue to tread the sand as though he did not care who it was. "Good thinking," Ademola thought, coming out from behind the tree. Then he saw the silhouette of a man approaching them, holding what looked like a bell and a long staff. Ademola recognized him as an *Aladura*—a priest of the Cherubim and Seraphim, a break-away Christian sect that believes in the existence of a celestial being having three pairs of wings, one of the first order of angels. The Old Testament's description of the cherubim emphasized their supernatural mobility and their cultic role as throne bearers of God, rather than intercessory functions. The followers wanted the rest of the world, including Jews, Christians, and Muslims, to believe that the cherubim were ranked high among the attendants of God.

In the early fifties they broke away from another sect which believed that Jesus Christ had been reincarnated into the form of a Nigerian, *Jesu Oyingbo*, who hitherto was a destitute carpenter. He preached frugality, hard work, and abstinence from coital interaction. Members were forced to disown their families and move into a communal residence at Ikeja. The membership grew. So did the collective wealth of the sect. When it was later revealed that the bulk of the sect's wealth belonged to the leader, a group broke away to form a new creed that retained the basic tenets of the sect. Their frugality manifested itself in their distinguishing characteristics: white robe reaching down to the ankles; clean-shaven head; the ever-present hand-bell; and the establishment of their holy shrine on the beach at Victoria Island where they roamed barefooted.

"Have you come to repent your sins, my children?" the man asked as though he already knew the answer.

"Nope," Crowder snapped.

"Are you then a member of the military?"

Crowder did not answer.

"Are you a soldier or not? If you're civilian, you shouldn't be out. They kill curfew breakers on the spot!" The preacher blocked Crowder's passage.

"Get the—"

"Let me handle this." Ademola stepped forward, wondering why Crowder was always so blunt. He switched from English to Egba dialect, suspecting the man hailed from Abeokuta. "Good morning, sir. Please, don't mind my brother, he is tired and confused."

"Are you troubled, my son?"

"Indeed. And I hope you might be able to help us," Ademola replied.

"Are you from my village also?" the preacher said and quickly added, "That does not really matter because we are all children of God."

"Amen." Ademola spiced up the bait.

"How deep is your trouble, my son?"

"Deep as the length of a rain-drop from the sky." Ademola pinched himself at the uncanny similarity between the preacher and his father in their manner of speech. Loneliness enveloped him at the thought of his father, and his voice broke when he said, "Will you help us?"

The preacher stared at Ademola. He clasped both hands around the mid-section of his staff, looking like one who was about to strike, or to give a blessing.

Ali got on his knees and gently pulled the preacher's robe. "Please!" His voice sounded supplicatory, anguished.

A smile tickled Ademola's mind as he locked eyes with the older man who bent forward to help Ali up. "What is your trouble? If it is God's command, I will help. But you must repent first."

"We will and—"

"Lord in Heaven, protect us from evil!" the preacher said in a voice laden with panic as he shifted his gaze.

Ademola turned to look over his shoulder and his heart skipped a beat when he saw headlights speeding toward them.

5

Sakara's heart missed a beat. He held the telephone receiver against the side of his head like a suicide weapon. He nodded several times before hanging up, shadows of fatigue under his red-rimmed eyes. He had not slept in the last twenty one hours. With a cryptic glint, he glanced at Lieutenant Ben Achibong seated in front of him and murmured, "When elephants fart, Lagosians defecate, eh?"

"Sorry, I don't believe so, sir," Achibong said, pronouncing the word as though the letter r scratched his throat, a phonetic inability which compelled most people to assume that he was not as intelligent as he really was. Like Sakara, Achibong took full advantage of the imperfection by emphasizing the drawl.

"Why not?" Sakara's voice sounded harsher than he intended. He was not fooled by Achibong's antics. But he accepted them as a necessary device.

"Lagos has never been a natural habitat of elephants, sir." Achibong smiled, glaring back at Sakara without disrespect. "But you're right, when a towering calamity befalls one, smaller ones do not wait for invitations."

Sakara watched him, noting that the lieutenant was his only subordinate who did not cringe in his presence. That in addition to Achibong's natural inadequacy was why Sakara felt a kinship toward him. At first he felt challenged by the young man's conduct, which at times bordered on defiance. But as he got to know him he realized that Achibong respected him as much as, if not more than, the others serving under him. Sakara tolerated him once in a while but never let him get away with any infraction. He brought him under his wing mostly because of his abilities and loyalty. "I want you on this case, Ben. Your expertise will be helpful. But we only have twenty-four hours to get the files and bring those two fugitives in. Balewa is an idiot. I shouldn't have allowed Dikko to talk me into giving that drunkard the case in the first place."

"Thank you, sir. I will do my best."

"What have you got so far?"

"With the information procured from the ambulance driver—He's been very cooperative, by the way. I have the address where he dropped off both Mrs. Ogawa and the doctor's fiancée."

"I doubt if they're still there. Ademola's fiancée is a very smart woman."

"Do you know her, sir?"

"What kind of question is that?" Sakara snapped, feeling the need to regain control.

"I didn't mean to imply anything untoward, sir."

"Good."

"I agree with you, chances are they have relocated since the driver dropped them off. But I'll find her."

"What about Ademola and Crowder?"

"I believe they're still here in Victoria Island."

"How's that?"

"They have not been to Embassy Row or anywhere near the bridges. It's safe to assume they're here, sir."

"Could they have found someone to hide them?"

"Not very likely, sir. The homeowners here are happy with the status quo. They won't do anything to jeopardize their positions. But their servants could be bribed. I will spend more time searching the boys' quarters."

"What about the worshippers on Bar Beach?"

"Highly probable even though the soldiers on patrol at the beach claimed that they did not see anything untoward there lately. Don't we have an informer among the worshippers, sir?"

Sakara opened a file, pulled out a sheet and handed it to Achibong. "That's him, a sergeant from Special Unit who went undercover among the worshippers. Be careful not to expose him. Comb the whole beach."

"Shall I bring them in for interrogation?"

"Not yet."

"Should Balewa be allowed to continue interrogating the patients that were *re-arrested*, sir?"

"Yes. He can't do much more damage there."

"What about the ambulance driver?"

"What about him—do you need anything else from him?"

"Nothing I can think of just now. He's been most co-operative. My concern though is that he talks too much."

"So?"

"Maybe he should be—"

"Let him go," Sakara said with finality, dismissing the five-foot-three-inch-tall lieutenant whose large head seemed an overcompensation for his height.

⤳

"Over here!" The preacher waved at Ademola who was on his knees behind a palm tree a few paces away.

Ademola filled a hole at the foot of the tree with sand. He pressed the sole of his foot several times over the spot before dashing away. He swam to where the preacher stood chest-deep in water, helping Crowder put Ali inside one of four boats that rocked as the waves slammed against them.

The boats were tied to a part of the pile of rocks erected by the British over a century before. The two-hundred-fifty-foot-long and ten-foot-high wave-breaker separated the Atlantic ocean from the lagoon which surrounded the island of Lagos.

"I pray that you're all safe and alive when I return." The preacher helped Ademola into the boat.

"Thanks." Ademola began to pull the wet tarpaulin over his head. He stopped and looked out in time to see approaching headlights.

"You are in God's hands now." The preacher took off his soaked robe and stuffed it under the tarpaulin. And clad only in his underpants and a crucifix dangling from a chain around his neck, he swam ashore.

Ademola ducked his head beneath the tarpaulin as several vehicles came to a halt on the beach. He heard the muffled sound of car doors slamming.

"Where do you come from?" an authoritative voice barked.

"From my usual predawn swim," the preacher said.

"Didn't you know there's a curfew?"

"But the work of the Lord must continue, doesn't it?"

"I ask the questions, not you!"

"Yes, my son," the preacher said.

"Where are the rest of your congregation?"

"We are not a congregation, officer. We are a flock following our Lord Jesus to salvation."

"Answer my question! Where are your people?"

"They are all sleeping as the Lord so ordained."

"Then why are you not with them? You're breaking the law. There is a curfew in effect."

"The law of God is supreme, my—Yes, His will must be done before anything else. I am the shepherd of our flock, officer. It is my duty to be up earlier than the rest."

"Have you seen any stranger about lately?"

"Yes, officer, two men and a boy."

"Where—when?"

"I don't know where they are now," the preacher said, looking away from the edge of the wave-breaker, a few paces from where the boats bobbed like toys. "Two of them were limping very badly. I offered to help but they refused."

"When was this?"

"Before I went for my swim."

"They must still be around somewhere then." The officer turned around. "Spread out!" he screamed.

Ten soldiers materialized from behind the vehicles.

"Search everywhere. You, sergeant, take two men into the water and search those boats."

The preacher looked up to the sky.

"Yes, sir. But I can't swim—" the sergeant began.

"The water is not deep. The rest of you, spread out."

The sergeant beckoned two soldiers toward him and the three started to take off their boots.

"What are you doing?" the officer asked.

"Taking off our clothes."

"Get in there!"

"Yes, sir," the three answered in unison and went in. The closer they got to the first boat, the deeper the water and stronger the waves. They held their rifles with both hands above their heads. The sergeant reached one of the boats first, but a strong wave surged toward him as he peered inside, making him lose his balance and then drop his rifle in the water before he could grab the edge of the boat. He cursed several times in his native language, bent over to look for the gun, and the surf swept him, smashing his body against the boat. He opened his mouth to scream and ingested a gush of salt water as he went under.

"This one to my right is empty. Find out what's under the tarpaulin in the boat next to you."

"Where's the sergeant?"

"He was over there a second ago—SERGEANT!"

No answer.

"Sergeant, where are you!"

The voice became clearer as it got closer. Ademola heard a metal-on-wood sound as the barrel of the soldier's gun hit against the side of his boat. His heart leapt when the boat rocked as the soldier grabbed the edge. He heard, "I am going to search this one."

"Corporal!" The soldier sounded alarmed.

"What is it?"

"The sergeant has gone under. I can't see him."

"What do you mean, you can't see him? Oh my God, he can't swim!"

Ademola felt a slight pressure as the corporal dropped his rifle into the boat, landing it on the tarpaulin over Ademola's head. He held his breath, expecting the soldier to pull off the cover. He waited. And waited.

The soldier turned around and swam toward his comrade. The two went under water and remained there for a brief moment. The corporal's head surfaced first and he took a deep breath before going under again. The other soldier came up, gasping. "I got him!" He wrapped his arm around the neck of the sergeant. "Corporal!"

"Right here, what—is he dead?"

"I don't know." He shook his head to clear the water off his face. "We better get him ashore. Get my gun from the boat."

The corporal reached a hand into the nearby boat, grabbed his rifle and then swam to the boat containing Ademola. As he reached a hand in, a huge wave crashed down on him. He went under, bumping his head against the side of the boat. Before he could regain balance, the surge of the wave took hold and swept him ashore.

Ademola raised his head and peered out. He saw the soldiers on the beach in frenzied movement, looking like evil spirits in a ritual dance. More soldiers came into view, accompanying a herd of robed worshippers who looked like sacrificial lambs ready for slaughter. They lined up along the edge of the beach.

Suddenly, he felt the boat bobbing, and the edge dipped as water rushed in. "We've got to get out of here. The rope is broken and the boat is drifting toward shore."

"Did the soldiers leave yet?" Crowder raised his head above the rim of the boat and ducked. "Dammit!"

"We must get off." Ademola jumped into the water. He grabbed the stump of the rope as the ocean-bound surf pushed the boat farther away from shore. He looked up and saw Crowder drop Ali into the water. "Can you swim?"

The boy shook his head in fright.

"Don't be afraid. Just hold onto my neck and I'll do the rest." Ali trembled, holding onto Ademola. "Ayo, let's try to hide behind that one." Ademola pointed to the boat a short distance away. He looked up and saw another wave approaching. He swam faster and reached the boat just as the wave started to descend. He saw Crowder looking up to the sky, immobilized. A black wall of water loomed above them, its top curved like the head of a cobra ready to strike. "Come on, swim!"

Crowder went under. A moment later his head surfaced next to the boat just as the wave crashed down, its noise drowning other sounds.

⌒

Dawn is a busy time for the residents of Lagos. People busy themselves folding sleeping mats, greeting each other at the top of their voices, older siblings bathing the young ones, women cooking and sweeping homes and housefronts. Early morning activities are always festive and frenetic.

This Saturday morning was different. By the time the sun negotiated the horizon, yawning away its slumber, its light supplanted the darkness that had given cover to the curfew-enforcers. The air had become filled with dread. Residents crowded hallways and backyards, anxiously awaiting the arrival of family members whose fate remained a mystery. The few that ventured outside ran back indoors to report their findings to their families. Several people had been found dead, their bullet-riddled bodies littered the streets. Mothers joined their babies in their tears, fearful lest the same befall their loved ones.

The sky wept with them, splattering on the rusted corrugated sheet-iron that roofed the houses, where the residents cowered inside in silent desperation. Grownups were too scared to spread rumors, their voices muzzled behind closed doors. An ominous force had seized control of their space as the families huddled together in their rooms.

Nobody seemed to pay much attention to the black sedan parked on the side of the street. A huge house that looked out of place in a neighborhood filled with wretched dwellings loomed a hundred feet away. The windshield wipers of the sedan glided back and forth. Rain splashed the tinted windows, which concealed Sakara, seated in the back, as he observed the front entrance of the big house.

"Knock on the door and, whoever answers, ask if Eniola is at home. Chances are she's not. Leave the message: She's expected to come to DMI headquarter not later than noon. Take a look inside for any sign of others in the house. Go!"

The driver dashed out of the car, bent forward, and held his hand like a visor to shield his face from the rain as he ran to the house.

Sakara watched as his driver banged on the door and waited. He banged again. Still no response. The driver wiped the water off his face, which looked contorted with rage. He banged once more and, getting no answer, walked to the window. As he commenced to peer inside, the front door flung open and a young man in pajamas stood in the doorway. The driver walked back to the door, and a heated argument ensued. The soldier slapped the young man. Sakara cringed and his lips curled into a curse, "You dung-eating buffoon!" He reached forward and pressed the horn which trumpeted like an enraged elephant. He peered through the windshield and saw a small crowd begin to gather. The young man stepped forward and struck the soldier on the side of his head. The soldier responded with a backhanded swat, and grabbed the young man's neck. Two neighbors who had arrived at the scene pulled them apart. Fingers started pointing in different directions. An old woman, whom Sakara recognized as Eniola's mother, came out, her headscarf tied around her waist.

"I wish this idiot would come back here before someone has the audacity to do what this type of crowd normally does. They will burn this car in an instant with me inside. Why in God's name do I have imbeciles as assistants?"

And then, quite suddenly, the commotion stopped and all heads turned to stare at the sedan. Sakara saw his driver push his way back to the car, under the intense scrutiny of the crowd. They looked at the top of the car, their eyes hypnotized by something seemingly astounding. "What's going on?" Sakara asked himself, wishing he could roll down the window to look. But he dared not. He waited for his driver to rush back to the car. "What the hell is going on?" His anger was spiked with curiosity.

"That stupid boy came out of the—"

"Dammit, I didn't ask you about that. You idiot! What on earth are they staring at?" With the corner of his eyes, he saw that the people had shed their inertia and had started to come forward. "Start the bloody car and get us the hell away from here."

The driver engaged gear and took off. Sakara turned in

his seat and looked back. At first he did not see anything. Then his eyes caught a strange image up in the sky, a half-formed rainbow which radiated strange colors. "What manner of happenstance is this? There had been the sudden downpour of rain while the sun looked like it was ready to burn the sky yesterday. And now this," he pondered, worry furrows creasing his forehead. His mind became a bewildering cyclone. He tasted bile in his mouth as his stomach churned.

Throughout his life he had felt this type of fear only once—in the presence of his father the day before he left for Mayfield School. He shut his eyes, and yet he couldn't expunge the images that began to pierce the fog in his head. With the clarity of a full moon the face of his father loomed, eyes as big as oranges, and lips twice the size of a blacksmith's bellows. His voice, clear as though he was there with him, said, "No matter how red your eyes get, you cannot light a cigar with it! The world is disgusted with failures whose mouths are full of excuses—"

"Shut up!"

"I—I beg your pardon, sir?" the driver looked over his shoulder, bewildered.

"Drive on," Sakara snapped as he shut out the images in his mind. "A problem is never so weighty that one can slice it with a knife. What I need to do is pay the old man a visit on his farm where it all began. It's time I cast off his spell, and even the score," he promised himself.

Ademola, Crowder, and Ali stood on the beach, water dripping down their necks. The preacher looked at them, anxiety and anguish in his voice: "Why do they want you?"

"The less you know the better off you are," Ademola

said, knowing that was far from reassuring. He stepped
toward the preacher, then wiped the water off his face with
the back of his hand. In a conspiratorial tone of voice, he
said, "We are in possession of damaging information."

"What type of information?"

"I can't tell you that."

"Is it the thing you buried there?" The preacher nodded
to a nearby palm tree.

"Yes."

"Why don't you dig it up?"

Ademola walked to the tree. He got on his knees, dug a
hole, and extracted the manila envelope and a wad of currency. He got up and walked back to the preacher. "What
kind of information is it?"

"We don't have any idea."

"Then how do you know it's damaging?"

"That's neither here nor there, sir. We need your help,
and if you're going to do something let's get started before
those soldiers come back," Crowder said.

"How can I help you?"

"First, we need to get off Victoria Island."

"Then what?"

"We'll leave the rest in the hands of God. As I said, it's in
your best interest that you don't know who we are, or what's
in the envelope."

"Don't you mean, for your best interest only?"

"True," Ademola responded.

The preacher got down on his knees, looked up to the
sky, palms pressed together in supplication, his lips began to
tremble as he prayed. Crowder rolled his eyes, shook his
head, and moved closer to Ademola to whisper, "We are
wasting precious time. Daybreak will be here soon, and if we
are not off this island by then we are easy targets."

"What do you suggest we do?" Ademola whispered
back.

"We need to disguise ourselves."

"How?"

"If only we could grow beards and—"

"Wait a minute. Look at the preacher."

"Yes, what about him?" Crowder asked.

"He's bald."

"So what?" Crowder asked.

"We do the same."

"No!"

Ademola looked over his shoulder to make sure the preacher did not hear them. "Let's get real. Your idea of growing a beard is not a viable option right now. Later maybe. In the meantime, we have to become incognito."

"And Ali?"

"What about him?" Ademola asked, not liking his friend's tone of voice.

"We have to lose him."

"Not until we're sure of his safety," Ademola said with uncompromised determination.

"When will that be?"

"We—"

There was stirring. Ademola turned as the preacher got off his knees and beckoned them to approach. "Here's the situation. Our Lord in Heaven has spoken to me. He has appointed me as His Messenger and Prophet of Mercy to help you. But not before you repent."

"Thank you very much." Ademola reached out for a handshake. The preacher walked away, toward the ocean. He beckoned and Ademola followed, wading in the water until he was knee-deep. He stopped beside the preacher who placed his hand on the back of Ademola's neck. "You shall be cleansed of your past sins." He pressed the other hand against his stomach and pushed his head down into the water. He held it there for a moment. He looked up to the sky and commenced to pray:

"Baptism, which corresponds to this, now saves you, not as a removal of dirt from the body but as an appeal to God for clear conscience, through the resurrection of Jesus Christ, who has gone into heaven and is at the right hand of God, with angels, authorities, and powers subject to him."

Ademola shook the water off his face, gasping. The preacher repeated the exercise two more times, prayed some more, and finally pronounced him purified.

Crowder and Ali refused to come forward when the preacher waved at them. "Your brother and the boy will cause you a lot of trouble in the future if they refuse to repent, my son," the preacher said. He waited for a brief moment before shrugging his shoulders. He held Ademola's hand in his and the two walked back to the beach.

The preacher got on his knees, and punched three holes in the sand with his index finger. He connected the holes with lines, forming a triangle. "This is your escape route." He looked up. "This is Victoria Island." He pointed, "From here you will travel in a boat to Takwa Bay."

"Why must we go to another island instead of crossing to Lagos or the mainland?" Ademola asked, concerned.

"That is what I gleaned from the Message, my son. Don't question His will."

Ali stepped forward and nodded his acquiescence.

The preacher smiled. "The people after you are very clever. By now they must have known that you intend to cross to Lagos in a boat."

"How do you know that?" Crowder interrupted.

"It's a guess. Don't walk into a trap that I suspect is already set. From Takwa Bay a fisherman's canoe will take you across the lagoon to Ebute Meta on the mainland. At that point you are on your own. Praise the Lord!"

"Thank you very much."

"Don't thank me, be grateful to our Lord Jesus Christ

through whom you will gain entrance to everlasting peace, Amen." The preacher got up, walked to a nearby tent and came back with three white robes. He handed them to Ademola and asked him to go into the tent and change.

Ademola did. And when he emerged, Crowder started to laugh. "What's so funny?"

"You should see yourself. You look like a *serafu* who has not accepted God," Crowder said. "You have a head full of hair."

"Oh, that." Ademola smiled, wanting to laugh but not wishing to annoy the preacher. He turned to the old man. "Do you have a razor blade, sir?"

"Of course, my son. I will be glad to rid you of your human vanity. Come with me."

Moments later, Ademola emerged hairless.

"Now you look just like one of the congregation." Crowder laughed with tears in his eyes.

"It's not funny at all. Our lives are on the line and we ought to be grateful." Ademola stopped and looked surprised as he saw Ali going into the tent.

"Do you suppose he's going to let the preacher shave his head also?" Crowder asked in mockery.

"Ali has demonstrated better judgement than you and I under the circumstance," Ademola responded, miffed.

"You're right. I didn't mean to belittle our problem. It's just that you look so strange and funny," Crowder said, bursting into a cackle.

"Stop it!"

Crowder's laughter waned into a chuckle.

Ali came out shaved. He held out his hands for the robe which Ademola handed him, and he put it on while Ademola wrapped his ankle with a piece of the material he tore off his shirt.

Sakara stood in the middle of his office glaring at Achibong, whose facial expression resembled one who had just swallowed a glass of quinine.

"I take total responsibility for the mishap, sir. Even though it was inevitable," Achibong said, finishing his report.

"The only thing that is inevitable is your demotion to the rank of sergeant," Sakara said, surprised at how calm he sounded despite the inferno raging inside him. He walked to the wall and stared at a map of Lagos. He took a yellow marker out of his pocket and stabbed it at a point on the map. "That's where you should have gone first instead of wasting precious time searching the houses."

"No doubt that's true, sir. But—"

"Don't speak unless I ask you to." A wrathful smirk twisted Sakara's face. "That old preacher did not tell you the whole truth."

"Shall I bring him in?"

Sakara spun around and banged on a table nearby so hard the telephone flew off and crashed to the floor. He yelled, "I told you not to speak."

Achibong backed off a few steps and stood rock-still.

Sakara walked back to the wall and stared at the map with the intense frustration of a famished lion looking at a gazelle behind an impenetrable fence

"They have left Victoria Island," he said in a broken murmur. "But where are they?" He leaned forward and studied the map, concentrating on a spot, another island connected to both Victoria Island and Lagos by the Atlantic ocean and the lagoon. The word Takwa Bay loomed in black. He looked at his watch and saw both fingers of the dial pointing at five-twenty-five. "It's already morning and the curfew is off. Dammit, the streets will soon be filled with eight million people. Finding the bastards will be like looking for a pinhead in a sackful of woodshavings." The word FAILURE flashed in his head.

Sakara had always had the fear of failure since his father warned him not to come back from Mayfield without accomplishing his goals. But he had failed at the end of his first year. All because he had listened to that son-of-a-fornicating-canon who conspired with his bastard brother to mislead him. He had trusted Crowder. Over twenty years later, he could still hear the sound of the cane as his father lashed his body until he had thought he was going to faint. Yes, that was old history, but he had waited long enough to get even. Crowder and Ademola must pay with their lives, NOW! They owed him that much. That devious prank at Mayfield had cost him a year and an unforgettable lashing from his father. Yes, his fornicating father who'd acted as though he was better than anyone else in the village. What a joke! But he was right about failures with empty excuses. HE WOULD NOT FAIL! A head for an eye, that was what he promised the bastard and his spoiled friend, Crowder. "But what about Achibong? Is he a spy? A detractor? Or just another bumbling nonentity in army uniform? And we have plenty of them here, especially the officers at the top. Generals! What a farce! There are more generals in the Nigerian Army than in all the countries on the continent of Africa combined. Lazy bastards who have turned an honorable institution into a parody of the Salvation Army! But I am a member of that infamous club as long as I wear the uniform, and kiss the black rear ends of dimwits like Dikko, Idi Amo, and Bukha." He turned to Achibong. "Come with me to the beach." He snatched up the special edition of the daily newspaper on his desk before walking out the door. "Stealing the file from my office, Ademola and Crowder are egg-snatchers without a doubt," he fumed, remembering Dikko's story about the eggs.

Their canoe ride from Takwa Bay to the mainland of Lagos was uneventful. The fisherman was reasonable in his demand for the fare, and knowledgeable in his navigation of the waters. Ali never stopped staring at the water, mesmerized by the school of fish that followed the canoe. It was mid-morning when they arrived at Ebute-Meta. The sun was up in the sky, heated like a leaky radiator.

Ademola was the first out of the canoe. The bandage around his ankle had helped to reduce the pain but he still walked with a limp, his white robe already soaked in sweat from the heat and humidity. But Ali had stopped limping, causing Crowder to pull Ademola aside. "We need to lose this boy. He's a trickster, without a doubt," Crowder said.

"Why do you say that?" Ademola asked, not liking his friend's tone of voice.

"Haven't you noticed that he does not limp anymore?"

"Yes, I did."

"Isn't it strange?"

"Granted, the boy is a little mysterious, but he hasn't caused us any trouble so far. Besides, I still don't feel that it's time to lose him as you so put it."

"I don't like mystery. And the boy is full of it. I hate to say this, if we don't get rid of him soon, I'm going it alone. If you want to play surrogate father to a seven-year-old boy that looks like he came straight out of an Ethiopian refugee camp, that's your privilege."

"Don't say that, it's wrong and you're being unfair. Look at what he's done to help already."

"What?" Crowder hissed.

"Sshh. If we had not followed him toward the beach, chances are, we would have walked into a trap."

"So we did, but I still think our best bet is to find a place in Takwa Bay to hide for a while," Crowder said, his voice lacking conviction.

"That's not a viable option, and you know it."

"Have you got a better idea?"

"Not yet. But it will be easier for us to find a safer and more reliable place to hide here on the mainland."

"Where and for how long?"

"I don't know. Let's think. You and I have lots of friends. There's bound to be one that will help."

"Like who?" Crowder grimaced as he scratched his head. "I feel like the bald-headed, blind old diviner atop the hills of Arinota."

"That's it!" Ademola grabbed Crowder's arm as though he stumbled on the most brilliant idea yet. "Why don't we go to the village? Arinota will be our best bet."

"There's only one thing wrong—it's too obvious. We have to think in diabolical terms. We have to imagine what they expect us to do and then twist it backward."

"Let's go back to the beginning," Ademola said, his mind already set in motion. "After escaping from DMI, we headed for the American Embassy but then decided against it because of Ali, right?"

"That probably was a bad move. We were way ahead of them. Chances are we might have made it there before they got started."

"But they followed us to the beach. And we got lucky."

"Some luck. Look, let's get off the street first. I feel exposed and vulnerable despite our silly disguise. There's a taxi." Crowder waved to a passing yellow car which did not stop. "Our immediate problem is getting off the street. But we have to know where we are going before we get into a taxi. We can't discuss that in the presence of the driver."

"Let's head toward Yaba. We'll ask him to drop us off in front of the asylum," Ademola said.

"Maybe we should check in there. We are mad enough to be admitted." Crowder started to laugh at his own joke.

"Very funny indeed."

Crowder shrugged and took a step forward. "TAXI!" He

waved. Four taxis cruised by, one after the other, without stopping. "Dammit. I think it's time to find a food canteen nearby. I'm famished."

Ademola agreed. And they continued walking for a while. Nearing a white house that looked like a hotel, Ademola noticed that the mass of pedestrians on both sides of the street had stopped walking, and were staring at the center of the road behind them. Then the air was deafened by the sound of a siren as a convoy of military vehicles approached. There were several soldiers brandishing their rifles in the air. Ademola ducked, pulling Crowder down with him. As the last of the six vehicles sped past, Ademola looked at Crowder and shook his head in disdain. "Are they already this close on our trail? Let's get in there." He pointed to the hotel, and then commenced to cross the street.

They were halfway across when a yellow Peugeot 504 sedan screeched to a halt, almost hitting Ali. The driver's hand shot out, palm spread wide in a local non-verbal assault on the culprit. He then stuck his head out the window and yelled, "*O ba'ya e, om'ale* (To your mother, you bastard)!"

Ademola and Crowder ran to the other side of the road. Ali stood still, refusing to yield.

"Get away from my front, stupid *serafu*," the driver yelled in pidgin English.

Ali remained rooted to the spot. The driver jumped out and was about to do violence to the boy when Ademola said, "Is your taxi available for hire?"

"I no *dey* go Victoria Island," the driver snapped contemptuously.

"We are not either." Ademola quickly opened the back door and got inside. Crowder followed, and Ali slipped inside and settled in the front passenger seat.

"*Na* where you want go?"

"Yaba," Ademola said.

"Say that again, eh?" The driver turned around to stare at

Ademola.

"I said Yaba," Ademola repeated.

"I hear you the first time. Your voice familiar."

"What voice, what're you talking about?" Crowder grabbed Ademola's hand.

Ademola turned sideways to look out the window.

"I *fit* say—" the driver started.

"Will you go!" Crowder snapped, interrupting the driver who immediately accelerated.

"Where in Yaba, eh?"

"The asylum," Crowder responded.

"The hospital for mad people, eh? The reason I no want go to Lagos *na* because military checkpoints plenty for road. Big trouble *dey* for country and I think say those soldiers *wey* just passed will be setting up checkpoints all over town soon." The driver looked in the rear-view mirror.

A disquieting fear engulfed Ademola.

The driver repeated, "Checkpoints plenty for road."

"So?" Crowder snapped.

"No problem, if you no get nothing to hide." The driver slowed down. Then he pulled over and stopped.

"What's the matter?" Crowder asked.

"I know you. Why, you no recognize me, eh?"

"You know me?" Crowder asked.

"*Na* the doctor I *dey* talk to."

Ademola reacted as though someone hit him on the chest with a powerpunch, his body reeled backward.

"Your voice sound like a doctor I *sabi*. His name *na* Dr. Ademola. He be your relation?" the driver asked.

"No! Will you get back on the road and take us to our destination?" Crowder snapped.

"No problem." He drove on.

For a short while there was silence. Then Ademola saw the driver's face in the rear-view mirror, frowning as he suddenly turned to look over his shoulder at Ademola.

"Keep your eyes on the road," Crowder barked.

"*Chineke*, help me *o*! *Na* you."

"I beg your pardon," Crowder said. "What sort of nonsense is this? This man is mad. I think you should stop the car right now and let us get out and find another one."

"Please, make you no vex with me *o*. This *na* the way God *dey* do His miracles. Look at this." He grabbed a newspaper from his lap and handed it to Crowder who started to read the front cover, and his eyes bulged instantly.

Ademola reached over and his reaction was the same.

"This *na* miracle *o*. Dr. Ademola, make I remind you who I be. Last year my two-year-old pickin was brought to your hospital at Ikeja. She for die if not for you. You not only saved her, you even give us money for her medicine. And you came twice to the house to see if say her progress good. How I *fit* forget you? You still no remember me, eh?"

"I'm sorry, I don't," Ademola whispered, his eyes glued to the newspaper.

"My name *na* Uche Okpara. The name of my pickin *na* Ngozi. Now, you remember?"

"Faintly. You have to forgive me, I see so many patients daily, it's impossible to remember everyone." Ademola felt uneasy.

"I understand. You are a good man, doctor. Me I no care what the paper say. Them *dey* offer one hundred thousand *naira* reward for your arrest. The BASTARDS! But you no *fit* blame them *o*. Our people *fit* do anything for that kind money. The soldiers done turn the citizens of this country into *asewo wey fit* do anything for money. But not me *o*. Wherever you want to go, I go take you, doctor."

"Thank you." Ademola's voice cracked.

"No, it's I which must thank you. And I do, everyday. Dr. Ademola, we Ibos never forget a debt. I owe you plenty. You see, my wife get four children *wey* died before Ngozi was born. All of them *na Agbanje*, the same pickin Yorubas call

109

Abiku. So my little daughter who is alive and in robust health, thanks to you and God, *na* my only child. Even though our culture say that I must get plenty children, I no *fit*. But thank God, one is better than none."

"I am glad to hear your daughter is doing fine."

"Doctor, you no *fit sabi* how important Ngozi is to me." His voice broke. He ran a palm over his face, wiping away tears, and was quiet for a while.

Ademola patted him on the shoulder. "You're a lucky man. And you should be proud of your daughter. Now I remember. You live at Mushin, don't you?"

"Yes, behind the railroad track. You visited us once."

"You spoke to me in Yoruba when I came to visit you, didn't you?" Ademola asked.

The driver nodded yes.

"Your daughter was a fighter who refused to die. I'm glad for you and your family. How's your wife?"

The driver hesitated before answering in fractured Yoruba. "There's not a day she does not thank God for sending you to help us."

"I was only doing my job," Ademola said, embarrassed.

"You don't understand. If I had died before Ngozi, that would have been the end of my clan in this world."

"How's that, don't you have any relatives?"

"It's a long story, doctor. I was born in Jos and lived there with my family until 1965 when we moved to Kaduna. A year later, all the members of my household, including the children, were slaughtered like animals. I still have nightmares. I—I saw—"

"It's okay, Uche. You're fine now," Ademola said, feeling the man's pain, and sharing it.

When the driver spoke again, his voice was only a shade above a whisper: "I was only ten when it happened. The mob came at night brandishing all types of weapons, stabbing, slashing and cutting everyone in sight. I escaped by hiding inside the drum we used to collect human waste. But I saw two men press my m—mother to the ground and cut her throat like a goat. She was six months pregnant. I still hear her cry, a choking, bloodcurdling sound as she died in her own pool of blood." His hands began to shake, and he stopped the car in the middle of traffic.

The hot air was permeated by noises as the drivers behind the taxi blared their horns, their heads stuck out the windows as they yelled curses at Uche in different languages.

Ademola took one look out the window and his heart began to race. Two men had jumped out of the vehicle three cars behind the taxi. As they got closer, Ademola saw one of them pull out a *bulanla*, long leather whip, his expression as awkward as his army uniform.

"Move the car, Uche!" Ademola slapped the driver on the shoulder. Getting no response, he yelled, "For the love of God, move the car. Two sold—"

The soldier with the whip yanked the driver's door open. The other soldier bent forward to stare at Ademola. He yelled, "You, who are you?"

"We are passengers." Crowder dropped the newspaper in his hand to the floor.

Ademola heard Uche's strained voice, his teeth gritted, "I beg you, officer."

"All of you, come out," the soldier with the whip barked in his Hausa-accented broken English, his hand clamped on Uche's shirt. There was a struggle as Uche grabbed the hand and yanked it off. The soldier's face contorted with rage. He took a step back and was about to lash Uche with the whip when the car surged forward and sped off, knocking the soldier to the ground.

Ademola looked over his shoulder and saw the two running back to their Land Rover.

"They are coming after us."

"Let them. God will punish the bastards." Uche accelerated.

"I hope you know what you are doing, Uche." Ademola's fright mushroomed as the Land Rover came flying after them.

"I was once a soldier in the Biafran army. These bastards are no match for me, doctor."

"But you're not—"

"This is war and I'm not afraid to die fighting."

"Oh, my God!" Crowder said.

6

Within the last twenty-four hours everything connected to the investigation had met one form of failure or another. Though the dead journalist had gotten his comeuppance, the objective of the operation still eluded Sakara. The file remained at large. And Ademola had stolen an even more damaging document right from under his nose, a revelation that would cause an uproar among the generals and their fellow kleptocrats. But more significantly, it was a situation that would ignite a bloody *coup* from within the junior officers, who had been seeking such an excuse to take over the country. Another *coup d'etat*. Another page in the never-ending saga of inhumanity at the highest level. Ademola must be captured soon, and the files recovered. Now, seated in his office, Sakara began to review the case, acknowledging the mistakes. Personal sentiment had been allowed to impede the investigation.

Facts: Lade Ogawa had the file. Most likely, he had given it to his wife, who must've given it to Ademola. Ademola must have given it to Eniola (an unconfirmed supposition, but highly probable). Eniola and Ogawa's wife had escaped from the hospital (possibly with the file). An army officer had been set ablaze on the grounds of Ikeja General Hospital. The officer had been taken to the Military Hospital in Lagos where he remained in critical condition. Presently Ademola was guilty of attempted murder. If the officer died (which could be arranged), the charge would elevate to first-degree murder. No lawyer in his right mind would come forward to defend him. After all, wasn't the attempt premeditated. PENALTY? Death by Firing Squad. Ademola and Crowder were guilty of obstruction of justice; theft of government property; the attempted murder of another officer who had almost drowned at the beach; and finally, an iron-clad first degree murder of the officer whose death occurred during a car chase on the mainland of Lagos. The taxi driver of unknown identity was also being sought.

Sakara worked at his desk for an hour before leaving the DMI building for Dodan Barracks. The roof of the black sedan received the violent rays of the sun full blast, turning the inside of the car into a furnace despite the air conditioner. He rolled down the window, hoping to get relief from the heat, only to smell the stench that filled the air. The combination of the heat and his frustration had given him a headache. He could do nothing about the sun. It was God's way of showing a sample of the hell that awaited a people who must have committed the ultimate sin. Military dictators with parboiled brains had taken over the task of finishing the job. Wholesale annihilation.

The closer he got to Dodan Barracks, passing the tangle of houses on Awolowo Road, the more people there were crowding the streets in spite of the presence of armed soldiers. He rounded the corner into Obalende Street, a narrow road that led to the gate of Dodan Barracks, and the traffic crawled to a stop. Several soldiers lined both sides of the road, the expression on their faces mirroring the anxiety that had gripped the nation. He looked up and saw two red-headed lizards on the roof of a house locked in a deadly battle; the prize, a green-headed female, watched and waited for the winner. He shook his head. "I bet that nymphomaniacal reptile could easily satisfy both those red-headed idiots without any problem. The lizards have no solution because they lack understanding. Or else they would unite, and together, force the female to service both of them."

He glanced at the clock on the dashboard and realized that he had three minutes to get inside the gate. At the rate the soldiers at the check-point were moving, he knew he would be late for his appointment with General Bukha. He pulled off the road, parked the car and walked to the barricade. "Where's your vehicle?" he interrupted the captain who was snapping at a driver.

"What the—" The captain looked over his shoulder, his voice thick with venom. But he quickly changed the expression on his face, saluted Sakara, and pointed to a Land Rover behind him.

Sakara did not acknowledge the captain's greeting. "My car is over there. Here's the key. Get someone to bring it inside at once." He gave his keys to the captain and accepted the one for the Land Rover. He crinkled his nose as the stench of horse manure and hay from the Polo Club adjacent to Dodan Barracks attacked the air like an army of invading locusts. He got into the Land Rover and sped off, leaving a cloud of brown dust behind.

When he drove through the security gate and entered the grounds of the official residence of the head of state, he saw that the news people from the state-controlled television station were already unloading their camera equipment for the taping of Bukha's address to the nation. He parked the vehicle behind a white van with NTS inscribed on its sides, and hurried toward the building entrance.

The editor of the *Nigerian Times* called out to him, "I hope you like the cover of today's paper, major."

"Good job," he said over his shoulder without stopping.

Inside, he had expected the taping to take place in the conference room on the ground floor, but instead, a major told him to go upstairs to the residential section of the building. He did so with apprehension. "This bastard didn't tell me he was coming here," he thought.

Dikko, who sat next to Bukha on an over-sized sofa said, "Welcome, major."

The head of state waved him to the side of the room. The ash from the tip of Bukha's cigarette dropped to the carpet. "Hand over the document."

"I don't have it with me, sir."

"Why not?" Bukha got on his feet. He strode toward Sakara as though he was going to slap him, his face hardening. "You deceived me all along. I know full well you don't have the document."

"I—I—"

"Shut up," Bukha roared. "You are off the case, and as of this moment you're demoted to the rank of captain." His face had become so vicious that Sakara expected the giant to shoot him on the spot. "Do you take me for a fool? I should have you court-martialed." Suddenly the door opened and the second-in-command, Major General Idi Amo and the new head of security guarding Dodan Barracks, Brigadier Babasa, strode into the room. "You were right, he does not have the document," Bukha said to Idi Amo.

"Well, the reason is clear. The two fugitives are not only from the same village that the major hailed from, they are known to be best friends." Idi Amo sounded even more obnoxious than his superior. "He's treacherous." Idi Amo's *persona* swelled with the sardonic temperament of a drill-sergeant.

Sakara's fear of immediate execution diminished as he felt the scorching fire of hatred in his head. "This whore-mongering bastard is Yoruba. Or is he really? Coming from a state wedged between the Hausa-north and Yoruba-south, no wonder his people are schizophrenic. They are Yoruba and/or Hausa, depending on the prevailing opportunistic circumstance. So is Brigadier Babasa, who comes from another state, a smaller one north of River Niger, but equally afflicted with their kind of divided personality. A hitherto inferior people who hunger for power and superiority," he thought silently.

"You crossed the line when you lied to me." Bukha was irate. "A line that separates life and death."

"I can explain the—" Sakara began.

"Silence! Should I get one of the officers in my unit to escort him to his residence and keep him under house arrest, sir?" Babasa stepped forward.

⌒

A cloud of wine-colored dust hung over Iddo market as several hundred traders transacted their business in a uniquely African fashion. There were lots of women in colorful blouses and wrappers. The men, whose polyester trousers and dashikis were spotted with dark blotches of sweat, carried neck-breaking sacks of rice or *gari* on their heads.

The women measured their *gari, elubo*, rice, flour, couscous, corn, millet and several other grains with locally-made tin cups which had been dented so as to reduce their retention capacities.

The aroma of *moinmoin*, yams, and plantain (fried in groundnut oil) competed with those of spicy goat stew, *jollof* rice, *fufu, amala,* and the assorted tropical fruits balanced on the heads of teenage hawkers who paraded the grounds between parked passenger lorries. The sound of wooden pestles as the women pounded boiled yams against the hollow surfaces of mortars was drowned by a band of mendicant drummers who serenaded the traders with sycophantic ballads that got more laughter than money. The noise from two loudspeakers in front of a music-for-hire shop drowned every other sound with the music of King Sony Ade. Young boys and some adults wiggled their buttocks to the tune, their faces expressing joy and ecstasy.

"Make you forgive my behavior, eh?" Uche said in pidgin English, wiping sweat off his face. "I be like a man possessed. Those soldiers bring out the worst in me *o*. I had to do what I did, my brother."

"I understand, Uche." Ademola marveled at the speed which Uche drove the taxi while the two soldiers pursued them with such determination it was apparent that something dreadful was bound to happen.

And it did. Halfway into the hot chase, Uche drove into a crowd of pedestrians, barely missing a woman, and made such a daring U-turn the taxi looked like it was going to turn over. But it only swayed for a moment before regaining balance. The driver of the military vehicle tried to do the same thing and Ademola saw the Land Rover skid and swerve to the right and left before turning over. "It would be a miracle if either of the soldiers survived the crash," Ademola thought.

"Why are we going back toward Lagos?" Ademola had asked, breathless.

"As I *don* say before, I be once a soldier in Biafra, doctor, so I know well well how these nonentity in Nigerian Army uniform think. They no go expect us to travel back to town." Uche pressed hard on the gas pedal. As he drove, Ademola tasted bile in his mouth, and felt the squeezing of his heart. He looked at Crowder whose lips trembled as though he were locked inside a butcher's freezer.

Uche had driven the taxi straight into a mechanic's shop, an old friend from his village. Ademola and Crowder were asked to remove their white robes and were given mechanics' overalls. Ali made do with an oversized dashiki which made him look like a dwarf. Uche had a quick discussion with his friend in Ibo, and after much gesticulation, a sudden eruption of laughter, and finally a handshake and a bear hug, an agreement was reached.

Uche drove off in a blue Volvo station wagon with Ademola seated next to him, Crowder in the back seat and Ali concealed beneath a pile of old newspapers in the rear of the vehicle.

"Where do we go from here?" Ademola asked.

"Doctor, God *dey* for your side. The devil *dey* on the side of the government. And they win sometimes. But only because our people *don* give up hope. No be so?"

"Where do we—"

"The way I see your problem for this moment be like your chance for escaping from *dem* soldiers small like a groundnut if you stay here. You must leave the country through Cameroon."

"Cameroon?" Crowder asked.

"Yes, my brother, Cameroon. As I say before, I was a soldier in—"

"Yes, you were in the Biafran Army. But the war ended twenty years ago," Crowder said without tact.

"You are wrong, that war never end so long as the bastards *wey* kill all my people remain free."

"Well, with all due respect to you and your people, life goes on," Crowder said.

"The thing you say *na* why we Ibo never trust Yoruba. Even though Dr. Ademola is an exception like the old man who risked his life to rescue me in Kaduna twenty years ago. And I am always grateful to him, and you too, Dr. Ademola," he finished in Yoruba.

"Thank you," Ademola said, meaning it.

"As I say before, we Ibos never forget our debt. And we never forget past mistakes. My advice to you to escape to Cameroon is because that country is at war with Nigeria as we speak. But also because all the borders in the south will be loaded with soldiers by the time you get there."

"Don't we have to travel to the east to cross to Cameroon?" Ademola asked, not liking the idea.

"No. You must go all the way to the north—"

"What, are you out of your mind?" Crowder shouted.

"Dr. Ademola, this man is not nice *o*. But I no go pay him any mind. As I was saying, the *Nigerian Times* get your pictures on its cover, as you already saw. The good news be that that edition *dey* only for the south now. Not until tomorrow morning before it reach the north. If you travel now, you go reach the border before the cock start waking people up."

"How do we get there, and what part?" Ademola asked.

"Like I said, God *dey* for your side. My friend, the mechanic, told me that my brother-in-law, the one who transports kolanut to the north, is ready to leave for Yola as we speak. You must go with him. The journey no go be too nice, but I hope it will save your life," Uche concluded like a school teacher giving his student a difficult homework assignment.

Sakara walked out of the building a broken man. Outside, in the parking lot, Babasa, who had escorted him out, put a hand on his shoulder. "I wouldn't worry too much about what just happened. You must not abandon your search for the document." His cold stare said plenty, raised a lot of questions, but left no room for discussion.

Sakara saluted and started to walk out of the gate when he heard Babasa crack his fingers, and a lieutenant materialized from behind a green Mercedes Benz sedan. "Drive Major Sakara to the check-point where he left his car and bring it here. Let him have yours. Major, you can keep the Benz for as long as you wish. But you must find the document as soon as possible." He returned Sakara's salute, turned around, and disappeared into the building.

"Why would Babasa take such a chance?" Sakara asked himself as he drove off in the green Mercedes Benz. "Was he helping me or giving me a longer rope with which to hang myself? Or is his name on the list? One does not look a gift horse in the mouth. But this is not the time for idle speculation. I need hard facts fast. But how—where?" He glanced at the clock on the dashboard and realized that he was already late for his regular Saturday afternoon meeting with his old boss.

Retired General Akin was not just another soldier that rose to the top, he was one of the finest and best men in uniform. Sakara had met Akin right after graduating from the Defense Academy. He was then a lieutenant and had been posted as the *aide-de-camp* to the then Brigadier Akin who was also the GOC in Ibadan, the second most populous city in Africa, second only to Cairo. The brigadier took the young lieutenant under his wing, teaching, advising, guiding, often scolding, but mostly, mentoring him. And Sakara reciprocated with unconditional loyalty. He did anything and everything for his boss. Once, he introduced a beautiful young lady to the GOC. An undergraduate student at the university whom he would have liked to keep for himself. Eniola was sweet, smart, but above all, ambitious. She craved success and power. And she had her way with Akin, who later became a general after the coup that ushered in the short-lived rule of Murtala Muhammed.

Akin had shared a compromising secret with his protegé during one of their regular afternoon lunches, which they never ate until after a game of squash. The two enjoyed the game with the abandon of overeager adolescents. "Be ambitious but realistic," Akin had said. "Being a southerner has its limitations especially in the military. Don't aspire to be what is deemed an exercise in futility—becoming the king of the land. Do the next best thing. Be a kingmaker by keeping your ears close to the ground. Listen with your brain, not with your heart. The north has come to believe that the country belongs to them. And it does, as long as the Ibos and Yorubas maintain a destructive distrust between themselves."

"How?" young Sakara had asked.

"Pay attention to history. It has a way of repeating itself especially within the walls of the barracks. Offer to help those you know harbor achievable ambitions. But don't stick your neck out too far, or it will get chopped off. Don't, and I repeat, don't allow yourself to be used."

"Is that how you survive?"

"I do not survive, young man, I live. With confidence, self-respect and pride. I am a Yoruba!"

Then the shocker came.

"There has not been a *coup d'etat* that I either didn't know about or participate in. Most succeeded. But when there was failure, I was miles away from being implicated."

"Were you part of the first *coup* in '66?"

"Of course, Lagos was under my command. The Prime Minister was mine. So was the president, but someone warned him and the Premier of Eastern Region, and they escaped from right under our noses the night before January 15. The Prime Minister was not so lucky. He died, and I placed his body under a tree. It was sad because the killing took place during the month of Ramadan. He was fasting. As you know, the Premiers of the West and North were also killed along with several ministers and senior army officers. Most of us were exuberant in our patriotic duties. It was time for a change. But the operation was not a success. We were betrayed by some officers, mostly from the east. After the *coup*, we all agreed that Ironsi should head the nation. Six months later there was another bloodbath, Ironsi died while visiting Fajuyi, who was then the governor for Western Region. He too died. Though I was the most senior officer in the army, a couple of years ahead of

Gowon, I chose not to be considered for the number one post. That was how Gowon became the head of state when he was just thirty-two years old and a lieutenant colonel. Am I boring you?"

"Not at all, sir."

"You're not paying attention."

"I don't understand, sir."

"If you were paying attention, you would have asked the most significant question."

"I'm sorry, it's just that I did not wish to interrupt you," Sakara said earnestly.

"Now seize the opportunity to ask," Akin had said, openly testing his protegé.

Sakara did. "Who initiated the *coup* plans, and if not you, how were you approached?"

"Good question. Nzeogwu initiated the plan for the first *coup*. But it was Banjo that approached me. Those two were known to be serious. I could not question the veracity of Banjo's proposition. Besides, we all knew a change was inevitable. The country was drifting toward disaster."

"What about the second *coup*, sir?"

"That was a surprise. Lieutenant Babasa masterminded that one. Keep your eyes on him. He's obsessed with power and must never be underestimated. He wants to be king, and he will be one day, mark my word."

Now, ten years later, Sakara knew that this visit to his old boss was not going to be business as usual.

﹏

"Have you read it?" asked Akin, holding the manila envelope in his hand like a father about to open his daughter's report card.

"No!"

"What about that?" He nodded toward a copy of the

Nigerian Times on the coffee table. His soft eyes, peering over the rim of his reading glasses, locked with Ademola's in the picture that covered half of the front page of the newspaper.

Eniola nodded and looked about to weep. "You have to help him, please. He is innocent." She hoped she hadn't lost her magic touch with the retired general, who had done everything possible to assist her in the past. She trusted him then as now.

As soon as the ambulance driver dropped her and the Ogawas off in front of a house somewhere in Ikeja, she waited for the ambulance to drive off before hailing a taxi that drove them to a second location. And then they took another one to yet another location. In all, the trio had driven in six different taxis before Eniola parted company with Mrs. Ogawa and her son in front of the house of one of Ogawa's old classmates. Eniola proceeded to Surulere where she found a nondescript hotel and checked in using an alias. She had stayed up all night wondering what could have happened to Ademola, tempted several times to take a taxi to Ademola's house. When she couldn't stand the wait any longer, she had gone out only to find the street deserted. The darkness and eerie silence added to her fear, forcing her to rush back to the drab room and wait until daybreak. She couldn't stop worrying about Ademola, missing him more than she had ever missed any man, hoping he was safe, but doubting it.

"*Naira* for your thoughts." Akin interrupted Eniola's reverie.

"Pardon me. The last ten hours have been terrible," she said, her tired eyes meeting his gaze.

"What will you do with this piece of dynamite?" He waved the document in the air.

"Ola told me to give it to someone I trust with my heart."

"He said those exact words?" Akin's voice was husky.

"Just about," she said.

"Do you?"

"Do I what?"

"Trust me with your heart?" He was watching her.

"I did once. Why shouldn't I now?"

"I thought you love this doctor friend of yours?"

"I do. More than I've ever loved anyone else," she said earnestly, not wishing to hurt him.

"I see." He sighed.

"Will you help him?"

Akin reviewed the pages again, and whistled.

"It's really bad," Eniola thought, sensing the danger, hoping she had not made the wrong decision by coming to her old sugar daddy, as she used to call him years back.

As though he'd read her mind, Akin put the papers back in the envelope and returned it to her. "I can't keep this, Eniola. I am retired from military service. And I wish to spend the rest of my life in peace and tranquility." He took a deep breath. Eniola held hers for a moment. "You are not drinking your coffee?"

She picked up the cup as though commanded, and smiled.

Akin smiled back and leaned forward in his chair. "When was the last time you saw Major Sakara?"

"I—it's been a while, why?" She wondered why she stuttered. More importantly, she wondered why the sudden change of subject.

"We play squash every week. He should be here soon."

Eniola's cup of coffee stopped halfway to her mouth. "Is he really? I thought he was out of the country."

"Who told you that?"

"A close friend of Ola's. The other man being sought by the government in connection with this document. He was at DMI yesterday and—"

"Eniola, this is way over your head. Take my advice,

don't mess around with these people. They're more dangerous than you can imagine." He got to his feet.

Eniola put the cup on the table and stood to face her old
lover. There was fire in her eyes though her voice cracked
when she asked, "Does that mean you won't help?"

Akin looked away. "I didn't say that."

"Then take it and do something with it, dammit."

Akin looked at her, then sat down.

"Are—"

He struck the table with an open palm, producing the
sound of an exploding firecracker, and sending one of the
two cups crashing to the floor. Eniola's face mirrored her
shock and anger. She spun around and started for the front
door.

"If they find you, and they will, you'll be killed like a
pestering fly." His voice cracked.

"Am I a pestering fly?" Eniola yanked the door open.

"Wait wait wait—"

"For what? If you can't help, why should I? I thought
you could, apparently I was wrong," she said over her shoulder as she walked out.

"Stop right there, young lady. How dare you speak to
me like that?" He took his glasses off the bridge of his nose,
glaring at her. "I didn't say I would not help you."

Eniola turned around, hesitated before taking a few steps
toward him, and thrust out her hand, again offering him the
envelope. "Take it, please. I don't need—I don't want it. You
said it yourself, it's dynamite. Take it, you are the soldier, not
me."

"Not anymore." He refused to take the document from
her. "Do yourself a favor, Eniola, take it to DMI on Monday
and hand it to Major Sakara. He would know what to do."

"Why don't you give it to him when he gets here?"

"It's best the offer comes from you. That way he will be
obliged to help your fiancée. I shouldn't be the one to give

it to him. And you must not let him know that you came to me first. Trust me on this." He paused. "You have to leave now. Where are you staying?"

"I am at—never mind. I will telephone you later."

"How are you with money?"

"I have enough, thanks."

"Don't go near your house or the doctor's. I'm sure they have guards watching both places. And don't go to any of your close friends."

"Thanks."

"Call me two hours from now."

"I will do that."

"Eniola, don't take risks." He went into the house.

ᴄᴏ

"Uche, there is something I need to do before we get on that lorry," Ademola said, savoring every bit of the blade of a sparerib in his hand.

"*Wetin* be that, doctor?" Uche swallowed a ball of *fufu* dipped in a mixture of okra, bitterleaf, and peppered goat stew. He put a piece of meat in his mouth and chewed with his mouth open. Sweat of satisfaction beaded the bridge of his nose. "I don't think you get time for do anything."

Crowder put his bottle of cold Star beer back on the table and frowned. He pushed away his plate, now empty of the stewed catfish and rice he had just consumed. "What do you mean we don't have time to do anything?" He fanned a fly away from the bottle with his open palm.

"My brother-in-law's lorry go leave for Yola in less than ten minutes. He no agree easily to let you people go with him. And so therefore he is not going to wait or stop anywhere for you."

"I need to see Eniola for a brief moment, to give her a message for my family," Ademola said. "I can't just leave the

127

country without letting them know what's going on." He gave Uche a pleading look.

"As for me I am happy to take the message to her or your family. But as for my brother-in-law, the man no go wait a second longer, he told me that already."

"Ola, where do you intend to go looking for her? Didn't you ask her not to go home? Eniola is smart, once she sees the papers she will understand why you are still on the run. Same with your parents," Crowder said.

"You don't understand, I can't just leave without—"

"Yes, I do. There's another problem we also need to address," Crowder said.

"What's that?" Ademola asked.

"What to do with this little chap." Crowder nodded toward Ali, who was at the advanced stage of devouring his hefty serving of *jollof* rice and fried plantain. The boy had already downed two bottles of Fanta and he looked like he could do damage to another without any problem.

"I'm hoping that Uche will take care of him."

"*Wetin* you want make I do?" Uche swallowed yet another ball of *fufu*.

"Find where his parents live."

"What? He no be your child?" Uche snapped.

"No, he is—" Crowder began.

Ademola shook his head, bit his lower lip, then grimaced. He grabbed a bottle of Fanta, opened it and handed it to Ali. He stroked the boy's head, and choosing his words carefully, afraid that Ali might storm out, he said in Yoruba, "Ali, how's your food?"

"Good, very good." The boy smiled.

"I'm going to ask you a question and I want you to be honest with me," Ademola said, his voice soft and tender. "Promise me you won't walk away."

Ali nodded.

"Very good. Now tell me, where do you live?"

128

"Everywhere," the boy said simply.

"What do you mean? What I want to know is—"

"You mean, where is my father and mother?"

"Yes." Ademola reached a hand out to touch Ali's shoulder. The boy did not flinch.

"My mother is dead." He became silent.

Ademola stole a glance at Crowder who looked like he was going to say something but changed his mind for the moment.

"What about your father?"

"I don't have one."

"Really?" Ademola leaned forward in his chair. He looked Ali straight in the eyes and said, "My friend and I have to leave the country, the government is looking for us as you already—"

"I know."

"Then you must know that we can't take you with us." Ademola's voice was solemn.

"I can help you get away from the wicked soldiers if you take me along."

Ademola sat back, folded his arms against his chest, and asked, "How?"

"I don't know, but Allah will tell me."

"Allah, are you a—do you speak Hausa?"

Ali nodded and immediately looked away.

Uche glanced at Ademola first, turned to glare at Ali, and then back to Ademola. "The boy is a bloody Hausa, a mosquito like the rest of his people. They sit their bottom at the top in government and at the ground for the streets, sucking our blood. I no go lift a finger to help anyone of them no matter what."

Ademola ignored Uche's diatribe. He looked at Crowder, expecting him to join ranks with the taxi driver. But Crowder looked nonplussed, as though the conversation was not nearly as important as the bottle of beer in his hand.

"What do you say?"

Crowder shrugged and continued to seem unconnected.

"Is that yes or no?"

"What's the question again?"

"Do we take Ali with us or not?"

Crowder sat the bottle down on the table, scratched the middle of his left palm with an index finger, and remained silent. Ademola recognized the signal of acknowledgement, and disagreement, an old trick from their school days. He took a deep breath, wishing his friend would not make the situation more difficult than it already was. Convincing Crowder that Ali should be taken along would not be easy. But Ademola was not about to let Ali go just as yet now, especially after gleaning the essence of the boy, mysterious as it was. But of equal importance was the fact that Ademola couldn't think of anyone else kind enough to take the boy in and care for him.

"We must hurry *o*, the lorry is going to leave now now." Uche looked at his watch. He turned to Crowder and asked, "*Wetin* you say make we do with the boy?"

"That depends on you. After all, we are at your mercy, isn't that so, my brother?" Crowder said, looking at Uche.

Ademola smiled with his eyes, thanking his friend for not expressing his objection openly.

"The parasites no deserve any help from you or me *o*, so therefore, I no go take him anywhere."

"Is it okay if we take him along on the trip?" Ademola asked.

"That one depend on my brother–in–law *o*."

"He doesn't have to know, Uche," Ademola said.

"I no *fit* lie to him." Uche sounded adamant.

"You don't have to tell him anything about the boy," Ademola offered in compromise.

"As I say before, I go do anything inside my power to help you, but withholding the truth from my fellow Ibo, especially to help a Hausa, that one is something I no go do." Uche's breathing became labored.

"I thank you for what you've done so far, and I do appreciate your point."

"You no *fit* understand my people. If they ever find out that I did the thing you *dey* ask me to do, I will be a dead man. We Ibos are—"

"You are a tribalistic and parochial bunch." Crowder got up, his face mirroring his anguish and frustration.

~

"I hope you don't mind if we skip the game today, sir." Sakara stepped into the marble-floored foyer of his old boss' house.

"Aren't you well? Actually you look terrible." Akin shut the front door.

"I feel worse, sir."

"Let's go into the family room." Akin eased past Sakara to lead the way. "It's more comfortable in there."

"Can I have something to eat first, sir? I haven't eaten in twenty-four hours." Sakara trailed behind Akin out of the foyer into a hallway leading to the parlor.

"Sure, but you'll have to prepare lunch for us both." He stopped to let Sakara catch up with him. He put his arm over his shoulder and they continued through the parlor, past the formal dining room furnished with a magnificent Chippendale bonnet-top mahogany highboy, wide table with twelve chairs, and an assortment of original oil paintings on the walls. "My wife is in London with the rest of the family. They'll be gone another two weeks," Akin continued as they entered the family room. It was comfortable indeed; exuding the warmth and beauty only good taste and lots of money can generate. Two sumptuous slipcovered wing chairs which turned a formal style into everyday seating were separated by a hand-tufted sofa in a classic paisley fabric. The floor, thickly carpeted in sky blue, was overflowing with throw pillows of assorted colors and sizes.

Sakara mentally tuned out the subtle and complex opera by Mozart, *The Marriage of Figaro*, offering a rich blend of humor and seriousness, as the music floated out of Nakamishi speakers on top of a stereo cabinet. He was preoccupied by an unsettling thought that pierced his mind, sending him a warning signal. "The general has never put his arm around my shoulder in all the years we've known each other. And come to think of it, he did not say anything about the Mercedes Benz I parked in his driveway. I know he saw it. Why?" he thought, but said, "Did you know there's a state of emergency on the island, sir?"

"I heard about it last night. What's going on?" Akin asked as they entered the kitchen. The automatic coffee maker on the ceramic-topped counter was half-full, the warm dark liquid emitting its rich aroma into the air.

Sakara saw two cups in the sink, one with dark red lipstick stains on its rim. He turned toward the counter. "Coffee, sir?"

"Yes, major." Akin opened a cabinet above the stove.

"Do you have company, sir?"

"Not anymore, I did. Why?"

"Lipstick stains."

"One of the young girls you introduced to me years back came to visit."

"Which one is that, sir?" Sakara relaxed at the general's openness with him, a characteristic he believed the general shared only with him. The man was known to be close-lipped.

"The beautiful undergrad with midnight skin, Eniola—"

Sakara spun around, dropping the cup to the floor, the sound of broken china filled the room. "Eniola was—" He swallowed whatever was choking him and tried to speak again but remained quiet when he saw Akin's hand raised in the air, gesturing him to silence. Sakara's head jerked left and then right, looking for the sign of someone else in the kitchen, his crossed eyes becoming enlarged.

"There's nobody but us in the house," Akin answered his silent question. "You need to tell me what's going on, young man, quickly."

"As of an hour ago, I have become *persona non grata* at DMI."

"What are you talking about?" Akin slammed the door of the cabinet with a bang.

"General Bukha not only took me off the case, he—"

"Start from the beginning, son."

"Someone stole a file from Brigadier Dikko's office—a file that contained the detailed account of how General Bukha conspired with officials of the Nigerian Oil Corporation to divert a total of two-point-eight billion *nairas* from the country's foreign reserve into a private account. That's almost four billion American dollars. The money stayed in the account for a total of two hundred days, generating a daily interest of over six hundred thousand dollars before the principal was returned to the government's account. Lots of money, sir. The document showed the *PIN*, personal identification number, the general's fingerprints, and everything else that would make the case indefensible."

"What else?"

"There is a document containing the names of ten senior officers who have planned to overthrow the present regime, including the operational logistics." Sakara stopped.

"Does Bukha know about this list?"

"I'm not sure. It's not unlikely that Dikko told him something to that effect, sir."

"Dikko is a whoring son-of-a-fornicating-nomad. He's capable of playing both sides against each other. Who are the architects of the *coup*?"

"I have not seen the document," Sakara said, furrows of frustration creasing his forehead. "But something strange happened this afternoon. Brigadier Babasa, who is now heading the security unit at Dodan Barracks, gave me the Mercedes Benz that I drove here despite General Bukha's order that I be demoted and placed under house arrest. Strange, isn't it?"

"No, it's not."

Sakara looked up and met Akin's stare. "Why not?"

"Make us a tuna sandwich and let's continue the conversation in the family room over lunch." Akin handed Sakara two six-ounce cans of albacore solid white tuna. "There's a jar of mayonnaise in the refrigerator. The bread is over there." He pointed to a wooden container next to the coffee maker. "I'll go up and change since I can no longer kick your black butt on the squash court today," he added before exiting the kitchen.

Sakara put two sandwiches on a china plate. He wiped tears off his face as the sharp spiciness of chopped onion filled the air. He poured ginger ale into two Waterford crystal tumblers and placed them on a silver tray along with the plate containing the sandwiches. He left the kitchen happily anticipating the imminent defeat of hunger.

Though Akin was yet to offer any specific solution, the family room looked brighter and more welcoming than Sakara had ever seen it, and he felt his burden had lifted, having confided in Akin. Akin never failed to amaze him. The retired general was like the Rock of Gibraltar. Sakara sat and leaned his back against the sofa like a piece of the fabled rock.

"Something here smells delicious," Akin said, coming down the staircase, dressed simply in grey gabardine wool trousers and a starched white linen collarless shirt. The retired general looked much younger than his sixty years.

Sakara gazed at the wall and smiled at the picture of his old boss as a young cadet in training. The serious-looking young man stood against the background of the entrance to the Royal Military College at Sandhurst.

Akin, at nineteen, had been admitted to R.M.C. along with other carefully selected young men from the Commonwealth overseas territories. He was one of the few southern Nigerians sent to the village in the Workingham parliamentary division of Berkshire in England, nine miles north of Aldershot, immediately after Nigeria gained independence from Britain in 1960. The trainees' military courses included British history, organization and administration, military law, tactics, drill, signals and weapon training. The cadets-in-training from outside of England worked hard, believing that upon graduation they would return home to protect the sovereignty of their motherland against any threat from within or outside, but especially from within. Unbeknownst to them, they were being trained as neocolonialists whose main objective was to protect the economic interest of Her Royal Majesty. And upon graduation and subsequent arrival back to the now-independent former colonies of Great Britain, they did their best to help God save the Queen. This they did with the never-ending *coup d'etats* that continued to slash the jugular veins of third-world countries.

"I hope you like the sandwich, sir," Sakara said.

Without any preamble, Akin said, "Babasa is not the one to watch even though he is the architect of the *coup* plan. The one you must keep your eyes on is Hakabala."

"How do—" Sakara held half of his sandwich like a rectangular mathematical instrument.

"Yes, he is on the list. Eniola wanted me to have it. But I refused."

"You didn't take it from her?"

"Nope. And don't ask me why, son. Now, back to the

two schemers. Babasa is shrewd, cunning, but above all, ambitious. He's always wanted to be king. If I didn't know better, I would have said I am surprised Bukha didn't retire him two years ago. I would have. And to let him head the security unit guarding Dodan Barracks is the height of folly. Without a doubt, Bukha and that chronically angry deputy of his need to be overthrown."

"But why is Hakabala the one to watch, sir?"

"He's the most senior Berber in military service. His people are known to be straightforward, honest, but by no means opposed to money-making. And they are not scrupulous in the methods they employ. Hakabala must always be respected and suspected as well. He's a very resourceful and unpredictable man. Most dangerous. Be careful in your dealings with him. He has an inferiority complex the length of River Niger."

"Thank you, sir, but where do I go from here?" Sakara asked, trusting his old boss' judgement.

"Let's hope that Eniola does not spring a surprise on us. She holds in her hands the file that could determine your future. And possibly that of a whole nation."

"Where is she?" Sakara asked.

"That's neither here nor there, son. Her concern is the welfare of her fiancée. If she knows that the doctor will be left alone, I believe she will cooperate."

"But I still have to find the bastard, sir."

"Why?"

Sakara grimaced. "Ademola took another file from my desk in the observation room."

"What file?"

"One that is more damaging than the one Eniola has."

"How's that?" Akin sipped his ginger ale.

"It contains the names of military officers whose foreign—Swiss bank accounts add up to ten billion dollars."

"Phew!"

"Your name is on the list, sir."

"Is that a fact?" Akin said, edge to his voice.

"Yes, sir."

"Who else is on the list?"

"Nineteen other generals, half of them retired like your-self. But you're the poorest with only seventy million dollars in your accounts at four banks in Switzerland, and one at Midland Bank in Great Britain, sir."

"And who else knows about this list?"

"That depends on whom Ademola has shared it with."

"Aside from him, who else?"

"Officially, nobody else."

"Well, major, you better make sure the list does not fall into the wrong hands. Destroy whoever gets in your way if you have to!" Akin instructed.

"Will do, sir."

7

At six-fifteen the sun descended like a ball of fire, threatening to set the green cap of the tropical forest ablaze. The top branches of mahogany, walnut, *iroko*, and *sapele* trees that reached two hundred feet into the sky swayed with the breeze, their stems rigid below the leaves, which looked like ceremonial umbrellas. Several dwarf antelopes and duikers panted, wishing to slow down to catch their breath, but not daring, as if running from a pack of leopards in hot pursuit. A family of monkeys watched from the branches of ebony, wild *kola*, and *camwood* trees, thanking the god of monkeys, gorillas, and chimpanzees for enabling them to dash from one tree top to another without setting foot on the dangerous jungle earth. Pythons and giant vipers slithered over the dark soil, their hearts filled with envy as green mambas and black cobras blended with the vegetation, their fangs filled with venom as they lay in wait for their next meal.

Instantly the ever-present symphony of bush fowl, guinea pigeons, ducks, and wild geese yielded to the sound of lorry engines with enough horse power to fill a racecourse, their tires threading the asphalt of the highway that wound through the jungle like a black snake.

Ademola's heart began to race as the engine coughed, and slowed down, indicating that the driver was approaching yet another roadblock, the fifth in their journey so far.

"Where are we?" Crowder whispered, his lips almost touching Ademola's ear.

"Sshh!" Ademola felt the sting of Crowder's breath which competed with the stench of kolanut. He sneezed, wishing in vain that the musky smell would stop irritating his sinuses. His back had stopped aching and had become numb from lying inside a wooden box the size of a coffin for the past six hours.

"Ola, I have to use the bathroom, and don't shush me. Have I stopped you from sneezing since we left Lagos?"

"We are nearing another checkpoint." Ademola strained his ears as the voice of the driver and the hot, dank air joined on their way towards the back. He sneezed again.

"You haven't said one single word since we left Lagos, little boy. Are you deaf, mute, or both?" the driver said in Ibo, knowing that the boy who sat next to him did not understand a word. "We are approaching the point on the trunk-A highway that all drivers dread the most."

"What is he saying?" Crowder whispered. "I am serious, I have to go." His voice had a threatening ring to it.

Ademola held his breath to prevent an impending sneeze.

"This is serious!"

Ademola felt a jolt as the engine coughed again and died. "Sshh, listen!"

"I am not sure which one I fear more—the terrible police at the checkpoint or the old bridge," the driver said to Ali who was fast asleep, his head wedged in the space between the window and the front passenger seat.

"If this is not a checkpoint the driver will send a signal and might let you out. Remember, it's quite a task for him to lift the two sacks of kolanut above us," Ademola said, his ear pressed against the box, making the muffled voice of the driver a bit clearer.

"I wish to God I no listen to Uche *o*. If this foolish people find out I carry contraband for inside my lorry, I go be in big trouble *o*," the driver said in pidgin English to no one in particular as he got out of the lorry.

Ali sounded as though he were sucking a mango. He opened an eye dreamily, closed it and went back to sleep.

Ademola heard the driver's footsteps as he approached the front of the lorry. Then another voice greeted the driver in Ibo, "*Kedu*, my brother."

"*Odinma*."

Ademola tightened his grip on Crowder's wrist.

"Something terrible has happened, my brother. I just heard from the driver ahead of us that they are searching every vehicle for some prisoners that escaped from Lagos, and it is believed they are heading this way," the driver said in Ibo.

"Which kind prisoner?" Ademola's driver switched to pidgin English.

"I no *sabi o*, but I hear say the driver *wey* fail to do as he was commanded was shot to death an hour ago."

Ademola's driver crossed himself and said, "Hail Mary," three times. "Only God can punish this government *o*. Anyone of our people among them, eh?"

"I heard that soldiers took over the checkpoint."

"Soldiers?" Ademola's driver sounded alarmed.

"Yes, my brother, and every single one of them is Hausa. Bastards! Instead of going across the border to fight the Cameroon who *don* seize our land and the oil inside it, they are here harassing innocent Nigerians."

"God is the judge *o*." Ademola's driver looked up as though expecting an agreement from Him. The sun staggered toward the horizon, smearing the sky crimson. The skyline resembled cindered trees standing against the fading daylight. "It will be my turn next. Pray for me *o*, my brother."

A burst of rifle fire cracked a short distance away, followed by the agonized yelp of a man.

"What was that?" Crowder asked.

Ademola listened to the alarming sounds that filled the air. Then a powerful voice commanded, "Corporal, get that lorry off the road. And tell the next driver to move forward."

"*Chineke!*" the driver said solemnly just before the lorry surged forward.

"What's going on?" Crowder asked.

"I think the driver of the lorry ahead of us was just shot at the checkpoint. I feel like a trapped animal." He felt an irritation in his nose and held his breath in a futile attempt. He failed and seconds later, after the engine was turned off, he let loose a sneeze.

"What was that noise?"

"W—Wh—Wha—" the driver stammered.

"Come out!" the soldier said in Hausa-accented English.

The driver's legs started to shake.

"What do you carry?" The tribal marks on the sergeant's face twisted in proportion to his anger.

"Ko—koko—ko—kol—"

"Move! You carry kolanut?"

"Yes, sir." The driver's whisper was muted by the sound of the water raging under the bridge.

"I will check!" The sergeant climbed the lorry.

The driver's knees buckled and he collapsed on the asphalt ground with a thump. "God have mercy on me!"

Ademola heard the driver's cry first, then the sound of movement above him. He felt the squeezing of his bladder as his heart began to race. He heard as the sergeant lifted the first of the two sacks of kolanut above their hideaway. The sergeant dropped the sack on top of the piles to his left and bent down to lift the second one.

Suddenly, the dusk air was filled with a solemn voice:

Allahu Akbar Allahu Akbar

I testify that there is no God but Allah.

I testify that Muhammed is Allah's messenger.
Come, let us pray.
Allah is the Greatest
La ilaha illa lah!

Ademola shut his eyes as he recognized Ali's voice. "What is he doing now? I should have listened to—" He felt the warmth of teardrops snaking down his upturned face.

The sergeant's voice whipped the silence, "Is it *Magrib* time already?"

⤳

Sakara sat in a recliner covered with black vinyl, staring at the images of female dancers, their buttocks gyrating across the television screen. He got up and went into the kitchen, opened the refrigerator door, and his mood took a dive. He slammed the door shut, turned around and went straight into the bedroom where he searched the pockets of his jackets in the closet. He found a stick of marijuana the size of a cigar, the only vice he indulged in. He turned the switch on the wall, flooding the sparsely furnished bedroom with light. He looked around as though he was seeing it for the first time. "This is all I have to show for a bloody eighteen-year service in the army," he muttered. "While I work myself to death, the bastards at the top enrich themselves." He stormed out and headed back to the kitchen, the cigar clasped between his lips. He found a box of matches and lit the marijuana, taking a long drag as he removed the contents of a plastic shopping bag he had brought back from Akin's house. "What a laugh, six cans of tuna fish from a man who has seventy million dollars stashed away in European banks." He exhaled and then took another drag. "The man I have looked up to all these years. Now he wants me to find and destroy the document that will tell the world how crooked he's been, like all the rest."

He continued to smoke, feeling the hallucinogenic effect of the cannabis taking hold. The tips of his fingers and toes tingled, he became light-headed and his stomach grumbled. He became hungry and thirsty at the same time. He took a can opener out of the kitchen cabinet and opened one can of tuna, the jagged edge of the lid scraped his finger, lacerating it. He giggled as he pressed the finger to his lips, sucking the blood mixed with salty tuna water. He took a bag of *gari* (roasted and floured cassava) out of the cabinet, poured a cupful into a ceramic bowl, added water and several cubes of sugar, and started to hum his favorite Yoruba poem as he ate.

After the meal, he finished the rest of the joint and went back to the bedroom for another stick, lit it and continued to smoke it in the parlor. Gradually, his eyelids became heavier and the rest of his body seemed buoyant. The light on the television screen split into a million iridescent stars, swirling as they emerged from the box, filling the room. He opened his mouth to say something and his voice sounded as though he were in a tunnel: "Major General Akin, I have the document you requested. But I must be paid before I hand it over. The price is ten million dollars. Do we have a deal?"

There was silence as the twinkling stars became a kaleidoscope of lights, all colors of the rainbow, illuminating a space the length of a football field, and the width of his parlor. The ground turned into a white cloud. He sat in his swivel chair at the end of a giant conference table made of solid gold. Then clanking cymbals preceded the sound of an approaching military band. He tried to get off the chair but couldn't, his hands were nailed to the sides of the chair, and his feet cuffed to the legs of the table.

A familiar voice, young and seductive, rose above the military marching music. "Look!" She directed his attention to the other end of the table. Sakara recognized the voice as

that of Eniola when she was eighteen years old. He looked
around the huge room, needing to connect her face to the
voice that was everywhere. "Just listen!"

He looked and beheld his old boss, dressed in the uniform of a cadet-in-training at Sandhurst College. Young
Akin looked handsome, his eyes hungry and determined.

"Welcome, major." Akin's voice sounded deathly. He
held a half-eaten tuna sandwich in his hand. "This is imported tuna. Want a bite?"

"Hell, no!"

"Watch your language, young man. What has gotten into
you? Have you forgotten in whose presence you are?"

"No. You are a thief like the rest of the generals."

"I am not! Only those caught stealing are called thieves.
We all steal, you know. You, me, and the rest of humanity.
But those that are stupid enough to be caught in the act are
thus cursed."

"What do you call enriching yourself with seventy million dollars that belong to the people of Nigeria?"

"Insurance, young man, insurance!"

"Against what?"

"Poverty."

"What are you—"

"SHUT UP!" The sound was deafening. "How dare you
speak in *our* presence."

Sakara looked up and saw a seven-headed phantom seated where Akin had been only seconds before. From the
neck down, the monster was dressed in the ceremonial uniform of a general. The head farthest from the neck on the
left reminded Sakara of the warlord from the horn of Africa.
The next one looked like that of the butcher of Entebe, irritating its neighbor, the five-billion-dollar-man from
Kinshasa. In the middle was the obnoxious head of the
sleeping giant of Africa from Lagos, flashing an effeminate
smile at the sergeant-turned-general from Monrovia. Next

was the Tuareg colonel-turned-president-for-life from Tripoli. The phantom head of Akin, which sat farthest from the neck on the right, spoke first:

"Major Sakara, meet some of the very best the continent has to offer the world. We are—"

"Let me speak," the nomad from Tripoli interrupted. "We are the security guards in charge of the priceless commodity on the continent. The PALM GROVE!"

"Why don't we start from the beginning?" asked the giant from Lagos. "General Akin should tell the fable since he speaks the major's language."

"I agree," said the butcher of Entebe.

"Me too, as long as our beautiful secretary records everything." The billionaire from Kinshasa licked his lips.

"Very well! The mess you see all over the continent is not of our making—"

"Cut the crap," the sergeant-turned-general snapped.

There was murmuring as all the heads turned back and forth, agreeing to disagree, until Akin silenced them with a shrill whistle and then began:

"The WORLD was once a river that was joined to the sky by the rain that never stopped. And because the rain was part of the sky, there was only darkness. Then one day that was still night, the cloud that was the gate of heaven erupted and *Olodumare* emerged with three calabashes. As the angels wept, lamenting the loss of innocence and heavenly tranquility, the rain fell in torrents and the river that was the world rumbled as the Creator opened the lids of the calabashes that contained sand, figures of animals and humans, and all the natural resources that only He could create. He splashed a handful of sand on the surface of the river and formed the land of *oyinbo* that humans later called Europe. He put a white figure there, sprinkled some coal, oil, a bit of minerals, and lots of snowflakes on the land. He repeated the exercise the next day and the land of Asia came to be. The

Creator was frugal. He became benevolent, however, when on the third day, He planted a brown figure on the land of the Americas.

"He continued until the sixth day when He created the land of Africa where He put the only black figure and all His animal creations including the lion-king. He turned the half-full calabash upside down and all the natural resources rained down on the land—"

"Where is this silly—" Sakara began.

"SHUT UP!" all seven heads roared in unison.

"Don't ever interrupt *us* again, major," Akin said and continued as though he had never been interrupted. "Then *Olodumare* breathed life into His creations. The animals roamed the lush jungle in search of plentiful food. The humans could talk. They could hear. They could see. They could feel. But most importantly, they could ask questions. And they did. All but the black one asked The Creator why He gave so much to the African. They reasoned that since the black one was so endowed, he would rule the world. Why didn't God redistribute the wealth equally among them all?

"*Olodumare* smiled understandingly, but assured His creations that they didn't need to worry since they were all equal in His eyes. They disagreed and were relentless in their supplication. The Creator in His infinite wisdom decided to alleviate their fears by adding a palm tree of special genius to the plethora of the African vegetation.

"'Why? Why do You love the black one so much that You give him more? Why?' they demanded.

"'Have faith. More is less! This tree will shed sweet-tasting but intoxicating tears. Your black brother will turn the tears into PALM WINE, and in a state of stupor and inebriation, he will be of no threat to you.'

"*Olodumare* then added yet another of His creations to the landscape, the indomitable tse-tse fly. Satisfied, He told them that as long as the black giant slumbered they could take anything they needed from the land, including the strong progeny of the drowsy giant. But there was a *caveat*: They could pillage the land for thousands of years as long as they did not overindulge, and only God could determine when enough was enough. But if they did, their worst nightmare would become reality; the giant would wake up and rule over the world in perpetuity.

"When the time arrived, *Olodumare*'s omnipotent voice calmed the rumbling river: 'LET THERE BE LIGHT!' The rain stopped, and the black sky was suffused with an explosion of a million stars, and there was light everywhere except in the African continent which was darkened by the shade of the PALM TREE. So it was at the beginning as it remains."

A bang at the front door snatched Sakara from his hallucination, trembling with beads of perspiration covering his body. He ran a palm over his face, trying to wipe off the effect of the cannabis. He succeeded but only partly. He struggled off the recliner, went to the bathroom, ran cold water over his face and took a deep breath before he went to answer the door. "Who is it?"

"Lieutenant Achibong, sir."

Sakara opened the door. "What's the problem?"

"I found the driver, sir."

"Which driver?" Sakara wiped the water off his face with the collar of his shirt.

"The taxi driver that helped the fugitives get away, sir. His name is Uche Okpara."

"Where is he?"

"At headquarters, sir. But he refused to talk. The only person that can get anything out of him is you, sir."

"Did you try everything to make him talk?"

"No, sir. I didn't want him to die before you could have a go at him."

"Good! Let's go."

"I can't believe this." Femi's voice was drowned by the noise from the black-and-white television set. The panoramic shot of the stadium showed the spectators on their feet as the semi-final match raged on between Brazil and Italy for the World Cup championship.

Eniola sat on the bed, her back propped against a pillow. Her brother paced up and down the room of the hotel in Surulere, holding the document in his hand. He read the three pages again and was about to turn the volume down when an announcer's voice cut in:

WE INTERRUPT THIS PROGRAM TO BRING YOU A SPECIAL ADDRESS BY THE CHAIRMAN OF THE SUPREME MILITARY COUNCIL AND HEAD OF STATE OF THE FEDERAL REPUBLIC OF NIGERIA, MAJOR GENERAL AHMED BUKHA!

There was a brief silence followed by static, and the Nigerian National Anthem filled the room:

Nigeria, we hail thee...

"They should change that bloody thing to Nigeria we HATE thee." Femi snapped the set off just as the screen was filled with the face of Bukha.

"I want to hear what he has to say."

"He's going to lie to us until he's black in the face."

"He's already black in the face." Eniola laughed.

"All the damn generals are liars and thieves."

"In fairness, they're not nearly as bad as the civilians. You should have been here three years ago."

"What happened?"

"Everybody in Nigeria got down on their knees begging them to take over from those civilian thieves. Some of the top party stalwarts did incredible things. One of them flew a plane-load of champagne into the country to celebrate the day he became a billionaire. He accomplished this heroic feat in three years."

"Where is he now?"

"In London where the rest of them are hiding. Those

guys were so bad, they made the soldiers look like boy scouts. And they were the dumbest the country had to offer. Check this, on the day of the *coup* in December, 1983, Uba Bauchi was enroute back home from London. The pilot of his private plane was told by someone from the control tower that the airport was shut down because of the *coup* and the plane should not land in Nigeria. The idiot had the audacity to tell the pilot how important he was in the country. The pilot relayed the information to the authorities in Lagos and was given permission to land."

"Why?"

"They wanted to lock his butt in the slammer. And they did. That's how arrogant and stupid they are."

"Incredible. But I still believe the soldiers have no business ruling the country."

"Don't get me started on politics, please. Enough! I just want to rest before I see Major Sakara."

"Eniola, we can't just sit here doing nothing. Granted, it is dangerous for you to be caught with this dynamite, as you say General Akin called it. I agree with him that you should give it to Sakara. He'll know what to do with it and more than likely he'll be able to help Dr. Ademola. After all, they're friends."

"I don't want to go to his house."

"Why not? I'll go with you. Plus, I'd like to tell him about the stupid soldier in mufti that came to the house this morning. You should have seen mom, she came out of the house ready to do battle. That fool was saved by that strange rainbow I told you about." Femi drank the rest of his Pepsi straight from the can.

"I don't think it's a good idea for us to be out there tonight. Someone might recognize us."

"How? I borrowed a nondescript car from a friend of mine. But I have to return it in the morning. Between now and then we will have found Sakara, hand him the document and be done with the whole thing."

Eniola shook her head before getting off the bed. "I don't feel good about this. What if the soldiers at the road-block decide to do a body search?"

"Give me a break. A body search?"

"I wouldn't put anything past those recruits. I don't have the energy to argue with you, so let's go. But if we botch this and anything happens to Ola, I will kill you."

⤚

Sakara struck a match, lit a candle and waited for his eyes to adjust to the sudden change before he walked in. He saw Uche tied to a metal chair, his lips were bleeding from several cuts. One eye was swollen shut. In all, his face looked like someone had used it as a punching bag. "What happened to him?" He sounded concerned, gentle, friendly. He did not wait for an answer from his assistant but reached a hand behind the chair to untie the steel rope that was cutting into Uche's flesh.

"The prisoner was uncooperative, sir."

Sakara got on his knee to unbuckle the belt wrapped around Uche's ankles. He covered his nose with a palm as the stench of urine exuded from between Uche's legs. "Who did this to him?" he asked, feigning anger.

"I don't know, sir," Achibong lied.

"Liar!" Uche's throat rasped.

"What did you say?" Sakara leaned forward, his ear closer to Uche's brutalized mouth. The smell of blood mixed with saliva and bad breath breezed past his face to fuse with the rancid smell of urine in the room.

"He's a liar." Uche raised a hand which fell back to his side. He recoiled in pain.

"You mean this officer lied?"

Uche nodded, and his Adam's apple went up and down.

"Tell me what happened then." Sakara sounded like a priest in a confession room.

"This *na* the man *wey* beat me like—" Uche stopped as Achibong started to laugh.

Sakara swirled around. "What's so funny, lieutenant? You think this is a game, don't you? Do you like to play games?" He repeated the question as he faced Uche.

Confused, Uche stammered, "W—who, me?"

Sakara nodded. "What kind of games do you like to play? Table tennis, squash, soccer?"

Uche shook his head twice and nodded once.

"Oh, you like soccer, eh?"

Uche nodded again.

"Good, let's go play some," Sakara said, and exited the room. He went straight to his office, picked up the telephone and spoke for a minute. He left the office, got in his car and drove across the bridge to the stadium. He unlocked the gate, drove in and turned on the lights, flooding half of the field. He waited by the goal post, on the dark side of the field, singing his favorite poem.

A Black Maria drove through the gate. Three soldiers jumped out and dragged Uche to the field. A tall soldier alighted, carrying a black ball. He went to stand between the posts. "This shouldn't take long, sir."

A dark cloud seemed to envelope Sakara. He nodded at the soldier, then said to Uche, "The game is simple, the man at the goal will throw you the ball, and all you have to do is score. Three goals, and you are free. But before you leave, I'll ask you one simple question. If I'm satisfied with your answer, you'll be allowed to go home. It's that simple. Do you understand?" He became congenial.

Uche looked confused, standing six feet away.

"Are you ready?" Sakara asked.

Uche nodded.

Sakara blew the plastic whistle in his mouth. The soldier threw the ball in the air with both hands. Uche raised his right foot, arched it sideways in readiness to kick. The ball curved on its descent and just before it hit the ground, Uche aimed and kicked with all his might. "*Chinekeee!*" His voice filled the stadium. Mouth wide open, head tilted backward, eyes enlarged, staring at the black sky in horror. He fell to the ground, writhing. He grabbed his foot which dangled at an obscene angle from his ankle, screaming.

Sakara's black eyes looked dead. "In America they call that a bowling ball. You didn't score. We must try again!"

Uche's body went into a seizure, his lower lip caught between his teeth, trembling. "B—ba—bastard!"

"What did you say?" Sakara leaned toward Uche.

"God will punish you, Yoruba bastard!" His face contorted with pain and fury as he pointed a trembling finger at Sakara.

"You didn't score. You must try again." Sakara's voice was a whiplash. He beckoned the soldier toward him. "You will tell me the whereabouts of Dr. Ademola, Dr. Crowder, and the boy."

Uche shook his head violently. "You will have to kill me, son-of-a-harlot."

"I will, stupid idiot," the soldier said in Hausa with a chilling smile.

Sakara pointed to the bowling ball. He mopped his brow, took a deep breath, controlling the inferno raging inside him. He saw a flash of horror in Uche's eyes but something told him this Ibo man would not be easy to break. He nodded at the soldier, who hastily picked up the ball and raised it above his head. With a determined malevolence, he whacked it against Uche's left foot, pulverizing it.

Uche screamed, tears of terror and pain running down

his face. Sakara nodded at the soldier, who got on his knees and lifted Uche into a sitting position.

A pair of headlights appeared at the gate, and a green Peugeot 505 sedan drove onto the field. Achibong got out of the car and hurried toward the goal post, carrying a bundle in his arms. He was breathing quite hard. "Here's the package, sir." He unwound the wrapper around the bundle.

"We will see how much you are willing to sacrifice for the safety of those you don't even know." Sakara's eyes were icy cold. He studied Uche, whose eyes were shut as he continued to scream in agony. Sakara waited.

The tiny voice of a child rose above Uche's cry. His eyes widened in horror. "Oh my God, please, don't touch my baby. Please!"

Sakara reached and touched the girl's head. "Where are they?" he said with a smile.

"I go tell you everything, but please, don't—"

"You should have cooperated much earlier."

"Don't hurt my pickin." Uche looked up, cold sweat running down his bare back, shock contorting his face.

"Where?" Sakara glared down at him.

"Y—Yo—Yola."

"Kill him." Sakara walked toward his car.

Achibong ran after him, panting. "What about the little girl, sir?"

"Let her go. After all, we are not murderers. Clean things up and meet me at the airport, we have a plane to catch, lieutenant."

༄

8

Raising his forehead from the ground after the sixth time, the sergeant said, "*Assalam Alaikum wa rahmat Allah*," over his right shoulder, and the left. He was about to hurry toward the lorry to resume his search when Ali said in Hausa, "Please, allow me to say a prayer for you, sergeant."

"What's that for?" The sergeant picked up his rifle from the ground.

"All prayers are for Allah's ears, sir."

"Okay, but make it quick." He got on his knees in front of ten soldiers who squatted on the dirt along the highway.

Ali raised his hands in the air, open palms connected at the sides: "Oh, Allah, we thank you for our lives."

There was a chorus of "amen."

"Please, forgive us for our sins
   As you have Forgiven the sins of those before us.
    Protect the sergeant and his men as
     They continue to serve you,
     And our beloved Nigeria."

"Amen."

"Grant the sergeant wealth,
   And promotions as he carries out the
    Commands of his superiors."

"Amen."

"On the Day of Judgement, Oh, Allah,
    Please, repay the sergeant
        Fully for all his
            Deeds in this world—"

"That's enough!" The sergeant got up. "What's your name, boy?"

"Ali, sir, Ali Mohammadu," he replied earnestly.

"Where are you heading?"

"I am escorting the driver to Yola, sir."

"I see." The sergeant scratched his stubbled-face. "I like the way you called the *Adhan*. Keep it up."

"Thank you, sir."

They walked toward the lorry, the sergeant a few steps ahead of Ali. "Why is your driver so nervous?"

Ali quickened his steps. "Don't mind him, sir, he's been like that ever since I have known him."

"How long is that?"

"Very long, sir. You must accept a gift of kolanut from us. I'm sure the driver won't mind."

"You are a good boy," the sergeant beamed.

Ali smiled. "*Yanminrin*, give the sergeant a bag of kola-nut," he snapped, using a derisive word to address the driver whose legs refused to stop shaking.

The sergeant burst into uproarious laughter that lasted a few seconds. He wiped tears off the corners of his eyes, laughed some more before patting Ali on the back. "I like you, boy."

"Thank you, sir. I like you too. On my way back, I will remember to bring you some *suya* from Kaduna." Ali promised a delicacy; peppered and roasted lamb meat.

"That will be nice, *mugode, mutumi*," the sergeant thanked Ali, calling him friend in Hausa. He received the sack of kolanut from the driver, lifted Ali up and placed him on the front seat before waving at the driver. "Go!"

Crossing the bridge over River Niger seemed to take a lifetime. Toward the end, Ademola released his grip on Crowder's wrist. "That was a close call."

"You can say that again. Ali is something else. I'm glad you insisted on bringing him along. Can you imagine what would have happened without him?"

The lorry slowed to a stop.

"Another checkpoint—" Crowder started.

The driver's voice slashed the darkness: "So, you be Hausa, eh? Stupid nonentity, you called me *Yanmirin*! I want you and the criminal doctors off my lorry, right now."

"Trouble," Crowder said.

"Let me handle this." Ademola braced himself as the driver's footsteps approached the back of the lorry.

"What are we going to do?"

"Leave him to me." Ademola suppressed a sneeze.

There was movement above as the driver lifted the sacks of kolanut, panting and cursing. "Get up! Both of you. Off my lorry!" He pulled the plank, exposing Ademola and Crowder who lay on their backs like Siamese twins.

"What's the matter?" Ademola asked.

"I want all of you off my lorry. You caused me plenty trouble already."

"What have we done to—"

"Up!" The driver shook with anger

Crowder started to get up but Ademola pulled him back. "We're not moving. You might as well get back to the front and drive like you're paid to do. You accepted two thousand *naira* to take us to Yola. Until we get there, nobody is getting off this lorry." Ademola sneezed.

"Bless you," Crowder said as though they were in a Boy Scout camp. "I need to get out there to relieve—"

"If you no get off my lorry, I promise you when I get to the next checkpoint, you go see how wicked I be."

"You'll be amazed what the soldiers will do to you

when they find out that you have two thousand *naira* in your pocket. They will take the money and then kill you."

"*Chineke*, which kind trouble is this, eh?!"

"You are the one trying to make the matter worse than it already is. Tell you what I'll do; you get us to Yola safe and sound, and I'll give you a bonus of one thousand *naira*," Ademola offered.

"Why did Uche lie to me?"

"About what?" Crowder got up. He climbed the bags of kolanut and jumped off the truck.

"He no tell me say the boy *na* Hausa."

"What difference would that have made?"

"I for not accept take him along."

"That boy saved your life," Ademola said.

"Did the driver ahead of you at the checkpoint have anybody with him?" Crowder zipped his pants as he got back on the truck.

The driver shook his head.

"But they killed him anyway, didn't they?" Crowder said, making the point that was all too apparent.

"Which one of you go pay for the kolanut the boy gave to the bastards?"

"What kolanut?" Ademola asked.

"That little Ha—the boy ordered me to give the foolish sergeant a sack of my merchandise. He even called me *yan-mirin*, the little goat!" The driver fumed.

"Which would you have rather given away, a sack of kolanut or your life?" Ademola asked.

"The kolanut, of course, but that's a lot of money."

"How much?" Ademola snapped, showing his revulsion.

"One hundred and fifty *naira*."

"Take it out of the one thousand I promised to give you at the end of our journey. You need to get started, we're wasting time talking about kolanut and little goat in the middle of the jungle. How much longer before we get to

Yola?" Ademola got up to stretch himself.

"Eight hours," the driver said.

"Thank—" Ademola sneezed again.

The driver shook his head, and then took a small square tin box, the size of a match box, out of his pocket. He opened it, dipped his right thumb inside, picked up a chunk of yellowish-brown powder and guided it to his nose. He inhaled, both eyes shut. When he opened his eyes, they were misted and bloodshot. Then he sneezed.

Crowder flinched.

"Here." The driver tossed the can to Ademola.

"I'm not putting that in my nose," Ademola said.

"Make you no waste my time, doctor. The snuff *fit* help you relax and you no go smell the kolanut again."

"Thanks, but no thanks."

"If you want to continue to sneeze like a goat, then you no go come to Yola with me *o*."

"I can't."

"Try the damned thing, Ola," Crowder coaxed.

Ademola took a deep breath before grabbing the can. The moment he inhaled the substance his head felt like it was going to explode. He let out such an explosive sneeze, he felt as though a chunk of his brain had exited through his nose. Tears ran down his face.

"Bless you." Crowder laughed.

"My face is on fire."

The driver smiled.

"I hope that means you won't harass me any longer with your sneezing." Crowder laughed again.

The driver took back his little box, replaced the sacks of kolanut, jumped down, and shook his head in astonishment before driving off.

"I don't think I can survive another eight hours in this box. We should go back to Lagos, give the documents to the soldiers, and go on with our lives."

"You're kidding me, right?" Crowder said.

"I'm serious. After all, we haven't really committed any crime, other than petty theft of government documents which nobody cares about anyway."

"It's a fact that we have been involved in several accidents where not one, or two, but three—at the very least—three soldiers have either died or have been visited with bodily harm. Setting a soldier ablaze is not a misdemeanor. It's a capital offense punishable by death, especially in this tropical Gulag."

"We should be able to defend ourselves in a court of law." Ademola flinched at the naivete of his argument.

"And which white-wigged, black-robed solicitor will defend us at the military tribunal?" Crowder laughed.

"At the right price someone would be greedy enough to take the case. I don't make any sense, do I?"

"Nope," Crowder said.

"But there has to be a way out of this mess."

"That's what we are seeking."

"I mean, other than running away like cowards."

Crowder's voice choked with rage. "We're not cowards. Two-legged predators with big guns are chasing us out of the land as they've done in the past."

"Which past?" Ademola asked grimly.

"In the beginning—"Crowder coughed, and his voice sounded like that of an old *griot* readying to tell a bunch of children a folk tale under the shade of a baobab tree. "In the beginning, all humans were one people. God created man in his own black image. There was peace when we were equal. But after some time, a few came to believe that they were stronger, superior, and more important than the rest. They amassed wealth and with it they became mighty. With their power they became conceited and tyrannical. They waged wars against each other and the weaker ones were forced to work the land for the benefit of the few. The less powerful were chased out of the land of Africa onto the barren region to the north where the sun seldom shone and the climate was always cold. Most perished. The few that endured became one with the new world; their skin, whitened and covered with hair, protected them from the bitter cold. The more they suffered, the more they were forced to learn the art of survival, and the more their bodies mutated. Over generations they became white. But they never forgot how they came to be. So when they finally came back to the land where it all began, most of them came with vengeance in their hearts. Just as you and I will one day."

⤳

Femi looked at the envelope in Eniola's hand. "Are you sure it's safe to do that?"

Eniola nodded, covering the mouthpiece of the telephone. She hesitated before continuing with her conversation. "It's my brother... Yes, he's back from London... I'll tell him. Give me the address again... Yes, I know the house, but—" She held the telephone to the side of her head with her shoulder, freeing a hand to grab a pencil. She scribbled the address on the manila envelope. "Thanks, I'll meet you there in about thirty minutes." She hung up and started for the door.

"Eniola, I don't think it's a good idea to hand the document to someone you don't know," Femi said.

"I know Brigadier Babasa. I introduced my best friend to him two years ago, and they're still friends. She's meeting him at his guest house at Ikeja. So are we, to give him the document."

"If you say so," Femi agreed with reservation.

"I do. After all, his name is first on the list. It looks like he is the mastermind of the *coup* plan. I should have thought of him first."

"But what if Sakara is not in good terms with Babasa? Or better still, what if Sakara is against the *coup*?"

"I'm not concerned about that. We went to Sakara's house to give him the document as suggested by Akin, but he wasn't home. I'm not sitting around until Monday with this dynamite on my lap. Come on, let's go."

As soon as they exited the hotel parking lot in the blue Nissan 260ZX, Eniola shook her head in bewilderment. The streets were empty and eerie as they drove past the National stadium, past Ojuelegba, and were about to negotiate the roundabout when Femi grunted, "Here we go!"

"What is it?" Eniola peered through the windshield as they stopped at a makeshift checkpoint. "Leave this to me."

"Do you have a pass?" asked the corporal, a short and stocky man with the face that looked like that of a toad, who materialized from behind a green Land Rover. Three other soldiers stood in front of the Nissan, their rifles held firmly in their hands.

Eniola leaned towards the driver's side and smiled. "We're on our way to deliver a message to Brigadier Babasa."

"What message?" The corporal grabbed the door handle.

"It's for the brigadier, not you," Femi said smugly.

"Get out!" The soldier yanked the door open.

"Not so fast, corporal." Eniola pulled back.

"It's against the law to be on the streets without a pass. If you have one, show it to me—"

The sound of rubber screeching to a stop behind the Nissan interrupted the corporal. The horn blared and he looked over his shoulder. He straightened and walked toward the car, a green Mercedes Benz. Reaching the driver's side, he bent over and quickly saluted, then waved at his men. They removed the barricade from the middle of the road.

Eniola rolled down her window to see who was in the

car as it sped past her. "That's Sakara in the Benz." She stuck her neck out the window and screamed, "Segun!"

The Mercedes Benz did not slow down.

"Go, Femi!"

"B—but—" Femi slammed the door shut.

"Now!"

Femi stepped hard on the gas pedal and the car surged forward, speeding after Sakara's car. "Are you sure that's Major Sakara?"

"Yes, go after him, please," Eniola said, then looked back and her hand gripped the steering wheel. "Faster, the corporal is coming after us."

"Sure, but you have to let go of the steering wheel."

Eniola released her grip.

Femi sped after Sakara's Mercedes Benz just as fast as the corporal's vehicle was chasing after the Nissan. The trio sped past Mushin, past the night market, and as they approached the intersection of Agege and Airport roads, the Nissan coughed and jolted.

"Why are you slowing down?" Eniola asked.

"I think we're out of gas."

"What?"

"The needle is on zero."

The car jolted again. Then the engine died. Warning signs on the dashboard filled the dark interior of the car with glowing red lights.

"Now what?" Eniola's chest began to heave.

"Big trouble!" Femi said with dread as footsteps hurried toward them.

"Get out!" The corporal's breathing was labored.

"We—we—"

"Out, I said." He yanked the door open.

"Go, get out," Eniola said to Femi. "Do as he says." And as Femi exited the car, Eniola extracted the three pieces of paper from the envelope, stuffed them under her seat, and opened her door. She heard Femi's groan as the corporal punched him in the stomach.

"You two will smell pepper tonight." The corporal grabbed Femi's neck.

⤻

The aging Boeing 737 took off in readiness to defy the law of gravity, vibrating as it sped down the runway, screaming as it rose above the darkness of the swampy coastal belt. Sakara shifted in his aisle seat, tensive. "Is there any chance the taxi driver gave you misleading information regarding their point of exit before he died?"

"None whatsoever."

"Good, we should be there soon." Sakara became quiet.

"Is there anything else the matter, sir?" Achibong asked.

"This is a dangerous flight. There aren't any landing lights on the ground at Yola airport. The last time I went to Yola like this, the plane almost crashed. But if anyone can get us there, it's this pilot," Sakara said as though he were speaking to himself.

"Why don't we land at Jos airport and telephone the GOC in Yola to send a battalion to the border, sir?"

"It's much easier to telephone London from Lagos than it is to get through to Yola from Jos. The system is in shambles." Sakara sounded frustrated and furious. "It's ironic that we're on this flight, chasing Ademola."

Achibong looked confused.

"Do you know why we're on this mission?"

"To arrest Ademola and Crowder before they cross the border, sir."

"But why do we need to do that?" He tested Achibong.

"To recover the file stolen from DMI yesterday."

"Didn't you speculate that the file was given to the doctor's fiancée?"

"I'm speaking of the second file, sir."

Sakara glared at Achibong. "So you know there's another file missing?" he mused, but said, "What other file?"

"There must be, sir, since the one we were after is known to be with the doctor's fiancée somewhere in Lagos."

"You're very resourceful, Achibong."

"Thank you, sir. If there's anything you wish for me to do, you only have to ask. My loyalty is absolute."

"Good. Now let me level with you. The doctor stole another file from the observation room, a file as damaging as the first one. The irony of the matter is that one of the generals whose interest would be compromised by the content of the file is also the one that's putting our lives at risk as I speak."

"Why is that, sir?"

"Six years ago the government gave OTT the contract to overhaul the country's telecommunication system."

"The Overseas Telephone and Telegraphic Corporation?"

"That's the one. The chairman of the multi-national company was a close friend of General Muhammed before he was assassinated."

"The wealthy Yoruba man."

"Well, the general that succeeded Muhammed gave the contract to OTT. The government paid over one billion dollars to the company, but the job was never started. The chairman of OTT took the money, gave some of it back to the generals, and they got away with impunity."

"If OTT had done at least half of what they were paid to do, we would have been able to telephone Yola. I see your point, sir."

"It's sad, isn't it?" Sakara said, needing to talk freely. "But I am chasing after the document in order to use it later against all the thieves."

"There are a lot of them, sir. Do you think we will ever be able to stem the tide of corruption drowning the country?"

"Yes, with the right leadership, we will, despite all the stories and jokes."

Achibong smiled.

"What's so funny?" Sakara was astounded that he could be so open with his subordinate.

"I beg your pardon, sir."

"It's okay. What is it?"

"This is so out of place, but I just remembered a joke I heard from a friend of mine who lives in California."

"Let's hear it." Sakara relaxed, feeling the need to be closer to Achibong.

"It's about a Nigerian businessman who visited his partner in Seoul, and was amazed at the palatial home of the Korean. 'How did you get the money to build such a big house?' the Nigerian asked. The partner told him to look out the window. He did, and the Korean pointed to a new bridge, 'I got the contract to build that for the government. My commission was ten percent of the cost.' Two years later, the Korean was in Nigeria, visiting his partner. 'Your house is ten times bigger than mine, how did you do it?' The Nigerian opened the window and pointed, 'I got the contract from the government to install that telecommunication satellite.' The Korean looked, shook his head, and said, 'What satellite? I can't see anything.' The Nigerian smiled, and said, 'How can you, my commission was one hundred percent!'"

Sakara was surprised that he could laugh. He wiped tears from the corners of his eyes, patted Achibong on the back, and unbuckled the safety belt. "Jokes aside, the madness must stop." He dashed toward the cockpit, plunging through the door. He stood beside the captain, who was busy punching the buttons on the instrument panels above the windshield.

The plane flew over the hilly belt clothed in dense evergreen rain forest, and stopped vibrating as its nose tilted downward when it reached cruising altitude. Sakara glanced at the navigational instrument panel and saw that the plane was heading north. He then looked through the windshield but saw only darkness as they flew over Jeba, south of River Niger. With his mind's eye, he saw the high plateau rising three thousand feet above sea level as the plane cruised over Jos with its open vegetation of tall grass and deciduous, fire-resistant foliage.

In just an hour they travelled the one thousand eighty three kilometers between Lagos and Jos, a fourteen-hour journey by land. Judging from what Uche told Achibong, Ademola's lorry should be exiting the township of Yola by the time the plane touched down there.

"How long before we get to Yola?" Sakara asked.

The pilot pressed another button, waved Sakara to silence before pulling the lever beside him. "Less than fifteen minutes." He pulled the lever to begin their descent toward Yola, a zone in the dry savannah region of the country. Sakara looked through the windshield again, but the darkness prevented him from seeing the thorn thicket interspersed with bare patches of sandy soil as the plane approached the airport.

Sweat beaded the pilot's forehead as he shifted the roaring engine into reverse, slowing the forward thrust of the plane, which vibrated violently. He bit his lower lip as the tires scraped the asphalt, and the plane bounced off the runway, heading toward the terminal building like a blind vulture. It skidded, bounced again before screeching to a stop, barely missing a fuel truck. "You owe me big time, major," he said, wiping sweat off his face.

"Thanks, I'll remember this, believe me." Sakara patted the pilot on the shoulder before exiting the cockpit to join Achibong. They trooped out of the plane, Sakara running toward the terminal.

An old man, who looked angry enough to kill an elephant with his bare hands, came out from the side door of the terminal. "Who are you people?" he asked in Hausa.

"I need a vehicle right away." Sakara ignored the man's question.

"Who—"

"That's none of your business," Sakara snapped in fluent Hausa. "Where's the fastest vehicle here?"

"The manager's car is over there," the man said, his face expressing the acknowledgement of authority and present danger.

"Where's the key?"

The old man turned and disappeared into the terminal building. He emerged a few seconds later, a bunch of keys dangling in his outstretched hand. Sakara snatched it and ran to a white Peugeot 505 sedan in the parking space marked Manager. He got behind the steering wheel, started the engine, and threw it into gear just as Achibong got in. Sakara rolled down the window, and yelled, "Captain, I'll be back soon. Refuel the plane before I get back."

"Are we going to the barracks for reinforcement in case the fugitives resist arrest, sir?"

Sakara's foot pressed hard on the accelerator. "Who said we're going to arrest anybody?"

The roadblock on the northern bank of River Benue, just outside of Yola, was manned by four policemen whose appearance was as sloppy as their blue uniforms. Sakara pulled up, got out of the car, and approached one of the officers, a lance corporal. "Has any lorry been through here lately?"

"Who wants to know?" the policeman said in Hausa.

"Major Sakara from DMI—"

"What's BMI?" He laughed. "Hey, *mutumi*, do you know what BMI is? This one says—"

"Shut up, you stupid idiot! It's *DMI*, Directorate of

Military Intelligence. Is this how you conduct yourself in the presence of a superior officer?" Sakara pulled out the pistol from his pocket.

The lance corporal ran a hand over his face as though wiping away his ignorance. He stepped back, and saluted. Two other policemen joined him, and the three stood at attention. The lance corporal offered an apology.

"Did you allow a lorry carrying kolanut to pass through here within the last hour?"

"No, sir, but a passenger car—a yellow Mazda station wagon went that way, sir," the corporal said. He did not tell Sakara that the driver had given them a one hundred *naira* bribe, a huge amount considering the fact that there was no contraband in the car.

"How many people were in the car?" Sakara snapped.

"Not counting the driver who—"

"How many?"

"Three, sir, a little boy and two men. The driver—"

"How long ago?"

"Oh, about twenty minutes, sir."

"It's more than that, I will say twenty three minutes," the shortest of the three corrected the corporal.

"Where were they heading?"

"This road goes straight to the border with Cameroon, sir. The next town is Garoua on the other side."

Sakara spun around and ran to his car. He slammed the door and sped off into the night.

"The border is closed for the rest of the night. You have to come back in the morning," the customs officer on the Nigerian side of the border said.

"Isn't there any way you can accommodate us, officer?" Ademola asked, hoping that the man could be persuaded.

"We don't have any accommodation here. You'll have to go back to one of the hotels in town," the officer said.

"I don't mean that kind of accommodation, my friend."

"What do you mean, then?"

"Let me handle this." Crowder stepped forward. "What does it take for you to search the car for contraband?" he asked, exposing the wad of currency notes in his hand.

"It all depends, but your problem is with the immigration and security officers who are sleeping and don't want to be disturbed." The officer eyed the money.

Crowder peeled off five twenty-*naira* notes, which he then spread out like a fan.

"That's not enough." The officer's countenance assumed that of an extortionist. "If you want to go across now, it will cost you more than that."

"How much more?"

"At least ten times more. And I'm being kind. Remember, I would have to explain to the other officers why I did not let them do their jobs."

"We understand." Crowder added more to the notes, counted it and handed the officer the sum of one thousand *naira*. He smiled.

"Thank you for your understanding. It's a difficult job we do here for our country," he said, taking the money.

Ademola, Crowder, and Ali got back into the yellow Mazda, and the driver drove through the barricades, under a long metal pole which the officer had raised. The car stopped, and the officer lowered the pole. He then walked to the front of the car, bent over and commenced to remove a long chain spiked with what looked like several sharp nails that zig-zagged across the road for several yards. As the driver navigated the treacherous path slowly, Ademola looked behind him, and saw what looked like the headlights of a car speeding toward them. The officer had almost completed the task when a car horn blared half a mile away.

"Faster!" Ademola said to the driver.

"I can't, it's dangerous to drive any faster." The driver continued to maneuver the car carefully.

Crowder looked over his shoulder, and pointed to the headlights. "Oh, my God, is someone coming after us?"

9

"Why did they have to cut the elastic from my underwear?" Defiant, Femi tried to keep what was left of his Fruit of the Loom briefs in place, the only clothing concealing his nakedness. The jailroom reeked of urine, old perspiration, and the stench of stale cigarette smoke.

"We don't want you to commit suicide with the rubber," said the military police officer, a Yoruba, judging from the three short scars on his face.

"Are you out of your mind? Where's my sister?"

"Pompous brat! You are very lucky to be alive." The military police officer looked like he was having difficulty holding his temper. He marched away from the steel bars separating him from Femi. "I would show more respect if I were you, young man," he said with a sneer.

"You didn't answer my question. What have you done to my sister?" Femi repeated in Egba dialect.

The officer turned. "Are you from Arinota or Abeokuta?"

"Abeokuta—Please tell me what has happened to her."

"Last time I saw her, she was in the interrogation room. That's no place for anyone to be, especially a stubborn woman like her." He took a cigarette out of his pocket, lit it, and exhaled the smoke which spiraled like a stick of licorice candy.

"Why are you treating us like this? Why?" Femi asked.

"You're as stubborn as your sister, aren't you? Unfortunately for both of you, the physical evidence we have does not corroborate your story."

"What evidence? What the hell are you talking about?"

The officer pursed his lips. "Why is Brigadier Babasa's name on the envelope you were supposed to be taking to Major Sakara?"

"What kind of question is that? Didn't my sister tell you?" Femi crinkled his nose as though the officer fouled the air, and not by the cigarette smoke.

"I want to hear your answer," the soldier snapped.

"I don't understand all the intrigue, I just came back from a four-year stay in London, and—"

"Don't waste my time on frivolous discussion about your stay in London." He dropped the cigarette to the floor, and ground it with the sole of his boot.

"You don't sound like you want to help us."

"Is that a fact?"

"Yes, and I wish to exercise my constitutional right."

"What is that?"

"I have the right to call my solicitor."

In spite of Femi's seriousness the officer burst into laughter. He lit another cigarette, and laughed some more. *Johnny Just Come*, you're not in England. This is Nigeria. Our law is different here. The courts and the stupid constitution are for civilians. Nigeria is under military rule, in case you haven't heard. We have DECREES, military justice, the same thing that those pseudo-intellectuals in their ivory towers call jungle justice. Not civilian laws or a stupid constitution. And anyone that breaks them dies. Now, do you still wish to call a solicitor?"

"Yes." Femi remained defiant.

The officer walked out of the room, the glowing cigarette clamped between his lips. He rounded the corner and entered the interrogation room where Eniola sat at a table, facing the door. "Your brother corroborated your story." He exhaled cigarette smoke through his nose.

"What did you expect?" Eniola was indignant.

"But you didn't tell me the whole truth. Like what happened to the content of the envelope."

"You're too low on the hierarchy to have that information," she thought, but said, "Your people at the checkpoints need to be trained on how to handle law-abiding citizens," admonishing the officer.

"You think you are superior to them, don't you?"

"Don't you also, officer?" Eniola snapped back. "And put that thing away, please. The smoke bothers me. Besides, it's bad for your health."

The officer smiled benignly, hesitated, then dropped the cigarette into an over-flowing ashtray. "The Nissan has been impounded, and I will get my boys to search it for the document which I believe you've hidden somewhere in there."

"Are you asking for my permission?" Eniola taunted.

"Don't push your luck. I can have you flogged."

"You can have me killed also, that much I know. But what you don't know is that someone other than my brother knows I'm here, and the person is surely going to tell Babasa and Sakara that I am in your custody."

"Do you think I am afraid of that?"

"You should be." She rubbed her temple.

"I beg your pardon?"

She raised her right hand as though about to take an oath. "If anything happens to me or my brother, you'll pay dearly for it, I assure you." She dropped the hand to her side. "But let me say this; I've read the document, and I believe that you'll be better off not knowing what it's all about." She stared at the officer. "Now, you're curious," she thought.

"That's a chance I'm willing to take, so why don't you tell me what it's all about. After all, we're from the same town." The officer sat down at the table to face her.

"So what? That doesn't mean I should trust you."

"Why not?" The officer sat forward.

"I don't know you. And I was specifically instructed to hand it to Major Sakara, and that's what I was about to do before those idiots arrested me. One of them went as far as to beat my brother. He'll pay for that." She sat still.

"You speak with confidence and arrogance," the officer said, "but you shouldn't threaten me."

"That was not a threat, it's a promise."

"I am a military police officer, not a regular soldier. I investigate cases, and arrest accused soldiers—"

"I'm not a soldier. Why am I under arrest?"

"You are in possession of a military document, and that falls within my jurisdiction."

Eniola turned from him to stare at the wall. "Where's the Nissan?"

"I told you, it's been impounded."

"Where is it?" She got off the chair.

"Sit down," the lieutenant said with subdued violence.

"Where?" Eniola remained on her feet.

"Here, in the parking lot."

"The document is under the front passenger seat."

He pulled a cigarette out of his pocket, and was about to light it when Eniola screamed, "I told you that stupid thing bothers me!"

He shook his hand, killing the flame, but remained seated.

"Aren't you going to get it?"

"Perhaps," he sounded cryptic. "What's that supposed to mean?" Eniola asked, not liking the sudden glint in the officer's eyes.

"Didn't you just say you don't know me?" For a brief moment, he looked indecisive, troubled. Then he reached a hand into his trouser pocket and extracted the three pieces of paper, folded in half. He spread them open, looked into Eniola's eyes then commenced to read the first page.

Eniola rushed toward the officer, who shifted sideways, preventing her from grabbing the papers from his hand. "You idiot, you've had it all along," she said between clenched teeth. "I warned you!"

"I'm a detective, not a stupid soldier, remember?"

"Now what are you going to do?"

He smiled, and then waved her to sit down.

She did.

"I have several options: I can take the document straight to Dodan Barracks, and hand it over to the head of state personally. The consequence, of course, is that heads would roll before the end of the day, including those of Babasa and Sakara, not to mention yours and your brother's."

"And what do you think Bukha will do to you? Promote you to general for knowing his secret? They kill fools like you without batting an eye," Eniola raged.

He ignored her. "My second option, of course, is to give the document to Brigadier Babasa, enabling him to proceed with his *coup* plan, in which case, General Bukha and the other members of the Supreme Military Council would be killed. But since you're so smart, why don't you tell me which of the two choices is better?"

"You have four other choices."

"Four?"

"At least." She took a deep breath. "You can share the information with other junior officers like yourself. And being the mastermind, you could become the next head of state. Don't look at me like that, it's happened in other countries in Africa. Granted, you have your work cut out."

"I'm sure you're kidding me, right?"

"You'll never know." Eniola decided to prolong the exercise. "Another option is to give the document to your unit commander. You might be promoted to captain. Isn't that the next rank?"

The officer nodded, and picked his nose.

"You are not only stupid, but also filthy." Eniola squirmed inside, but said, "You can hand it over to Major Sakara, for whom it was intended in the first place."

"That's not a good one."

"Why not?" Eniola studied him.

"Major Sakara is known to be a dangerous man."

"Lucky for you. At least you know who he is and where he stands. Would you rather take a chance with Bukha?"

"And the fourth?"

"Give me back the documents and let's forget this ever happened." She smiled.

The officer shook his head and smiled back.

Sakara was in a state of despondency, having exhausted all his resources pursuing Ademola and failing. Despite the warmth in his parlor, he shivered, and rubbed his arm before going into the kitchen. He put a kettle on the stove, and made a cup of coffee, which he took back to the parlor. He sat heavily on the recliner, spilling the coffee. "Dammit! There's no need to even think about how Ademola escaped at the border," he thought. What good would that do? But he needed to think of what to do next. The official word from the head of state was that he was under house arrest, which meant he shouldn't leave the house. It was already Monday morning, and he needed to get into his office to clear his desk, especially the classified files in the observation room. Granted, no one else could open the steel door. He had not only installed a special lock but he had also changed the combination, which he alone knew. But Dikko or Bukha could order him to hand over everything. And one of them would soon.

He sipped the coffee, got off the recliner and was halfway to the bedroom when the doorbell chimed. He ignored
it and went into the bedroom. He heard the sound of banging, then a familiar voice commanded, "Major Sakara, you're
ordered to open the door!"

He grabbed his pistol from the bed, went into the bathroom and splashed cold water on his face, wiped it off with
the tail of a cotton shirt hanging on a nail on the door, and
then went to answer the door.

Captain Balewa stood on the step, flanked on each side
by three armed soldiers, none saluted Sakara.

"What is it, captain?"

"You're ordered to come with me to HQ."

"Whose order is that?" Sakara snapped.

"That, I'm not at liberty to divulge, major."

"So, I'm still a major," he thought, perceiving a ray of
hope. He looked at the dark eyes of the captain. "Let's go."
He took a deep breath, inhaling the hot, moist air before
stepping forward.

The trip to Victoria Island was quick despite the usual
Monday morning traffic jam. Captain Balewa used the siren,
and a long whip, landing it on the roofs of the vehicles that
did not yield the right of way fast enough.

At DMI headquarters, Dikko wasted no time as soon as
Sakara entered his office. "Who gave you the authorization
to commandeer a plane?" He did not offer Sakara a seat.

"Nobody, sir, but—"

"There's no but, major. The head of state made it clear
that you were under house arrest, didn't he?"

"When I received reliable intelligence regarding the possible whereabouts of the fugitives I had to pursue them."

"By disobeying the commander in chief?"

"I assumed the end would justify the means."

"Did it?"

"Under the circumstances, no."

"So you still haven't got the document."

Sakara assumed that his boss was making a statement. He pursed his lips, and waited.

"You did not give me an answer regarding our little chat on Friday."

Sakara's insides churned, but he remained silent.

"Are you with us or not?" Dikko pointed to a chair.

"About what, sir?" he asked, but thought, "So this is what it's all about? Let's see how Machiavellian you are."

Dikko leaned forward, resting his elbows on the desk to support his face. "Don't tell me you forgot about the plan." Then, he whispered, "The *coup*."

"I beg your pardon, sir?" Sakara feigned dismay.

"Hold it!" Dikko held up his hand, gesturing for calm. "I'm not trying to entrap you. There's no listening device in this room. I thought we took care of that already."

"Am I still under house arrest, sir?" Sakara needed to further pierce Dikko's armor.

"Well, the head of—"

"Am I?"

"Officially, yes."

"I should be home then." Sakara started to get up.

"Sit down, major!"

Sakara obeyed.

"This is a difficult time—a dangerous time for us in this department. I disagree with the head of state's decision to take you off the case. And I told him so. But he's not likely to change his mind, however, mostly because he doesn't know you as I do." He looked at Sakara as though he expected him to express appreciation.

None came.

Dikko got off his chair, and walked to the window. He parted the blinds, peered out as though looking for something. Without turning around, he said, "You are a very resourceful and hard-working officer, an asset to this department, major, and I hate to see you treated badly."

"Thank you, sir," Sakara said, only because it was the appropriate thing to say at the moment.

"I mean every word. Your loyalty to me has been unquestionable, and I need it now more than ever." Dikko's voice cracked. He looked rattled as he turned around. He dashed straight to the bar, poured half a glass of scotch, and took a sip.

"What's the matter, sir?" Sakara asked, puzzled.

"General Bukha is getting ready to make a move. He knows about the *coup* plan. And he suspects that I know more than I've shared with him."

"Like what, sir?" Sakara got up.

"The names of the architects—the names on the missing document. We've got to get that file back before Bukha gets it. He has assigned someone from the NSO to find it."

"I don't see how I can be of any assistance if I'm off the case, sir."

"I said you're *officially* off the case. Why do you think I sent Captain Balewa to bring you here?"

"That was quite unnerving, sir." Sakara's heart pumped harder against his chest, hurting. He had a revolting taste in his mouth and wondered how far he could trust Dikko. "Balewa was—"

"Balewa is loyal to Bukha, he's the mole. And I intend to use him to *our* benefit. If Bukha suspects that you're still working on the case, he's liable to have you locked up, and possibly executed. He's a paranoid bastard."

Sakara took a couple of steps backward, feeling strange, and needing space. "Given sufficient time, I will get the file back," he said calmly, but not feeling calm at all. "How much time do I have?"

Dikko gulped down the rest of the scotch. He wiped his mouth with the back of his hand and said, "A couple of hours at best. What else do you need?"

"Lieutenant Achibong." With a deliberate sneer, Sakara's eyes probed, daring his boss to look at him.

Dikko looked away. "You have it," he said, his voice barely audible.

Sakara saluted, and reached for the door.

"Major!"

Sakara stopped but did not turn around.

"You're still under house arrest, and off the case."

Sakara grunted in feigned appreciation, saving his rage for later. He exited, slamming the door behind him. He rushed through the reception area of his office, acknowledged his secretary's greetings with a grunt, and marched into the inner room. He sat at his desk and checked to make sure all the files that he had been working on the previous Friday were still there. They were, undisturbed. He picked up the phone, dialed, waited for the first ring, and then hung up. The phone rang, he picked it up and snapped, "Come in here immediately," and hung up again.

Achibong rushed into the room, saluted Sakara, who waved him to a chair. The two sat facing each other. "What do you have?" Sakara asked with contained impatience.

"You were right, sir, Brigadier Dikko is playing both sides. He had supper with the head of state last night, very late. But he had already met with Brigadier Babasa in the afternoon. The meeting was not congenial—I have the tape. Brigadier Babasa sounded very strange, suspicious. You were also right about the missing document, sir, it was the only copy made. Babasa ordered Dikko to find it before the end of—yes, end of today."

"And if not?"

"Brigadier Babasa said, and I quote, 'We'll have to scratch the project,' that was it. They said their goodbyes and Dikko left. But listen to this, Babasa telephoned Brigadier Hakabala and told him just the opposite."

"What?"

"He said, 'We strike at 0200 hours, on the dot.' I think he meant tonight, sir."

"Where's Brigadier Babasa?"

"Dodan Barracks."

"I need to see him, alone and soon."

"Should I make the appointment, sir?"

"No! I will contact him myself. Get—"

The telephone shrilled.

Sakara spun round in his chair, grabbed the receiver, and barked, "Who is it?"

He listened, and the dark spots in his crossed eyes looked like they were going to disappear into the bridge of his nose. "Are you sure?" He listened for a moment then said, "Let them in!" The intensity in his eyes bored into Achibong's. "Do you know anything about this?"

The lieutenant's eyebrows soared, apprehensive. "About what, sir?" he asked sharply.

"Dr. Ademola's fiancée is here."

"What?"

"She's here with her brother, and a police officer—military police."

The door creaked open and Eniola strode in like a real estate agent about to show the office to her brother and the military police officer who trailed behind her looking like prospective buyers.

Sakara nodded at his secretary, who peeked from behind the officer, flashed a nervous smile, shrugged, and eased the door shut.

"How are you, major?" Eniola asked pleasantly, her voice a shade above a whisper.

He swallowed, and his Adam's apple looked like a lemon squeezed up and down a rubber tube. "H—how are you?" He smiled back, tightly.

The officer approached Sakara, stopped a couple of feet away, saluted, and stood at attention for a moment.

"At ease, lieutenant," Sakara commanded. "What brings you here?"

"I need to speak with you alone, sir," the officer responded, spreading his legs apart, hands locked at the base of his back.

Sakara looked at him with incredulity. "What about?"

"Alone, sir," the military police officer repeated, this time, in Yoruba.

"Does that include the civilians you came with?" Sakara asked in English.

"No, sir."

"Then you better tell me what's on your mind. Now!"

"Very well, sir."

"Sit down." Sakara pointed to a chair.

The officer did.

Achibong got up, removed some files from the sofa, and Eniola and Femi took their seats.

"The lady has something to show you." The officer nodded at Eniola. "She was arrested two nights ago at a road-block on the mainland, sir. And she claimed that she was on her way to give an envelope to you."

"What envelope?" Achibong asked, and immediately stopped, his face mirroring his bad judgement.

Sakara acknowledged it, flashing a disapproval look.

"When I saw the document, I knew I had to do something quickly. First, I thought of taking it straight to Dodan Barracks." The officer swallowed.

Achibong flinched.

"I also thought of showing it to Brigadier Babasa." He looked as though he was enjoying the suspense.

"That means you've already read it. Too bad!" Sakara thought, and the first verse of his favorite Yoruba poem pierced his mind. He shut his eyes and recited the rest of the poem without parting his lips. He remained silent until he finished. Then he opened his eyes and saw Eniola glaring at him. Her face mirrored her awareness of the police officer's predicament. "After so many years, she's still so ravishing, and she seems to have retained her intuitive abilities," Sakara thought, and then felt a stirring in his pants. He quickly crossed his legs.

Eniola smiled faintly.

Femi turned from his sister to stare at Sakara, and back to his sister. He frowned, then coughed. "Is it okay if I use the men's room outside?" He waited for Sakara to grant him permission. "Can you show me where it is?" He nodded at Achibong, who glared at him and looked about to say something. Sakara waved him into silence.

Femi waited for Achibong to open the door and was about to exit when Sakara said, "My secretary will let you know when to come back inside."

Femi looked over his shoulder and winked. "Sure."

Sakara scratched his stubble-sanded cheek. He stared at the tip of his nose, watching Eniola attentively. Her perfect eyebrows arched, adding beauty to her almond-shaped eyes and her thick and long lashes.

Her voice caressed his maleness, "This belongs to you and—"

"That was wise to send those two out," the lieutenant interrupted Eniola. As she handed the three pieces of paper to Sakara, the door creaked open, and Achibong came in and took his seat. "I thought you asked him to stay out," he said in Yoruba.

Sakara's face suddenly looked like a carved stone. "Get out," he fired, getting on his feet.

The officer remained seated.

"I think you should know that the lieutenant made copies of the document," Eniola said.

"Is that a fact?"

"Yes," the officer answered.

"And why did you do that?"

"Insurance, sir," the officer said smugly.

Sakara cocked his head, scrutinizing the officer. "Against what?"

"Well, you never know," the officer responded in Yoruba, defiant.

"You like to play games, don't you?"

"No, I don't."

"I do. And I particularly like American sports. Take baseball and fishing for example. They are both fun." Sakara turned to Achibong. "Aren't they, lieutenant?"

"Indeed, sir," Achibong got on his feet, smiled, and saluted.

Sakara smiled back, appreciating Achibong's understanding of his command. "The sharks in the ocean are famished, it's feeding time," he thought.

At Dodan Barracks Babasa nodded several times as he listened to Sakara. He accepted the file. "You are absolutely sure this is the only copy in existence?"

"Absolutely? No, sir. But the military police officer who brought them to my office was made to talk after a brief interrogation. He had made two copies of each page which he kept with a friend."

"And?"

"We got them and they've since been destroyed, sir."

"What about the officer and his friend?"

"They will never be a threat to anyone again, sir."

"Good. What do you intend to do with the young lady?"

"She's a good source of intelligence, sir."

"Don't harm her."

"Yes, sir."

"How's DMI?"

"It's due for a shakeup, sir." Sakara read between Babasa's words.

"Get me a report and your recommendations. I'll contact you soon," Babasa said in Yoruba.

BOOK TWO

10

Three blind men, a one-eyed man, and Ali sat in a circle on a rug around a bowl of meatless *jollof* rice. The leader, the one-eyed man, whose face looked as smooth as a baby's, garbed in the combat uniform of a general, grabbed Ali's hand. "You've had enough," he snarled.

"But I'm still hungry." Ali withdrew his hand.

"We must be full before you can eat again." The leader pointed an admonishing finger at Ali.

"His Excellency is right." Ali's surrogate father stuffed his mouth with rice. He then whacked the side of the boy's face with the back of his greasy hand.

"You are wicked. You've had more to eat than me," Ali cried. "Why should I stop eating? I'm still hungry."

"Because you're not blind like us, and you speak the language of southern *kafirin*," said another beggar whose blind eyes looked like burnished copper. "Your father has the right to do as he wishes. And we're lucky indeed that the leader has taken time out of his busy schedule to visit us, rich and powerful as he is."

"Then why doesn't he help us to live better than this?" Ali wiped tears off his face.

The leader swallowed hard. When he spoke, his voice sounded amplified, like the voices of several men: "It is the wish of Allah that you should roam the streets as beggars. I cannot do anything about that. But you must be grateful that I am one of you—the CHOSEN TRIBE, naturally endowed by the Almighty to rule Nigeria forever. I am the king and you are the paupers, both from the same kingdom!"

"But I'm still hungry—" Ali twisted as he dreamt, his head resting on a pillow propped against the window. He barely felt the vibration as the Boeing 747 plane screamed toward the sky. Below, the plateau rose two thousand feet, bounded by broken, rocky mountains with peaks up to eight thousand feet. The surface of the Atlantic ocean shimmered as the plane left behind the land mass of Cameroon, en route to the land of the white man made rich by imported sagacity and brutal force.

Ali did not remember being so exhausted that he had to be carried aboard the plane fast asleep. But he smelled the appetizing aroma of the food as the flight attendants wheeled loaded carts down the aisle. He twisted his body again, nose twitching as the aroma became stronger. He yawned, and then woke up famished. "I am hungry, *dokito*."

"I bet you are." Ademola stroked the boy's tangled hair. "From now on, it would be more appropriate if you called me dad, daddy, or *baba*."

"Why?" He looked suspiciously at Ademola.

"Because I have adopted you." Ademola eyed Crowder.

Ali frowned, and shook his head.

"What does that mean?" Ademola asked.

"What is adopted?" Ali asked, stretching.

"It means I am your father, officially."

"Does that mean you get to beat me if I am bad?"

"I will never lay my hands on you, but if you ever do anything bad I'll talk to you about it."

"What if I'm really bad?"

"You'll be punished, especially if it's deliberate."

"You'll beat me then?"

"No."

"How would you punish me?"

"I would take away some of your privileges."

"My food?"

"No. No television, for instance."

"I get to watch television? But you don't have one."

"I will when we get to our destination."

"And I can watch it all the time as long as I'm good?"

"You'll be restricted to watching it for a few hours on weekends only—if you are good, that is."

"But what if I'm really really really bad?" Ali asked.

"I'll be in charge of that department. And I do not spare the rod. So you'll be well advised to be of good behavior." Crowder looked serious.

"Would you let him do that?" Ali's eyes bored into Ademola's, pleading with childish innocence, and succeeding. He smiled when Ademola shook his head no. "I approve."

"You do, eh?" Ademola laughed.

"Yes, *baba*. I like that the most."

"You have to understand that I've never done this sort of thing before."

"Me too."

They both laughed. Crowder snickered.

Ali started to get up but was restrained by the safety belt. Ademola helped him unbuckle it. He showed him how to use the belt, rebuckling it, and Ali tried, and succeeded in unbuckling the belt by himself.

"Very good, son. You learn fast, don't you?"

"I'm smart." He tapped his head with his index finger.

Crowder looked at Ademola and shook his head. "When someone says something good or nice about you, the appropriate thing to say is thank you."

"Even if the person does not give me anything?"

"A compliment is a gift."

"What is compliment?"

Crowder shook his head again. "You've got your work cut out. I have a feeling I'm going to enjoy this."

Ali got on his feet and his eyes grew large upon seeing so many people in what looked like a long room without an end. He quickly sat down. "Who are all these people?"

"They're passengers like us."

"Why are they here?" he asked suddenly, apprehensive.

"They are going to New York."

Ali's eyebrow soared.

"It's a big city in America. We'll be there soon." Ademola nodded at the window.

The expression of surprise did not leave his eyes as Ali turned again, and grabbed Ademola's arm.

"What is it?"

"The wicked soldiers killed us, didn't they?"

"What are you talking about?" Ademola looked at Crowder, who looked back, his brow creased with confusion.

"The sky is below us! We are in heaven—dead, and on our way to meet Allah," Ali whispered, and began to recite *Al-Fatihah*:

"*A'udhu billahi minash shaitanir rajim*
In the name of God, the Merciful, the Most Kind.
All praise is for God, the Lord of the Universe,
Master of the day of judgement. You alone we—"

"You've got your hands full." Crowder laughed.

Ademola shushed him to silence, and immediately raised both hands together, joining Ali for the rest of the prayer:

"—From You alone we seek help.
Guide us along the straight way—
The way of those whom You have favored,
Ghairil maghdubi alaihim wa lad dallin."

Ali rubbed his face with open palms and said, "Amen." He turned, and pressing his face against the plexiglass window, peered out and beheld an endless bed of white clouds.

"Look!" He opened his mouth in awe as he pointed upward to the glorious blue sky. "God is great!" he whispered, and tears welled up in his eyes.

Ademola caressed the nape of Ali's neck, and the boy's tears ran down the plastic window, smudging it.

"We're not dead. We escaped from the wicked soldiers, and we are fleeing to America. You'll like it there."

"But we're up in the sky, in heaven, yes?"

"In the sky, yes; in heaven, no."

"Honest? But how come we're standing on the cloud?"

"That's what happens when you are in a plane." Ademola turned to Crowder for assistance.

"Don't even try," Crowder said, hands up in the air.

"Some friend you are." Ademola smirked.

"*Bon jour, monsieur. Parlez vous français?*" asked the flight attendant, pulling the cart to a stop.

Ademola nodded.

"I didn't know you speak French," Crowder said.

"I don't."

"Then why did you nod your head? The lady asked if you speak French."

"Since you speak the Gallic language so well, why don't you tell the lady that I didn't know what she said."

"You're pissed, aren't you?"

"Why should I be?"

"I don't know, you look miffed," Crowder said.

"I'm not miffed or pissed, or whatever else you want to call it." Ademola looked away. "Damn, my life has been turned upside down. I miss Eniola and my family. I feel so empty and alone. All because I did what I needed to do—it's my job to heal people. But you can't understand."

"What's that supposed to mean?" Crowder snapped.

The attendant started to push the cart to the next row of seats. Crowder shook his head vigorously. "Don't go yet, lady, I want—I need a drink." He pointed to a miniature bottle of vodka on the cart.

The attendant's smile radiated warmth and friendliness. "*Pardonnez moi.*"

"That's a very beautiful smile." Crowder winked.

"Thank you."

"You speak English?" Crowder asked.

She nodded, handing him a transparent plastic cup filled with ice. Crowder picked up the bottle from the cart. He offered her a five-dollar note. She shook her head. "Compliments of the airline, sir. Enjoy your drink."

"Thanks." Crowder looked up, openly appraising the attendant's face. "You do remind me of my friend's fiancée. She's just as beautiful."

The attendant smiled. "*Merci, monsieur.*"

"Can I eat now?" Ali interrupted in Yoruba.

"Yes, what would you like?" the attendant replied in a different dialect of Yoruba.

"I'll be damned, you speak Yoruba too?" Crowder asked.

"My father was from the southeastern part of the Republic of Benin."

"You're talking too much. Can I eat now, please?" Ali interrupted again.

"Yes, what would you like, fish or beef?"

"I want food," Ali said importantly.

"Of course." She smiled. "But you must also eat meat or fish, yes?"

Ali smiled back, liking her, glad that she did not treat him like a beggar.

"After I finish my food, I'll eat the beef and fish."

"That's asking—well, it's possible. And what would you like to drink?"

"Fanta!"

Her smile widened. "I don't believe we have Fanta, but there's something similar. Would you like to try it?"

Ali nodded.

The attendant handed him a tray and a can of orange soda. She looked at Ademola questioningly.

"I'll take the fish."

"Let me have the beef," Crowder said.

Ademola helped Ali to remove the thin aluminum foil, exposing the steaming dish of broiled halibut steak, fried rice, and baby carrots. Ali eyed the tray suspiciously.

"Don't you like it?" Ademola asked.

Ali pointed at the plastic bowl of salad. "This, no. Only goats and cows eat leaves. And you shouldn't eat it either. It's not good for you." His importance soared.

"Says who?" Crowder asked.

"That's a fact," Ali replied, knowingly.

"Salad is very good for you. Trust me on that, I'm a doctor," Ademola said.

"Can I have the beef instead of the leaves?" Ali looked at the attendant.

She nodded and took the salad bowl from him, gave him a plate filled with beef steak marinated in mushroom sauce, three pieces of asparagus and mashed potato.

"Thank you." Ali smiled. "I like her very much. Why don't you take her as your wife, *baba*? I think she will be a good woman for us. We need one, yes?"

Crowder laughed. "Is that a fact?" He looked up, meeting the attendant's eyes. She shook her head, moving the cart away with a smile.

"I think you embarrassed the lady, Ali," Ademola said seriously. "After your meal you should go and apologize to her, okay?"

Ali nodded. "What should I tell her?"

"Tell her you didn't mean what you said."

"But I do mean it. She's a good woman and—"

"Lady."

"Yes, she's a good lady, and so are you."

"I'm not a lady, son." Ademola chuckled.

"You know what I mean, *baba*."

They ate in silence. Another flight attendant, a male, took away the empty trays. Ali ate his dessert of chocolate ice cream, liking it enough to beg Ademola for more. Crowder gave him his. The male attendant came back and gave them three earphones for the in-flight movie.

"Ali, it's time to go and apologize to the lady," Ademola said. "Excuse me, please, would you show my son where the lady attendant is?"

"Yes, sir, no problem at all." The attendant smiled.

Ali unhooked his safety belt, got up and stretched before following the man toward the front of the plane. He heard Crowder's voice, "I don't think it's a good idea to let that boy loose."

"What damage can he possibly do?" Ademola asked.

"You never know. There's something about him that sets warning signals off in my head," Crowder said.

"I'm sure he'll be fine."

Ali did not wait to hear the rest of the conversation. He trailed behind the attendant to the first class section of the plane. He saw the beautiful lady from Benin serving a tall, white man who looked rich and important. If not for his bulbous nose he would have been considered handsome. Ali saw him take a wine bottle from the lady, and then reach a hand out to pat her buttocks. She moved deftly away from him. He flashed a smile. Ali grabbed the man's hand, and snapped, "That's very rude. Don't ever do that again."

"I beg your pardon, who is this thing?" the man asked in French.

Ali shrugged, not understanding a word. He looked up and smiled at the lady.

She smiled back and shook her head.

"Who's this boy?" the man asked again.

"He's the son of a passenger, please, excuse him," the attendant responded in French.

"Did I cause you any trouble?" Ali asked in Yoruba.

"Yes, and you shouldn't be here."

"But I came to tell you that I did not mean to embarrass you. I'm sorry."

She held him by the wrist, and gently pulled him toward the back of the section, to the service area. She took a bar of ice cream out of a box, handed it to him, and said, "I accept your apology, now run along."

Ali took the bar, looked up and said, "Thank you."

"You're welcome, now, go!"

"Can you please open the door? I need to go out." He looked down sheepishly.

"Out where?" she asked, and started to laugh.

"Outside, you know, to—you know—" he said, not looking at her.

"You can't go out there, we're thirty-five thousand—oh, I see. Listen," she said gently, "there's a bathroom aboard. Let me show you."

"But I can't, you know, do it here in the room."

"I understand," she said, the smile never leaving her eyes. She stopped in front of a door, pushed it forward, and pointed to the toilet.

Ali remained standing.

"Go on, that's the toilet. You know how to use it, don't you?"

Ali hesitated before shaking his head, embarrassed. He saw the corners of the lady's mouth twitch ever so slightly, concerned. She held the door open, nodded to Ali, beckoning him to go inside. He did hesitantly. "After you take off your pants, sit on this thing here. When you finish, use this paper to—"

"But I need water to, you know," Ali said, still not meeting the attendant's eyes.

"Are you a Muslim?" she asked.

Ali nodded.

"I am too," she said, comforting him. "Wait here for a second, I'll be right back," she said, and left. The door shut automatically.

The pressure in Ali's bladder increased. He pulled down his pants to his ankle, and was half way through when the door opened and the lady entered.

"Ooops, I'm sorry."

Ali turned to sit down. He sat there long after he finished, waiting for the door to open. It didn't. And he waited. And waited for what seemed a lifetime. He heard voices outside, but the door remained shut.

Someone tapped on the door. He heard a male voice which sounded like that of the man with the big nose. He shut his eyes, disliking the man. "What happened to the lady, and the water," he thought. He got on his feet, pants down to his ankle, and pushed the door as he'd seen the lady do. It did not budge. He tried again. Nothing. He panicked. "Oh, Allah, please, open the door," he started to pray. He smelled his waste. He pulled the tip of the roll of toilet paper down and grabbed a handful. He bent over to wipe himself, not feeling clean. He pulled up his pants, and pushed at the door again. Then, he banged it. He heard Ademola's voice, "Son, are you all right in there?"

"Yes," he said faintly.

Then he heard the voice of the lady attendant. "I don't think he's okay."

"Other people need to use the toilet. Hurry up and come out, son," Ademola said.

"I can't!"

"What d'you mean, you can't?" Ademola's voice sounded concerned.

"The door, it won't open."

"Are you all done?"

"Yes."

"Step back."

The door swung inward and there was a sudden applause as several passengers clapped their hands. Ali wished the ground would open up and swallow him in one gulp. No luck. He saw the attendant smile and wink at him, which added to his embarrassment. He ran back to his seat and quickly covered his head with the blanket.

Ademola returned to his seat without saying a word.

After a few minutes the lady attendant stopped by. "Is my friend okay?" she asked, her smiling eyes locked on to Ademola's. "He's a wonderful young fellow."

"Thank you." Ademola returned her smile. He reached a hand under the blanket to touch Ali. "We've got a visitor."

Ali pulled down the blanket slowly, just enough to expose his face. His lips twisted into a nervous smile.

"I brought you something. But first, I need to know your name," she said, her voice teasing, affectionate.

"Ali," he said, barely audible.

"Mine is Taiwo, but my friends call me Tai."

"You're a twin?" Crowder asked. "Is your—"

"She died right after we were born," she responded as though she'd been asked that question innumerable times in the past.

"Oh, I'm sorry to hear that," Ademola said, the expression on his face conveying sympathy.

"Thank you." She handed a package to Ali. "I hope you like what's inside. You're a very special person, Ali. It's been a pleasure meeting you."

"Thank you." Ali responded to Ademola's subtle nod.

"You're very welcome," she said and started to leave.

Crowder asked, "Where are you staying in New York? I'd like to treat you to a nice dinner. No strings."

"The Roosevelt on Lexington Avenue. But I'll be away visiting a friend in Brooklyn. Thanks for the offer." She walked away gracefully.

"Are you not going to open your gift?"

"I will when she comes to visit us," Ali said.

"What makes you think she will do that?" Crowder asked.

"She will, I just know. Can you tell me what that man is saying?" Ali pointed to the movie-projector screen.

"You have to use the earphone, like this." Ademola showed him how to use the gadget.

"But I don't understand the language, *baba*."

"It's French, and I don't understand it either. Let's just enjoy the picture."

"We have to learn French, yes?"

"Yes."

⌢

The plane landed safely at John F. Kennedy International Airport. The immigration officer smiled and congratulated Ademola on his new status, stamped the passport, granting him and his son, Ali, political asylum in the United States with rights to gainful employment.

Clearing customs was a different and humiliating experience. Crowder's American passport assured him a trouble-free passage through customs.

"Where's your luggage?" the custom officer asked.

"I don't have any," Ademola answered.

"None at all? Not even an empty bag like your people?" The officer's tone was contemptuous and condescending.

"None."

"What do you carry on your body then?"

"Only my clothes."

"Very funny," the officer said tightly. "In that case, you'll be subjected to a body search."

"What does that mean?" Ademola asked.

"It means checking to see if you have any plastic down your throat or up your you-know-what."

"I don't know. What?"

"Up your butt, buddy, move!"

Ali and Ademola were subjected to the humiliating body cavity search. Nothing was found, but no apology was offered. They joined Crowder outside. Ademola told him what happened and learned that Nigerians were subjected to the same treatment at every airport in the world. Cocaine trafficking was the reason. Nigerians had become kingpins in the business, supplanting the Italian Mafia.

Getting a taxi was equally frustrating. Several empty cabs cruised past them, only to stop for white passengers a few feet away.

"Welcome to America," Crowder said finally.

"Is it this bad?" Ademola asked.

"This is the appetizer, my friend, the main course awaits us in the city."

Finally, a "gypsy" cab driven by a newly-immigrated Haitian stopped. "*A wey you go, mine friend?*" he asked in French-patois-accented broken English.

"Manhattan," Crowder said.

"Fifty *dola*, no meters." The driver flashed a smile, exposing the largest set of teeth Ali had ever seen.

"Deal!" Crowder jumped in the front seat. Ademola and Ali followed.

The taxi, a not-too-old Chevrolet Impala that looked as though it had seen better days came off the on-ramp to join the traffic on the highway. The afternoon was hot, humid and cloudless. Nauseating exhaust fumes filled the air.

"Turn the air conditioner on, will you?" Ademola said, covering his nose.

"Sorry, no work, compressor broke. But I repair tonight, eh eh." The driver sounded as though he was either laughing or coughing. "You *Afrique?*" He looked over his shoulder.

Crowder nodded. "Please keep your eyes on the road."

"No problem, me good driver. Drive well, *monsieur.*"

Crowder rolled his eyes.

"Haitian driver the best." He flashed the teeth again.

Ali, seated behind Crowder, looked at Ademola and forced a smile. He covered his mouth with his palm, and turned to look at the back of the driver's head. Somehow, the driver reminded him of Uche back in the land of the sleeping giant, and he wondered if the *yanmirin* ever met this one. He noted the similarities: Uche and this driver are talkative and reckless. Maybe taxi drivers all over the world come from the same womb, he mused. They certainly must, he concluded, and then turned his attention elsewhere.

He looked out the window and became enthralled by the strange scenery, the majestic skyline of the jewel in the crown, the land of the white man people talked of with reverence back home. The tops of the buildings looked as though they could be seen only if one took off one's hat. Otherwise, the hat would fall to the ground since the back of one's head had to touch the neck in order for one to look so high. He saw so many of them racing toward the sky that he began to reason that the white man was so rich and happy because he could reach God in heaven faster than anyone else in the world.

"*C'est la vie,*" he heard Crowder say, looking as though he knew the wrong words came out of his mouth.

The taxi stopped as a throng of pedestrians crossed the street. The driver burst into a strident laughter. "New York never change, *monsieur*. The same."

Ali continued to look out the window. He saw many people sleeping on the concrete floor and park benches, some pushing grocery carts, fighting each other over discarded empty soda cans. White women who looked as though their minds were filled with madness, overstuffed brown bags hanging dangerously on their bloated arms, walked lazily about. And soot-covered children ran around, scavenging like mad dogs. He saw black and brown men dashing from car to car, washing windshields, while the drivers waited nervously for the lights to change, their faces creased with hostility and fear. "Allah must be angry," he whispered.

"What is it?" Ademola asked.

"Look, all these people, hungry in the land of the most rich. Why?" And warm tears stung his eyes.

11

LAGOS

August, 1985

Sakara suppressed a yawn. "I'd suspected that someone other than Balewa was the mole, but Dikko?"

"It's quite simple, sir." Achibong kept his face guileless. "Brigadier Dikko would not call his actions as those of a mole. I'm sure he believes that he's just being expedient, sir."

"By giving a classified document to a journalist?" Sakara paused. "The nerve of the cow-dung-eater to get me listening to his speech about eggs."

"I don't believe he expected you to find the document." Achibong studied Sakara. "If the owner of a house sets it on fire, it behooves those who wish to put it out to pay attention to the direction of the smoke. You did, sir."

Sakara stared at Achibong. "Good theory," he thought. "Dikko gave the document to Ogawa to divert everybody's attention from what, the *coup* plan?"

"What if General Bukha read about it in the dailies, only to find out that Brigadier Babasa, who had told him about another one planned by Babasa's enemies in the army—I mean, what if Bukha had killed Babasa and his cohorts? Mind you, Dikko's name is not on that list. But he was in on the plan."

Sakara rubbed the back of his neck. "The bastard wanted to entrap me."

Achibong looked as though he couldn't believe that his boss failed to see the obvious. "Asking you to join the group was not Dikko's initiative. He spoke the truth when he told you that Babasa asked him to recruit you. The problem with that, of course, was that Dikko realized that Babasa preferred you to him. He had to get rid of you by dumping a potentially fruitless assignment in your lap."

"Your supposition ties in everything neatly." Sakara got off the recliner. "Come with me." He headed toward the kitchen. "The long and short of it is that Dikko wants to be the next head of state, right?"

"There you go, sir."

"Tuna?"

"Yes, thanks, sir."

They went back to the parlor and ate the tuna sandwiches in silence. They then spent the next hour poring over the documents Achibong had brought from DMI. With black markers, names were encircled to be scratched off the list of employees, including Dikko's and Balewa's.

Redundant divisions were scrapped and new ones formed. Operations were identified as overt or covert depending on their level of confidentiality and seriousness. All deletions, additions, modifications, and potential actions were assigned budgetary figures. In all, the new, stronger, better, and more efficient DMI was recreated to be the central power base of the intelligence-gathering arm of the new republic. The NSO, CID, Army, Navy and Air Force Intelligence, all were to play second fiddle to DMI. And Sakara intended to be at the helm of affairs with Achibong as his assistant.

"I'm scheduled to meet with Brigadier Babasa in thirty minutes." Sakara looked at his watch. "Come with me!"

Achibong became instantly attentive. "What if Brigadier

Babasa objects to my being there, sir?"

"Let me worry about that." Sakara suppressed the urge to tell his subordinate that he was being tested. "Is that fear of being associated with the *coup* planners, or just his concern for my welfare?" Sakara thought, but said, "Why are you not married yet?"

Achibong looked surprised at the sudden change of topic. "I have not f—found the right girl."

"Interesting that he would have difficulty answering such a simple question," Sakara thought.

"To be honest with you, sir, the reason is because I do not wish to be encumbered, compromised. I do harbor the ambition to be the head of state of this nation."

"Don't we all, but what's that got to do with being married?" Sakara picked up a file.

"Everything, sir. Marriage in my culture means a family with lots of children. And that in my view has been the weakness in our leadership to date."

"Explain that." Sakara warmed to the conversation. "This young man really has balls," he thought.

"To rule Nigeria, the leadership has to be suicidal. Zealots with absolute belief in the way things should be. Family is a hindrance, sir." Achibong accepted the file from Sakara. He put it in the leather bag he'd brought from the office. "Why are you not married, sir, if I may take the liberty?" He met his boss's crossed eyes.

"Ditto," Sakara said simply. "Every military leader or civilian president since independence has had to take chances, compromising their ability to retain power long enough to effect even a semblance of meaningful change. Enemies and detractors abound, all snapping at the heels of those who wish to do the best for the masses, most, if not all, wanting to lead for no other reason than just merely to hold the title. I agree with you, one who wishes to do good must not be compromisable. Yes, a family would make one vulnerable as it has done in the past."

There was a knock at the front door.

Achibong's brows creased. He zipped the bag, stuffed it under the sofa, ironed out his trousers with his hands and went to the door. "*Idem fo?*" he greeted in Efik, holding the door.

"*Oson, sugsug-o,*" Eniola replied, surprising Achibong.

They smiled together. "Please follow me, the major is in the parlor," Achibong said pleasantly, leading the way.

Sakara stared at her as she walked gracefully into the parlor. "I'm glad you could come." His penetrating gaze softened. "How are you?"

She acknowledged him with a smile, her perfume sweet and enrapturing. "I'm fine, thanks." She sat on the sofa.

"You look more beautiful than ever," he stuttered.

"Thank you. You look a bit tired," she said in her kind, silky voice.

He stared at the engagement ring on her finger.

With refined subtlety, she crossed her hands, palms down on her lap.

"Thanks for bringing the document to me. How's Ola?" Sakara's nod was almost imperceptible.

Achibong pulled the leather bag from under the sofa. "Is there anything else, sir?" He headed for the door.

"I'll be with you in a few minutes," Sakara said, appreciating his subordinate's tact.

"I'll wait in the car, sir." Achibong saluted, then smiled at Eniola. "*Kadi.*"

"Good-bye, lieutenant." Eniola smiled back.

"I'll have to go out. I'm meeting someone in a few minutes." Sakara held her hand in his, and a wave of heat swept him. "You must wait here for me."

"For how long?" she asked.

"I don't know, but I want you to promise me that you'll be here when I get back." He squeezed her hand. "My house is not the best in the world but it's all I've got to offer for now." He laughed.

She laughed and the sound thrilled him. "Boy, she still has the magic touch," he thought. "Slow down, she's got you going." He got on his feet. And she did also, facing him. He put both hands around her waist, and pulled her closer. He landed a kiss on her forehead, then slowly moved down to her lips. He felt her hesitate. He clasped his hands around the back of her neck before kissing her again.

She pulled herself back and looked up at him. "We shouldn't." Her voice was soft and cautious.

Sakara looked into her eyes, wondering about her, wanting her, needing her, remembering how sweet she was the first time so many years ago, regretting passing her on to Akin. "Shameful," he thought, but smiled and said, "Please don't leave."

She shook her head. "You were the first," she said with endearing innocence. "But I belong to someone else now, please understand. I came to speak to you about Ola."

"Really? Don't go, okay? We will talk when I get back. Brigadier Babasa is waiting for me." He tempted her, remembering her astuteness and insightfulness. He knew she would add things up with remarkable accuracy. Despite her concern for Ademola, he suspected she still craved power, and she must know that it was within his grasp. He walked out the door, wondering if she would be there when he returned.

The evening hurried toward sunset, the moisture in the air promising a night of displeasure. Sakara drove through the streets crowded with motorists and pedestrians, most hoping against all hope that they would get home before the curfew enforcers took possession of the night.

"Stop! Who are—ah, so sorry, major!" The armed guard at the entrance to the air force barracks saluted.

Sakara nodded and drove on. Throughout the barracks soldiers and air force recruits manned several checkpoints.

"Stop! Who are—ah, so sorry, major!" Another guard bowed, saluted, and waved Sakara through.

"Without a doubt a senior air force officer is part of the plan." Sakara glanced at Achibong seated next to him.

"Indeed, sir."

"Stop! Wh—"

"It's me, sergeant, open the gate," Sakara snapped. He drove through the barricade and stopped in front of an office building. Ten armored vehicles with mounted machine guns were parked around the building. Sakara stole a glance at the vehicles and noticed that they were manned by junior officers from Special Unit. He recognized one of them as the captain who Dikko had promised would be demoted for insubordination. He smiled and went into the building.

The moment he entered the office leading to the conference room, the smile evaporated. An inferno of abhorrence enveloped him when Balewa said slyly, "Go right in, major."

Sakara hesitated. "Think," he said to himself. "What is this traitor doing here? What kind of game is going on?" He decided to gamble. "Captain, go inside and inform them that I seek permission to bring my assistant with me." He stared at the tip of his nose, glaring at Balewa.

"I don't think that—"

"Now!"

Balewa obeyed. Seconds later, he came out to inform Sakara that he could take Achibong along.

The two marched in side by side, and froze as they saw Babasa seated at the table, a short, squat man with piercing dark brown eyes. The forty-four-year-old Babasa was a street-smart Nupe, a minority tribe whose people were known to be of mixed tribes, part Yoruba and part Hausa. Babasa's self-esteem bordered on narcissism, a characteristic that was both a strength and a weakness: Strength because he was filled with the insatiable desire to look good and be seen as such by those around him; and a weakness because he attracted sycophants who were ready to tell him, with embellishment, what he wanted to hear.

Babasa's dominating figure was flanked by his vassal, Hakabala, an equally shrewd but functionally psychotic man, paranoid to the core. Hakabala's tribal facial marks looked as though a mad shaman had used a blunt dagger to incise his face when he was only a few days old. It was rumored that his soul escaped with the bleeding. Now at forty-six, Hakabala was a mean-tempered, treacherous, and unpredictable man. Sakara remembered what General Akin had told him: "Hakabala is a Berber whose ego and ambition are the size of an elephant. He's a dangerous man. Be careful in your dealings with him."

"Welcome, major. You look fit as usual," Dikko said in Fula. He was seated to the left of Babasa.

"What's this two-faced bastard doing here," Sakara fumed. "How dare he speak to me in the foul language of nomads?" But he flashed a fractured smile.

"Is it true you refused to accept Brigadier Dikko's offer to participate in a plan to overthrow the government?" Hakabala asked in English.

"Be calm, use your brain," Sakara told himself. "This is a trial. Your survival depends on how you handle this. Dikko is an enemy. But on whose side is he?" He turned his gaze to Hakabala. "Yes, sir."

"Do you have the report?" Babasa asked in Yoruba.

With subtlety, Sakara shifted his gaze to Dikko. "I bet no one here knows you speak Yoruba," he wanted to ask, but said, "I do, sir."

"Do you have it—" Dikko started in Fula, then stopped. He looked nervously at Babasa, and continued in English, "Do you have any idea why you are here?"

"Bingo!" Sakara exclaimed to himself. "You just showed your hand. But this is not a game of poker, it's as real as life and death," he fumed. "No, sir," he replied.

"There's a Yoruba proverb, major, as a matter of fact, it's my favorite," Babasa interrupted.

"There are over six thousand Yoruba proverbs, sir, no one knows them all."

Sakara heard superiority and threat in Babasa's voice, who picked up a piece of paper from the table, frowned, looking as though he was having trouble with his thoughts. He looked over his left shoulder, and smiled at Dikko. He turned his attention back to Sakara, and said in a whisper, "A bed wetter does not snub the person who does his laundry. Have you heard that before?"

Sakara swallowed hard. "No, sir. That, like most Yoruba proverbs, is full of riddles." He read between Babasa's words, decoding the message. He smiled.

"You didn't answer the question." Hakabala looked as though he just joined the party.

"My apologies, but which question, sir?" Sakara asked, not wishing to alienate the Berber.

"The report and your recommendation, do you have it?" Hakabala demanded.

"You sand-eating desert Napoleon, Akin was right about you. You are a dangerous lizard," Sakara thought, regaining his concentration. "Yes, I have the report. Shall I hand it over right now?" He gambled, knowing the report had Dikko's head under the cleaver.

"That won't be necessary," Babasa said. "You're responsible for the airport." He leaned over and handed Sakara the piece of paper. "These are the logistics of your operation. Captain Balewa is your second-in-command. The plan activates at 0200 hours. I want everyone to assemble at the location identified in the document I gave you at exactly 0500 hours."

With peripheral vision, Sakara saw the sudden shift in Dikko's countenance. "You're a dead man," he said to himself. He wished that he could have the honor of driving a bayonet through Dikko's heart.

As though Dikko sensed the danger, he asked, "Why don't we go through the logistics again, and as a matter of principle, we should demand that Major Sakara express his intentions openly."

"Never mind that." Hakabala looked as though his patience hovered dangerously at a breaking point with Dikko. "Balewa is your second-in-command, major, make sure there's no problem." He dismissed Sakara and Achibong.

"I'll do my best, sir." Sakara saluted and headed toward the door.

Achibong did likewise.

As the two neared the exit, Babasa coughed. "Major, do you know the remedy for a stomach ache?"

Sakara stopped, suspecting that Babasa was about to pass on a message. "That depends on whose ache, sir."

"Yorubas say that all lizards press their bellies to the ground, but no one knows which one has a stomach ache, have you heard that one before?" Babasa said in English.

"Yes, sir. There are known remedies, sir." Sakara smiled, knowing that he read the instruction accurately.

Balewa met Sakara and Achibong at the door, and the three marched out of the building together.

"Sir, I have the cure for that stomach ache," Achibong said, confirming Sakara's suspicion.

"Do you have a stomach ache, major?" Balewa asked.

"Yes, but Achibong has the remedy, don't you?"

"What is it?" Balewa asked stupidly.

"I'll tell you when we get to the airport, captain," Achibong said contemptuously.

"Captain, you drive." Sakara handed his keys to Balewa. "Lieutenant, ride with Captain Jaja in the armored vehicle and head straight to the south entrance of the international airport. Secure the area and post your men at these designated posts." He took the paper Babasa gave him out of his chest pocket, unfolded it and spread it out for Achibong to read.

"May I see that?" Balewa asked.

"Not right at this moment." Sakara folded the paper, put it back in his pocket and said as though it was a second thought, "Since Captain Balewa is my second-in-command, the two of us should not ride in the same vehicle. You and Lieutenant Achibong must go together in the armored vehicle. Jaja will ride with me."

Balewa gave back the keys and marched away.

"He should be the first casualty, lieutenant. Don't let him out of your sight, or allow him to get within whispering distance of anyone. He's inclined to pass on vital information to the other side. Terminate him as soon as you get to the airport. Good luck!"

⤳

At precisely two hours past midnight, the first shot rang out, heralding another page in the never-ending history of the country, a history replete with false promises by yet another self-ordained do-gooder in olive-colored uniform. A single bullet lodged between the astounded eyes of the first victim. Achibong booted Balewa's body out of the armored vehicle and drove off to join others who had already commenced massacring military officers deemed hostile to their cause. The sound of gunfire shattered the night, forewarning the citizens that a pogrom was in the making.

As soon as dawn shanghaied the night, the news of the *coup* reached every corner of the globe, forcing the rest of humanity to shake their collective heads at the mindlessness of a people who have condemned themselves to hell on earth.

Achibong joined Sakara at the roadblock in front of the local airport. The whole area had been sealed off. Sakara got into the armored vehicle and the two headed toward Lagos. Achibong turned into Obalende Road and continued past the cemetery. The streets were littered with bodies: over a hundred people sprawled on the ground. The air was filled with gunsmoke. Several soldiers crouched behind military jeeps, combat-ready. Achibong slowed down as they approached Dodon Barracks. The walls of nearby buildings were poked with bullet holes, and more lifeless bodies had been piled on top of each other along the sidewalks.

At the gate, Sakara told Achibong to stop as three soldiers in combat uniform leveled their gun barrels at the vehicle. Sakara identified himself, and the three soldiers snapped military salutes. He exchanged a few words with the shortest of the three, whose three stars emblazoned on his shoulder identified him as a captain.

"You can go in, sir." The captain opened the gate and Achibong drove in, straight to the steps of the main building. Two soldiers standing by the door snapped to attention. Sakara's nod to the soldier to his right was coldly polite. The soldier was equally glacial.

The two marched into the official residence of the military head of state. The walls were splattered with blood and flesh. Halfway into the main reception area, a woman sprawled dead on the couch, her cold eyes staring into nothingness. Parts of the left side of her head were gone, exposing bloody brain matter. Sakara recognized her as the wife of General Bukha. A few yards away Sakara's lips rounded into a whistle when he saw the bullet-riddled bodies of Dikko and Idi Amo on the floor. Containing the dread that overcame him as they approached the door at the end of the reception area, he stepped aside as Achibong knocked and stood at attention.

The door swung open and a giant of a man, also a captain, appeared and saluted. "Welcome, Major Sakara. The rest of the members of the junta are all here." He stepped aside to let Sakara in. Achibong followed. Both men approached the round mahogany table in the middle of the room and saluted. Hakabala nodded to a chair next to an air force officer, Air Commodore Maxwell Gideon, a tall, gaunt man in his late forties. Sakara sat down and looked behind him. He nodded to Achibong who took backward steps to the wall and sat next to a junior naval officer, whose boss, Commodore Andrew Spiff, the oldest man in the room, sat at the round table next to another army officer, Colonel Christian Emeruwa.

The atmosphere in the room was tense, the air thick. Abruptly the doors flung open and Babasa marched in, surrounded by twenty mean-looking, combat-ready soldiers whose eyes shone with near-supernatural brilliance. The fiercest looking of the pack charged forward, and with the gruffest voice announced:

"I present Major General Raheem Babasa, head of the Provisional Ruling Council (PRC). Mr. PRESIDENT!"

Everyone in the room jumped off their seats, stood at attention and meted out the stiffest military salute to the new strongman of Africa.

~

12

ARINOTA

September, 1985:

Ademola's mother wiped tears off her face. "You're pregnant?" She squinted as though blinded by a sun blast.

Eniola nodded twice.

The older woman pressed the palm of her hand against her knuckles and cracked them. "Allah does His work in miraculous ways," she said, her voice barely audible. "This has been the only news I've heard since I last saw my son." She began to sob. "Are you sure?" She met Eniola's stare.

As though afraid someone was listening, Eniola whispered, "I double-checked before coming here to share the news with you, mama—" She hesitated as she sensed a stirring at the door, and clasped a hand over her mouth when the stirring turned into footsteps. "Who is out there, listening?" she thought. But before she could answer her own question, Ademola's father was already three steps into the room. His face looked leaner from sleeplessness. His eyes lacked their usual fire.

"Sit down, please," his wife said with a broken voice.

The old man did not move. He did not speak.

Eniola became consumed by the sense of intrusion that

216

had invaded their lives, casting its hex on all three. She got on her knees in quiet supplication, but her prayer was cut short by the old man's gentle voice, "An elder does not sit idly and allow a child's head to lie crooked. My son's pain is my pain. And so is yours. What secrets have you whispered into the ear of my wife?"

Eniola bowed her head. "I'm pregnant with Ola's child." Then she looked up and her heart skipped a beat as she glimpsed the pain in his eyes.

"Is it true?" he muttered under his breath, looking as though he knew with the certainty of a diviner that Eniola was telling the truth, but that he also knew that she was not beyond intrigue. "Tell me what happened."

Eniola looked in the direction of the older woman. She took a deep breath and told the story:

Three nights before Tunde's birthday party she had visited Ademola. The two had eaten the supper she prepared and since it was already late in the evening, Ademola asked her to spend the night. Before going to bed he gave her an engagement ring, promising to tell his parents the news on the day of his brother's birthday celebration. Her happiness was beyond description. So was his. She spent the night with him in the same room. She woke up the next morning happy but fearful of his feelings about her not being a virgin. He assured her that he felt the same as before. And that made her even happier.

"How did you meet my son?" His eyes bored into hers.

"I—I met him through his friend, Ayo Crowder."

"So you knew Ayo before Ola?" he asked.

"Yes, sir. Crowder had asked me if I knew any young lady from a respectable family from Abeokuta that was ready to settle down. I knew such a person and I told him so. He asked me to introduce her to Ola. All four of us met at Crowder's house and as things turned out, Ola insisted on talking to me more than to my friend. Later, he told

Crowder and me that he liked me more than my friend. I liked him too, but it was not the right thing to do, and I said so. Crowder asked me not to reject his friend's offer on account of his having known me first—please, believe me, Crowder and I never did anything together. Our friendship was very new."

"I see," was all the old man said.

She told them about the document, how she had gone into hiding as Ademola had wished. Without hesitation, she told them about her meeting with Akin and what he had suggested.

"You know Segun Sakara too?" he asked suddenly.

"Yes, I met him a long time ago while I was a student at Ibadan." She became uncomfortable when Ademola's mother sighed. Eniola felt a snap as though a bond was beginning to break. Something screamed from deep inside her, warning her to be more discreet; but she couldn't hold anything back. She told them she had been forced by a military police officer to give the document to Sakara. She told them that she had visited Sakara later, hoping that he could help Ademola, but Sakara had left the house before she could ask him for help. She told them how uncomfortable she felt staying at his house, and how she had left and had not gone back to see him. She told them how she discovered that she was pregnant.

"And you're sure the baby belongs to my son?"

"Yes, without a doubt, sir."

"How can—"

"Please, Baba Ola, this is a matter only a woman knows best," his wife appealed gently.

Eniola told them how she had become restless during the last two days worrying about Ademola's whereabouts. She was unable to sleep having exhausted all her resources in the futile attempt to find out what had happened to him. Ademola seemed to have disappeared for good. She dreaded the possibility of his being dead, killed by the soldiers that took him and Crowder away from the hospital.

Ademola's mother covered her face and began to sob again, and then went to her prayer mat in the corner of the room, knelt in supplication and began to pray.

"This is not a matter for one God. We must ask all the gods to come to our aid." Ademola's father got on his feet. "There are things that need to be done." He left the room.

⌇

Ademola's father tread the moist forest ground, his chanting throaty as he approached his destination.

> The dog stays in the household of its master
>> But does it know his intentions? No!
> The sheep does not know the intentions
>> Of the man who feeds it.
>>> I myself follow Sango,
>>>> Though I do not know his intentions.
> It is not easy to live in Sango's company.
>> Rain beats the Egungun mask,
>>> Because he cannot find shelter.
>>>> The masker cries: "Help me,
>>>>> Dead people in Heaven! Help me!"
> But the rain cannot beat Sango.
>> They say fire kills water.
>>> Sango rides fire like a horse.
>>>> Lightning, with what kind of cloth
>>>>> Do you cover your body?
> With the cloth of death.
>> Sango is the death that drips—
>>> Like indigo dye dripping from a cloth.

As he chanted, he glimpsed the past, and felt the present

219

invading the future. He opened the door to his soul so that his spirit could touch the face of sadness and anguish that resided there, and his essence witnessed the loss of young lives. He felt the helplessness in the land where law and order had gone on vacation, leaving the people in the hands of the polytheistic curfew-makers who have tasted blood, and thirst for more. "The warthogs, having taken over our stream, have muddied it. Fear is the weapon of tyrants. I am not afraid to fight the purveyors of carnage. I will protect what is mine!"

As he walked through the forest covering the distance between Arinota and Abeokuta, he felt as though the ago-nized voices of his ancestors had deafened him as they spoke in unison. He became blinded by the spirit of the jungle. But slowly, as he neared his destination, he felt his hearing return, and he saw through the fog that enveloped the boul-der at the end of the plateau, a steep rise where the town of Abeokuta joined the sky.

It was before dawn when he stopped in front of the three-legged *akee* tree, each leg the size of an *iroko* tree. All three merged into a stem that reached forever into the sky, forming an entrance into the most sacred cave in the Yoruba cosmos. Gloom engulfed him. The wind was quiet. His heart burst open and a profusion of colors invaded his soul:

Silence that spoke in colorful tonality.
　　Coral red the color of a newborn baby,
　　　　Inflicting the hearts of mothers with felicity.
Indigo blue the heart of a young lady,
　　　　Saddened by the silence she loves for eternity.
　　　　Brown mud walls of a hut with roof so thatchy,
Pervious to the invasion of the rain so noisy.
　　African black kite blinded by a fire so smoky,
　　　　The roaring yellow flame burnt it mercilessly.

The sound of silence was deafening yet cleansing, enabling him to enter the cave, announcing the presence of the one whose aid he needed the most. The silence grew louder in his soul as the butterflies in his stomach began to fly helter-skelter.

At once, a human voice tapped him on the shoulder, old but steady: "Welcome, my son. The gods have spoken, and their words will fill many hearts with sadness."

"But which words are meant for Ola?" Ademola's father asked, chest pounding.

"Silence, my son. Come closer and feed my blindness with your presence," the voice said.

"But I can't see you, my venerable master."

"Come forward, but be careful not to step on the bowls of fetish all around," the voice said in old Yoruba.

Ademola's father groped in the dark toward the voice, touching and feeling the rough surface of the cave with his palms. "How is my son?" he cried out.

"Which son do you speak of?" the voice asked.

"Ola, of course!" He stopped as his palm touched something that felt different. He pulled on a sharp piece of rock. It gave and became a narrow opening. He stuck his head into the hole. He pried more stones off the wall, enlarging the opening enough to crawl through. "Where am I?" His voice echoed in the new chamber. He waited a few seconds to adjust his senses to the new environment, both darker and bigger than the cave entrance. "Where—"

"Where only the chosen few dare to enter. But is it true that your backside has better sense than your head?" the voice chastised.

"What, my master?"

"It closes its doors after discharging waste matters, does it not?"

He turned and quickly replaced the rocks without argument. Stench of old palm oil, stale palm wine, rotten meat, and decaying vegetation hung in the air.

"The *atupa* is a few feet to your left. It has a box of matches sitting next to it," the voice said.

Ademola's father lit the lamp. He jumped and his jaw dropped when he beheld the figure of his master. The master diviner barely weighed more than the wooden *Ifa* divination tray which lay beside him on the raffia mat. But his skin was firm and healthy. He sniffed the air like a famished dog in search of a hidden morsel of meat. And since there was no wind in the cave, the master's nose seemed to work harder. He was as blind as a bat at high noon. His dead eyes looked like the ripe fruits of the *akee* tree, coppery-yellow with dark rings.

Ademola's father trembled as he stared at his master, who sucked in the air through his clenched gums. He'd been toothless for as long as Ademola's father had known him.

"Ola is not *your* son." The master diviner's dead eyes glared at his acolyte.

"W—wh—what do you mean?"

"Ola is an *Abiku* sent here for a purpose. He's the child of the world—a world which had been turned upside down. His job is to try to put it right again. He should not be constrained by your claim of exclusive ownership of him. He needs more to survive than you. Does that mean you shouldn't do your fatherly job? Of course not, he's alone but there are others who have also been assigned to assist him to navigate the treacherous path he treads."

"But where is he?"

"He is where he should be."

"Where?"

"You ask the question a woman would ask, my son. Are you not a diviner? Have I failed in my job? Didn't I teach you to think like the gods?"

"My venerable master, with all due respect to you and the gods, I think as a father, unlike you or the gods. My heart aches and so does that of Ola's mother."

"What is that supposed to mean?"

"I do not wish to sit idly by without knowing my son's whereabouts."

"Did I ask you to do that?"

"No, but he had accidentally stumbled upon—"

"There are no accidents in this life. Everything happens for a purpose. Do you think Ola is your son by accident? Did I not say that you have a job to perform?"

"Yes, my master."

"One does not pry the palm kernel from the nut by tender means. Ola needs all the help he can get. His enemies are strong and powerful and they are getting more powerful and dangerous by the day. The first thing you need to do is to make sure no one in your family discusses his problem with anyone. Secondly, as soon as you get home, offer sacrifice to appease the gods. You know what to offer. And finally, be patient until he can come home, provided he survives. It is going to be a long while before Ola acquires enough strength to face his enemies, and even then only the gods know who the winner will be."

13

LAGOS

September, 1985:

From behind the corner window of the reception room leading to Babasa's office, Sakara watched with uneasiness the soldiers on duty on the grounds of Dodan Barracks. He spotted one who looked out of place. He was white and in charge. "How can this be allowed here?" he fumed, but shelved the problem for later scrutiny. The walls in the room had been repaired and painted in a soothing earth tone. Handsome pieces of furniture replaced the ostentatious ones that adorned the place during the regime of Bukha. Since the *coup*, Sakara had been named Acting Director of DMI. Every morning at 1000 hours he met with Babasa to discuss and analyze the various proposals put forward by members of the Provisional Ruling Council (PRC). Babasa's first order of business upon assumption of office was to promulgate a decree honoring himself with the title of Mr. President and Minister of Defence. Until today, he had not met with the irascible Inspector General of Police. And so when Sakara found out that Babasa was to meet with the police chief at 0900 hours, he knew the time had come for the final showdown.

Sakara had recommended that the I.G., one of a few

department heads from the previous regime to survive the first round of purge, be retired immediately. Babasa had listened but had yet to act. "No doubt, the axe is about to fall," Sakara thought, and turned around. Then he saw the three plainclothes detectives from the C.I.D. seated on a sofa like patients in a dental clinic. They looked nervous. "What are they doing here?" he asked himself, studying their faces for future identification.

"His Excellency will see you now, major," Babasa's *aide-de-camp*-turned-administrative-assistant announced.

Sakara marched into the president's office, snapped a sharp salute, and waited. He noted that he was called in ten minutes before the scheduled appointment. The fifty-six-year-old I.G. was on his feet beside Babasa, who sat behind a mahogany desk. The room was dimly lit, and the wall-to-wall bookshelves were stacked with military, law, constitution, history, and psychology books. "This is a different era in the history of the nation," he thought. "The country finally has a thinking president."

"Have a seat, major," Babasa said circumspectly.

Sakara did, facing the president. He turned his gaze ever so slightly from Babasa and before he got to the police chief his jaw went rigid. Standing between the ends of the bookshelves was a man, a white man, whose dark clothes blended with the bookshelves. But for his face, it would have been impossible to know that he was there. "He's one of the C.I.A. agents on loan to Babasa," Sakara remembered reading in the memo Achibong had passed on to him.

Babasa's commanding voice snapped his attention away from the walls. "Major Sakara, the I.G. has brought certain allegations about your conduct to my attention."

Sakara's eyes instinctively focused on the tip of his nose, glaring at the marks on the police chief's face. "I hope the I.G. will share the same information with me." He flashed a smile laced with abhorrence.

"With pleasure," the police chief said ebulliently, rounding the desk to stand with arms akimbo between Sakara and Babasa. The vulgarity of his countenance further infuriated Sakara, who remained poised in his seat. "If this hyena is allowed to stay in office longer than the setting of the sun, I will kill him," he promised himself.

"Isn't it true that you commandeered a plane, forced the pilot at gunpoint to take you and your assistant, or more appropriately, your lover, to Yola?"

"I—I am at—"

"Stop stuttering! Did you not?" The police chief's face expressed feigned repugnance.

Sakara turned to look at Babasa. "Do I have your permission to respond, sir?"

Babasa leaned forward in his chair, scratched his temple, and shook his head. "Is there anything else, I.G.?"

"Yes, Your Excellency, the major is not only a known homosexual, he's also a drug addict. There's enough evidence in this file to prove my point."

Sakara's inner grenade detonated but he managed to smile. "With all due respect, in our business, you and I screw a lot of people, and for the most part, they are almost always males. I therefore suggest to you that you and I are homosexuals both."

Babasa smiled with his eyes. The police chief laughed with hysteria. Sakara remained chagrined.

"Are you mad?" The I.G.'s face contorted with rage.

Babasa said, "That'll be enough, Major Sakara." He jabbed his index finger in the air like a pistol aimed at the Inspector General. "I want your resignation on my desk in thirty minutes. Get out of here!"

The police chief looked like he was hit on the chest with a sledgehammer. He recovered quickly, mortified. "How dare you think you can get rid of me like that? You will pay for this!" He glared at Sakara before storming out.

"He's all yours, *colonel*, congratulations."

Sakara's heart missed twice but he said nothing. Holding his breath, he thought, "Is this a slip or have I just been given a double promotion?" For a split second he had thought his career in the army was at an end. "What does one make of this?" he thought. He had expected to be compensated for participating in the *coup*, but getting promoted from major to colonel, skipping the lieutenant colonel rank, was more than he had expected. He sighed.

"Congratulations are in order, Colonel Sakara." Babasa broke into his thoughts. Waving his finger in the air, he said, "In the matter of the I.G., I want you to take care of that old fart personally. Come on, let's sit on the settee, it's more comfortable. I need your advice on some important issues."

Sakara jumped to his feet, flashed another salute, a shade sharper than the previous one, then marched to the sofa. He waited until Babasa was seated before he joined him, leaving a respectful three-foot space between them. "Thank you, sir. I pledge my loyalty to you once again."

"And I pledge mine to Nigeria. But the business of governing this country is a rather nasty one, major—excuse me, colonel," Babasa said with his easy charm. "A new title is always difficult to get used to."

Sakara watched his new commander-in-chief, and decided that there was something congenial about him. The man seemed honest and genuine.

"I like the thoroughness of your report and analysis. It's shameful that our intelligence was allowed to get so appallingly loose and inefficient. But let me ask you this, who in your opinion is this government's worst enemy?"

"Journalists, sir," Sakara replied at once.

"Now I know why I like you, Segun." Babasa smiled and patted Sakara on the shoulder. "They are at the top of my list too. Whoever said that great minds think alike was right, isn't that correct?"

"Yes, sir."

Babasa's smile widened. "Perception is reality. I want every citizen in this nation to believe that we at the top are the servants of the people, not the other way around. To do this, we must not only tell them what we are doing, we must be perceived as honest. And the bridge to that goal is the media." Babasa paused. There was eloquence in the silence, which was louder than his words.

"I agree with you, sir." Sakara decided to test Babasa. "I believe that the first thing the government needs to do is to establish the necessary trust—mutual trust between us and the media, sir."

Babasa nodded yes. "And how do we achieve that?"

"In my opinion, the draconian, vindictive, and restrictive Decree Four of the last regime, the law against the practice of journalism, should be abolished, sir."

"Perfect. I will publicly make the announcement today. Excellent! Contact all the top media executives in the country and tell them that henceforth they must feel free to come to you for anything they want. The public believes them more than they believe the government. That must change. I'm sure you know how suspicious and arrogant some of our journalists are, so you must be careful how you approach them. I am confident of your ability."

"Giving back to the journalists what was rightfully theirs in the first place cannot be seen as compromise," Sakara told himself, responding to a warning bell that went off in his head. "Caution, Babasa is smooth without a doubt, and dangerous as Akin had warned. Abolishing Decree Four is cosmetic at best," he realized, and decided to test Babasa with something more concrete. "Sir, the public will believe what the journalists tell them only for a short while. Soon there will be clamoring for something more substantial—"

"Like what?"

"Many things come to mind, sir."

"Give me three examples." Babasa looked stern.

"How about telling them how long this regime plans to stay in power? Be specific as to when you will hand over the government to a duly elected civilian regime."

"Go on." Babasa's lips thinned, and his countenance became guarded.

"Release all political prisoners, at least those that we know can get the government the loudest applause."

"Compile a list and have it on my desk before the end of the day. One more, I said three, didn't I?"

"You did, sir. Conduct a national census, a real, honest-to-goodness census."

"You think the people of the north are ready for that?"

"It's not for them to be ready, sir, it's for you, the most powerful leader in black Africa, to show them how and where to march." Sakara was surprised at how calm he was.

"Are these all your ideas, colonel?"

"No, sir. All three belonged to Lade Ogawa, the journalist that died in the bomb blast three weeks ago."

Taking charge when expediency required it summed up Babasa. He patted Sakara on the shoulder again before getting on his feet. "You and I are going to get along real fine. We have much work to do. Segun, let me share one of my personal aspirations with you."

Babasa's tone of voice made Sakara become alert once again. "I feel privileged, sir."

"I want to make a difference. When I leave office, I want to be remembered for having done something significant for the nation. All the three suggestions you made are easy to implement. I want big ideas. Think about it."

"There are a lot of wonderful ideas out there, sir."

"I only need a couple. Find me one, colonel. Remember what I said about perception being reality?"

Sakara nodded yes.

"Rumors and innuendoes are the enemies of such realities. Take that stupid statement about you being a homosex-ual as an example. It's nasty, don't you agree?"

"But it's not true, sir."

"I know it's not, colonel, and that's my point. We can't allow that sort of nonsense to distract us from our job. I want every member of the PRC to project a wholesome image—a family image, that is."

"I understand, sir."

"Do you? I'm glad to hear that. I like you. As a matter of fact I feel like a big brother to you. Find yourself a good woman to marry. Good day!"

Sakara saluted his boss and marched to the door. And just before he exited, Babasa said, "You should be the first to inform your assistant, *Major* Achibong, on his promotion."

"Will do, sir!"

It was past noon when Sakara marched into the reception area to his office. "Ask Achibong to come here right away," he told his secretary.

She said to Sakara, who was about to disappear into his office, "A man has been waiting to see you since nine."

"Give him an appointment for next week." He slammed the door shut and went straight to the filing cabinet con-taining his most confidential files, extracted two, and was about to sit down at his desk when Achibong barreled in. "Have a seat."

Achibong saluted and remained standing.

"I said have a seat." Sakara looked up.

"I thought you might want to see the man outside."

"I already asked Iyabo to give him an appointment."

"It's Eniola's brother, sir. He was here last week."

"Do you know what he wants?"

"He said he has a letter from Dr. Ademola for you."

Sakara picked up the receiver. "Iyabo, ask the young man to wait." He turned to Achibong. "Sit down, *major.*"

"Ye—sir?" Achibong did a double-take.

"There are four pieces of news; two good, and two bad. Which do you want to hear first?"

"How about the bad ones first, sir?" He sat down.

"Did you sweep the office for bugs today?"

"The very first thing, sir."

"Good," Sakara said, but thought, "Why should I trust you when I always told Dikko the very same thing, knowing fully well that his office had been bugged." He sighed. "President Babasa will make the announcement about our promotions shortly. You have been promoted to the rank of major. Congratulations."

"Thank you very much, sir." Achibong jumped to his feet and flashed a salute. "I appreciate your recommending me for the promotion."

"I didn't, major. That's one of the bad news. Your promotion is compliments of President Babasa. The other one is that you and I have to find some young ladies to marry. And that's not a suggestion or request, it's an order."

"How can there be any good news after that one, sir?"

"The Inspector General of Police is ours to feed to the sharks. That's also an order, major."

"Wonderful! I'd love to take care of that personally."

"He's all yours," Sakara said with a chuckle. "And lastly, Babasa has agreed to conduct a national census."

Achibong looked astonished. "Do you—I mean, are you sure about that, sir?"

Sakara nodded twice.

"Oh boy," was all Achibong managed to say.

"There's an old Yoruba proverb, major, and I'm not particularly crazy about proverbs. Their mixed messages have a way of confusing the issue. But think about this one: One whose head is used to crack a coconut is most unlikely to eat the nut. What's your reading of that one?"

Achibong's Adam's apple bobbed up and down. He looked as though a shiver went through him. "You have my absolute loyalty, and I hope I don't need to prove that anymore."

"That's what I believe, major," Sakara said, but thought, "If you ever allow Babasa to use you to get to me, you'll be in pain as the head that is used to crack the coconut." He smiled.

"I mean that, sir," Achibong said with emphasis.

"I believe you, major. Now let me tell you something else that Babasa wants from *us*. He wants to make a difference during his term in office. And to achieve this, he needs—he wants me to come up with one or two big ideas. What do you make of that?"

Achibong's cheeks expanded like a pair of balloons. "If he *really* means that, sir, he should be speaking to the intellectuals at the various think tanks in the country, not us. Unless he wishes to use that as a criterion for membership into the PRC, sir."

"My thought exactly," Sakara said, liking Achibong's responses. "In what area do you suppose he wishes to pursue this seemingly inordinate ambition? Politics, social issues, economics, or foreign relations?"

"It depends on who the primary beneficiary is, Babasa or the masses?"

"What if it's for the people?"

"Then without a doubt it should be economics, sir."

Sakara smiled. "And?"

"There's an idea waiting to be plucked from the mind of a brilliant Nigerian. Can I send out the word, sir?"

"Yes, major, do that. But remember, time is of the essence." He looked at his watch and smiled. "Tell Iyabo to send the young man in."

Achibong saluted his boss again before barrelling out.

The secretary held the door open for Femi to enter the office. She coughed softly to announce the presence of the visitor and immediately shut the door.

"Good afternoon, Major Sakara," Femi said.

Sakara waved him to the chair vacated by Achibong.

"I almost believed that it would have been much easier to see God than to see you, sir," Femi said, not smiling.

"I'm busy, young man," Sakara said, not liking Femi's impertinence. "You arrogant brat, with your Oxford education that means absolutely nothing in this country," he thought. "You should be lucky you get to come into my office without your sister." Then he looked up and was immediately astounded by the similarity between Femi and Eniola: the almond-shaped eyes, perfect oval face and the skin's velvety black hue of midnight softness. "I understand you have a letter from Dr. Ademola for me."

"That's correct, sir." Femi handed him the note.

Sakara took his time to read the note. When he finished, he leaned back in his chair, eyes trained at the tip of his nose, and studied the young man seated in front of him. "What the hell is Agric/Econometrics?"

"It's the application of mathematical and statistical techniques to economics in the study of agricultural paradigms, problems, and theories. Simply said, sir, it is the new trend in the use of modern technology to maximize agricultural yield and utilization," Femi said dazzlingly.

"I see," Sakara said, but thought, "I don't have time to waste with this pompous brat! "Why didn't you apply for employment at the ministry of agriculture?" His tone was condescending.

Femi's left eyebrow soared. "My sister told me you're the perfect person to talk to about my idea first."

"What idea?"

"It's rather revolutionary—"

"Give me the abstract. I've got very little time to spare."

Sakara contained his impatience momentarily.

"What if Nigeria embarks on an agricultural project that in a matter of ten years, makes us not only capable of feeding the whole continent of Africa, but also capable of creating millions of industrial jobs?" He paused. "There are nineteen states in the country, right?" He did not wait for an answer. "Suppose a specific agricultural commodity is found to be indigenous to a state. Take the coconut tree in Lagos, or cassava in Oyo, or cattle from Sokoto."

"We don't have to imagine anything, young man, those are well known facts already." Sakara felt his impatience turning into anger.

"What you don't know is how revolutionary my idea is. Imagine that a multipurpose machine is created, a machine that when the coconut tree, and I mean the whole tree, is fed into it, nothing will come out on the other end as waste. In other words, every part of the tree is turned into a consumable commodity. Bear in mind that each part of the tree represents an industry." Femi smiled.

Sakara had become attentive. "What would have been a waste product from one plant in say, Imo state, could now be a raw material for an industrial plant in Plateau, right?" Sakara asked, liking the idea.

"There's a catch, though."

"Like what?"

"Government's involvement has to be at the minimum."

"If I understand you correctly, Femi, this idea is a very costly one. There's not enough money in the private sector to implement it."

"Of course not. However, that does not mean the government has to foot the bill. The Federal government's involvement will be to create the infrastructure at the onset, set the guidelines and let the state governments and the private sector go at it. Inevitably the true spirit of entrepreneurship will be unleashed."

"What kind of budget are you talking about?" Sakara smiled at Femi, liking him, thankful for the idea. He believed this was something he could take to Babasa.

"Over a ten-year period, the first phase would cost twenty billion dollars."

"Whew! How do you figure that?"

"One billion dollars would be needed for each state. That includes the cost of land acquisition, seeding, planting, fertilizer, industrial machinery, etc."

Sakara sighed. "Do you have all this in writing?"

"Of course, it is the proposal for my doctoral dissertation," Femi said with pride.

"The figures don't add up. You said twenty billion. But you've spent nineteen."

"Oh, that. The one billion is for research and development, project coordination, management, administrative, etc. Don't worry, sir, every penny is accounted for. And there are checks and balances—accountability. At the end of the day, the margin of error, and if you will, the chances for corruption, would be almost nonexistent."

"Good. Bring me the write-up, shall we say, tomorrow morning?" Sakara was having a hard time containing his excitement. "How about nine o'clock, here? And ask Eniola to come with you."

꯭

14

The corrugated iron sheets roofing an old building rattled as the rain started. The wind pounded the window, threatening to yank it off the hinges. A man's hand reached out and rescued the window from the gust, shut and latched it. Inside, a soldier stood beside the door, facing an officer who sat behind a wooden table on which were a wire clothes hanger, a jagged knife and a white towel. A hurricane lantern burned below the window-sill, its lazy light casting shadows on the walls like the paintings of cave dwellers. The door opened and two soldiers in mufti dragged Eniola inside. She looked dishevelled as she fought to free herself. She was blindfolded. They shoved her forward. Unable to break the fall with her cuffed hands, she crashed to her knees on the concrete floor. "What do you want from me?" Her voice cracked from exhaustion and fear.

One of the soldiers nodded to the officer before stepping back to flash a salute.

The leader waved the late-comers away. He stood up, walked in a leisurely way toward Eniola, and pulled her by the elbow to her feet, rearranging the shadows on the walls. "Congratulations on your pregnancy," the officer sneered.

Eniola spun around. "Who are you?"

"I asked my boys to bring you here in order to pass on a

very important message to you," the officer whispered.

"What message?" Eniola's chest began to heave.

"You must do everything possible to endear yourself to your old friend."

"What are you talking about?"

"You must become Major Sakara's wife!"

"You are mad!"

The officer walked away. He stopped beside the table, picked up the hanger, rearranged its shape before walking back to her. "Do you know what this is?" He placed the hanger in her cuffed hands.

She began to shake her head, then recoiled.

"I'm impressed," the officer smirked. "It's true that you are smart. Thousands of women have died or became mutilated after using the hanger to rid themselves of unwanted pregnancies. I am sure you don't want the same to happen to you. And it won't if you do what I command. Sit down!" He grabbed the chair and set it next to her.

Eniola remained on her feet.

"You are not in any position to refuse—"

"Help!" Eniola dashed toward the door, bumping into the soldier who grabbed and dragged her to the chair.

"You've wasted enough of my time!" The officer gripped her left shoulder. "Here's your order: At the appropriate time, you must pay Major Sakara a visit at his house to congratulate him on his recent promotion. Be nice—be very sweet to him. Get him to want you enough to want to marry you. And married you will be to him."

"I will die before I do any such thing," Eniola flared.

"No, you won't. But your brother and mother will, I assure you. This is not a game, young lady. This is a direct order from the top—presidential, if you will."

"I can't." She began to cry. "I will tell him—"

"You're not as smart as I was led to believe, are you?" There was a renewed threat in the officer's voice, more ominous. "If you ever breathe a word of this to him, you will personally witness the slow death of your family, especially that cute brother of yours."

Eniola covered her face with her cuffed palms. Her body went into a spasm which lasted for a good minute. The voice of the officer was a shade louder than her sobs as he gave the details of his instruction. "Do you understand?" he asked finally.

Eniola nodded several times.

He turned around and was at the door when Eniola managed to pull down the blindfold. Her eyes rounded upon seeing the unmistakable back of General Hakabala's head.

Sakara should have been happy as he paced up and down the parlor. But he was gloomy and troubled, looking without perceiving the opulence that surrounded him. He saw the image of the fabled king who sat on his throne under the sword hanging from a thin thread. He shivered at the realization that the power he craved would boomerang on him someday. Hastily, his mind raced elsewhere to recapture the event that led to where he now stood.

Babasa had received the file, read the proposal, and exclaimed with exuberance, "Full marks, Segun. This is the best idea yet." He'd closed the file and placed it on his desk. "I want you to present it to the members of the PRC today. I will approve it, and you can get started. Excellent! Move your belongings to your new residence. You have been assigned the house on Luggard Avenue in Ikoyi."

"Which house, sir?"

"The one General Idi Amo lived in before the *coup*."

"Isn't that the official residence of the second-in-command? General Hakabala—"

"He chose another house. Yours is bigger and more comfortable, enjoy it. It'll be big enough for you and your family. You're working on that, I presume?" Babasa smiled.

"Yes, sir." Sakara began to feel uncomfortable.

"Excellent, colonel."

Sakara flashed a salute and was about to turn around when Babasa said, "You took care of the I.G. personally, didn't you?"

A shiver coursed through him. "Yes, sir," he lied. Babasa smiled but the coldness in his eyes sent butterfly wings flapping in Sakara's stomach.

"Excellent. By the way, tell Major Achibong to move into the vacant house on Victoria Island immediately."

"Will do, sir." Sakara was instantly on guard.

"Congratulations again. This is brilliant." Babasa turned affable, the smile returning to his eyes. He waved Sakara away.

That was yesterday. He blinked himself back to the present and went to the French windows, parted the blinds, and looked out. The manicured yard was the size of three basketball courts, and the Olympic-size swimming pool reflected the rays of the setting sun. He took a deep breath, filling his lungs with the smell of new furniture; two large sky-blue velvet-covered sofas arranged in an L-shape which looked even more beautiful on the blue-grey wall-to-wall carpet. A black leather recliner sat next to the music console. The walls were filled with paintings of villages, markets, and traditional Yoruba themes, all by young Nigerian artists. Sakara turned to stare at the *faux* mantlepiece which looked ridiculous in a mansion in the middle of the hottest part of the tropics. He laughed at the similarity between the adornment and his presence in the house. "I can't grant myself the luxury of depression," he said to the empty house, before dashing upstairs to the master bedroom, which was as big as his old house. He picked up a box of cigarettes from the king-size bed and took out a joint. He went back downstairs, sat on the recliner and lit it. Halfway through the joint, the bell chimed. He went to the door with the cigarette held between his fingers and eased it open.

᠎᠆

Eniola smiled and entered the house. "Do you still smoke that thing?" She sniffed the air.

"Yep, my only vice." Sakara shut the door.

"Congratulations!" Her hand swept the air. "This is huge, Segun. I'm happy for you. Here." She handed him a bottle of Dom Perignon. "For your promotion."

"Thanks, but you know I don't drink." He put the joint in his mouth and inhaled. "This is much better, and cheaper than that French water." He laughed.

She sat on the sofa, feeling its softness with the palm of her hand. "I really like this place. Oh my, you even have a fake fireplace. I love fireplaces even if they are just for show. This is beautiful." She got off the sofa. "Why don't you show me the rest of the house?" He held her hand and squeezed. She squeezed back.

"That's the formal dining room. But let me show you the kitchen first."

Her brow creased. "Why, does that mean the first place a woman should see is the kitchen?" she said playfully.

"That's right," he said, but the seriousness in his eyes was softened by his smile.

She followed him into the kitchen. "This is bigger than the parlor of my house."

"Wait until you see the five bedrooms." He took the bottle from her. He opened a cabinet door and took out a funnel-shaped champagne glass.

"Just one glass?" She sounded pained.

"I don't drink alcohol at all. I tell you what." He took

out another glass. "There's a case of Seven Up in the refrigerator, get me a bottle."

She did. He popped the champagne bottle clumsily, poured her a glass, and then filled his glass with the effervescent soda. "Cheers!" He smiled and his crossed eyes looked like the eyes of a black mamba ready to strike. But Eniola did not cringe like most people. She laughed with both her mouth and her eyes. She wanted to be happy for him. She saw the melancholy in his eyes.

"How sad," she thought, "The talk in town is that he's third in command in the country. So why the gloom?" Then she remembered, "Major Sakara needs to get married, have a family, that's what he needs now," Hakabala had said.

"But I know just the perfect lady that would make him happy," she had said.

"Nobody else but you will do," Hakabala had snapped.

"I can't take a chance telling him that I'm pregnant with Ademola's baby," she concluded her thoughts with a forced smile.

"What's that all about?" Sakara asked.

"What's what about?" She looked at him.

"The smile, you look like you're up to something devilish, and if I remember you correctly, you probably are." He opened the door to the master bedroom.

Eniola gulped down the rest of the champagne and placed the glass on the nightstand. She embraced the room with her arms and spun around, "This is marvelous, Segun. You must be very happy, tell me you are." She stopped and went to him. "What's the matter?"

"Nothing." He shrugged. "Here, let me pour you some more champagne." He did, and then set the bottle down beside the glass. He put the roach into an ashtray and lit another joint. He inhaled deeply, and then handed it to her. She shook her head no. He insisted. She began to shake her head again, but stopped when she saw the pain in his eyes.

She accepted the joint, took a drag and started to cough. Her throat felt scratchy and dry. She held the joint out to him, but he shook his head and urged her to try again. She did and coughed again. She felt a burning sensation in her throat. She picked up the glass of champagne, took a sip, and then inhaled again. He took back the joint from her hand, and took a couple of drags. The room was filled with the smoke and smell of cannabis and the aroma of expensive French champagne.

"I'm hungry." Her voice slurred. She felt her head begin to swell. She giggled. "This is really weird, isn't it? I want to tell you something."

"What?"

His voice sounded faraway. "Come closer, I can barely hear you." She giggled. "I'm pre—" She felt dizzy and swayed like the stem of a young plant.

"Sit down for a moment." She heard Sakara's voice as though he was speaking from the other end of a tunnel. Then she felt his arms, strong and hard picking her up and, placing her on the bed. A scream went off in her head as she saw the ceiling swirl. "I f—feel d—dizzy."

He bent over her and kissed her on the lips, then stroked her forehead.

"You shouldn't do that." She became apprehensive.

He sat at the edge of the bed and put her head on his lap. Gently, he took off her lace blouse, exposing her near-nakedness. He turned her over and unsnapped her bra.

"What are you doing?" she asked feebly, helpless as the cannabis took hold.

"What do you think?" He continued to undress her patiently until all she had on was a gold chain around her waist. She took a deep breath as though already asleep. "You can't do that, I'm pregnant with Ola's child," she thought she said. "God, please give me strength," she prayed. Then she felt his hands caressing her body, his sweet and pungent breath warming her face. Like Ademola's. She saw the face, happy and serious. He wore a long white jacket, like a doctor's overcoat. Ademola's. He took out a ring and slid it on her finger. "Will you marry me, Eniola?" Ademola asked.

"Oh, yes, my darling, yes," she replied, feeling the hands, Sakara's hands, caressing her breasts. She gasped, "What are you doing?" She closed her eyes and her chest heaved, faster. And the warmth travelled down to her groin. "We will have three beautiful children together," she heard Ademola whispering into her ear.

"Yes," she whispered, and arched her back as Sakara's strong hand caressed her thigh.

"No more Abiku, I want three children that will grow old," Ademola said with candor.

"Yes, darling, anything you want," she mumbled as Sakara's finger parted her lips.

"I want two girls and a boy, okay?" Ademola asked.

"Yes, I like that," she acquiesced as Sakara mounted her, his chest heaving as he readied to take her.

"They will be tall and big," Ademola said.

"Oh, very big, yes," she hollered as Sakara's oversized hardness thrusted powerfully into her. His Olympian body crushed her breast as he rode her. She screamed as his hugeness pumped rhythmically again and again and again, filling her with pleasure until she felt the squirting of his masculinity.

"Go to sleep, my sweet mango," Ademola said.

Tears ran down her upturned face, and her eyelids became heavier while Sakara caressed her.

⤴

15

NEW YORK

The little boy stood on a tin drum, head tilted forward, and hands joined together concealing his face in prayer. The sky rumbled and the rain fell in drizzles from the cloud hanging above his head. He began to scream while a girl, whose features resembled that of the boy, came from the darkness and knelt beside the drum. As the rain fell, the girl grew bigger as if sprouting from the black earth. The taller she grew, the louder the boy's screams became. Then, he raised his face to the sky, arms stretched sideways, and dared the gods to bring down the cloud. The girl became a woman full with child. She looked up and just then, the black cloud crashed down, breaking her neck and that of the boy.

It was midnight, Ademola woke up shivering, his body covered in beads of cold sweat. He closed his eyes, settled back onto the pillow, and tried but failed to remember the identity of the boy and the girl in the dream. He got up and headed for the bathroom.

Ali yawned. "Is it morning already?" The boy lay on a daybed in the small room he shared with Ademola.

"No, son, go back to sleep. I have to return the cab to the garage."

244

"Don't go out there tonight, *baba*. Please, stay home!"

"Why not?" Ademola sat on the edge of the daybed.

"I just have this thing in my stomach, *baba*."

"What thing?" Ademola looked into Ali's face which seemed creased with an inexplicable foreboding. "We will talk about your stomach when I get back. I won't be gone long." He got up, tensed his muscles to fight off the cold, and disappeared into the bathroom.

Faintly, he heard Ali's voice, "Don't go, please."

A little after sunset, white flakes had started to drift downward from the sky. Soon after, the snow had become heavier, filling the streets.

Ademola pulled up the zipper of his ski jacket and hobbled out the door of his Stuyvesant village apartment building on the lower east side of Manhattan, his unsteady steps crushing the ankle-deep snow as he walked the four blocks to where the yellow cab was parked. At first, he couldn't find it. All the vehicles on the street were covered with snow. Muttering under his breath, he searched for almost ten minutes before he found the cab. Rubbing his gloved hands together for warmth, he spent the next few minutes removing snow off the windshield. The wind blew harder, turning the air colder, stinging his skin.

Once inside the cab, which seemed colder than his freezer, he felt as though his teeth were going to shatter. He gunned the engine to life, turned on the heater and quickly turned it off as cold air blasted his face. He gripped the steering wheel and waited for the engine to heat up, willing his internal combustion to warm his body and kill the pain that seemed intent on freezing him to death. He shut his eyes and imagined himself back home in Nigeria where the temperature always hovered around ninety degrees. That didn't help. He switched his mind to a more immediate necessity. He opened his eyes to look at the clock on the dashboard, and the dial read twelve-thirty-five. He had almost an hour to get the cab to the garage in Brooklyn, an easier and less painful exercise than the agony of his subway journey back to Manhattan. He shivered at the thought of waiting for God-knows-how-long at the desolate train station in Brooklyn. He shivered again, then engaged gear, pulling the car away from the curb with difficulty.

The streets looked different, empty, soundless, and brighter, as the yellow phosphorescent street lamps glowed with surreal brightness against the snow-white background. "Why should I be driving a taxicab for a living, for crying out loud? I am a surgeon," he thought, his mind drifting back to another space and time—

He remembered his exuberance at the possibility of working in one of the children's hospitals in New York after he arrived from Nigeria. He sent copies of his typed resumé and applications to three hospitals, two in Manhattan, and one in Brooklyn. A week later, he telephoned the hospitals and was shocked to hear that he could not practice medicine in the United States until he passed the FLEX exam.

"What's that?" he had asked the secretary. And he was told that all non–American-trained doctors were required to take the grueling test. He applied and found out that the test was deemed by many people to be as strenuous as the combined tests of a four-year medical school experience. He was challenged and optimistic but he needed the time to study just as much as he needed to have an income. Getting a full-time job was not prudent if he wanted to have enough time to study and pass the test within two years. He did not have to agonize over the issue for long. He needed regular income in order to feed himself and Ali, and also to send money home to his family in Nigeria. Crowder had made it quite clear that he was not going to allow Ademola to worry about the rent or anything else.

Crowder did not have Ademola's problem. As soon as they arrived in New York, he had gone back to his former employer, the *New Yorker Daily Times*, the newspaper with the largest daily circulation in the world. He had worked for the *Times*, as it was called, for four years before landing a two-year contract job in Nigeria. His boss, also an alumnus of Columbia University, was reluctant to let Crowder go to Nigeria. But he relented after getting the assurance from Crowder that he would be back at the end of his contract.

As assistant bureau chief in the West African department, Crowder's salary was more than enough to take care of his needs and those of Ademola and Ali.

But Ademola needed the income. As serious as he was about his studies, he couldn't bring himself to just stay home and expect Crowder to take care of him and his family back home. "I found out that I only need a valid driver's license to drive a cab," Ademola told Crowder one evening after dinner.

"Don't tell me you want to drive a taxi," Crowder had said, an edge to his voice.

"I applied today and—"

"Get that idea out of your head. Why do you have to get a job? Isn't passing the FLEX exam paramount?"

"I still need to send money home for Tunde's school fees and my parents' upkeep. Also, it's going to cost me a lot of money to bring Eniola here. I can't possibly ask you to shoulder that burden also."

"How do you intend to find the time to study?"

"Driving a cab, I can work at my own pace, a few hours a day during the week and longer hours on the weekends. I believe I can bring home seventy-five dollars a day."

"Do you know how dangerous it is?"

"At night but not during the day. And that's why it's the best thing for me right now. I study best at night." Ademola had already made up his mind, and although Crowder opposed the whole concept, he knew he had no choice but to accept his friend's decision.

Perhaps thirty minutes passed before Ademola navigated the taxi through the snow-filled streets of Chinatown, and out of Manhattan over the Brooklyn bridge. The streets looked desolate and eerie. Since he left Manhattan, he had seen only a few cars and a handful of pedestrians who dared to brave the cold and the snowstorm that had turned into a blizzard. "Ali is right, I shouldn't be out on the streets tonight." He became infused with foreboding. "I'm almost at the garage," he reassured himself. "I'll ask one of the drivers on night shift to take me back to Manhattan. It will be cheaper than keeping the taxicab all night."

He continued to drive south on Flatbush Avenue and did not see a black car that sped past him. A few minutes later, as he was about to turn into a side street, he saw the figure of a woman running toward him. A few yards behind her, a man was brandishing a gun in hot pursuit. Ademola rolled down the window.

"Help, I've been attacked!" the woman screamed.

He slammed on the brakes. The woman yanked open the front passenger door and rushed into the cab. "Go!" Ademola hit the accelerator and zigzagged on the snow-covered road before speeding off. He slowed to stop at a red light a block away. "What happened?"

"Pull over," the woman ordered gruffly. "Now!"

Ademola turned to look at her and his heart skipped a beat upon realizing that the person was a man disguised as a woman. "What do you want?"

"Your life!"

Ademola's hands began to shake. So did his lips.

The back door flew open and the other man jumped in. "Here's a present from home!" He said in Hausa-accented broken English before wiping his nose with the back of his hand.

"I—I—I—" Ademola was gripped by fear. Without a doubt, the two men were assassins.

"Did you think you could get away for ever?" the assassin seated next to him asked.

Then the one in the back shouted violent obscenities and pointed the revolver at the back of Ademola's head.

"Please, don't hurt me. I'll give you all my money."

"Good! Let's make it look like a robbery. Your wallet!"

"We must take the cab too," the skinny assassin in the back seat interrupted in Yoruba, the left side of his face twitching.

Ademola hastily handed over his wallet to the one in the front seat who yelled, "Get out!"

He hesitated, and was about to say something when the assassin in the front snapped, "Gimme that," grabbing the gun from his partner. "Now, get out!"

Ademola was halfway out of the cab when a shot rang out. The bullet barely missed his head. He spun around to stare at the assassin. The gun looked more lethal as silver-colored smoke curled upward from its muzzle. He saw the assassin's index finger curled around the trigger. A second explosion erupted, and he sucked the cold air into his mouth in horror as he felt the impact of the bullet against his chest. He reeled backward before collapsing to the ground. He clutched the right side of his chest with his left hand and felt the warmth of the blood oozing out of the wound just as two more shots rang out before the taxi drove off. "I've been shot!" He stared in disbelief at his blood-soaked hand. His breathing became labored as he staggered toward the lamp post a couple of yards away. "Help, I need help," his brain screamed out. "Get out of the darkness, go under the light where someone can see you." He felt the warmth fleeing his body and the brightly illuminated lamp started to blur. His head ached and he bent forward to stop himself from falling. The fear of falling down where no one could see him made him panic. "Help, somebody, help me, please." Warm tears stung his cold face. He looked up to the sky overhead, and the snow crystals fluttered down like petals onto a grave. Fear fueled his resolve and he managed to get closer to the lamp post, scanning the deserted street for the help that was locked away behind the closed doors of apartments nearby.

Barely a few feet from the post, his legs stopped moving. His brain screamed the order: Move! Move! Move! But the order was refused. Both legs went out from under him and he collapsed on the ground, face up, his left hand fisted over the gaping wound in his chest. Panic engulfed him. "I'm going to die!" he whispered to himself, his arms numb as his hands and feet. He took a deep breath, ignoring the pain in his chest, and exhaled. And again. "Keep breathing," an inner voice whispered, "If there's life, there's hope." He remembered the words of his mother. And her face suffused his mind, growing clearer and sharper. He saw her sitting on her goat-skin prayer mat in the middle of the parlor, her smile radiant and her words soothing and loving: "My husband, of all the sons and daughters of Arinota, you have the most caring heart. You're the well of happiness that your father and I drink from every day. We love you so very much."

"I love you too, mom. Please tell dad and Tunde that I love them too," he whispered, lips frozen as he lay on his back in the middle of a deserted street in Brooklyn. His eyelids fluttered as he tried in vain to look up to the sky. "Please, God, don't let me die here," he managed to say, as the cold continued to spread to the rest of his body. He shut his eyes and the dream came back: The boy screamed to the gods to bring down the cloud and as it descended, Ademola saw the face of the woman whose stomach bulged. He smiled as the snow continued to fall, transforming the city into a Christmas postcard. "Isn't this beautiful, Ali? Come, let me introduce you to the woman that will take care of us. Come on, son, don't be shy."

And Eniola smiled back.

16

ARINOTA

As soon as Babasa made the announcement, the country was gripped with fever-pitch vitality. Sakara, recognized as the mastermind behind the ambitious agriculture program, became a celebrity overnight, surpassing even the head of state. Every journalist wanted to interview him. He refused most, but that did not stop them from splashing his face on the cover of every newspaper and magazine in the country. Everyone was happy for him. Sakara knew that Babasa was watching with mixed feelings. At first the president appreciated the popularity that his regime was receiving, and thus diverting the people's attention away from his main objective. But competing with Sakara for space in the newspapers was bound to have its repercussions. "I must do something about those pestering journalists as soon as I get back," he said aloud.

He gripped the steering wheel of his black Mercedes Benz 380SE sedan as he drove the car through the verdant streets of Lagos. It was a little past dusk, and he was heading toward Arinota. It was his birthday. Every year on the anniversary of the deaths of his mother and sister, he observed the sacred ritual of visiting the graves alone and at night. He never forgot how Crowder and Ademola intruded on him on the day before he left Arinota. Their insistence that he should join them for the celebration on the village playground had landed him in trouble with his father. He never forgot the humiliation. But the visit tonight was going to be different.

As he approached the outskirts of the village, his melancholy loomed. "It's time to even the score." He felt the heat that seemed to radiate from his soul. He opened the glove compartment and pulled out a revolver fitted with a silencer. The coldness of the metal chilled his heart.

A flash of lightning pierced the sky as Sakara pulled off the potholed road and parked the car in front of a mud house. He remained seated for what seemed much longer than one minute before a haggard-looking middle-aged sergeant approached the car. The soldier came to attention, then flashed a salute. Sakara nodded and the man got in.

"Is the old man on his farm?"

"No, sir—" The sergeant seemed ill at ease.

"What's the matter?"

"A strange thing happened, sir. Your father—"

"He's *not* my father, you idiot!"

"I am sorry, sir—the old man left his farm before dawn yesterday."

"Has he returned?" Sakara glared at the sergeant.

"No sir. Bandele and I followed him to Abeokuta—"

"Where in Abeokuta?"

"That's the strange part, sir. He went up the hill to the forbidden cave and hasn't come out since."

"What's so strange about that? The man is a *babalawo*, and it's a known fact that his master, the blind wizard, lives in the cave." Sakara's patience began to ebb.

The soldier swallowed. "As we waited, other people came up the hill and entered the cave. One of them is the father of your friend."

"Which friend?" Sakara yelled.

"I—I am sorry, sir. It was the father of the doctor. Also, two people, the pediatrician from Abeokuta, Dr. Awoyinka, and a woman who is known to be a witch followed. Then came two other women from Ijebu. All six stayed in the cave. A little before dusk a man that looked like an American arrived. He wore a black patch over his left eye. He's as tall and big as an *iroko* tree. His skin is the color of red clay. He looks different indeed. But the strangest part is that this man carried a baby that couldn't be more than a year old into the cave, a white child, mind you, sir, who was either dead or terribly ill." His Adam's apple bobbed up and down. He looked as though he expected Sakara to ask a question.

Sakara remained silent, pondering the meaning of the information. "Is it possible that these people are what they are rumored to be?" he thought angrily, remembering what he had been told about his mother's death.

"I think the witches are going to eat—"

"I'm not interested in what you think! Tell me what you saw." He had difficulty controlling his rage, remembering, when only about seven years old, that his mother's death and that of his twin sister had been rumored to be at the hands of the blind diviner who lived in the cave high atop the black hills that loomed over Arinota. The people of the village often spoke about it in whispers, and Sakara had wanted to confront his father but couldn't, mostly because he had always been afraid of him.

He stopped the car. "Get out and go back home. I will pick you up in an hour. You still have a rifle, don't you?"

The sergeant nodded, and was out of the car instantly. As a passing car honked, the soldier made a pained sound and quickly looked over his shoulder like one who felt stalked by an evil spirit.

Sakara drove off toward the edge of the forest. He parked the car and traced the footpath to his father's farm. He went straight to the graves of his mother and sister and got on his knees. He prayed and shared some of the news about his fortune with the spirits of his mother and sister. He informed them that Eniola, a pretty woman from Abeokuta, was pregnant with his baby. Even though it was against his wish, he had no choice but to marry her. The wedding was to take place the following day. He promised his mother that it would be a simple affair. He also promised that if the baby was a girl they would name the child after her. As on his previous visits, he shed tears, feeling desperately alone and sad that he could never bond with anyone. There seemed to be a void inside him that could never be filled by the love of any human being. And he blamed his father for it. He shivered as the sky rumbled and a flash of lightning pierced the darkness before it began to rain. He bent forward and kissed the grave, promising to bring his wife and child to visit soon. A somber threat of vengeance glinted in his eyes. "Soon, the diviner and my father will join you with screams of agony on their lips. I know he conspired with the diviner to kill you because of that hag who gave birth to that bastard Ademola." He got up. He remained rooted to the spot for a while before hurrying back to his car, soaking wet, astounded by the suddenness of the rain.

He took off toward the village and skidded to a stop in front of the mud house. The sergeant rushed out of his house fighting the wind with his tattered umbrella before getting in the car. He wiped the water off his face with the sleeve of his dashiki.

"Put the gun in the back seat and throw that useless umbrella away," Sakara commanded, racing over the pot holes that poked the muddy road to Abeokuta as the steady rain beat on the roof of the car like arpeggio. The moment they reached Abeokuta, the rain stopped as if the gods had given up trying to discourage Sakara from proceeding with the deed that lurked in his mind.

"We have to walk the rest of the way through the forest,

sir." The sergeant got out of the car. "Do you have a torch-light, sir?"

"You didn't bring one?" Sakara snapped.

"The corporal has a kerosene lantern with him."

The forest was dark and silent as if the rain had chased away its spirit, filling the void with dread. The smell of wet vegetation filled Sakara's lungs as he trod the soaked earth. The sergeant kept looking over his shoulder as though he expected a phantom to materialize from behind the trees. The two ascended the hill slowly until they reached the spot where the three-legged *akee* tree stood like a sentinel at the entrance to the cave. The sergeant looked around for a while before spotting his assistant a safe distance away.

"What's that idiot doing all the way over there?" Sakara whispered.

"There's a better view of the cave from there, sir."

"Ask him to bring the lantern. We are going in."

"I'm not going into that cave!"

"I beg your pardon?" Sakara snapped.

"You heard me right, sir. I am not going into that for-bidden cave. There is no one in this world that can make me go in there," the sergeant said, walking away.

"You will pay for your insubordination!" Sakara ran to Corporal Bandele. "You, come with me into the cave."

Bandele looked up and his face registered his shock as though Sakara had asked him to piss on the grave of his father. He shook his head no and proceeded to walk away.

"Stop right there!"

The corporal continued to walk away.

"Okay, let me have the lantern then."

Corporal Bandele stopped and pointed to a tree close to where Sakara stood. "It's useless," he whispered as though afraid to disturb the darkness.

Sakara picked up the lantern and shook it. "There's no kerosene left in the damn thing!" He dropped the lamp, shattering its glass enclosure. He walked toward the cave. And just before he went through the legs of the tree, he turned and said, "You will regret your refusal."

The sergeant looked as though he wanted to tell Sakara to go to hell, but instead, he said, "Inside that cave dwells the protector of the children of Egbaland. Invading her space would be asking the gods to piss on all of us. It's a sacred place, colonel. No one that is not a member of the secret society of wizards and witches has ever gone in there. Don't do it."

"Superstitious idiots!" Sakara pulled out his revolver and disappeared into the cave.

Once inside, he took a moment to adjust his senses to the darkness and stillness. The silence surged about him in waves. So did the dampness and the chill. His head began to swell when another wave was punctuated by sounds that seemed to come from the walls, the ceiling, and the floor of the cave. Sakara was enveloped in a harmonious chanting that seemed to ooze out of the rocks, its throaty humming rising and falling intermittently.

He felt the hair on his skin rising in proportion to the intensity and nearness of the sound. Fear gripped his mind. He groped in the dark toward the wall, and pressed the side of his head against the rough surface of the rock. The chanting did not change. He inched forward to another spot and got the same effect. He did it yet again, and again until he became dizzy. The pitch and intensity of the sound was the same everywhere. He tiptoed to the center of the cave, which appeared to be shaped like a round bowl. He remained rooted to the spot for what seemed eternity, immobilized by the sound. He was startled by an infant's cry that interrupted the chanting. The silence that followed was ominous. Then all at once a sound like that of a volcano exploded. The ground shook with such violence that Sakara lost his balance and fell down. He struggled to his feet and felt the burning heat that seemed to emanate from the walls of the cave. Then millions of glittering stars whirled above with centrifugal speed. He shut his eyes and the stars multiplied in number, filling his head. He tried to scream but nothing came out. When he opened his eyes, the cave was as dark as a tomb. He took off on wobbly legs heading for a ray of light.

Outside, the chanting began again, louder than before. He looked around, and realized that the sound was inside his head. Directly in front of him appeared the figures of the two soldiers who stared in awe at Sakara as though they had seen a ghost. The night had surrendered to the morning sun. The air was moist and warm. He looked at the sergeant whose hand seemed frozen in midair, eyes ready to pop out of his face. "I'm hallucinating," he mumbled. Weird noises seemed to issue from the sergeant's throat, and his index finger pointed to the sky behind Sakara, who turned around, and to his horror, beheld a black mountain that seemed to be floating toward him, turning daylight into night. The mountain infused the dank air with the smell of a dreaded insect: millions of screaming hungry locusts.

⌇

17

NEW YORK

Crowder came into the living room dressed in a navy pinstripe three-button Brooks Brothers suit, starched white shirt, and a maroon silk tie. The room was cold and gloomy. Ali sat stiffly on the sofa, fingers interlocked on his lap. He looked preppie in a pair of olive corduroy trousers, crimson cardigan over an eggshell button-down shirt, and a pair of black tasseled loafers. On the other side of the sofa sat the flight attendant, Taiwo, her face filled with sadness. She leaned over and gently wiped away the tears from Ali's eyes.

Crowder went to Taiwo and bent down to kiss her cheek. Ever since they met on the flight to New York, Taiwo had telephoned the house every time she was in the city. She had hinted her interest in Ademola under the guise of playing surrogate mother to Ali. Ademola had acknowledged her generosity. But he had made it known that he intended to marry Eniola, who was having difficulty procuring her visa from the American Embassy in Lagos. Crowder and Taiwo liked each other, platonically. She looked beautiful and ethereal in her long, deep green velour mock-turtle-neck dress, accentuating her velvety black skin.

"Ola was a fool," Crowder thought, and hastily forced a smile as he looked into Taiwo's almond-shaped eyes. She did not smile back. She only nodded and allowed Ali's fingers to slip into hers. They headed for the door. The phone rang. Crowder ignored it, holding the door open for her to pass through. She arched her eyebrows.

Crowder dashed to grab the phone. His forehead creased and his voice sounded hollow when he whispered, "Oh my God! Are you sure?" He shook his head several times and then nodded as if forced to agree with the party on the phone. Dejected, he dropped the receiver and went back to join Taiwo and Ali by the door.

"Was the call about Ola?" She asked in a whisper.

Ali started to weep before Crowder could nod yes.

"What did—"

"Not now, please. We must hurry." The three trooped out to the curb where a taxi waited. "King's County Hospital in Brooklyn." Crowder pressed his face against the window, frosting it with his breath, trying to deaden the dread that filled him as he stared at the snow-covered street. He shuddered as he imagined his friend lying on the cold ground, bleeding from three gunshot wounds to his chest. His sadness became anger, first toward Ademola for driving the cab the night he got shot. It'd been over twenty-four hours since the crime, but it wasn't until an hour ago that he'd found out what had happened. He turned the anger toward himself, remembering their painful and dehumanizing escapade, like corpses amidst sacks of kolanut, fleeing from the soldiers all the way from Lagos to Cameroon. Ademola had suggested that they should seek political asylum from the British High Commission in Yaounde, but Crowder had disagreed. "We will be better off in America," Crowder had said, insisting that they would be safer in New York. "Have you forgotten the story of the politician who was found in a crate in England? The reason the attempt to kidnap and send him back to Lagos failed was because the Nigerian Airways plane was late."

"I'll take my chance in England anytime. The British government doesn't allow every citizen to be armed with guns as they do in America where innocent people are shot and killed every day," Ademola had said.

"You've been watching too many detective movies, Ola. New York is one of the safest cities in the world. I lived there for almost ten years without once encountering any violence. Besides, you can't compare the salary in England with that of New York," Crowder had said lamely.

"Who cares about that?"

"There's another compelling reason why you should go to New York though. They have the best children's hospital in the world there. I'm talking about state of the art medical technology and equipment, and a never-ending supply of patients." Crowder had laughed, knowing that Ademola was bound to swallow the bait.

"You win." Ademola had agreed as he always did with Crowder. "But the main reason I agree with you is because I'm realistic. After all, you're an American citizen already. It would be more difficult for me to become a British citizen than an American. And I suspect that we will be gone for a while. However, it will be the height of irony if either one of us got shot in America."

Crowder had appreciated Ademola's candor, and his voice had been filled with exuberance when he said, "Trust me, New York is the safest city in the world and a fun place to be. The shops, theaters, and gorgeous women from all over—"

"Yeah, right." Ademola had laughed.

Now riding in a cab toward Brooklyn, Crowder felt the tears in his eyes at how prophetic Ademola's words had been. And he felt responsible.

"Good evening, ma'am, we're here to see Dr. Ademola." Crowder spoke through the holes in a bullet-proof plexiglass that separated the clerks from visitors at the hospital.

The clerk, a pleasant black lady with grey hair arranged into a bun atop her head, looked up from a pile of files on her desk, regarded Crowder over the rim of her reading glasses. "It's nice to hear such courtesy once in a while. The young men of today don't know such fine words as 'Good evening ma'am.' You must be foreign—Nigerian?"

Crowder nodded yes.

She bunched a fist and shook it in self-congratulation. "I've had the pleasure of meeting some of your countrymen. Fine gentlemen they are. What's that name again?"

"Dr. A-d-e-m-o-l-a."

"I don't believe we have any such doctor here. I should know, I've worked here since I finished high school. And that's a long time, young man. But let me check—"

"He doesn't work here, ma'am. He was brought in unconscious yesterday for gunshot wounds to the chest."

"We get lots of that here—wait a sec." She beckoned a nurse who had just entered the room. She looked up again.

"A-D-E-M-O-L-A?" Crowder repeated.

The nurse bent over, clutching the back of the old lady's chair. "That's the patient Simone donated her blood for." She looked up at Crowder. "Are you a relative?"

"My brother."

"He's a lucky man. He was brought in yesterday on his last breath. I believe he's still in ICU. Come, I'll take you to see him."

Crowder thanked the old lady, grabbed Taiwo's hand, and went through the door with Ali behind them. They took the elevator up three flights to the intensive care unit. They passed through the nurses' station to Ademola's room. The nurse pushed open the door and stepped aside to let

Taiwo in and then nodded to Crowder to go ahead. He insisted that she should go first. Inside the dimly lit room, Crowder saw the figure of Ademola in the bed. His face to his nose, chest, and arm looked serene as though he were in a coma with tubes running from transparent plastic bags that hung on stainless steel gallows.

Ali started to weep. Seated by the head of the bed was a woman who hastily got on her feet. She pressed her index finger against her lips for silence. Crowder swallowed, captivated. The woman was about five feet two inches tall. She looked stunning with a body shaped like an hour-glass and smooth skin the color of gold. Her jet-black curly hair cascaded down to her lower back. Crowder felt tempted to tell her she was the most beautiful woman he had ever seen, but forced a smile instead.

"This gentleman is a rela—"

The nurse was shushed to silence by the woman beside the bed. "Let's step outside," she whispered, looking at Ademola protectively. She eased the door shut after everybody exited the room. "My name is Simone Silva." Her voice sounded like a crystal bell.

"How is he?" Crowder asked, and with the corner of his eye glimpsed a narrowing in Taiwo's eyes.

"He has not turned the corner yet. He lost a lot of blood and—"

"Are you a doctor?" Taiwo interrupted.

"No, I'm a nurse."

"Does he need more blood? I will be glad to donate some of mine right away."

"That's very kind—and you are?" Simone asked.

"Taiwo, a good friend." She stressed the relationship.

"That's a pretty name," Simone complimented.

"So is yours. Where're you from?" Taiwo seemed to have difficulty with the woman.

"Here." She met Taiwo's stare, and smiled. "My father

was from Brazil, and my mother is Creole from Louisiana." She opened the door, looked in for a brief moment, shut the door again, and smiled. "Let's go over there where we can talk without disturbing Dr. Ademola." She pointed to the room across the hall.

"What's the prognosis?" Taiwo asked.

"The next twenty-four hours or so will be critical—"

"Critical?" Taiwo's voice cracked.

Envy and sadness pricked Crowder's heart as he looked at Simone and Taiwo. "Without a doubt these two are about to have it out over Ola. How lucky can one man be?" he mused with envy but quickly braced himself, reminded that Ademola was the brother he never had, and without a doubt his best friend in the world. He felt lonely and sad. "Even Ali accepted Ademola as though he had known him all his life. And speaking of the rascal, where is he?" Crowder looked around the room, and quickly opened the door.

"Where are you going?" Taiwo asked.

"To find Ali." He stepped into the hallway, looked left and right without seeing any sign of the boy. He strode to Ademola's room, eased the door open as he had seen Simone do earlier, and sure enough, Ali was there in the room, sitting on the chair vacated by Simone, staring at the figure on the bed. Crowder felt another jolt at his heart. Ali looked like a son visiting his father on his deathbed. There was love and fear in the boy's teary eyes. Crowder felt a lump in his throat and started to pray, something he had not done since his mother passed away when he was only ten years old. He wept silently.

⌐

18

LAGOS

May, 1986:

Eight months after Eniola discovered that she was pregnant with Ademola's child, a sharp pain shot down her thighs. A cramp. She rubbed her lower stomach to take the pain away but it became more intense. She screamed.

Her mother dropped the porcelain teapot she was holding and rushed upstairs. "What's the matter, honey? Are you—oh, my!" She rushed to the bathroom, soaked a towel, and dashed back to find Eniola sweating, her breathing labored.

"Please God, don't let me have the baby yet. Give me two more weeks. Please!" The contractions came closer together, faster than normal and the pain tore through her.

"My goodness, something is terribly wrong. I have doubled as a midwife several times but this is strange. It's as though the baby doesn't wish to be born," her mother whispered in Egba dialect. "Sweetheart, listen to me and do as I say. Take a deep breath—now, exhale as I count—one, two, three, push!"

"Segun is bound to wonder why the baby came prematurely." Eniola gritted her teeth as the pain shot through her lower abdomen.

"Push! One, two—bear down! Again, one—push! Here we are. Push." She reached her hands between Eniola's legs and expertly pulled at the baby's tiny head. "Keep pushing, honey," she coaxed as she pulled the baby all the way out, almost. The umbilical cord and the left foot of the baby remained inside. She pulled the leg. Clasped around the baby's left ankle was a tiny hand. "My God!"

~

Eight days after Eniola delivered the twins, a boy and a girl, Akin entered Sakara's home office. He took a seat opposite his host, who looked like he was either getting ready to go to bed or just rising from one. During their telephone conversation the previous night, Akin had told Sakara that he wanted to see him at dawn.

"Good morning, sir." Sakara yawned. It had been a long night. He had spent the better part of the night at Dodan Barracks where he was briefed by the twelve-member *ad hoc* committee on the decision to appoint the new minister of agriculture. The list of contenders had been shortened to three, and Sakara had to decide which one he wanted to present to Babasa for the president's approval. He left Dodan Barracks a little after 0300 hours without sharing his decision with the members. That was for Babasa's ears only.

Tired as he was, he couldn't go straight to bed when he got home. Eniola's family and friends had turned the house into a camp ground. People had travelled from different parts of the country to join in the naming ceremony that was scheduled to commence at dawn.

"You're a lucky man and I'm happy for you. You surely deserve every good blessing that the gods have showered on you." Akin was ebullient.

"Thank you," Sakara said calmly, but thought, "He's up to something." He suspected that Akin wanted something out of the ordinary. Otherwise, why would he get up so early, drag his wife along to assist Eniola's mother in performing the traditional naming ritual, and offer to pay for the expense of the ceremony?

Akin addressed the matter as though Sakara had voiced the question. "Who did you choose to be the minister of agriculture?"

"I beg your pardon?" Sakara loathed the retired general's audacious interference in his official business.

"Remember my advice to you about being a king-maker?"

Sakara gritted his teeth, sensing the reappearance of the chanting sound inside his head. Ever since he came out of the cave in Abeokuta he had not been able to shut off the sound that deafened him whenever he got angry. He looked Akin straight in the eyes and nodded.

"I'm glad to know that I wasn't wasting my breath." Akin looked up and frowned. "Are you okay, son?"

"Yes, why?" He forced a smile.

"Nothing." Akin smiled back. "Do I smell coffee, or is my nose playing tricks on me?"

Sakara got off the chair and walked over to the table by the door to the bathroom. A percolator spewed steam into the air and two mugs and a jar of honey were on the table. He filled the mugs, added a tablespoonful of honey to Akin's, and went back to join his old boss.

"Thanks." Akin sipped. "Good coffee."

Sakara sat down.

"What kind of plans have you made for the twins' future?" Akin glanced at Sakara, who turned sharply and flinched at the *non sequitur.* "Don't tell me you haven't thought of that."

"As a matter of fact I haven't. They are only eight days old. There's plenty of time yet." He wished Akin would be less intrusive.

"No, there isn't." Akin looked over his shoulders as though wanting to make sure they were alone. "I was a bit disappointed and hurt when your wife told me that Achibong had been chosen as the babies' godfather."

"Eniola should have let me tell him that," Sakara thought. "I apologize for the mishap. She had asked me to suggest a name and I told her to handle it. I had hoped that she would choose you."

"Don't worry about it, Segun, regardless of who the godfather is, I know what my duties are. Remember that talk we had about the missing files?"

"Yes." Sakara wondered what was on Akin's mind.

"Well, seventy million is a lot of money even for a man like me. I've decided to put two into a trust fund for the twins, a million dollars each."

"I beg your pardon?" Sakara got off the chair and came closer to Akin. "My kids don't need any trust fund, sir." He closed his eyes to shut off the sound in his head.

Akin heaved his bulk out of the chair to face Sakara. "Don't be a fool, of course they do. You are on top of the world today, as I was not too long ago, but you will not remain there forever. You are a soldier, Segun. Bad things happen to us."

"Granted, but I still cannot accept your offer."

"It's for the children's future, young man. They—"

"They don't need a million dollars each to be secure, sir. As you rightly said, I am on top of the world right now and I intend to use the opportunity to prepare them for a better world. There are millions of children in this country who are not nearly as lucky as the twins."

"Good. Perhaps I should do something for them too."

"That would be a good start," Sakara said tightly.

"Do you have any suggestions?" Akin's face hardened.

"As a matter of fact I do. You can use just a fraction of the two million to build a clinic in my village or anywhere else for that matter."

"Why a clinic?"

"That's something close to my heart."

Akin pressed his lips together and regarded Sakara as though thinking, "I didn't know there's a heart inside that body of yours," but said, "Tell me about it, Segun."

"About what?"

"The clinic."

Sakara cleared his throat. "Thirty-eight years ago, my mother and twin sister died minutes after I was born. The rumor in the village was that my father had talked the blind diviner who delivered my sister and me into putting a curse on my mother. Superstitious as it sounds, I believed it and I've blamed my father ever since. But deep inside I've been bothered by the thought that if there was a clinic in the village my mother and sister would have had a chance." He cleared his throat again. "The problem of a lack of medical facilities is not unique to Arinota. And it's worse in some areas. Those that do not die at birth end up starved or poisoned to death."

"Poison? How's that?"

"Nigeria, a country of over eighty million people, doesn't have a single sewer system. None! Where do you think all the human waste goes?"

"Underground, where else?"

"Drinking water comes from the same source, doesn't it? Take your house as an example. You have a well, don't you?

"A borehole, yes."

"Where do you think the waste in your neighbor's septic tank, which probably has never been emptied, ends up?"

"That's another fantastic project you should propose to Babasa. But, son, let's handle one thing at a time, all right?" Akin's face twisted into a forced smile.

A warning bell supplanted the chanting in Sakara's head, temples pounding. He forced himself to hear the rest of what Akin had on his mind.

"I want to head the ministry of agriculture."

"So that's what it's all about?" Sakara's eyes clouded suddenly with rage, the chanting filling his head.

Akin hastily raised a palm in the air. "Hear me out first, young man. Sit down."

"*He's an enemy. Kill him!*" The chanting in his head urged him. He dashed to his desk, opened the drawer and reached for his silencer-fitted gun, grabbing it, and was about to aim it at Akin when the door eased open and Eniola's mother walked in. "We are ready to begin the ceremony," she said with a smile.

Silence replaced the sound in Sakara's head. He shut the drawer and told the old woman they would be out soon.

Akin was unaware of how close he had come to getting shot. The fractured smile never left his face. "The agriculture project is a brilliant idea and if it becomes a reality it would change the balance of trade between Africa and the rest of the world."

"What do you mean, *if*?" Sakara snapped.

"Are you aware of the magnitude of your idea?" Akin looked like a school teacher trying hard to get a point across to a difficult kindergartner. "There are two problems with it though." Akin looked at Sakara's face and frowned. "Are you sure you're okay?"

"Yes, why?"

"You don't look too good, son."

"I'm fine." Sakara searched for the sound in his head without success.

Akin shrugged. "First, there's too much money involved and that's the honey that will attract the sycophants in the country. None of them would be qualified to implement the project successfully. I can, and you know it." He stopped and looked as though he sensed that Sakara's patience was wearing thin. "Besides, I'm the only southerner that Babasa would not object to if you nominated me."

"Why don't you ask him to appoint you directly?"

"Didn't he tell you that perception is reality? Babasa thrives on that belief. If you recommended me—"

"But I've already chosen someone else."

"And who may that be?"

"I can't tell you that." Sakara headed for the door.

"Sit down, Segun. What's the matter with you? Have you become so big that you've lost your bearings? Don't ever walk away from me again before I finish talking to you."

Sakara remained on his feet, wishing to end the discussion before the madness in his head took over.

"What's the matter with you? First, you insult me by naming Achibong to be your children's godfather. You refuse to accept my gift to your children, a gift which you misconstrued as a bribe. And now, you have the audacity to walk away from me. I come to you as a friend, Segun. I want that position, and I usually get what I want."

Sakara sat down. "What's the other problem?" he said, confident that the sound would not come back.

"As you brilliantly proposed, and correct me if I'm wrong, you intend to maximize the yield and utilization of every indigenous cash crop in the country. In addition to that the project is aimed at creating millions of jobs in the industrial sector, right?"

Sakara nodded.

"Western European and American economic interests in Africa would be challenged by your idea. Don't expect them to sit on their hands. You're talking about real economic independence for the continent."

"You don't believe the project will succeed?"

Akin remained quiet for a while. He got up and started for the door. "Come on, they are waiting for us to start the ceremony."

"You didn't answer my question."

"Total success? No. You hold the seed in your hand though. What is needed is someone to plant it and bring it to fruition. I hope I don't need to convince you that I am that person, son. However, if I do not get it, Babasa will give the job to someone from the north, and by then you won't need but a double-digit IQ to figure out what the outcome will be. You need someone who is capable of attracting the brightest minds in the country to the project. Not a bunch of idiots who would fill key decision-making positions with their unqualified relatives and friends. You've seen me in action before and you know how I detest *mediocracy*."

The parlor had been cleared and furniture rearranged to create space for Eniola's mother and Akin's wife, a light-complexioned middle-aged woman, who sat on a finely-worked quartz stool with a looped handle. This was the first time that the old Yoruba ceremonial stool that Akin had bought from a museum in Germany at a mind-numbing price had been taken out of his house. Eniola's old grand-aunt, Iya'gba, whose face looked like that of a featherless black owl, clapped her bony hands together, announcing the commencement of the ceremony. She took off her scarf and smiled, exposing both her baldness and toothless gums. Sakara and Eniola sat on the sofa, each holding a baby. Achibong winked conspiratorially at Femi, who stood by the window eyeing Chiedu, the vivacious and heavy-busted current girlfriend of Hakabala. Akin shook his head and smiled, looking as though he caught the subtle exchange between Achibong and Femi.

Iya'gba got up slowly and seemed to move like a snail to the center of the room, knelt down, spread a straw mat on the floor and produced several containers from beneath the stool. She asked Eniola to kneel beside her. "We will start with the younger one." She smiled. "According to our tradition, the first child of a twin birth is the younger one. Therefore the baby that came out of the womb first shall be named *TAIWO*, literally meaning the child that tasted life first to determine the appropriateness of the new world for both. Seniority is very important in our culture. The first child was sent out of the womb by the older of the two. Only older ones can send others of younger age and experience on errands. The second child will be named *KEHINDE*, the one that comes last, by implication, the older. These names have remained unspoken since the birth of the babies eight days ago." She gently undressed the baby. She nodded and Akin's wife opened a can containing palm oil. Iya'gba touched the oil with the tip of her index finger, tasted it and then smeared the baby's lips with it.

"The primary duty of a parent is to provide protection and sustenance. And in keeping with Yoruba tradition, the eight-day requirement is absolute because it's believed that it takes that long to consult the spirits through the medium of an *Ifa* divination. These two children are special—the girl wears two important spiritual caps, so to speak. First, she's an *Ibeji*, and because of her curly hair, she is also a *Dada*." She picked up a lobe of kolanut and handed it to Sakara. She asked him to kneel next to his wife on the mat before giving Eniola another piece and asked her to chew the bitter nut. With prolonged deliberation, Iya'gba shut her eyes and appeared to be off on a private contemplation. Her lips quivered as she cleared her throat, and with feeble resonance, the words of the poem of twins issued from her lips:

"Twins are rich children
   They give us happiness, as does a crown,
     Like one with a long, graceful neck,
  Like one with whom it is good to see in the morning

Like one that attracts attention,
 Like one with gloriously beautiful eyes,
At dawn, the owner of the house sweeps the ground.
 Don't touch my eyes or tail!
 You, who're honored at dawn with drumming,
Who sleep with the Kings, but never
 Roll up your mats at dawn.
 You, who're taller than others,
Who enter without greeting the King.
 Everyone is king in his own house.
 Tiny babies in the eyes of jealous others,
Who're treated with love and care by their mother.
 You shout, 'Insult me, and I shall follow you home.
 Praise me, and I shall leave you alone!'
You that does not despise the poor,
 Who are families of the cloth seller.
 You enter without greeting the King.
Ibeji, you belong to the world.
 A tiny pair that live in trees.
 Twin who cannot walk alone,
 Who needs others with whom to walk."

B y the time the sun stopped bearing down on Lagos and
disappeared behind the horizon, the temperature had
dropped to ninety degrees Fahrenheit with eighty percent
humidity. A soft breeze filled the air with the salty moisture
from the ocean. The catering staff from the Federal Palace
Hotel had finished setting tables and chairs on the grounds
of Sakara's house. Technicians tested the electronic
equipment on the elevated stage. Drums and guitars were
tuned to perfection. King Sony Ade was expected to enthrall
the guests with his musical arrangements.

Hundreds of guests, mostly top government officials and

foreign diplomats, trooped in through the tight security posted at the main gate. The men were dressed in bright flowing *agbadas*, and their female companions wore lace *bubas*, their heads covered with damask scarfs. The foreign dignitaries wore tuxedos and their ladies wore evening gowns. They laughed and talked in animated tones. The aroma of barbecued lamb chops, steamed lobsters, fish, giant prawns, shrimp, *moinmoin*, fried plantain, steamed rice, *eba*, pounded yam, stewed and fried fish, and roasted lamb filled the evening air. French labels competed with Italian wine. Imported liquor, wine and champagne outnumbered the local beers.

Great importance was given to the seating plan. The highest in rank and most prestigious in social standing were closest to the bandstand, which was separated from the first row by a rectangular dance floor. Babasa, flanked on both sides by members of the PRC and their wives sat on the first row behind the round table occupied by Eniola's family, Akin's wife, and two smartly-dressed nurses who held the twins in their expert arms.

Eniola wore a beige organza blouse; the wrapper, an ikat-dyed, hand-woven cotton in blue and green stripes interlocked with grey and red stripes, cascaded from her waist to her ankles. Her hair was concealed beneath a head scarf of the same fabric as the wrapper. She wore a pair of diamond and gold earrings. Sakara was attired in a voluminous light-grey lace robe with matching short sleeves, collarless shirt and pants. His cap was made of the same material as Eniola's wrapper.

"I wonder if they have Chivas Regal." The American ambassador, looking debonair in black tuxedo, beckoned a waiter, who took the order and disappeared. "This is some celebration. Can you imagine the cost?" he muttered under his breath to his wife, who shrugged and smiled with the corner of her mouth. "If that waiter brings me a shot of

Chivas I'll give you a good guess at the cost."

Moments later the waiter reappeared. He set a silver tray on the table with a thirty-two-ounce bottle of Chivas Regal and an equal-sized bottle of Perrier water on it, bowed and turned to walk away.

"Hold it, young fellow. I'm the only one drinking Chivas at this table. Just pour me a stiff drink and you can take the rest away."

"No, sir. We don't pour drinks here. Everybody gets a whole bottle of whatever is ordered. It's all yours, sir. If you need more, I shall bring another bottle," the waiter responded and walked away to take another order.

"I'll be a son-of-a-gun," the ambassador chuckled. He turned around and his face widened with amazement upon seeing quart-size liquor bottles and champagne on other tables. He locked eyes with his wife and muttered, "And these people have the gall to request a twenty-billion-dollar loan from the World Bank and IMF?" He shook his head before joining his wife in laughter.

The musicians played soft music while waiters hovered over the tables, efficient and silent, making sure that each guest was satisfied.

Later, the tables were cleared, drinks replenished and the Master of Ceremonies, Major Achibong, delivered a perfunctory opening address.

The musicians stepped onto the stage and the naming ceremony commenced. With regal bearing, Babasa walked to the dance floor. Over a hundred dancing women with their expensive colorful head-scarves carpeting the floor welcomed him as he stepped on the head-scarves, dancing, dropping crisp Nigerian currency in twenty-*naira* notes, *spraying*. The members of the PRC joined him, dropping more money on the scarves as they danced.

"It's your turn, Colonel Sakara. You and Eniola have to join the head of state." Akin's wife beamed.

"But I can't dance to juju music. I don't know how," Sakara said, looking at his wife for support. Eniola just shrugged her shoulders.

"C'mon, Colonel, Eniola, you can't keep General Babasa waiting," Akin's wife coaxed.

"I know I'm going to make a fool of myself. But what the heck, it's a party." Sakara stood and there was a roar of applause from the guests. He awkwardly adjusted his robe by throwing the loose material over his shoulders. He held Eniola's hand and gently pulled her toward the dance floor.

The music stopped, and Achibong said, "Ladies and gentlemen, it's my pleasure to introduce the parents of the special babies whose naming ceremony we celebrate tonight. Due to the special circumstances of the births of the infants—being twins, and the girl, a *Dada*—a rare phenomenon, let the merriment be limitless."

The applause was deafening. The music started again at a higher pitch. The women danced around Eniola and Sakara, their wrapped buttocks bouncing to the music.

The circle of women opened and the members of the PRC trooped toward Sakara and Eniola. The first person in was Hakabala, who rocked left and right and back and forth. He plastered their foreheads with hundreds of twenty-*naira* notes and beckoned toward the table where the twins nestled in the arms of the nursemaids. The maids exchanged glances, got up and walked to the dance floor with the babies. Hakabala smiled and *sprayed* the infants with money. He stepped forward and smiled at Eniola, who flinched.

Ever since Hakabala told her, "I was asked to inform you that if you refuse to marry Major Sakara, you and your entire family will pay a heavy price. And you must never reveal any of this to him," Eniola always felt terribly ill at ease in his presence.

"But I am engaged to another man," she had pleaded.

"The fugitive, are you out of your mind? You will never

be allowed to leave this country."

Eniola had said, "I do not love Major Sakara."

"Who says you must love him? What you must do is provide me with a weekly report about everything he does, who he sees, and what his plans and ambitions are."

"I will never do such a thing. You will have to kill me," she'd screamed.

The general's response chilled her, "The child in your stomach will be flushed out with this hanger and your stomach ripped with this dagger, young lady."

"Oh my God, how——"

"How did I know you are pregnant? The same way I will know if you whisper a word of this conversation to anyone else. Your secret is safe with me as long as you do as I order. Do you understand?" Hakabala had snapped.

Pretending to love Sakara was not quite as easy as she had imagined, but she managed. Passing the information to Hakabala was easier. The conduit was Achibong, who she later found out was also passing information about the generals to Sakara.

The pitch of the music increased and the dancing became feverish. Eniola was oblivious to all the eyes on her as she forced herself to dance in rhythm to the music. Everyone stopped. They clapped their hands and stomped their feet while her steps and body movements continued. Akin and his wife joined her on the dance floor. They danced, laughing with her, happy for her.

The clapping and the stomping became louder as the American ambassador and his wife joined in, enthralled by how Eniola danced as though in a trance, her whole essence swaying in perfect time to the music. Soon everybody stopped watching and resumed their dancing, *spraying* each other and the musicians.

A sudden cool breeze swept through the dance floor and Eniola felt an inexplicable calm wash over her. She stopped dancing although the music had not stopped. The people on the floor seemed to move in slow-motion. And her heart froze when she saw what appeared to be Ademola's father standing behind the bandstand. The old man shook his head and she saw recrimination in his eyes. She looked to her left where her husband stood and saw Sakara's crossed eyes as she had never seen them before. They bore into hers like the deadly eyes of a black mamba. For the first time in her life she cringed and looked away. She shook herself back to reality and the noise of merriment filled the air; and when she looked again the old man was gone.

19

NEW YORK

June, 1988:

Ademola pulled the envelopes out of the mail box and knew right away where two of the four were from. His heart pounded against his chest as he climbed up the stairs. Although it had been four months since he sat for the FLEX exam, and in spite of his optimism, he continued to study. Once inside the apartment, he shook the unopened envelope and wondered if it would not be a bad idea to let Crowder or Ali open it. "No," he muttered under his breath. During the three years of sharing the two-bedroom apartment with Crowder their relationship had blossomed beyond mere friendship. Ademola remembered the evening right after he was discharged from the hospital. Crowder had sat next to his bed, and in his brusque way said, "From now on, the only thing you're allowed to do is eat, sleep, and study."

Ademola's physical recovery was prolonged by the more devastating emotional wound. On the day Crowder, Taiwo, and Ali went to see him at the hospital, Crowder had received a phone call from Nigeria just before they left the apartment. But he had waited for a few weeks, allowing Ademola to regain his strength, before giving him the news. Ademola had gone into a deep depression upon hearing that

279

Eniola had married Sakara barely three months after their escape from Nigeria. Unable to eat or sleep, he walked around the apartment as though his life had come to an end. Then months later, he plunged into his books, which helped him to get his mind off Eniola. Everyone left him alone, including Ali, who proved to be a wonderful son. He was obedient, helpful around the house, and showed considerable interest in his school work. The boy was challenged at first, but Ademola was able to convince him that being the oldest boy in his class had its advantages. Whenever Ali saw his dad studying, he would sneak into the kitchen to make coffee for him; he would bring it into the bedroom where Ademola studied, and then would snuggle into his bed to read. At the end of his second year in school, Ali did well enough to be given a double promotion by the principal. That was when Ademola struck a deal with the boy: "From now on, I will give you ten dollars for every A you get at the end of the school year." Ademola had studied Ali keenly. "And for every B, you'll get five dollars."

Ali's eyes rounded. "Good." He smiled.

"That's not all, young man. For every C, you'll pay me twenty dollars—"

"Twenty dollars!" The smile turned into a frown. "How are you going to get the twenty dollars from me? I don't have that kind of money."

"Let's suppose that in your next report, you get three As, two Bs, and one C, how much would I have to either give you or get from you?"

Ali used his fingers to add and subtract. "Ten dollars for A, five for B, and minus twenty for C, right? You will owe me twenty dollars," he said proudly.

"That's right, son." They had agreed.

Crowder came out of his room and frowned. "Why are you standing in the middle of the room shaking the envelopes as though they are—Is that the FLEX result?"

Ademola nodded yes.

"Give it here. Come on, let me have it." Crowder snatched the envelopes from Ademola's hand. He dropped three to the floor, and ripped open the one in his hand. His eyes danced as he read the report. A soft whistle escaped his lips, and his face turned sour.

"I failed?" Ademola reached for the paper.

Ayo nodded and handed the report to his friend.

Ali came into the room, took one look at Crowder, and immediately looked as though he sensed something different in the air. He looked at Ademola, whose serious facial expression transformed into elation just before he screamed, "I passed!" and started jumping.

"This calls for a celebration." Crowder grabbed Ademola in a bear hug. The two swirled around the room, dancing with happiness. Ali joined in, grinning from ear to ear.

"Let me call Simone," Ademola said, breathless.

"Do that—better still, don't tell her yet. It should be a surprise. Good thing Taiwo arrived here this morning. Why don't the four of us go out on the town tonight?" Crowder said, and then seeing the fractured expression on Ali's face, he added, "I don't see why we can't take this little fugitive from the land of the sleeping giant of Africa with us. What do you say?" He stroked Ali's head.

Ademola ran across the room to grab the telephone. He dialed and waited. "Hi, how about dinner tonight? Ayo is treating... Why not?" He frowned. "Well, we can have an early dinner... Yes... I'm sure... no problem... He's ten years old now." He nodded. "She's in town... that's great. We'll meet you there at five... It's a surprise... that's right... I love you too." He hung up and turned to Crowder. "Simone has to participate in a ceremony tonight in Brooklyn. We're invited. Is five okay for dinner?" He shook a bunched fist in the air happily.

"Congratulations. I heard that not many people pass the

FLEX the first time around. But I never doubted that you would be one of the few exceptions. Now you can get us into one of those fine apartments on the upper east side," Crowder teased.

"Not so fast, buddy. I still have to find a hospital where I can intern at. Thanks for everything. You've been a real brother and a true friend."

"I didn't do any more than you would have done for me. Besides, I was investing in a sure bet." Crowder laughed.

Ademola's face twisted into feigned disappointment.

"I was only serious." They both laughed again.

Ali looked at the two as though he missed the joke. He forced a laugh.

The dinner was wonderful at the famous Tavern on the Green on the west side of Central Park. Crowder was happy with his New York sirloin steak and a baked potato as big as a grapefruit. Ademola ate half of his broiled salmon and asparagus. The ladies talked animatedly like old friends over the special chef's salad. Ali stuffed himself with chicken and wild rice and didn't stop until he finished every bit on his plate. He shook his head no when Taiwo pointed to his salad. After dinner, the ladies excused themselves to go to the powder room to freshen up.

"Why do you have to do that? You two look fresh already," Ali said.

Everybody laughed.

"I'm really glad to see Taiwo and Simone getting along so well. How did you know Simone was the right person for you?" Crowder asked as soon as the ladies left.

"It's simple, really. Once I decide that I like a lady enough to want to see her again, I do a personality check."

"What's that?"

"First you have to know yourself. And that is achieved by drawing a line down the middle of a piece of paper to create two columns. At the top of each column, write the words positive and negative, then list all the things you like about yourself in the positive column. And in the negative, write all the things you don't like. With a red marker, asterisk those traits or behaviors you would like to be rid of and those that you would like to nourish. And then set your goals. But you must be realistic by attacking the least difficult ones first. It's a well known fact that almost all we need to know about each other is right there during the first three seconds of the first encounter. After that, everything else is either an addition or subtraction." Ademola sipped his champagne. "Take Simone: The moment I decided that I liked her, I did the same thing about her; all the good and bad things I saw in her are on paper. I told her I was going to do it. She was happy to do the same thing about me. Honesty is important. Later we swapped envelopes, and I was amazed at how accurate her assessment of me was. So was mine of her. By knowing each other's strengths and weaknesses, it's easy to get along."

"How come you never shared that with me until now?"

"You never asked. Besides, you weren't ready for it."

"Thanks, I like it very much. I will try it on Taiwo."

"No, do yours first—here they come."

"You two look like you've been talking about us," Taiwo said, sitting down.

"How did you know that?" Ali looked at her with admiration.

"So they have, eh?"

"Yep, but it was good talk," Ali said importantly.

Everybody laughed.

"So when are you going to tell us about the surprise?" Simone looked at her watch.

"There's no better time than now. I—"

"*Baba*, let me tell them, please," Ali said.

Ademola nodded.

"My father has just become a doctor again!"

"You—did you pass the FLEX?" Simone jumped off her chair, held Ademola's head between her palms, and landed a kiss on his forehead. "Congratulations!"

"That's all I get for all the sleepless nights? I—"

The rest of the words muted as Simone kissed him on the lips. "I am so happy for you," she said.

"Now you can be our wife, Ms. Simone," Ali said.

Everybody laughed again.

Ademola wiped tears from the corners of his eyes. Simone made a toast, Ali said a small congratulatory prayer, and the bottle of champagne was emptied easily.

Crowder paid with his credit card and they left the restaurant for Brooklyn in a chauffeured limousine.

In 1636 Dutch farmers settled in the marshlands, taking up their residence along the shore of Gowanus bay, which reminded the immigrants of another settlement in the old world called Breuckelen. In 1645, the settlement, often called Breucklyn, Breuckland, Brucklyn, Brookland, or Brookline, was established near the site of the present borough hall. It wasn't until about the end of the eighteenth century that the place became known as Brooklyn. The borough later became home to Christian European, Catholic Irish, Italian, Orthodox Russian, Jewish, Caribbean, and South American immigrants, all coexisting in mutual respect and suspicion.

In 1986, an old brownstone turn-of-the-century Catholic church in the more affluent Brooklyn Heights section of the borough was purchased and refurbished by the latest immigrants, those whose religious belief and practice were bound to raise eyebrows. These were the descendants of African slaves who came to New York from Haiti, Cuba, Puerto Rico, Brazil, Trinidad, Louisiana, and Belize. They followed in the footsteps of their forbears in Yorubaland. They worshipped *Ogun* (god of iron), *Oxossi* (god of the hunt), *Osanyin* (god of herbalism), *Omolu* (god of disease), *Uxumare* (goddess of the rainbow), *Yewa* (goddess of water), *Yemaja* (goddess of the salt water), *Oxun* (goddess of fresh surface water), *Xango* (god of thunder and lightning), and *Oxala* (god of creativity).

Upon entering the church to witness the inaugural ceremony of the worshippers, Ademola, Crowder, Taiwo, Ali, and the rest of the invited guests were seated on metal chairs lined along the right wall. Devotees and their families sat on the other side, separated from the visitors by a space the size of a basketball court. Several candles hedged the center court, supplying the only source of illumination in the church. The smoke and fragrance of exotic incense competed with the scent of the candles.

"This reminds me of home. The incense is just like what my father used to burn on his shrine," Ademola said.

"Is that right? This place seem eerie and ominous. What do you think we're about to witness? I wish Simone were here to explain—"

Ali jumped as Crowder's voice was cut off by a ceremonial drum that sounded like the amplified heartbeat of an elephant, deep and pulsating. Moments later, a female's voice rang out, bouncing against the walls like the echo of a bell in a tunnel: "*Y'ago-o-o, Y'ago l'ana* (Clear, clear the way)," the voice sang in Bahian-accented Yoruba.

Everyone in the audience turned toward the door at the rear of the hall. Eleven women and ten men emerged into the *barracado* in a straight-line formation. The procession of the children of the gods solemnly approached the center of the court. All, except the woman at the head of the single file, wore white body-hugging gowns, their faces, necks, and exposed arms and legs marked with white dots. The *mae de santo* who looked naked but for her skin-colored tights, also marked with the same chalky dots, stopped abruptly and bent forward. She clasped a long metal sword with both hands, swirling in full counter-clockwise circles, slashing the air with the blade with practiced precision. She stopped and became erect before inclining her body toward a diagonal. She took a couple of strides and closed her feet to turn around.

Suddenly the twenty men and women behind her stood on their toes, arms outstretched to their sides, backs arched, like ballet dancers doing Swan Lake. They drifted a few yards back and stopped. Following the *mae de santo*, the ritual dance turned into a circular formation. They seemed to glide as they moved toward a chair where a man with a black patch over his left eye sat like the high priest. He nodded before getting to his feet, towering over the devotees like an *iroko* tree. He swirled full circle, clockwise first, and then counter-clockwise. The *mae de santo* stepped forward and got on her knees to reach under a small table from where she extracted a live white rooster. She handed the bird to the giant, whose right hand gripped the head of the rooster while the left held the body, exposing the long thin neck.

The pitch of the drum dropped, sounding like the throbbing of the rooster's heart, and the procession began to chant. *The mae de santo* invoked the gods in the Bahian language:

> *Ele come cru e nao lanca;*
> *Ele mata,*
> *Come e nao lanca,*
> *Nao se arrepende do que faz.*

(He eats food and doesn't throw anything away;
    He kills, Eats, and doesn't throw anything away,
      Doesn't repent for what he has done).

The drumming multiplied, growing louder and louder with the fever-pitch of a samba cadence. The devotees jumped in the air in unison, fists held together as though they were on horseback. They reconstituted into a single file behind the *mae de santo* who continued to slash the air with the metal blade in her hands. She approached the head priest in whose powerful hands the live rooster squirmed. Suddenly, with a quick and direct explosive thrust, she decapitated the rooster. The bird's eyes looked stunned in death. The devotees spread out, got on their knees, thrusting their torsos in circles while the rest of their bodies went into spasm as they lowered themselves to the floor horizontally. They wriggled on the ground, circling the *mae de santo* who was in full seizure, screaming gibberish. The high priest stepped forward and doused the *mae de santo* with palm wine. After what seemed like an eternity she got up, staggering toward the audience, amidst deafening applause.

Ademola gasped when he recognized Simone. She smiled at him the same way she greeted everyone else before exiting the *barracado*.

Later, she reappeared in a simple black dress, looking radiant and much more beautiful than Ademola had ever seen her. Her golden skin glowed as though polished. She had her black hair down, giving her the aura of a sun goddess. She held Ademola's arm possessively after planting a generous kiss on his cheek. She smiled at Ali who looked enthralled. "Come on, there's plenty food in the dining room. This is feasting time."

Ademola beamed. "That was an incredible performance, Simone. It reminded me of the ceremonies back home."

"So you've seen something like this before?" Simone

searched into his eyes.

"My father is a *babalawo*. He worships *Sango*."

"You're not kidding me, are you?"

"No." Ademola felt a bit uncomfortable. He looked away. "Why is that man over there staring at us?"

"Where?" Simone's eyes followed Ademola's gaze. "Oh, that's Clay." She smiled. "His real name is William Doss Johnson. He's the high priest, but he prefers the Yoruba title of *babalawo*. He's also my godfather."

"Why do you call him Clay?" Ademola looked away as the man's eye traversed the distance boring into his soul.

"Because of his skin, it's the color of red earth. You have something in common with him as a matter of fact. Come on, I'll introduce you." She pulled gently on his arm.

"Can we save that for later, please?"

"Well—oh oh, he's coming."

"Why did you say I have something in common with him?"

"He's a pediatrician like—"

William Doss Johnson's voice bounced off the walls like the rippling tone of a water drum. His mien was dazzling yet tranquil. His mouth curved into the shape of a crescent when he smiled. "My beautiful angel, why haven't you introduced your friend to me?" His eye locked with Ademola's.

"I was about to do just that, pappy. This is a very good friend of mine, Ola Ademola."

"*S'alafia ni?*"

Ademola was shocked. He looked at the man, then turned to Crowder, whose left brow elevated in proportion to Ademola's astonishment. "You speak Yoruba?" Ademola asked.

"Fluently. What part of Abeokuta are you from?"

"Close, I'm a short distance away from there, Arinota."

"What is your name again?" Johnson looked serious

without losing the smile.

"Ola Ademola, why?"

"Are you a physician?" Johnson looked astounded.

"Yes, I am." Ademola looked as though he expected the sudden revelation of an enigma.

"I'll be damned!" Johnson stepped forward and wrapped his arms around Ademola. "*Omo mi, baba e o so fun mi pe owa n'ilu yi.* (My son, your father did not inform me that you were here in this country)," he said in Egba dialect.

Ademola's curiosity soared, a disconcerting draft coursing through him. "Who are you?"

"Your father and I, along with another gentleman from your village, Chief Sakara, trained under Baba Agba, the blind master who lives in the cave atop Olumo rock. "Come with me, son." He held on to Ademola's hand as they exited the *barracado.* Johnson unlocked the steel door of a room and without letting go of Ademola's arm, he went in.

Ademola felt the walls with his palm, searching for a light switch. He found one and was about to flick it on when Johnson's throaty and portentous voice echoed in the dark, "Don't do that!"

BOOK THREE

20

LAGOS

August 31, 1995:

By the time Sakara arrived at his father's farm the mud hut and the trees were enveloped by predawn fog. Though not expecting anyone to be around so early he tiptoed over the forest earth as he approached the hut, shuddering to fight off the chill and the darkness. A crescent moon glowed against the black sky. He stuck his hand in his pocket and felt the coldness of the knife. How different it had been when he was fifteen, to come home from Mayfield to face his father's wrath. He was afraid of the old man then, and had longed for his affection and parental tolerance. Not any more. Now, he needed to talk to him, man to man, about his achievements in life and the hallucinations he'd been experiencing since he came out of the cave. "I hope General Akin is right," he thought, remembering his discussion with his old boss right after the naming ceremony. Akin had listened, nodding at intervals until Sakara finished the story of his experience. Akin had advised him to make peace with his father and beg his forgiveness. Only then would the curse be lifted. Sakara had agreed reluctantly.

As he was about to open the door, he took in the smell of cocoa pods and guavas, filling his lungs. He froze upon hearing a female voice. He cautiously walked around the hut and tried unsuccessfully to creep into the space between the wall and his father's *Ibeji* shrine as he had done several decades before. He dashed back to the door and pressed his ear against it. He covered his other ear with his palm to shut off the forest noise.

"... a vessel that voyages the ocean and the high seas must, sooner or later, return to port. It has been ten years since your son fled his fatherland."

Sakara gritted his teeth as his curiosity turned into fury. He recognized the voice of Ademola's mother. Spontaneously, he pulled the knife out of his pocket.

"Is that what you came all the way here to tell me, risking discovery?" his father demanded.

"No. I believe that Ola will come home soon—"

"What sort of belief is that?"

"Mother's instinct. We have to be prepared."

"For what?" The old man's voice became hostile.

"There's bound to be trouble when Ola arrives."

"Stop talking in riddles, woman!"

"I do not believe that Segun would give up the twins easily. The babies, who are now nine years old and call Segun father, are not his. They are Ola's children."

"What in the name of the god of evil are you talking about?" Sakara did not have to press his ear against the door to hear the anger in his father's voice.

"A month after Ola fled the country, Eniola came to tell me and my husband that she was pregnant by my son. That was before she married Segun."

"Are you sure?"

"*Sango* is my witness."

"Who else knows about this?" There was fear in the old man's voice. "If Segun finds out—I must think before—"

With a powerful kick Sakara struck the door which then opened with a crash. The flame of the kerosene lantern flickered as the air rushed in. Sakara's father stared into the darkness, stupefied. Sakara stepped forward into the circle of the yellow light, consumed with rage. The old man's mouth opened in recognition and horror, "You—"

Sakara slashed his father's throat, almost decapitating him. He bent forward to spit on the lifeless body.

Ademola's mother screamed, flattening herself against the rough mud wall, eyes shut, as Sakara approached. He rammed the blade between her breasts and spat, "Whore!"

He exited the hut, leaving the smell of blood and urine mixed with the overpowering presence of death behind. He felt a empty serenity descend between his ears. He slammed the door and bolted it. He hurried around the corner and bolted the two windows. Then, he ran the fifty yards or so to the barn. He came back carrying a jerrycan of lamp oil. He poured some of the fluid under the door and with the rest he doused the base of the hut. Panting, he ran back to the barn. This time he had two cans which he emptied, dousing the walls. He ran to his car and hurried back carrying a rifle. He crossed the clearing and stopped outside the door of the hut. He could smell the vapor of the lamp oil. Holding the gun under his arm, he took out a box of matches and a rag from his pocket, soaking it in kerosene. He struck the match, lit the rag, and the base of the wooden door burst into flames.

He ran around the hut, torching the kerosene-soaked base along the way until the whole hut was engulfed in flames. He walked away and stopped when he came to the graves of his mother and sister. He leaned against a cocoa tree that stood at the foot of his mother's grave, and lit a joint, the rifle held in his hand.

The hut was ablaze. The stench of sizzling human flesh filled the air. "Damn you!" Sakara shouted at the sky. The air was thick with smoke and he could hardly see the hut.

A terrifying scream deafened the forest.

Sakara held his breath, eyes trained on the blackness of

the hut. A yellow hole appeared in the center of the black smoke and a lone flame emerged. It got bigger as it licked toward the graves. Sakara glimpsed the human torch with both arms stretched out. His mind screamed: Run! Run! Run! But his body refused the command. The gun and the joint fell to the ground. The walking flame reached where he stood and he felt the flesh-burning heat and smelled the roasting of hair and skin. Hard as he tried, his mind could not will his body to move. Both her arms stretched out in an embrace. Sakara's bladder muscle opened up a flood of liquid at the moment the flame screamed. The front of his shirt caught fire, lungs filled with smoke, and he shut his eyes, trembling.

She screamed again before collapsing on her back, atop the graves, the knife stuck between her breasts as her dead eyes stared vacantly at the crescent moon.

"*Damn you to hell, Segun!*" Her scream echoed throughout Sakara's head as clearly as though she were still alive.

21

NEW YORK

September, 1995:

The croak of an African frog punctuated the surreal silence as the choir of the jungle grew louder. It turned into the sound of a metropolitan city. The images, an unfolding dream that filled the mind of Kathleen McFlarthey, became that of Cambridge in Boston: the annual ritual of the rivalry between the Crimson and the Eli was just halfway through. The Harvard team was out for revenge against Yale's Bulldogs. The score was 14-14.

The stadium was festive, a brass band playing, and the cheerleaders for both teams were at their best. Kathleen, head of the Crimson cheerleaders, was thrown in the air pom-poms and all. But there were no hands to catch her and she landed on the ground with a thud. Flat on her back in pain she stared up at the gray sky over a silent stadium. Then the players emerged like thunder. But the college football game turned into a deadly game of lacrosse. When the two teams of four each approached center field, Kathleen glimpsed the razor-sharp scythes in their hands.

"*Oh, my God! Not again.*" The dream stopped. She woke up in a cold sweat and rushed to the nursery where her fifteen-month-old son lay still in his crib. The boy looked dead when she found him. "No!" Kathleen ran to her bedroom, picked up the cordless telephone with trembling hands to dial nine-one-one. "This can't be happening." She ran back to the nursery, struggling to recall bits of CPR from a recent class, her delicate hands clamped over her mouth. She bent forward to pick up her son, lowering the side rail and turning him over on his back. She tilted his head back, checked his airway, pinched his nostrils and tried to breathe rapid breaths into his mouth. As she tried again, a sharp pain shot through her lower abdomen. Gritting her teeth, she lifted him up, pressing his limp body against her chest.

She held the telephone with her left hand, the right one clasping Jason to her chest. "My son is dying, please send an ambulance to—" She spoke rapidly, her blue eyes fixed on the child, hoping for any sign of life. At last she heard banging on the front door. With Jason in her arms she ran to open it. One of the paramedics took Jason from her, laid him on the floor, put a tube down his small trachea and bag-breathed for him.

"Children's Hospital," the paramedic said to his partner. "Fast!"

Outside, rain gushed out of the sky and crashed down on the earth, and the rumbling from the dark cloud surged above the Manhattan skyline. The paramedics transferred Jason to the ambulance and Kathleen sat besides him, holding his limp hand. With red lights flashing and sirens screaming they arrived at Children's Hospital on the upper east side of New York city with Jason drifting in and out of consciousness.

The double door to the Emergency Room hissed open and the paramedics ran through with Jason on the gurney and Kathleen close behind. The doors clanked shut on the night sounds of the city. Screams and groans of sick children permeated the waiting room with its oversized Disney characters on the walls. Several children with whooping cough, influenza, roseola infantum, and scarlet fever huddled on the laps of their mothers, coughing, faces pitiful with teardrop-shaped red lesions, noses dripping. The mothers' faces were creased with fear and lack of sleep.

In a flash, Kathleen took all this in.

"Put the boy in bed two." The nurse's voice startled Kathleen. "We'll hook him up to the monitor."

The paramedics shoved the gurney through the doors and Kathleen started to follow.

"Hey, Miss, are you a parent—I'm sorry, you can't go in there. You stay here to fill out the forms like everyone else," the night-shift clerk snapped.

Kathleen shook her head. Jason! She dashed forward and disappeared behind the yellow door.

Inside, a tall man stood next to the gurney as the paramedics lowered Jason's limp body onto the bed—an intern, judging from the boyish face that failed to conceal his frustration and anguish. He asked, "How's he doing?"

"He's going in and out. We haven't been able to stabilize him. Doc, this one is labile—he needs immediate attention!" the paramedic said.

"Please, help—"

"Are you his mom?" The young intern turned around with the desperate fatigue of end-of-shift. "You can't stay here!" His voice lacked authority, despite its loudness.

"Yes, I can. I'm not letting him out of my sight."

"Doc, we're losing him!"

"Quick, get another I.V. line going. Intubate him and get cardiology over here STAT! Get lab," the intern told the nurse.

Emergency Room staff surrounded Jason's bed. He was connected to a network of tubes and wires hooked up to a myriad of machines. The lines on the monitor danced up and down. "We're losing him! Rhythm is almost a flat line."

"Get me the paddles now and set it for ten jules!" the intern snapped.

The nurse gulped. "But he's only fifteen months old, doctor."

"Now!" He handed the nurse a tube of paste to smear over a pair of two-inch round silver paddles.

She placed one paddle to the upper right side of Jason's chest and the other paddle on the lower left side. "Clear!" And all personnel stepped away from the bed.

TCHIKIT! The baby's back arched, his legs and arms jumped, his face a death mask. The dancing lines on the monitor slowed but not enough.

"Give him epi and bicarb. STAT!" The intern's forehead was beaded with sweat. "Shock him again. Clear!"

TCHIKIT! Jason's back arched again, his face was lifeless and pale. There was brief commotion as the attendants made sure the breathing tube was ventilating properly. His eyes looked like those of a corpse, fixed and dilated. They repeated everything again, listening to the sound of the monitor indicating a flat EKG line with occasional cardiac activity for another ten minutes. They continued to bag him for air. Only the intern could stop it. For all practical purposes, Jason was dead.

Kathleen's eyes were glued to her son's chest, her lips trembling.

BEEP ...BEEP ... BEEP ...BEEP ... BEEP ...

"He's coming back," the doctor said cautiously.

"What do we do now?" the anesthesiologist whispered, sweat running down his forehead.

"We go right into epi, intracardiac and—"

"No, you don't!"

All heads turned to face Dr. Ola Ademola. His strong oval face, marked by two short fading scars on each cheek, was softened by his brown almond-shaped eyes. He had worked at Children's Hospital for seven years, now specializing in Pediatric Cardiology and Pulmonology. A quiet confidence enveloped him as he snatched Jason's chart from the foot of the bed. He took a deep breath before scanning it. As he replaced the chart and looked at the almost lifeless child, he heard a soft sound echoing in his head. It was the distant voice of a child calling his name. He took Jason's right wrist in his hand, and as the two bodies connected, a sudden blast of light blinded him. He blinked and jerked away, losing his balance.

"Are you all right, Dr. Ademola?" a nurse asked.

He closed his eyes and told himself not to be alarmed. *"It's been three years. This has to be a coincidence."* There it was again—the last time this happened the explosion was devastating. He had passed out. A week later, he found out the little girl's death was listed as SIDS. But he knew better. Closing his eyes, he relaxed and let himself float. Enveloped by a warm fluid, he drifted back in time, back to the womb, where all babies felt the most comfort. He stayed there long enough before drifting back, *informed.* When he opened his eyes the room was quiet except for the background clicks and beeps of equipment attached to Jason's little body. *"He's breathing. We might have just enough time."*

Without a word, Ademola rushed out of the room, straight to the nurses' station, rounded the desk and picked up the physicians' directory. He flipped through the pages, found what he was looking for and told the station nurse to page Dr. Fall.

"Dr. Ademola!" A powerful and aristocratic voice called from behind him. Ademola turned to look into the probing eye of the Chief of Staff, Dr. William Doss Johnson, whose other eye was covered with a black patch. "I want you and Jason's parents in my office," he said in a fatherly tone. "We will speak with Dr. Fall there. Put him through as soon as he calls," Johnson said to the nurse and left.

"Mrs. McFlarthey, I'm afraid we have to move your son to the Pediatric Intensive Care Unit right away." Ademola's voice was hesitant, and getting no immediate response, he coughed to draw her attention. Kathleen stared back at him. "Jason is stabilized and he's being transferred. I'll be back in a short while." He exited.

Kathleen stumbled toward the bed and collapsed as her legs gave way. She stared at her son's face with blank eyes. Her spirit had gone in search of answers, clues to unlock the mystery of the dreams, old and new. *It's been three years.* The dreams were the same: on the Harvard team, the leader was her son, looking vulnerable. The rest of the team consisted of her husband and a black doctor. She couldn't recognize the fourth member. She had screamed. The dream stopped.

Then she remembered: *last time, three years ago,* she had the same dream. But the captain of the Harvard team was her only child, fifteen-month-old Elizabeth. The leader of the Yale team had approached the captain of the Harvard Crimson team for the customary handshake. His body was human, bulging muscles pulsated under glistening skin. But fingers and toes were talons, scalpel-sharp. Kathleen tried to move but couldn't. Several pairs of hands held her down, spreadeagled on the ground. She was pregnant. The referee signaled to begin. But where was the ball? Then it dawned on her what the game was all about. She writhed as the players walked backward to the end of their respective side of the field, then charged forward. The applause from the spectators was hushed and eerie. Scythes raised, the applause changed. The scythes made hissing silver arcs in the air, decapitating the Crimson team. The body of the leader, her daughter, Elizabeth, stood rigid, unaware of the loss of her head. Kathleen had screamed herself awake as the dream ended. She'd rushed to the nursery and found her daughter barely alive. Elizabeth had died at Children's Hospital exactly three years ago.

"Mrs. McFlarthey, your son suffered a heart stoppage but he's stabilized now. I've ordered additional tests. He'll be transferred to a private room in PICU. Meanwhile, I suggest that you take a breather. Come with me to the doctors' lounge and—"

A woman's voice, younger and desperate, interrupted Ademola. "We need you for a preemie in bed six."

"How much does the baby weigh?" he asked the nurse. "If he's over five hundred grams page a neonatologist—Mrs. McFlarthey, follow me, please. We both need a break."

Kathleen obliged. Her voice shook as she said, "I need some answers, fast, Dr. Ademola."

They entered the doctors' lounge, which seemed less frenetic. Kathleen sat on a sofa much too big for her despite her bulging stomach.

"How about a cup of coffee?"

Kathleen looked down at her stomach, shook her head and asked softly, "Who are you?"

"Dr. Ademola. I specialize in—"

"That's not what I mean. I've seen you before. You walked into the emergency room and fainted after touching the hand of my daughter."

Ademola's eyes widened. "That was three years ago. That was your daughter? Elizabeth, right?"

"Elizabeth, and now Jason. I saw you both times. I want answers. You can start by telling me who you are."

"I thought I answered that already. My name is—"

"Were you at Harvard?" Kathleen stared at Ademola as if she hadn't heard.

"No, why?" Ademola asked, confused.

"For starters, Dr. Ademola, you were in my dreams, twice. Both times my children were—"

Ademola placed his cup of coffee on the table and walked across the room. He started to sit down next to Kathleen when she said, "I wouldn't sit here if I were you.

Like I said, I want to know what's happening here."

"Mrs. McFlarthey, hard as it might seem, I need answers too. Your daughter was already dead when I touched her. Tonight, I didn't pass out, but my mind was invaded by strange voices."

"You were in my dreams before I met you. That's invasion, if you like!" Her forehead gleamed with perspiration, betraying her desperation.

"I believe you. We need to go upstairs and speak with someone," Ademola said with reassuring kindness.

Ademola and Kathleen found Dr. Johnson, whose aura radiated inexplicable energy, seated behind a mahogany desk in his office. He pointed toward two green leather wing chairs. Ademola and Kathleen sat down facing him.

"Why did you page Dr. Fall for a pediatric cardiac arrest case? Isn't he an ophthalmologist?" Johnson asked without any preamble.

The telephone rang. Johnson pressed a button and a voice filled the room. "*This is Dr. Fall. For crying out loud, it's midnight. What's so urgent that can't wait until morning?*"

"Dr. Fall, we need you here to check the blood vessel patterns in the eyes of a fifteen-month-old child in PICU. I will furnish you with the details as soon as you get here." Dr. Johnson pressed the button and there was silence. "Dr. Ademola, I want you back here with the results of the retinal image test. This case has to be handled with the utmost discretion." Johnson turned his gaze toward Kathleen. "In due course you will be informed of your son's condition. While Dr. Fall is testing Jason, I want you to get your husband here fast."

She shifted in her chair.

"Don't be alarmed. Jason is fine meanwhile. The results of the test will determine his prognosis. Dr. Ademola will take you to my conference room next door and you can speak with your husband in private. You can get hold of him right away, can't you?" Johnson stood.

"Of course. He's at a fund-raising event with the governor and the vice president," she said matter-of-factly.

Ademola didn't need to be told to escort Kathleen out.

"William, it's me." Kathleen's hand shook as she spoke into the telephone, her knuckles white from the grip.

"*Where are you? I tried to reach you at home a few minutes ago,*" a man's voice chimed through the telephone.

"I'm at Children's Hospital. Jason is downstairs. William, it's the same thing all over again. Everything that happened to Elizabeth is—"

"*Oh my God! I'll be right over, honey. How is he?*"

"Barely alive. They're having tests done on his eyes, I don't know why. I'm in the Chief of Staff's office."

"*Go to Jason's room and stay with him.*"

"Dr. Ademola, I'm glad you're back. We lost the preemie a few minutes ago. The boy in bed two has been moved to PICU," a nurse said, meeting him in front of the elevator door that clanged shut.

"Dr. Ademola, may I have a word with you?" One of the doctors who worked on Jason appeared. "What's going on? Three pediatric deaths in less than ten minutes. I understand you spoke with Dr. Johnson concerning the patient in bed two. And what do you need Dr. Fall for?" The physician was shaking. "And—"

"Is it true you guys lost three babies already? The price of baby spare-parts must be high."

Ademola turned around, his eyes darkened as he stared at the man a few feet behind him. "Dr. Fall, if your professional sense is as bad as your jokes you should be out peddling oranges at intersections."

"Point taken! Is the patient ready? It takes five minutes to hook up the machine. I'll have the report in sixty minutes."

"Dr. Johnson wants the results in his office. I'll be in E.R. or elsewhere in the building. Just page me."

⤫

Kathleen sat on the edge of Jason's bed, her son's hand in her grip. "Be strong, my pumpkin. Mommy loves you." Jason's body had tubes and wires that connected his legs, arms, and the upper part of his body to all kinds of machines. Kathleen stared at her helpless baby, watching his chest. The boy was barely alive.

Suddenly, something stirred at the doorway, scratchy and urgent. All the machines in the room seemed to stop and listen. The sound came again. And again, three times in all. The machines gave up listening and resumed their humming and clicking.

Jason's body underwent a subtle change. He stirred ever so slightly, his eyelids opened and the eyes moved sideways, slowly at first, and then faster, as if in pursuit of something. Then they stopped moving, blinked, stared, then focused on the ceiling. There was fright in them.

Kathleen looked up and panicked when she failed to see what had her son's attention. Jason's eyes kept opening and closing, staring into space, looking away, back to the ceiling, away again, as though searching for something. He seemed to be listening. And communicating. And just before he shut his eyes and became still, three luminous forms bobbed to the ceiling, their shadows dancing on the walls.

22

LAGOS

September, 1995:

By the time the sun blazed to the center of the sky Sakara had smoked a joint and gulped down a full glass of Johnnie Walker Black scotch in a futile attempt to deaden the pounding in his head. The pain in his left shoulder throbbed. The taste of burning flesh in his mouth, the smell of locust, the chanting, and Eniola's horrific look hunted him. And he knew what he had to do. The fourth drum was filled to the brim—

As he waited for Achibong in his office at DMI, the door to Sakara's soul flung open, recapturing the events of the last ten hours: after burying the charred bodies of his father and Ademola's mother, he left Arinota, and stopped midway to Lagos. He had gone to the interrogation bungalow located in the middle of the forest. He took his time deciding which of the several torture contraptions he would use. He finally decided on the simplest one. He rolled three empty oil drums outside the building and spent the next hour digging a hole deep enough to bury the drums with their brims a foot below ground level. He pulled out a wheelbarrow from the warehouse and piled bags of cement on it. He wheeled the barrow to the drums, dumped the cement on the ground, and went back for more bags. He filled each drum with cement and water.

He was panting and covered with cement dust by the time he felt satisfied with the level and texture of the mixture. He went inside the bungalow, showered, dressed in one of the clean army uniforms stacked in the closet, locked the gate, and drove off.

As he approached Ikoyi a lone voice coming from the depth of the earth infiltrated his mind, sorrowful with angry words. He shut his eyes as the voice ululated:

Segun Sakara, the kingmaker,
  One that makes the king makes the rule.
The rule of the law breaker.
  The law that does not obey the wishes of the gods.
The law that snatches the suckling young
  From his mother's breast.
The law that allows the lawmaker to drink
  The blood of the unborn.
The law that turns people into flesh-eating weeds.
  The law of the land of the walking dead.
Segun Sakara, husband of a woman whose seed
  Could not be fecundated.
The maker of the king of doom.
  Son of one who is no more.
Your father awaits your arrival
  In the land of silence!

The lamentation got louder as he screeched to a stop at the foot of the circular driveway. And when he reached the bedroom and saw Eniola sleeping peacefully in their bed the pounding in his head grew unbearable. "Get up! I want you and the twins to come to Arinota with me right away."

Eniola yawned herself awake. "What's the matter, Segun?" she asked, becoming alert.

The sound of her voice further infuriated him. "Do as I say and stop asking me stupid questions."

"But the kids have school to—"

"Now!" His voice rattled the walls.

Eniola jumped out of bed and dashed to the bathroom. As she got ready to get in the shower, he barrelled into the bathroom and grabbed her shoulder, digging his nails into her flesh. She cringed. "You're hurting me, Segun. Will you tell me what's going on, please?"

"Put on your clothes and meet me downstairs right away." He let go, stared contemptuously at her nakedness, and then stormed out.

Minutes later, Eniola and the nine-year-old twins came into the parlor to join Sakara, whose heart began to grind nastily. He felt sick with hatred upon seeing them.

It was early morning when they exited Lagos and the sun was already blazing down on the city, promising to deliver yet another sizzling day. The streets were lined with market women. Pedestrians weaved in and out of the slow-moving vehicles whose drivers filled the air with the stridency of their horns. The furrows of frustration on the faces of the people were masked by laughter as they went about negotiating, cajoling, intimidating, frustrating, bamboozling, flattering, and doing all the other things that helped to make their lives a little less painful. They whispered the rumors of *coups* and counter *coups*, fearful of the possibility of their secret conversation being heard by the ubiquitous enforcers in olive-green uniforms.

By the time Sakara drove through the gate of the brown bungalow hidden within an eight-foot-high brick wall, the sun had made good on its promise, blazing down with such ire the sky looked as if it were on fire, portending a black Friday. "Come with me." He got out of the car, hurried back to the gate and locked it with a padlock. He found Eniola and the kids still waiting in the car. "I said come with me!"

The menace in his voice was unmistakable.

"Where? What are we doing here?" Eniola looked as though she sensed something tragic was about to happen. She quickly locked the doors, an act which made Sakara even madder. He slammed his fist against the front passenger window. The girl, Taiwo, began to cry in the back seat. Seething with rage, he ran to the rear of the car, opened the trunk and came back with a crowbar and slammed it against the window, smashing it.

"What the hell is the matter with you?" Eniola screamed, scrambling to the driver's side. She yanked the door open. "Come with me," she shouted at her children.

"I'm scared, mommy. What's the matter with daddy?" Taiwo cried.

Sakara rounded the car to the driver's side and grabbed Eniola's wrist with such violence that she screamed, "You're going to break my hand. For God's sake, tell me what is the matter."

"You bloody whore! You lied to me. These bastards are not mine." He jabbed his index finger at the twins.

Eniola's eyes enlarged in proportion to her fright. "Of cour—" The rest of the word got sucked down her throat. She coughed, spitting a tooth to the ground. She covered her face with both hands, blood dripping through her fingers. "Segun, please, hear me out."

He pulled her hair, jerking her head backward, and was about to strike the side of her head when she groaned, "Hakabala made me do it!"

He froze.

"Hakabala made you do what?" His voice sounded like that of a masquerader.

Quickly, Eniola told him everything.

"You've spied on me and passed information to Hakabala all these years?" His rage reached a level unknown to him before. "That scumbag Achibong is as good as dead!"

"I didn't mean to hurt you. I've grown to love you—"

"Shut up!"

"It's the truth, Segun, please!"

"You are a common whore like Ademola's mother. And you must join her now."

"Please forgive—join her where?"

"In hell!" he spat. "And you must be there too."

"Why?" Eniola sounded as though she knew Sakara was going to kill her. "I am innocent. Hakabala threatened to kill me if I did not cooperate."

"Like you, Ademola's mother lied to her husband about her bastard son. Ola is the son of the thing I called father." His demonic laughter filled the air.

"Segun, you and I are the victims," she cried.

To his astonishment, he believed her. He hesitated before raising his hand up in the air, and was about to throw the crowbar away when the boy, Kehinde, rushed out of the car, smashing the door against Sakara's back. "Don't, daddy, please, don't hurt my mommy," he screamed.

Sakara spun around and the crowbar smashed against Kehinde's head, cracking it. The boy fell to the ground, writhing in pain, clutching his head.

"You bastard!" Eniola smashed her fist against the back of Sakara's neck, stunning him. The crowbar fell to the ground, and she grabbed it.

"Give it to me," Sakara said between clenched teeth.

Eniola shook the crowbar threateningly.

Sakara held his hand out to grab it and she whacked his left shoulder, sending an agonizing pain through his body. Stunned, he stepped back, reached a hand into his pocket, pulled out a revolver and fired. A crimson dot appeared in the middle of Eniola's forehead, and she crashed to the ground next to her dying son.

Taiwo did not resist when the man she called father yanked the door open, grabbed her, and carried her like a

311

rag doll to the drums. She did not scream or beg when her father ripped off her clothes and dumped her, head first, into the cold cement. Her body was submerged in the brownish-grey mixture that would take several days to harden into concrete. Putting Eniola's body into the drum turned out to be more difficult than he imagined. He had to fold her body into a V-shape. He spent an hour digging another hole and burying the fourth drum which he filled with the cement mixture for his next victim.

⟿

Sakara massaged his throbbing shoulder, not to deaden the pain, but to remind himself of how he was going to enjoy killing Achibong. Sitting behind the half-moon-shaped French hunting desk that once belonged to Dikko, he felt a blinding flash behind his eyes and the pounding in his head soared as he remained fixed on the rest of Dikko's furniture. He was no longer in control of his life. History was about to repeat itself and he had to deal with a personal vendetta that filled him with madness.

He got off the chair, poured himself a shot of scotch, and gulped it down in one swallow. The pounding in his head seemed to abate. He was about to light another joint when he heard a knock on the door. He shoved the joint into his pocket, returned to his seat. "Come in."

Achibong strode in and froze.

"What's the matter?" Sakara barked.

"Ple—plenty, sir." Achibong flashed a caricature of his normal smart salute and a tentative smile, stepped forward, opened his attache case, extracted some audio tapes, and handed them to Sakara who shook the tapes as though trying to estimate the seriousness of the content by its weight.

"What is this?"

"A bombshell, sir," Achibong said angrily.

A twist appeared at the corners of Sakara's mouth. He inserted the tape into a cassette player on his desk, pressed a button, and listened to Achibong's taped voice. He recognized the codes that identified the location as the head of state's official residence in Abuja. The recording had taken place late the previous night:

"*Lafia, ko?*" Hakabala's voice replaced Achibong's as the head of state greeted someone in Hausa.

"*Alhamdulillah, rankadede.*" Sakara recognized the voice as that of Maitama Kano, the effeminate political adviser to Hakabala who was rumored to have provided sexual services not only to Hakabala but also to two other leaders from the north dating back to the sixties.

A choleric voice shot out, "*Your Excellency, the trial of Ken Saro-Wiwa and the eight Ogonis should be used to silence southern opposition once and for all.*"

"Who's that?" Sakara asked Achibong.

"Umaru Barawo, sir. He's a very dangerous man. Just wait until you hear the advice he gives Hakabala."

"*That troublemaker and the eight others must be executed immediately after the verdict is made public tonight.*" Barawo's voice sounded important.

"*But what if they are not found guilty?*" Kano's voice asked.

"*The trial is just for show.*" Sakara recognized the third person's laugh as that of Uba Bauchi.

On the tape, Hakabala cleared his throat. "*There are two civilian judges on the panel. I know for sure that one of them will find the accused guilty. Brigadier Sakara is the one that I'm not sure of. His behav—*"

"*Sakara must go!*" Barawo's voice said. "*And I don't mean retired either. This trial should be his last assignment. The director of DMI must be from the north as it was meant to be. Once Sakara is accused of attempting a coup against the government, and while the trial is under way, that Efik assistant of his should be transferred elsewhere.*"

"*Why transfer him? Both of them should be charged and found guilty,*" Bauchi's voice offered.

"*Good idea,*" Hakabala agreed on the tape.

"*We must be careful how we handle the PR. The Yorubas will rally behind Sakara,*" Kano said weakly.

"*Nonsense! They will do no such thing. I have the perfect solution, General. You will invite all the traditional rulers to meet with you, promise them contracts, and instruct them to tell their people that Sakara and whoever else we decide to implicate are guilty as charged.*"

There was a pause on the tape. "*I don't believe they will all agree,*" Kano said.

"*Why not? Are we not speaking about the same Obas that sold their people into slavery not too long ago? Believe me, I know these people, they will,*" Barawo spat.

"*You're right about that, my friend,*" Bauchi's voice sounded elated. "*Your Excellency, have you seen the Yorubas demonstrating on the streets since you locked up the winner of the presidential election? Of course not, my friend is right about them. While we have the power, we must strike hard and fast. Kill many birds with one stone by implicating every Yoruba military officer above the rank of lieutenant colonel in the coup plot. In addition, the former head of state and the sympathizing traitors from the north must be equally accused and silenced forever. I've always believed that if you cut off the head of a snake the body will die faster.*"

"*But how do I explain the executions to the rest of the world?*" Hakabala's voice asked.

"*As long as you control the production of crude oil and allow direct access to multinational western oil companies their leaders will turn deaf ears to the clamoring,*" Barawo advised. "*Soon, there will be elections in England and the United States. You must find a way to contribute millions of pounds and dollars to all the political parties in the two countries. White people appreciate the language of money better than anything else. Once the British prime minister and the president of the United States pay lip service to the do-*"

gooders *in their countries, the rest of the world will develop laryngitis over the issue."*

"*What about the Ibos?"* Hakabala asked.

"*What about them? I do not believe the Ibos will raise a hand to help the Yorubas. Not after they've been made to believe that Awolowo betrayed them during the civil war. Our best strategy is to divide, destroy, and rule."* Barawo burst into laughter, scratchy on the tape.

It took much of Sakara's strength not to stop the machine and rip the tape to pieces. He felt chilled by the enormity of the scheme. He shut his eyes, hoping to deaden the pain that pounded his temples.

Achibong cleared his throat.

Sakara opened his eyes and his voice sounded faraway when he asked, "Now what?"

"There's something else I need to share with you before we decide what to do, sir."

"There's more?" Sakara looked aghast.

"Yes! Chiedu, a friend of your wife, died last night, sir."

Sakara's face contorted with rage and he was about to yell at Achibong when his subordinate raised an open palm in the air for indulgence. "The cause of death was a slow processing disease, sir. Rumor had it that she was HIV positive."

"And?" Sakara snapped.

"She was Hakabala's bedmate."

"What?"

"The general's got AIDS, or at the very least, he's HIV positive, sir."

"You just bought yourself some breathing space," Sakara thought. "Your death will be soon enough."

꘎

315

23

NEW YORK

September, 1995:

D r. Fall had just completed the first round of the retinal image test when Ademola entered the room. With the retinal scanner, Fall had sent a beam of low-intensity near-infrared light through Jason's pupils, illuminating the retina. The blood vessels did not respond to light as expected; they should have absorbed more light than the surrounding tissue. Fall couldn't understand why. The scanner must be defective, he concluded. "Dr. Ademola, I'm going to be here longer than I thought. I'd appreciate it if I could be left alone. This machine has never failed before. So, I've decided to try another one. Give me another forty minutes or so."

"Is it okay for the patient's parents to come and spend just a couple of minutes with him?"

"As long as they do it while I set up the machine."

"I'll get a nurse to bring them right away."

⏤

Johnson was at his desk when Ademola entered. "Sit down," he said in Yoruba.

Ademola stood transfixed. In the seven years since he had known the old physician he had never seen him look older and more distant. Johnson seemed cloaked in the vestment of a sojourner who had just received a missive from the gods. He seemed troubled. "One changes the course of destiny with one's hands. I'm about to make the most important decision yet. My life is no longer in the hands of the gods," he said cryptically.

Ademola stared at his mentor.

Johnson's essence radiated a waning hope. He got up, and with subdued humility asked Ademola, "Have you ever pondered about life?"

"Yes." Ademola wondered why the man seemed troubled.

"I wish to share my deep thoughts with you, son." Johnson cleared his throat and his expression became solemn. "From the beginning of time we have always known God exists. But we worship other deities. In our desire to be like God, who created all living things, we create our own gods to ease our simple, imperfect minds whenever the chores of living prove difficult. Our inordinate yearning to be like the Creator underscores our imperfection. It is this dichotomy that fuels human schizophrenia which in turn fuels our inner torments. Do I sound like a plebeian village philosopher?" He studied Ademola.

"No, but I fail to see how this connects to Jason."

"Not directly, but ultimately it does. Fifty years ago, after I graduated at the top of my class from Johns Hopkins Medical School, all sort of hell broke loose. It was bad enough being the only Negro there, but being better than all my classmates was another thing. It was even worse during the three years I spent in the army. Being the best was not good enough on account of the color of my skin. At the end of my third year I became so disillusioned and frustrated that I knew I had to get away for awhile. That's how I ended up in Africa, in search of a higher meaning to my existence. Like you, I am an *Abiku*. My mother had three children that died before the age of two. I was the last, and I believe she sacrificed her life for mine." He sighed, eye shut, as though he needed to rid himself of an inner torment.

Ademola felt a deeper connection to his mentor.

"My mother died right after I was born, and my father believed that I was the cause of her death. He never forgave me. He never loved me. Smart as I was, I didn't know who I was until I arrived at Abeokuta."

"Why there of all places?"

"Good question, son. I've asked myself the same thing over the years, but the answer has eluded me. However, I believe there's a mysterious power within the rocks of Olumo, which loom over the township, where people worship anything that presents itself in a cryptic, non-empirical form. As a young man with Western sensibilities, I castigated the people and their beliefs as simple-minded, atheistic, and superstitious. I quickly discovered how wrong I was after meeting the blind diviner who allowed me to experience the Yoruba belief in spiritualism. As an acolyte, I was allowed to enter the forbidden cave atop the hills, and son, that was one thing I would not exchange for all the riches in the world. I paid the price with my left eye—but it was worth it." He sat down to face Ademola. "Seven of us, including your father, spent twenty-one years under the tutelage of the old master. I learned not only to appreciate the fact that my presence in this world is not an accident but that I was sent here for a specific purpose. I felt connected to a people, a culture and belief that existed on a spiritual level. I became challenged, and ultimately, filled with a sense of direction. Knowing who I was filled me with self-pride. And over the years, I have come to believe that therein lies the difference between Africans and black folks here in America, or shall I say African-Americans. This latest nomenclature is but another stage in the ongoing social metamorphosis that our people are going through. We have gone from slaves, to niggers, negroes, blacks, Afro-Americans, *Akatas*, and now, African-Americans. The rest of the world must be weary of us by now. But when the butterfly finally emerges, it will bring forth a mind-numbing surprise."

"What do you mean?" Ademola asked.

"Of all the people in the world, the black folks in the Americas are quite different from the rest of mankind." He became silent for a while. His countenance grew somber. When he spoke, his voice reverberated with divine strength. "No other people have been so challenged and re-created as us. After all, it was the strongest among the African slaves who survived the terrifying journey across the ocean. And the strongest among those that arrived here survived the brutal near-genocidal attacks by their owners, who were also the strongest and smartest among their people. And when the two became one through cross-breeding, the inevitable result was a progeny stronger and smarter than the seeds. Yes, man re-created what God must've intended when He made the Africans in the Americas. The rest of the world needs to hurry up and see what happens when the butterfly emerges. And this is where Jason connects. That little boy's presence here, your being chased out of Nigeria, getting shot in Brooklyn, meeting and marrying Simone, who was the instrument of our association—all these things are not mere happenstance or coincidence, my son. And that's why we must be careful where we go from here. They are all parts of a mosaic."

An inexplicable uneasiness enveloped Ademola. He searched his mentor's eye for meaning but none came.

Johnson's face was expressionless.

Just then, Dr. Fall hurried through the door and glared at

Ademola. "I have the results of the test." His chest heaved as though he was having difficulty breathing. "What the hell is going on?"

"Sit down, Dr. Fall," Johnson said calmly.

"Not before I show you what I found. Come down to the lab and see." He turned around and exited the room.

A s soon as Fall got to the ophthalmology laboratory he set up his apparatus. Ademola and Johnson came in and took their seats. Without wasting any time Fall turned off the lights. His neck showed thick and tense. "I want you to pay attention to the screen." He stepped backwards to press the switch on the lower side of the white screen. A computer-generated image appeared. "This is a normal human *fovea centralis*, the center of the retina. It gives the sharpest vision. The eye is like a camera and the retina acts as a living photographic film. When—"

"Dr. Fall, this is all pretty basic. What's your point?" Ademola demanded.

"You dragged me out of bed, Dr. Ademola. The least I expect from you is to let me explain my findings my way."

"We don't have the time to be re-educated on the mechanics of the human eye. Tell us what you found out."

"I don't appreciate your interruptions, Dr. Ademola. As I was saying—"

The door swung open and hurried footsteps echoed in the dark. "You can't go in there, sir," a female voice said.

"The hell I can't—"

"What's going on here?" Fall switched on the light.

Johnson remained seated, resembling a king expecting a visitation from his subjects. He pointed to a couple of chairs nearby. "Have a seat, Mr. McFlarthey. You too, Mrs. McFlarthey." He waved the beleaguered nurse away.

Sixty-one-year-old William McFlarthey remained on his feet, towering over Johnson. At six feet five inches tall, his broad shoulders and muscular arms made him look like a football player. His face was angular, his neck thick. McFlarthey's greying blond hair was brushed back. He had a recently-acquired tan that made him look even more handsome in old age than during his younger years. His raw energy seemed tempered by good living. William McFlarthey was one of the most powerful men in the world, a man not used to being told what to do.

"Dr. Fall, here are Jason's father and mother. Please, have a seat, Mr. McFlarthey," said Johnson simply.

"The McFlarthey media empire?" Fall asked in awe.

Kathleen nodded. She sat down and gently tugged at her husband's sleeve. He did likewise, letting her ease him down though with pronounced reluctance.

Fall turned off the light and approached the screen. "Compare the human eye to a camera wherein the retina is the film; everything it sees, it should be able to record. The eye should perform just like that, but it doesn't." He pressed a button at the bottom of the screen. A multitude of dots and striations appeared. "This picture was the first image observed on Jason's retina an hour ago." He pressed the button again. The picture disappeared and was replaced by another that looked like the one before. Again, he pressed the button and the picture disappeared and then reappeared. All the previous pictures of dots and striations appeared on the screen in squared boxes side by side. Fall started to perspire as he crossed over to the left side of the screen and pointed to the top layer of the first box. "This was Jason's ganglion cell layer at twelve-fifty this morning when the first picture of his retinal image was taken. Don't bother to count the number of dots here. Believe me, there's a difference. The last box, the picture of the same spot on his retina, taken an hour after the first shot, has eighteen more dots than the first. The same difference is evidenced in the dense-ly-packed bipolar which is the layer directly below the gan-glion cells. Now, it's on the vertically arranged photorecep-tor that the most significant aberration is observed. Pay close attention to this one." He touched a single line among the cluster. "With the help of magnified optography, I decoded the hidden meaning of this line. I never believed the notion that the eyes could contain the portrait—"

"I believe we've heard enough, Dr. Fall." Johnson's voice thundered as he snapped the light switch. Everybody's atten-tion turned to his empty chair. They all looked surprised by the swiftness of his movement and stared at him standing by the door. "Thank you, Dr. Fall. Dr. Ademola, make sure the McFlartheys visit Jason. Then, bring them to my office. We have lots of work to do before sunrise."

The only one in the room who as much as blinked was Ademola. The others stared at where Johnson stood seconds before he exited the room.

"Mr. and Mrs. McFlarthey, if you would follow me I'll escort you to the PICU." Ademola's voice snatched them back to consciousness and they followed him, leaving Fall glued to the spot in a zombie-like state.

Jason lay still. Alone in the room, his breathing was forced. The ceiling lights above his bed dimmed. Three luminous forms hovered around the fluorescent lamps. They stopped moving and peered down. Enveloped in a gray halo were newborn babies ranging from a few hours old to two days old. The oldest weighed eleven pounds and she was sucking her right thumb. Her almond-shaped eyes were old. Her supple skin was wrinkled, just like all newborn babies.

Farthest from the girl was a black child. He was restless. At two hours old, his curly jet-black hair made him look older and solemn. His eyes were big, black, and piercing.

Floating between the two was the third baby, a six-hundred-gram day-old brown neonate. His body was a network of wrinkles. He looked prunish, deathly. He twisted involuntarily, eyes shut as the lips parted to expose a dark crimson tongue. "*Is he still alive?*"

"*Of course he is,*" snapped the black baby.

"*We wait!*" the Asian baby said with finality.

"I love you, pumpkin," Kathleen whispered into her son's ear. "So does dad and your baby brother inside me." She felt a kick from within. "Maybe I should've said sister." She smiled nervously, staring at the death mask that was Jason's face. "Mother of Jesus! Why? It's the same thing all over." Her voice sounded hollow as tears snaked down her cheeks. "William, I think Jason is—"

McFlarthey dashed to the side of the bed. His strong legs began to shake. "Is he still alive?" He wiped tears off his face.

Kathleen nodded yes.

"I can't bear another death in the family. What on earth is going on?" His voice was barely audible. "Please, God, don't take my Jason away," he prayed.

McFlarthey had every reason to be worried and sad. Two years after graduating from Harvard he had inherited the richest and most powerful media conglomerate in the world. Soon after, he married the beautiful daughter of an Irish industrialist and they had a son that was the spitting image of his father. McFlarthey was not only rich and powerful, he was happy. Then one day, disaster struck. His wife and son were killed in a plane crash while on a visit to Ireland. He naturally mourned the death, but being a realist, he knew he had to get married again. There was just too much family history and heritage to be left to strangers. He needed to have a son to be groomed to follow in his foot-steps. A year after the death of his wife and son, he met Kathleen, a twenty-eight-year-old with blue eyes and blond hair of Irish descent, who had just earned her doctorate degree in Anthropology from Columbia University. The courtship was brief. They married three months later, and nine months after their wedding their daughter, Elizabeth, was born. Fifteen-month-old Elizabeth was brought to Children's Hospital where she died a few hours later. The cause of death was Sudden Infant Death Syndrome. Now it looked as though tragedy was about to strike again.

McFlarthey watched Jason's chest and started to pray. Suddenly there was a change in the sound of the EKG monitor. Everything slipped into fast-forward. The dot on the monitor sped up leaving in its trail a luminous line as it disappeared on the right side of the screen only to reappear with the same flattened line on the left side.

"Dear God, he's fibrillating!" Kathleen screamed.

A nurse rushed in and pressed a button on the wall. The p.a. system came alive: Code Blue, PICU 2; Code...

Kathleen stood frozen beside the bed, her right hand covering her mouth, the left tight against the lower part of her bulging stomach.

McFlarthey watched Ademola and several nurses hover over Jason as they took turns performing all types of life-saving activities on his son.

Johnson and Ademola looked like father and son in the middle of a family discussion. There was love and wisdom in the voice of the older man. "I wish I could let you go to Nigeria in my place," Johnson said.

"I wouldn't know where to go."

"I've already made the arrangements. Dr. Awoyinka, who

was also one of the seven acolytes that our master trained will meet me at Lagos airport and—" He was interrupted by a knock at the door. "Please come in," he said.

McFlarthey and his wife strode in and took their seats facing Johnson. "I need answers fast. What on earth is going on?" McFlarthey demanded.

"Everything in due course."

"But, Doctor—"

"Please!" Johnson's hypnotic stare chilled McFlarthey. "You have valid passports, I assume. We'll leave for Nigeria tomorrow evening—yes, Mrs. McFlarthey?"

"Don't you think you're assuming a little too much? You're making arrangements for us to go to Africa while our son is dying, not to mention my pregnancy." Kathleen ruffled up like a bantam hen.

Johnson's eye narrowed but his voice remained soft. "Mrs. McFlarthey, I assure you, I'm not assuming anything. However, there is no technology in this hospital capable of saving your son. Correct me if I'm wrong; you had a daughter who died under similar circumstance, didn't you?"

"Yes, from SIDS."

"SIDS, Crib Death. Elizabeth, Jason, and the baby inside you are one and the same."

"What do you mean?"

"They're *Abikus*."

"Oh, my God! Not th—the Yoruba *Abiku*?" Kathleen's face looked painted with chalk.

"What the hell is *Arbeecoo*?" McFlarthey snapped.

Kathleen clutched her husband's arm. "It makes sense, William. I know about the—they are children born to die and born again only to die again. But I thought it happens only among the Yorubas?"

Johnson shrugged, eye locked onto McFlarthey's. "It does. But then, maybe it doesn't. The issue here is that Jason is an *Abiku*. And a special one at that."

McFlarthey stirred like a chained Great Dane. "What makes you think Jason is an *Abiku*?" Kathleen asked, struggling, disbelief in her voice.

"In due course, Mrs. McFlarthey. Meanwhile, you and your husband need to fully appreciate the importance and urgency of the matter. If you don't get to Nigeria and carry out the necessary rituals, Jason's chances of survival are nil and you'll face a childless future."

"I beg your pardon? But how can we take Jason to Africa in his present condition?" McFlarthey asked.

"You can, with me."

"You? We need an entire staff. Didn't you see how my son is connected to all those machines?"

"I am not only one of the best doctors here, I am also a diviner, having spent twenty-one years in Nigeria to become one."

McFlarthey swung himself around as if to attack. "That's it. I've heard enough of this poppycock. I can't believe we're sitting here listening to—"

"William, please, the mythology of *Abiku* exists among the Yorubas of Nigeria. I should know. I spent years with the people while I was working on my doctoral dissertation," Kathleen pleaded.

"I need to use your phone," McFlarthey snapped.

Johnson nodded and McFlarthey grabbed the receiver, dialed and waited. "Give me Richard Stormier in the Research department." His thick eyebrows rose. "Yes, Richard, this is McFlarthey. I need you to do a full background check on a Dr. William Doss Johnson and Dr. O-l-a-w-o-l-e A-d-e-m-o-l-a... Children's Hospital... Yes, do that... Also find out what the heck is the mythology of—" He turned to his wife and whispered, "How do you spell that word again?"

Johnson wrote A-B-I-K-U and Y-O-R-U-B-A on a piece of paper and handed it to McFlarthey, who relayed the information to his employee. "Yes, Richard, everything. Bring it to the hospital... Good idea." He hung up and his blank expression changed, eyes narrowed and lips pressed against each other. He stared past Ademola at Johnson, his countenance dark. "I need to know what this is all about."

"From what I know about the mythology of *Abiku*, the phenomenon occurs only among the Yorubas of West Africa, doesn't it?" Kathleen asked.

"Generally speaking, yes," Johnson said, not looking away from McFlarthey.

"Then why do you think Jason's case is what you claim it to be?" McFlarthey demanded gruffly.

"Here we are, William and I, we're both Caucasian. There's not a drop of African blood in us," Kathleen added.

Johnson sat back and smiled. "How far back in your genealogy did you check to make such a statement?"

Her face was bewildered. "Both my father and grandfather have blue eyes and blond hair. So do William's."

"Perhaps we should look at it from a different perspective." Johnson got on his feet and went to lock the door. "This country is presently the center of gravity. Millions of people from all over the world are flocking here. They all gravitate here to partake of the promise of a better life. What in the world makes you believe that only human beings of this world are attracted here? Is it just a coincidence that there have been more UFO sightings in America than anywhere else?"

Kathleen seemed about to break into hysterical laughter. "UFOs landing in America in search of a better life? Are you out of your mind?"

Johnson walked back and forth. All three in the room watched him. "I didn't say that. Listen. Every couple of thousand years, the center of gravity shifts. It was Europe. Before that, it was Africa. Now it's North America. Soon it's going to shift to another continent. That's an absolute certainty. Where next, nobody knows. What you call UFOs are not just the abstract Unidentified Flying Objects beaming down in their flying machines. The real UFOs are the Jasons and Ademolas of this world. The Yorubas believe that there's another world out there inhabited by intelligent and beautiful children. These children are called *Abikus*."

Ademola cleared his throat.

Johnson smiled. "Here in the West we call the phenomenon Sudden Infant Death Syndrome, in total ignorance. The Yorubas know about these children. They know the symptomatology and the treatment. They can identify them. And they know how to stop them from going back home. But most importantly, they respect them enough to worship them. The *Abikus*, like twins, are revered by the Yorubas. Do you think it's only coincidental that one out of every four twin births in the world are among the Yorubas?"

"Is that a fact?" McFlarthey looked astonished.

"Absolutely. The fact that the Yorubas worship the *Abikus* and twins does not make the phenomena exclusively theirs. The Yorubas only have a better handle on them. Their worship of the shrines of twins is not unlike the Cancer Centers in the United States. The reason cancer patients are brought here from all over the world is because the phenomenon is better understood and better treated here than elsewhere."

Kathleen leaned forward and frowned. "Dr. Johnson, that's comparing modern technology with native mythology. Isn't that like comparing apples and oranges?"

With majestic severity, Johnson said, "Is it? Mrs. McFlarthey, modern technology and native mythology have one thing in common. Belief! Without it, there is neither mythology nor technology."

The telephone shrilled. Ademola answered it and handed the receiver to McFlarthey.

"Yes, Richard?" His voice became more authoritative.

"Bring it here right away... No, do it yourself... In the office of the Chief of Staff." He hung up and smiled. "Your achievements are impressive, Dr. Johnson. Impressive indeed. But I'm not sold yet."

"I'm not trying to sell you anything, Mr. McFlarthey. The decision to take Jason to Nigeria is not yours to make." Johnson leaned forward in his chair. His eye bored into McFlarthey's. "That decision was made before Jason came into this world. Call it his life script, if you will."

"What the devil is that supposed to mean?" McFlarthey asked. "Who is this one-eyed black man?" he pondered as his discomfort soared. He felt the intensity of Johnson's numinous gaze, whose soul seemed to regard McFlarthey with serenity.

Johnson cleared his throat. "We need to proceed right away. Time is speeding off from us." He got up and took a cylindrical abstract terracotta object out of a concealed safe in the wall behind his desk. He closed the door of the safe and covered it with a framed oil painting. He gently placed the six-and-a-half-inch tall figure on the desk, stroking the sacred *Aroye Pot*: an elaborately decorated spiritual vessel that displayed a medium-relief image of a horned human head with its tongue protruding from a gaping mouth. Sixteen rosette centers with mica mirrors encircled the vessel.

"What is that?" McFlarthey asked.

Johnson turned the vessel so its human head faced the McFlartheys. The bulging left eye was the darkest shade of brown which made it look black and the right was deep yellow. Kathleen gasped and looked away, twisting the diamonds on her finger. She whispered, "Please put that thing away," not meeting the black-and-yellow stare of the terracotta head.

"You need not be afraid of it," Johnson said reassuringly.

"Is this some kind of a game?" Kathleen asked.

"This is not a game! The enormity of it is incomprehensible outside the *Abiku* world. The death of Elizabeth, the possibility of Jason's death, and that of the baby you carry, these are not accidents. There are opposing forces at work. Now listen. What I'm about to tell you is of enormous importance!"

McFlarthey looked into Johnson's hypnotic face.

"Mrs. McFlarthey, I want you to touch the eyes, one at a time. Go on, touch them."

Kathleen looked paralyzed by fear. Her chest heaved, betraying the speed at which her heart was racing. She hesitated, looking confused as though unable to identify the source of her fear. With a trembling right hand she touched the brown eye, then the yellow. She jerked her hand back and stared at Johnson.

He returned her gaze. "You won't need anything on your trip but these. They are not eyes. The brown one is kolanut, and the yellow is kaolin. Over a thousand years ago they were used as sacrificial offerings to ward off evil spirits. They have acquired great power over the millennium." Then he grew silent, floating off into a private reverie, staring at the fetish on his desk. He nodded abruptly to Ademola. "Take the kolanut and the kaolin with your left hand and place them together on your right palm."

Ademola did.

Kathleen opened her mouth to say something, but before any sound emerged from her trembling lips, the room darkened. The darkness turned licorice-colored, accompanied by a gentle wind which blew in through the window. The sound of a funeral procession filled the room, supplanting the noise of New York traffic and pedestrians.

McFlarthey shivered in the dark.

Ademola's right hand became luminous, the kaolin and kolanut in the middle of his palm began to throb evenly as if breathing. The luminosity concentrated on the kaolin, glowing and pulsating. Then the wind stopped and the light came back. Ademola closed his hand into a fist, covering the fetishes, his whole presence becoming even more powerful and protective.

"Dr. Ademola will accompany you and your wife to Jason's room," Johnson said as though oblivious of what had just taken place. "The power at your disposal must be used with the highest degree of prudence. You must realize and appreciate the first rule. You're a temporary custodian of the power that joins the two distinct yet inseparable realms of the Yoruba Cosmos, *Orun* and *Aiye*. Humans, not of the *Abiku* world, should not—I repeat—SHOULD NOT be allowed to come into contact with the kolanut and kaolin either separately or together. The consequence is death. The power increases with time."

"What do I have to do?" Ademola eyed the objects in his palm with trepidation.

"First, go downstairs to Jason's room and do the following: send everybody except the McFlartheys out of the room—" He stopped to look at the door as though expecting someone to barge in. He smiled faintly. "When it's safe, place the kolanut on the center of Jason's forehead. Keep it there for not more than thirty seconds. Replace it with the kaolin for sixty seconds. Then put them together for safekeeping. Afterwards you can all go home, catch some sleep and the McFlartheys can prepare to depart with me in the evening. Dr. Ademola will procure the required Nigerian visas. Give him your passports. Good luck."

With that Johnson bid them goodbye.

Before McFlarthey exited the office, he looked over his shoulder as Johnson's numinous voice echoed: "*Our destinies are at stake. We must be careful, my friend. Goodbye.*"

Tension weighed down in the room, compressing itself into the soul of every one present. Ademola felt his head swell as though sensing the presence of something inhuman. The faraway voice of a child under water echoed in his ears. He looked up to the ceiling but was unable to see anything.

Jason stirred, his eyelids fluttered and opened. Kathleen moved closer to the bed and touched his forehead with her soft hand. There were tears in her eyes as she looked at her son's face. She smiled and sat on the edge of the bed, holding his hand. She seemed anxious but hopeful. McFlarthey stood at the foot of the bed.

Ademola took two steps toward the bed. He reached into his trouser pocket and his cupped hand emerged with the kolanut and kaolin. A cool mysterious breeze blew across the room. His hand became luminous. The lights on the ceiling dimmed. The room filled with the fragrance of jasmine. He shifted his stance ever so slightly and opened his hands, and there was the pulsating sound of breathing. Movement. Wind. Colors. The room became flooded with a kaleidoscope of light that emanated from Ademola's cupped hand. The noise of an explosion competed with the sighing of the wind as Ademola lifted his hand, his breath now labored. With his left hand he took the kolanut from his glowing right hand. Gently, he placed it in the middle of Jason's forehead. It lit up. The luminosity spread until the whole of Jason's head shone. Ademola stood still, his left hand a few inches above Jason's head. Then he turned around and looked at the watch strapped to his right wrist. "Twenty, twenty-one, twenty-two, twenty-three," he counted, simulating the ticking of a clock, "twenty-nine, thirty." As his fingers touched the kolanut, the breathing sound stopped. The kolanut became dark again. He picked it up, placed it in his right palm. Then he picked up the kaolin and placed it between Jason's eyes. The boy's face beaded with sweat. The wind heaved and an explosion shook the room as the kaolin disappeared into his forehead. There were stars in the room, millions of glittering stars swirling all over. And there was the smell of burning sulphur.

"What the hell is that?" Fall snapped as he barrelled into the room, lunging toward Ademola.

"Get out!" Ademola said between clenched teeth. His left arm, from his shoulder to his fingers, in a slanted V-shape over Jason's body was illuminated by the stars. Power leaped out of the arm. In a flash the stars converged on his arm. All the energy in the room coalesced on the tips of his index finger and thumb. He lowered the arm. As the fingers touched Jason's sweat-beaded forehead, the kaolin reappeared. It had been there exactly sixty seconds. He picked it up.

"You son-of-a—Let me see that!" Menace darkened Fall's eyes.

Kathleen whispered, "Please, do what Dr. Ademola says!"

Fall whirled to look at her. "I intend to find out what's going on here." He started toward Jason.

"You take one more step and one of us will be carried out dead." Kathleen's face grew sharper, a mother animal guarding her helpless cub.

Ademola felt something brush against his outstretched arm. The kaolin flew off his fingers and smashed into Fall's chest, hurling him backward with deadly force.

"Oh, my God!" Kathleen screamed as Fall's body crashed against the wall. He slumped to the floor, eyes glazed, blood snaking out of his nostrils, filling his parted lips and dripping to his chin. He gasped. His body jerked, eyes staring into space, and pupils constricted.

Kathleen rushed to him, kneeling to grasp his hand. "Oh, my God, do something, please," she whispered as Ademola pressed two fingers against Fall's neck.

"Is he dead?" Kathleen asked, stricken with fear.

24

Ademola quietly entered the living room of his apartment on the upper east side, his doctor's bag hanging loosely in his left hand. He set it on the floor beside the door and waited to accustom himself to the darkness before entering the bedroom. He stepped toward the bed on which Simone lay on her side, her black hair merging with the creases on the pillow. She stirred. He tiptoed around the end of the bed, bent over and planted a kiss on her forehead and then sat on the edge of the bed. He closed his eyes, face rigid in concentration, and felt the door to his spirit swung open, enabling him to glean parts of the enigma inside; the power of the fetishes he had received from Johnson. He reached into his pocket and held the kolanut and kaolin in his palm. He rubbed them together.

Suddenly, the dream he had been having the past couple of nights wafted through his mind, the images magnified: He had dreamt that the boy standing on the empty oil drum, face raised to the sky in supplication, begging the gods to bring down the sky to break the necks of all his enemies, was now a giant. But instead of allowing the sky to fall, the giant held it with his strong arms, waiting for something to happen before letting go. The dream had repeated itself several times: same theme, different variations.

He opened his eyes to shut out the disturbing image.

The clock-radio on the nightstand played soft romantic rhythm-and-blues music. The red dial of the clock glowed in the dark like an ember. Simone turned around and sleepily pressed the snooze button. She yawned as she opened her eyes, and a smile appeared on her face. "Hi, honey, is it morning already?" She scooted closer to him, held his hand, and guided it to her lips. She kissed the palm, and took a deep breath. "You look bushed, honey."

"And you look beautiful."

"Guess what?"

"What?" he asked, his voice husky.

"Your nearness warms my essence always. Come closer. There's a fire burning under the sheet. Why don't you slide next to me and put it out?" She pushed the sheet off.

Ademola swallowed hard. "You're the most beautiful woman in the world," he said hungrily in Yoruba, then translated it as he slipped off his clothes.

"And the happiest, honey." She hugged him. "I love it when you're this close to me. I was dreaming about you, sweet dream," she whispered in Bahian language, furthering the hardening of his anticipation.

"That makes me feel so special, my darling." He touched her and she groaned. And again. "I love you, baby."

"I love you too, forever." She also touched him and they groaned in unison. Her touch was soft, and his was strong, and getting harder.

Finally, Simone gasped, "You're so good, honey."

"So are you, baby," he replied between breaths.

"I wish we could do this more often."

"Me too. You give me such satisfaction."

"So do you. But I want more, sweetheart." She got on her elbow and stared into his eyes.

"I have an idea." He smiled. "Let's go away for the weekend, Florida, Puerto Rico, you name it."

She smiled back and shook her head no.

"Why not? I'm not on call this weekend."

"You forgot? We're going to perform the initiation ceremony tonight. Pappy is handing over—"

"Don't count on Pappy being there."

"Why not?" She searched his eyes.

"He's leaving for Nigeria this afternoon."

"Are you kidding me?" She sat up.

"No, sweetheart, there's a boy that needs to be taken to Nigeria for treatment." Ademola became serious. He told her everything that had happened at the hospital. When he finished, he looked at her and quickly added, "It's not as bad as it sounds."

She pulled her legs up and rested her chin on her knees. "What's so special about the boy that Pappy would abandon the *obrigacao* he had planned and worked on since we moved to Brooklyn? Nothing can be more important than the ceremony. And Pappy knows that." She picked up the telephone. "I must speak to him right away."

"I left him at the hospital," Ademola said, admiring her energy and determination. A fire he had come to understand and that nobody had been able to put out, though many had tried. He had chosen to let it burn freely. But Simone always treated him reverently. He was the only person she could express her strengths and weaknesses to without feeling vulnerable. Their lives were filled with love and mutual respect.

Ademola was happy. So was Simone, always treating Ali, who had just celebrated his seventeenth birthday, as though he were her own son. They both wanted to have at least one child together, but that had eluded them since they got married a year after Ademola started working at the hospital. All the tests proved negative in their search for the root of the problem.

"I really want to have a boy that would call you grand-pappy," Simone once told Johnson.

"You will, my dearest," Johnson had responded. "But always remember that your child will choose you when it's ready to come into this world."

"When will that be?" Ademola asked.

"As soon as you two stop being so anxious."

So they did.

Simone dialed and waited. "Dr. William Johnson, please," she said into the mouthpiece. She listened, and then arched her eyebrows upward.

Ademola's lips rounded into, "What?"

Simone shrugged, then shook her head. She hung up. "He's not answering the phone. Maybe he left already. I'll try him at home in ten minutes. How about coffee?" She headed toward the bathroom.

"Good idea." Ademola got off the bed and turned on the light. The room looked clean and comfortable. He walked to the window and looked at the skyline. He took a deep breath and inhaled the familiar smell, a potpourri of clean linen sheets, starched cotton shirts, wool and cashmere, Simone's assortment of perfumes. He turned and walked away from the window. On the table beside the brass bed the dial on the crystal Waterford clock read five-twenty-five. A picture of his father when the old man was about Ademola's present age stood behind the radio on the nightstand. The pictures of his mother, Simone's father, mother, and Dr. Johnson hung on the wall facing the bed. Ademola's love for his mother swelled suddenly inside him, filling him with melancholy and an unfathomable uneasiness. He opened the closet door, took out a white terrycloth robe and put it on. He went to the kitchen, filled the automatic coffee maker with water and ground coffee, turned on the switch, and headed for the bathroom. He joined Simone in the shower. They lathered each other under the cascading water.

He shaved while she dried her hair.

"That stuff really works, doesn't it?" She pointed to the piece of alum crystal he rubbed under his armpits, and over his face.

"Oh, is that why you're so tight?" he teased.

"Get outta here. I've not done any such—"

"It works. I heard that women in Nigeria douse their you-know-what with it to retain their tightness in addition to it being friendly to the environment. It's nature's gift of deodorant, aftershave, and youthful elixir to mankind." He laughed.

"You're nothing but a lying, dirty sailor disguised as a doctor. There's always a diabolical reason why a man would choose to be a physician, aside from the power thing, isn't there? You are a sublimated sex predator, Mr. Sailorman. I rest my case." She bowed as though addressing a jury panel.

The air in the bathroom crackled with laughter.

"I love you too, Simone," he said.

She laughed. And then became serious again. "You didn't tell me what's so special about the boy."

"Jason is a unique child, his parent's wealth notwithstanding. He's an *Abiku*."

"Every child is an *Abiku*, isn't it?" she asked, her voice sorrowful.

"*Abikus* are everywhere, they are called many names by different people of the world, but not every child is an *Abiku*. Jason is. He has to be taken to Nigeria."

"Sweetheart, you told me that already."

"But what I didn't tell you is—you see these marks on my face? There's a reason for it and—"

"You told me that too. But why would Pappy drop everything in order to take this child to Nigeria? Why can't he treat him here? He's done it before."

"You should ask Pappy that. He's the one who's going to Nigeria. And I respect his judgement on that," Ademola said, concerned, knowing that his mentor's decision was made after weighty consideration. He held Simone's hand and pulled her toward him. "I'm sure Pappy has a good reason."

She nodded in acquiescence, going into the bedroom with him. They got dressed and went to the kitchen which was permeated with the aroma of freshly-brewed coffee. She filled two mugs, handed him one and they sat facing each other at the dining table. She picked up the receiver from the wall, dialed Johnson's home number and waited for a while, furrows of worry creasing her forehead. She said dejectedly, "He's not home yet."

"Try the hospital again." He sipped from the mug.

She did. And once again, there was no answer. "Will you come to the ceremony with me?"

"Of course, after seeing Pappy off."

The telephone shrilled. Simone eyed Ademola curiously.

"*Baba*, it's uncle Ayo on the line for you," Ali shouted from his room.

Ademola pressed the speaker phone button and Crowder's voice filled the room: "*Turn your TV to channel four! I'll be right over!*"

Simone was already beside the television set when Ademola pressed the off button on the telephone. She turned it on and switched to channel four. Ademola joined her on the sofa. Suddenly Simone's eyes rounded, mouth agape as she stared at the television. The still picture of Johnson filled the screen for a few seconds, and was immediately replaced by a young reporter at the entrance of Children's Hospital, a microphone barely touching her lips as she said:

"The first-ever African-American Chief of Staff of the finest children's hospital in the nation, Dr. William Doss Johnson, was found dead at his desk just a little over an hour ago in what the medical examiner claims to be an apparent cardiac arrest. But the bigger news, one that sends chills down everyone's spine, is the fact that hours before and since

Dr. Johnson's death, a total of five newborns, babies ranging from a few minutes old to ten hours, have died of what the hospital is calling SIDS. This figure represents over fifteen percent of the hourly delivery of babies in the hospital."

The incredulity in Ademola's eyes could have melted the television screen.

"A cloud of silence has descended on the hospital. Nobody is talking," the reporter announced.

"Any word from the administrator?"

"None yet, Walter. As soon as I get further clarification I will let you know. Bizarre is—hold one moment, Walter." She pressed her fingers to her left ear, nodded several times, and said, "I've just been informed that a fifteen-month-old boy was brought in drifting in and out of consciousness last night and was discharged before dawn even though his condition seemed to worsen. What makes this significant is the fact that the boy is the heir to the McFlarthey media empire. Mr. McFlarthey and his wife brought their son here late last night. But listen to this: An ophthalmologist, the famous Dr. Fall, who was called to perform some seemingly unrelated tests on the boy, was found unconscious in the room that was occupied by the boy. I understand that the doctor is still in a coma. Bizarre is the word—"

The door bell rang and Ademola quickly let Crowder into the apartment. "Did you hear the news? What's going on?" He sat next to Simone who looked as though she was going to break down and cry at any moment, her unbelieving eyes staring at the television screen. She looked broken, an angel garbed in funeral linen, her golden face turning coppery-red as tears snaked down her cheeks.

Ademola blew his nose. There were tears in his eyes.

"What's going on, *baba*?"

Ademola looked over his shoulder at Ali standing next to the dining table. "Something terrible just happened, son, come over here." He wiped tears off his face with a handkerchief, took a deep breath, and said, "I haven't the slightest idea where all this is leading."

"What happened?" Crowder asked again.

Ademola started to tell Crowder and Ali as much as he could. The telephone rang. Ali dashed to the kitchen to answer it. "It's for you, *baba*. It's a woman. She sounds like a newsperson." He handed the telephone to Crowder, who had left the living room for the kitchen.

"This is Dr. Crowder... Yes... No, he's not available... What... I don't think so!" He slammed the telephone back on the cradle, covered his face with both hands and squeezed. His voice sounded gloomy. "We all better get out of here right away. The whole place will be swarming with reporters soon—Simone, are you okay?" Crowder asked, because his friend's wife looked as though she had lost her mind.

She did not answer him right away but glanced at her husband and back to Crowder. "What are we going to do?"

"I haven't the slightest idea." Ademola's voice sounded hopeless.

"I'm scared, Ola," Simone whispered.

"I'm sure there's something I should do—don't answer that," Ademola said, nodding toward the sound of the telephone ringing in the kitchen. "It was as if Pappy knew something like this was going to happen."

"Why do you say that?" Simone wiped tears off her face.

Ademola reached into his trouser pocket and extracted the kaolin and kolanut. "He gave these to me and asked me to perform the rituals on the boy. Pappy had never done that before. As a matter of fact—" He cocked his head sideways, listening as footsteps approached his front door. He held his finger to his lips for silence and waited.

The knocks at the front door sounded as though whoever was outside needed to get into the apartment fast.

Ademola pocketed the kaolin and kolanut, nodded at

Ali, who strode to the door and eased it open.

"Pardon me, Ali, is your dad home? I tried to call from downstairs but there was no answer. These people insisted on coming up." The doorman looked uncomfortably over Ali's shoulder into the living room.

Ademola was on his feet. "That's quite all right, Carlos. Thanks." He stepped forward. "Please, come in, Mr. McFlarthey," he said as though he'd been expecting the family.

McFlarthey strode inside with Jason on his shoulder. Kathleen and another man followed. The doorman hesitated. "Is everything okay, sir?"

"Yes, and please, don't let anyone else come up here. Thank you." Ademola eased the door shut.

They all went into the living room.

"What the devil is going on?" McFlarthey locked eyes with Ademola. "I take it you've heard the terrible news about Dr. Johnson? As soon as we got home Jason's condition deteriorated, and he's getting worse."

"I still think the child should have been taken to—" The man's mouth gaped open upon seeing Crowder emerge from the kitchen. "What are you doing here, Ayo?"

"Hi, Richard."

"You two know each other?" McFlarthey asked as though speaking to a couple of naughty children.

"Yes, Mr. McFlarthey, Ay—Dr. Crowder works for you at the *Times*, sir. He's the assistant bureau chief in the West African department," Richard Stormier said importantly.

McFlarthey waved his employee to silence. "What do we do next? I am convinced that Dr. Johnson's prescription is the best remedy for my son. But I'm at a loss now that he's dead." He looked much older now than when Ademola first met him less than twelve hours ago.

Ademola sat at one end of the sofa, Kathleen at the other, and Jason between them, his feet on his mother's lap.

Ademola was deep in thought, a worried look on his face.

Richard Stormier said, "Dr. Ademola, we—Dr. Ademola! I believe Jason should be taken to Children's Hospital right away." He bent over to touch Ademola's shoulder.

"Yeah! What?"

"We should get the boy back to the hospital, fast."

"No! He's fine. Thanks."

"But, Dr. Ademola—"

"You heard what he said," McFlarthey flared.

Stormier shrugged, and remained quiet.

"Dr. Ademola, what's going on? I can't take any more," Kathleen wailed in exhaustion and fear.

"We have to get Jason to Nigeria."

"But Dr. Johnson is dead!"

"I will go in his place."

Crowder's eyes rounded. "Are you out of your mind?" he snapped. "Nigeria is the last place you want to go, Ola."

Ademola looked up at Simone. She nodded yes, and said, "I'm sure that's what Pappy intended you to do when he gave you those objects. I'll pack some clothes for you."

"I agree with mom, *baba*, you should go," Ali said, and smiled. "I will go to the mosque and say some *dua* for you while you're gone. God will be with you."

Ademola nodded and then turned to McFlarthey. "I shouldn't have let Jason out of my sight. Dr. Johnson made that very clear."

"What do you mean?" McFlarthey asked.

Jason's body stirred. His eyelids fluttered.

McFlarthey looked at his son, then at Ademola whose eyes were suddenly shut. "Dr. Ademola, are you all right?"

In a measured voice Ademola said, "Please bring Jason to the bedroom." He got up and led the way.

Simone quickly took off the comforter and straightened the sheet. McFlarthey placed Jason in the middle of the queen-sized bed. Ademola unwrapped the wool blanket around Jason. Suddenly, he looked over his shoulder, feeling the presence of a hostile force. He reached into his trousers' pocket and held the kolanut and kaolin. He rubbed them together, massaging them as he knelt beside the boy, his right fist holding the kolanut and kaolin.

There was a stirring and faint chirping in the room, Ademola looked up and followed the sound with his eyes. The cry of a jungle bird filled the room. Kathleen pressed Jason's hand to her bosom. An explosion of wind ripped through the apartment. The lights went out, and the air crackled with resinous luminosity. It was hot. Ademola opened his fist and the kolanut and kaolin in his cupped hand began to throb. The chirping hiccupped, then stopped. The flapping sound of birds' wings grew louder.

McFlarthey exchanged glances with Crowder, who gasped and covered his ears. Stormier crossed himself and mumbled, "I can't breathe!" He dashed out.

The mirror on the dresser shattered. Simone quickly sat next to Kathleen at the edge of the bed.

The kaolin in Ademola's cupped hand breathed evenly, louder. His hand looked like a light bulb. The chirrups and the throbbing competed for prominence. Violent energies filled the room. Ademola began to sweat. There was a growl from behind the door to the bathroom. Ademola crinkled his nose. There was the smell of burning feathers. The chirrups choked and died. A gentle wind issued from the objects in Ademola's hand. The wind blew harder and the bathroom door flung open. Burnt feathers blew everywhere.

"What the hell is this?" Crowder's mouth hung open.

⌐

25

LAGOS

September 3, 1995:

“**H**ow did you get this?” Hakabala eyed the tape recorder on his desk with shock and unrestrained rage.

“You cow-dung-eating-son-of-a-fornicating-Berber,” Sakara cursed silently, refusing to answer the question.

“I was wrong about you, *General* Sakara.”

Sakara’s outrage ascended at Hakabala’s antics. “Is that a bribe camouflaged as a promotion?”

“It’s a well-deserved promotion. I was not sure I could count on you to find those Ogoni criminals guilty as charged, but you did, and I’m glad.” Hakabala smiled.

“I do not wish to become a general. But more importantly, I do not wish to be bribed for doing my job. I am a soldier,” Sakara said defiantly, wanting to get back to the topic of the taped conversation, aware that he had only a few minutes to accomplish his objective and be out of there safely. “How dare you?”

The smile disappeared from Hakabala’s face. “You’re treading dangerously close to insubordination, Segun. I ask you once more, how did you get this tape?”

“Are you threatening me?” Sakara got to his feet.

“Sit down! I can have you shot this very second.”

Hakabala's face contorted with fury.

"Can you really?" Sakara asked with deliberate inso-
lence. "This is nothing compared to the other recordings I
have in my possession."

"Like what?" Hakabala also stood up.

Before coming to Abuja for an emergency meeting of
the members of the PRC, Sakara was informed by the head
of the Special Unit, a top ranking officer from a minority
tribe in the south, guarding the presidential villa, that
Sakara's personal safety would be guaranteed but only for a
short while. Though Sakara did not have any problem
believing the officer, he had instructed his most loyal sup-
porters in the military to be prepared for the first phase of
his plan to overthrow Hakabala. His personal safety was
therefore the least of his problems when he approached
Hakabala at the end of the meeting.

The two had gone into Hakabala's private office in the
presidential villa. At Sakara's insistence, no one else was
allowed in the room with them.

"In addition to the cassette, there is a video tape of you
massacring the three American Catholic priests in Onitsha
during the Biafran war."

"What the hell is that?" Hakabala's mouth hung half
open, and his unbelieving eyes widened upon seeing the
photograph Sakara held in his hand.

"Pictures don't lie. This was you then," Sakara spat contemptuously. "The original and the video tape are in the
hands of loyal associates in Rome who have been instructed
to pass them along to the Pope and the American ambassador in Italy," Sakara threatened. He believed however that
as long as Hakabala remained in power the foreign policy of
western countries, especially Britain and the U.S, would be
determined by economic interests and not by humanitarian
sentiments. And the terms of such foreign policies would
always be dictated by the multinational oil corporations

which had direct access to the Nigerian oil fields at rock-bottom prices. A weakened and compromised Hakabala was just what the doctor ordered. But Sakara had to gamble. He suspected that Hakabala would not dare call his bluff.

The tension in the room grew as Hakabala's cunning eyes probed Sakara's. His voice sounded broken when he spoke. "Who took the picture?"

"It doesn't matter who did," Sakara snarled. "For someone who lives in a glass house you must learn not to throw rocks in anger. I am the head of DMI, a fact you seem to have forgotten. Those that spy for you also owe their allegiance to me. The reason you are still alive and in power is because of the dirty jobs we do." Sakara flung the picture to the floor. "To have Achibong and my wife spying on me is the height of imprudence," he said with deliberate slowness, baiting the head of state.

Hakabala swallowed hard. Once again, his words choked him. Finally, he said, "That was Babasa's idea."

Suddenly the truth became repugnant. In a solemn voice filled with contempt Sakara said, "It doesn't matter whose idea it was, what matters is that you are the sole beneficiary of the treachery. And as you very well know, there's a price for that sort of thing in the military."

For an instant the sides of Hakabala's mouth twisted into a villainous smile, momentarily throwing Sakara off balance. "I am still the commander-in-chief of this nation, and I can have you killed with impunity."

Sakara hesitated, recomposing himself. "If I am not in my office within the next two hours my instruction to Italy will be activated," he said over his shoulder, and was about to walk out of the room when Hakabala reached for a button on his desk. He stopped short of pressing it. "You will stay here in Abuja to make the call," Hakabala ordered.

"You don't get it!" Sakara turned around. Like one speaking to a stupid child, he said, "Several officers have heard the tape and seen this and other evidence. If they do not see me in Lagos at the designated place, bloody hell will break loose all over the country. You don't have to believe me though. It's your move." He stormed out and slammed the door, rattling the walls.

~

Though he had not expected to be arrested by the armed soldiers at the gate leading out of the presidential building, the presence of the added security warned Sakara to be more cautious. He was and got away.

Aso Rock loomed ahead as he drove toward Abuja International Airport. He sped past the airport, and five miles later turned into the back streets in the residential part of Suleja. He parked the car behind the thick shrubbery that edged a house adjoining a groundnut farm. There were several soldiers guarding the building. Sakara acknowledged their salutes before hurrying into the bungalow. He entered through the door which was opened by an officer in mufti.

"Are you staying here until tomorrow, sir?" the soldier asked in Yoruba, shutting the door behind them as they entered the parlor.

"Is everything ready?" Sakara headed to the bedroom.

"Yes, sir."

"Wait until I have been gone for about fifty minutes before driving my car to the airport. Park it where it can be seen easily. I'll contact you later for Plan B," Sakara said before disappearing behind the door.

He emerged a few minutes later dressed in a white cotton flowing gown, black turban, and an old Quran clasped in his hand. The pair of fake tinted bifocal horn-rimmed glasses perched on the bridge of his nose made him look like a *mullah*. The thick mustache and goatee made the disguise a perfect ploy. He exchanged keys with the soldier and drove away toward Jos in a Volkswagen Passat. Halfway into his seventy-five-minute drive the thought occurred to him that this was the same strategy Ademola had used to escape ten years ago: going against the flow of traffic. The thought of Ademola's success and happiness in his profession and personal life sent a jolt of jealousy up his spine. The Nigerian military attache at the United Nations had befriended Crowder and through him he had been able to keep an eye on Ademola's activities in New York. The officer regularly sent progress reports to Sakara. When Sakara heard that Ademola had been shot, he was saddened by the news. But later when he heard of his miraculous recovery, he was relieved. "I have the bullet that will pierce that skull of yours in my hand," Sakara had promised. "Enjoy your glorious moments in America while it lasts, bastard son of a whore!" he cursed aloud.

His anger and frustration crested upon seeing the mountains of caked fertilizer that lined the highway. Nine years and twenty billion dollars later his agriculture program had become another government sham. Akin had failed to deliver on his promise to bring the project to a successful conclusion. Funds borrowed from the World Bank and IMF had found their way into the bank accounts of top military officers including Babasa and Hakabala. Akin and his cohorts had fled overseas right after Babasa left office.

Femi, who had originated the idea, had left in frustration. The young man had gone back to Britain, received his doctorate, and stayed behind to lecture at Cambridge University. Since his self-imposed exile, Femi's first visit to Nigeria was two weeks ago. Sakara wondered if the young man had gone back to Britain. He shrugged the thought away, satisfied that he was no longer bonded to Eniola's family.

Two hours later, the flight attendant announced the arrival of flight WT 604 from Jos to Lagos. Sakara, still in disguise, was the last passenger to step off the plane into the arrival terminal which was buzzing with soldiers whose manners were as fierce as the smell of their sweat-soaked uniforms. Speaking the language of a Muslim cleric, he talked his way through the military check-points at the airport.

As the sun looked like it was ready to explode, Sakara hurried through the outskirts of Ikeja, constantly looking over his shoulder, wondering if he was being followed. Finally he arrived at the home of the highest-ranking Itsekiri Air Force officer. He was welcomed at the gate by his host and they marched into the house where two dozen Army, Navy, and Air Force officers, mostly southerners, were waiting in the parlor.

"Everyone here agrees that Hakabala must go," the Air Force officer said. "But we wish this to be the last *coup* in the country. Hakabala and his predecessors have discredited the military. And yet we must acknowledge that every one of us here has also acted dishonorably. We have taken the country on a perilous ride to the precipice."

Several heads nodded in agreement.

A stocky lieutenant colonel with an Ibo accent spoke next. "Our job is to defend the nation against foreign aggressors. But in the absence of such an enemy we have turned our guns against the very people we swore to defend. What do we have to show for our stewardship? We have more generals than all the countries in Africa combined, generals that have become billionaires overnight. We have become the laughing stock of the world. Enough is enough."

Again, there was unanimous agreement. Sakara's plan was right on course. As he listened, his mind became filled with the lyrics of his favorite poem. Drumming his fingers on the attaché case on his lap, he kept tempo with the poem. A sudden thought set off an alarm in his head. He snapped open the case and searched its contents furiously. "Damn!"

All heads turned to him.

"There's a file in the observation room at DMI that should not find its way into Hakabala's hand. By now the building is undoubtedly secured by the units loyal to him." The black of his eyes burrowed into the bridge of his nose in fury. "Nobody other than Achibong knows the combination to the steel door. But as you all know, Achibong cannot be trusted."

"With your permission, sir, I would like to personally take care of him," a Hausa officer volunteered. "He is still under surveillance as you ordered, sir."

"Good!" Sakara became silent for a moment. "I have to have Achibong and that file, even if we have to storm the building." He waited for volunteers.

All the hands in the room went up.

⤚

Achibong had every reason to be paranoid. Like Sakara, he had paid a heavy price for his promotions in the army. Two days after the bloody coup that brought Babasa to power, Achibong was seated in the bedroom of his house late at night when he heard a stirring like someone tiptoeing outside. "Who's there?" He reached into his pocket for his gun, then remembered he had left it in the car. He stood still, straining his senses for further sounds. He was not afraid, only astounded.

Then the movement came again. "Ben Achibong?" said the voice of the man behind the door. "I bring you an order from the president. Do not open the door or turn on the light!"

"Why?" Achibong was surprised at how steady he sounded.

"This meeting must take place in absolute secrecy."

"Who are you?" Achibong asked.

"As I said, I am the messenger. I am instructed to tell you that the president has chosen you as the unofficial bridge that connects him to the director of DMI."

"What kind of nonsense is that? The head of state does not need—why should I believe that you are who you claim to be if I can't see you?" Achibong was about to open the door when the silence was shattered by the sound of a gun-fire.

"The next time I pull the trigger, parts of your brain will splatter the walls," the voice said with conviction. "You are instructed to do as follows: install the best listening and recording device in the house which Colonel Sakara will move into. Contact the young lady that will soon be his wife every week to receive the tape from her—"

"I will do no such thing!" Achibong yanked the door open and stood frozen upon recognizing the man.

"You shouldn't have done that." The scars on Hakabala's face twisted out of shape with outrage.

"I—I am—so—sorry, sir—"

Hakabala shook his head. "Your father and mother are in good health in Calabar as we speak. So is your brother in Kaduna. They will remain healthy as long as this meeting is never revealed to anyone. Your loyalty to Sakara is misplaced. It should be to me and Babasa. That must be the case hence-forth. I want the tape and your report in my hand every Monday morning. You do your part and I'll make sure members of your family are left in peace. Sakara is a danger-ous man. We need to keep him on a short leash. And the best way to achieve that is to know what goes on in his household on a daily basis. I can help you, and you can help me in return. Two dirty hands become cleaner if they hold a bar of soap between them."

"I won't do it!"

"Yes, you will. You are not stupid, Ben. You know I didn't come here to play a game with you. What I told you is an order which you will carry out to the letter. Good day!" Hakabala said with finality and left.

On this day, Achibong had been watching Sakara's house through the powerful lenses of his binoculars since dawn. The house appeared normal, but something was amiss. During the past nine years Eniola had never missed their rendezvous. Like the German trains, she had been timely on her delivery of the tape recording of Sakara's weekly activities. Every Sunday morning Eniola would deposit the tape in a designated hole outside the fence. But today was different. Achibong had found the hole empty. He had waited until 1000 hours before going to the house under the pretext of just being in the neighborhood. That was when he got suspicious. No one came to the gate. The nightwatchman had left after dawn. The domestic servants should've been in their quarters. He dared not climb the fence. So he went back to his black jeep parked three blocks away, and made himself comfortable in the back seat with his binoculars trained on the gate. A blue Peugeot 505 sedan was parked a few blocks away. The two men inside the car watched Achibong as he continued to observe Sakara's house.

Precisely an hour later, a convoy of six armored vehicles approached the house, each mounted with a missile launcher atop the driver's cabin. Squatting behind each launcher was a soldier wearing a black steel helmet with a protective tinted plastic visor. The mouth of each soldier was concealed by a gas mask connected to an oxygen cylinder strapped to his back. Achibong swung his binoculars to the lead vehicle and his heart took a dive when his gaze fell on Major General Bata, the first cousin of Dikko. The enmity between Sakara and Bata dated back to the *coup* that ushered in the regime of Babasa. Achibong knew that Bata believed that his cousin,

Dikko, had been betrayed and killed by Sakara, and he had sworn vengeance. It was also known within the military circle that Bata was one of the strongest allies of Hakabala. Achibong knew that if Sakara was compromised his own future in the military would be equally compromised. It took no great wisdom to appreciate the precarious situation.

The vehicles stopped in front of the gate, blocking the entrance, thus openly informing all onlookers that mayhem was about to be unleashed. Just as Achibong was about to drive off, he saw the gate pull inward. He held his breath, waiting, hoping that Sakara was not about to walk into this den of famished wolves. A green Lexus 300 sedan emerged. Femi got out of the car, walked back to lock the gate, and was about to get back into the car when Bata jumped down from his vehicle. The two men engaged in a heated argument, and Femi, in his characteristic arrogance, walked away.

Achibong got behind the steering wheel and chased after the Lexus. He caught up with Femi at the entrance to the bridge that connected Ikoyi to Victoria Island. He waved Femi to the curb, ran to the side of the Lexus, and spoke through the window. "Where is Brigadier Sakara?" He looked over his shoulder as though afraid someone else might be listening.

"I don't know," Femi said.

"What about your sister?" Achibong asked nervously.

"I haven't seen her either. I'm concerned though."

"Why?"

"What kind of dumb question is that?" Femi looked at Achibong with undisguised abhorrence.

"Don't get snotty with me, Femi," Achibong snapped officiously.

"That's it, you've wasted enough of my time." He started to drive off.

"Eniola might be in grave danger as we speak," Achibong said hurriedly.

"What kind of danger?"

"Follow me to my office and I'll tell you."

Femi nodded a reluctant yes.

Achibong ran back to his jeep and sped across the bridge. He was unaware of the passenger in the blue Peugeot following Femi's Lexus. The soldier flipped open a cell phone, spoke rapidly, and nodded to his partner.

At DMI, Achibong was somewhat relieved that there wasn't anything unusual at the gate of the building. The air was filled with salty moisture and the smell of the ocean breeze gave him a false sense of normalcy. As the gate swung open to let him into the grounds, a phalanx of armed soldiers materialized from behind the high walls, blocking his path. The leader, a bulky, light-complexioned major with a cherub face stepped forward. Looking as though he was in the middle of a Sunday morning sermon, he said, "Welcome, Lieutenant Colonel Achibong." His priestly smile widened. "You will do exactly as I say!"

Femi put the Lexus in reverse and smacked against the front bumper of the Peugeot. He shifted gear and was about to drive off when a soldier yanked his door open. "Out!"

"I don't—"

"Now!" The soldier grabbed his shirt collar and dragged Femi from the car.

"What's going on?" Achibong asked the priestly major, who he recognized as the undercover agent Sakara had planted among the Cherub worshippers on the beach.

"Brigadier Sakara wants you to open the observation-room and hand me the green file in the second drawer."

"Where is he—and who are these?" Achibong pointed to the soldiers seated against the wall with their wrists and ankles bound.

"They are Bata's boys. But you need not concern yourself with them just now." The gun in his hand refuted the pleasant sound of his explanation. He followed Achibong and Femi up the stairs to the floor.

Achibong unlocked the steel door and entered the observation-room with its red light hanging from the ceiling. He heard the sound of the convoy of six armored vehicles approaching the building in a formation of three abreast.

Bata gave the order that sent three missiles out of the launchers, detonating in a splash of explosion, blasting the gate to pieces of twisted metal. The soldiers inside the building returned fire, and the helmeted soldiers atop the vehicles gave agonizing yelps, fell, and died before hitting the ground. Onlookers shook their heads in horror as they witnessed the commencement of yet another massacre.

Achibong was nearly deafened by the explosion that shook the building. Bricks came tumbling down, leaving a gaping hole in the side of the building. Furiously searching for a way out of the cauldron, he grabbed the green file and was about to run out of the room when the telephone shrilled. He froze. "Only three people have the number to this line," he thought, and he was one of them. "Better answer that," he said to the major who hesitated. "It must be Brigadier Sakara wishing to speak with us."

The major nodded, giving Achibong permission to answer the phone.

"I can't hear you, can you say that again?" Achibong shouted as a volley of shots rang out. "Are you sure... When... How many... Yes, give the permission to land... You are sure the name is... I can't hear... Yes it's the same... I will inform Brigadier Sakara right away... Very good." He hung up the receiver and looked as if he just received a gift from God.

"Who was that?" the major demanded, nudging Achibong and Femi out the door.

"The control tower at Murtala Muhammed airport."

"And?"

"It's something I have to tell the brigadier personally."

Upon exiting the building, they immediately took cover beside a vehicle turned on its side. A good part of the building had been reduced to rubble and dead soldiers littered the grounds.

"We need to get out of here before a reinforcement arrives," the major said, crouching next to Achibong.

26

"They finally gave us permission to land," the co-pilot announced.

"Good," McFlarthey said, sipping his herbal tea.

"I suspect that the only reason they did was because Dr. Ademola is on board."

"Why is that?" McFlarthey asked, not liking the concern in the pilot's voice.

"I spent thirty minutes explaining to the control tower why we need to land at the airport. The response was a blunt no. But after I gave the controller the passengers' manifest, he gave me the permission to land as soon as he confirmed that Dr Ademola's first name is Ola—who is he?"

"Never mind that, Dick. What's our ETA?"

"I'm ready to commence our descent now. An hour."

"Good!" McFlarthey pressed a button to summon one of the attendants on board. A smartly-dressed man in his mid-thirties, who looked more like a dancer than an ex-FBI agent, sprinted into the cabin. His strong arms and easy carriage gave him away as McFlarthey's body guard. He smiled easily out of the corners of his mouth, but his ice-cold blue eyes belied his relaxed manner. "How's Jason and my wife back there?" McFlarthey asked.

"Jason and the doctor are getting along real well."

"We land in about an hour. And since we've never been

to this country before, how do we handle security?" McFlarthey studied the man.

"Nigeria is a backwater country. Your personal security is not a problem. How long will you stay there?"

"That depends on Jason's recovery. But I would guess not more than a couple days. Get me another bag." He tapped the edge of his mug. He got on his feet, stretched, and was about to sit down when the telephone on the arm-rest of his recliner chimed. He let it ring. "The world must learn to get along without me for a few days," he thought.

When the Lear jet took off the runway at La Guardia airport, McFlarthey spent the first two hours on the phone. There was the dinner with the chairman of the Democratic National Committee and the Sultan of Brunei which had to be postponed.

Cruising over the Atlantic, he had a fifteen-minute tele-conference with the editor-in-chief of one his newspapers in Australia and the CEO of his diamond mining company in South Africa.

Next, he authorized the Chief Financial Officer of his conglomerate to pledge ten million dollars to UNESCO, shocking the penny-pinching financial wizard. The specific terms would have to wait until McFlarthey returned.

Finally, he was informed that Dr. Fall did not regain con-sciousness before he died. Stormier told him that the NYPD had named Ademola as the prime suspect for Falls' death, and the mysterious deaths of the newborn babies at Children's Hospital. The police also wanted to question the McFlartheys in connection with Jason's untimely discharge. "It doesn't look good," Stormier had said.

"Thanks." McFlarthey accepted the bag from his body-guard, and headed toward the rear of the plane. He found Kathleen in a reclining position, staring out the window. Ademola was showing Jason how to use the stethoscope. The boy looked as though he had never been sick. "Are you a good doctor?" He smiled at his son.

Jason nodded, holding the round metal part of the stethoscope in the air.

Kathleen looked at both her son and husband, smiled, and shook her head as though she was surprised at Jason's apparent recovery. "How much longer before we touch down?" The nervousness in her voice betrayed her apprehension.

McFlarthey settled next to his wife facing Ademola in the section of the plane that looked more like a living room than the inside of an aircraft. "Dr. Ademola, I can't thank you enough for deciding to come with us. I know that this trip could turn out to be dangerous for you. I know what you risked when you decided to come," Kathleen said.

"You don't want to know how dangerous it is."

"We thank you nonetheless." McFlarthey held Kathleen's delicate hand in his. "Richard Stormier told me you fled from Nigeria about ten years ago. What happened?"

Ademola continued to play with Jason for another minute before telling the McFlartheys part of the story.

"I'll be damned!" McFlarthey eyed him with awe and curiosity. "There has to be a reason for this. I don't believe in coincidences. The young fellow whose life you saved was the son of a newspaper journalist, wasn't he?"

"I didn't save his life, I merely treated his wounds."

"But you stumbled onto something that caused you to flee your native land. And here you are, ten years later, escorting us back to where it all started. And as before, you're helping to save the life of the son of another newspaper man. I don't call that coincidence, Dr. Ademola."

"What do you call it then?"

"I believe it all adds up to the fact that the Nigerian story needs to be told. And I suspect that I've been chosen to do it," McFlarthey said importantly. "Do you suppose there's more?" he asked.

"Of course. The world already knows about what is going on in Nigeria. As long as the atrocities are confined within the boundaries of the country, the rest of the world doesn't give a damn. But it won't remain caged like that forever. Sooner or later it will implode, and when it does, Rwanda, Somalia, Ethiopia, Sudan and the rest of the African horrors will look like a Sunday school picnic in comparison," Ademola said sternly.

"What's it like in Nigeria?" McFlarthey asked.

"Upside down."

"What do you mean?"

"Just what I said, confused and sad. In the Third World, there's no such thing as government of the people as we have in America. There are only obsessed thieves in charge of the national treasury."

"That's sad. But what are the people like?"

"Most are hard-working, honest, but helpless. You'll find out soon enough. We are only an hour away from the corruption capital of the world where a few have the balls of the majority in their iron-fisted grip, and are always eager to squeeze."

"Is it ever going to change?" Kathleen asked.

"Not as long as the leadership remain brutal and inhuman. Most observers believe that the problems of the Third World would be solved if only corruption could be eradicated like malaria or yellow fever. Corruption is a symptom. The basic cause is moral indifference and intellectual laziness. We used to imagine where we might end up after graduating from the university. We knew that all the socially-conscious intellectuals who had the effrontery to openly express their beliefs had either been marginalized, jailed, or sent into exile. Would you believe there are over four thousand Nigerian doctors who are members of the Association of Nigerian Physicians in the Americas, ANPA? There's hardly any college or university in the U.S. where one would not find a Nigerian professor. It was just recently revealed by the Census Bureau that Nigerians represent the most-educated new immigrants to America. That's equally true in Europe. With such an alarming exodus of intellectual manpower, you don't have to be a rocket scientist to understand why the country is in such terrible shape. The decision to emigrate is not made without serious thought. People are forced out. What is left is a hemorrhaging giant."

"Is it that bad?" McFlarthey asked.

"It's worse." Ademola's voice was barely audible.

"What happened to the documents?"

Ademola smiled. "I must have told my story to at least a dozen people and no one has ever thought to ask me about the documents. You're a real newspaper man." Then he fell silent.

"Are you going to tell me or not?"

"I gave the document you speak of to the lady I was engaged to. She has since married an old friend of mine so I don't know what happened to it. The document with the financial information on the twenty military officers who embezzled the government's money is with Dr. Crowder in New York. And if I do not contact him twenty-four hours after my arrival, he will get it published in the *Times* and—"

"No he won't—he can't." McFlarthey became serious.

"Why not?"

"Any story with the potential of embarrassing the leaders of foreign governments, especially a friendly one like Nigeria, and your country is an important business and strategic partner of the U.S.—"

"Nigeria is not friendly to the U.S."

"Dr. Ademola, did I argue with you about medicine? International politics and commerce are my business. The last time I checked, Nigeria was regarded as our close trading partner on account of their crude oil, which is among the purest and cheapest in the world. Any story about the

leaders of such a country would have to get clearance from
the Department of State. And your friend is not going to get
that kind of clearance. As long as the average American citizen
is able to purchase a gallon of gas for a buck and a half,
despots like the one in Nigeria will remain in power. That
doesn't mean that I don't intend to do something about
what you told me."

The intercom rang and McFlarthey hastily pressed a button
and the voice of the pilot filled the air:

"*Mr and Mrs McFlarthey, welcome to Murtala Muhammed
International Airport. Please remain seated until the aircraft has
come to a complete stop at the gate. There's a Nigerian Airways
plane ahead of us—*"

McFlarthey looked out the window and saw the sun
high in the sky, casting no shadows. As the plane rumbled
down the runway toward the gate, he scanned the landscape
with his wife's binoculars. "What the hell is that?"

"What?" Kathleen leaned toward the window.

"Take a look over there," he pointed at a convoy of military
vehicles racing away from the airport a few hundred
yards away. He handed her the binoculars.

"They're soldiers, William. We're in Africa."

"I know that!" He took the binoculars back, but the
vehicles had disappeared. He turned around and caught a
glimpse of worry on Ademola's face, which he quickly
replaced with an innocuous smile.

The plane bumped to a stop and Ademola carried Jason
on his shoulder through a plastic tunnel to the arrival terminal.
A queue that looked like a funnel on its side had
formed, enveloping the immigration desk, turning it to
chaos. Everybody was first in line. Bodies squeezed bodies,
voices competed with one another and the smell of perfumed
perspiration saturated the air.

As McFlarthey fought his way out of the funnel to find
an empty space a few yards away, he caught several people

staring at him. His family, escorted by Wayne, was buried in the mass of shouting, squeezing and jabbering black humanity. He took another look at the funnel and the people and his face reddened. He felt like someone had punched him. He stood there, dazed. "Why do I feel so vulnerable?" he asked himself.

"Mr. McFlarthey, are you all right?" Wayne asked.

McFlarthey tried to speak but couldn't.

"William, maybe you should sit down." Kathleen felt his forehead. "What's the matter with him?"

"I think I know what it is," Ademola said.

At the sound of Ademola's voice, McFlarthey shook his head slowly.

"For goodness sake, William, speak to me, will you? What's happening to him? I've never seen him like this before," Kathleen said.

"I don't feel good about us being surrounded like this," McFlarthey said finally, pointing to the throngs of people that enveloped the immigration desk. A sick feeling gripped him. The skin color of the people inside the arrival terminal was not only of the darkest hue but they spoke differently as well. McFlarthey was unable to comprehend the exotic facial expressions that seemed totally incongruent with their loud verbal exchanges. Arms flailed in the air as though ready to strike while the faces expressed happiness and joy. His fear rose in proportion to his shock at being the only minority in the hall.

Ademola smiled.

"Now, Dr. Ademola, what's so funny?" Kathleen asked.

"Your husband has just experienced culture shock."

"What?"

"Look around, you're the only white folks here."

"Well, yes, but I don't mind. Granted this whole scene is rather strange, but I'm prepared."

"You were inoculated on your previous trip here."

Kathleen loosened her husband's tie.

"Let's clear immigration and get out of here." Ademola started to walk away then looked over his shoulder.

McFlarthey remained seated.

"I think we better move," Ademola said.

Suddenly all the lights went out and they were plunged into darkness. "What the hell is that?" McFlarthey asked.

"That's the normal power failure here," his wife said.

"Normal?" McFlarthey's voice echoed in the dark.

Then there were tiny flashes as the immigration officers lit candles. They waited and waited but the lights refused to come back on.

"I don't like waiting in the dark like this. We should get the hell back on the plane and get out of here. Mr. McFlarthey, I think—" Wayne was cut off by the sound of a generator. The lights came back.

"Well, thank heaven for modern technology." Kathleen smiled nervously.

"Let's get out of here," Ademola said anxiously.

The immigration officer was courteous as he stamped their passports, allowing them a temporary stay in Nigeria for a maximum of three months with no right to employment.

"Thanks," Ademola told the man.

"No problem. Now you go to that place over there for your yellow card stamps."

"Let's see about the inoculation approval. I have a feeling that's not going to be quite so easy," Ademola said.

There was no line at the health department desk. Only foreign visitors were expected to be inoculated. The health officer was a huge man with a bulging stomach, dark-complexioned with a face that resembled that of a hippopotamus. He took the yellow cards from Ademola, laid them on the desk and took the better part of two minutes to read the first one on the pile. He stared at Ademola, then Kathleen, then McFlarthey, then Wayne, and finally at Jason on Ademola's shoulder. He put the card back on the desk. He cleared his throat, rubbed his face with both palms and stared at Ademola. "Your documents are not in order! No inoculation for cholera, malaria, yellow fever, leprosy, tuberculosis, meningitis, AIDS, and more." The authority and threat in his voice were undisguised.

"I think you're mistaken—"

"What! Me, mistaken? Who are you? Who is your father in this Nigeria?" he snarled, his water-hose nose swelling.

"I beg your pardon? What's that got to do with anything? I'm a physician. The list—"

"I don't care if you're God. You want to teach me my job, eh? Do I come to your hospital to teach you your job, eh? So if you are a doctor, *nko*? I am the officer in charge here and what I say is what I say. So shut your mouth, you hear?" He looked over his shoulder as though expecting someone to come charging in.

Wayne moved closer to McFlarthey and started to whisper in his ear.

"Shut up!" The officer banged on the desk and the cards flew to the ground. "What did you tell the big man?"

"I don't—" McFlarthey started, his face turning red.

"Shut up!"

McFlarthey's inner combustion flared, consuming him with an outrage and fear that he had never experienced before. He was enraged to be so contemptuously treated in the presence of his wife and employee. And alarmed because the big black man in front of him had the power to visit unimaginable grief on him with impunity. He felt like a man who fell into the ocean and was confronted by the king fish who wanted to know if the man ever ate seafood. If the answer was yes, the man knew he would be fish bait. McFlarthey wished he could tell the bully to go to hell, but a glance at Jason reminded him that much more was at stake. His apprehension soared again when he remembered the story Ademola told him on the plane. "Without a doubt, this black monster is waiting for someone else, possibly a much more wicked brute," he thought. Despite all his wealth and power the feeling of vulnerability overpowered him.

"What do you want?" Ademola asked.

"I say shut your mouth. Or you don't hear well?" The officer ordered Ademola to pick up the cards.

Ademola did quickly. The officer snatched them from his hand, stared at Ademola again, and then smiled. He looked over his shoulder once more before handing the cards back to them. "You can go," he smacked, a diabolical smile on his face as he stepped away from the desk.

Ademola waved to a man standing a few feet from the exit door. "That's Dr. Awoyinka, our host, over there."

The man waved back and hurried toward them.

McFlarthey was amazed at the similarities between the man and Johnson. The two men could've been brothers. Not in their physical appearance, but in their aura and mien: stoic, aristocratic, self-assured. Both men's almond-shaped eyes were alert yet celestial.

Wayne pushed the luggage cart toward the exit door. Kathleen and Ademola, with Jason on his shoulder, followed amidst a crowd of anxious relatives awaiting the arrival of family members. McFlarthey walked behind them.

Quite abruptly, there was a commotion around the exit door. A draft of disquiet chilled McFlarthey, and his heart lurched upon seeing two soldiers sprinting toward them.

"Welcome back, Dr. Ademola, this must be the unluckiest day of your life. Welcome home!" Achibong glared at Ademola.

"Do I know you?" Ademola asked lamely.

"I am Lieutenant Colonel Achibong, DMI. It's been ten years. Let's hope this time you do not try to run away!"

"Why would I do such a thing?" Ademola's voice was steady as he looked Achibong straight in the eyes.

"You're under arrest!"

⸏

27

"This is a special bulletin from the BBC! We have just received word that the Nigerian capital city of Abuja is under siege. The BBC correspondent stationed in Lagos is standing by—Judy, what is the latest?" The nasal British-accented voice of the announcer filled the room.

Brigadier Sakara nodded to Air Commodore Ebutie, who hastily turned up the volume on the short wave radio. "Another bloody *coup* is in progress in the West African nation of Nigeria. From what I've been able to gather so far, soldiers loyal to General Hakabala are locked in a deadly battle with those of Brigadier Sakara, the hitherto second-in-command of the Nigerian Ruling Council. Here in the city of Lagos, several top army officers have already lost their lives in what is seen as a successful attempt by the southern faction to control the city. The building housing the Directorate of Military Intelligence, DMI, was reduced to rubble during the battle between the unit led by General Bata and the soldiers loyal to Brigadier Sakara early afternoon in a failed attempt by General Bata to arrest or execute Brigadier Sakara—" The female correspondent stopped to catch her breath.

"Any news of the whereabouts of the leaders of the two factions?" the announcer asked.

"It's safe to assume that General Hakabala is still in

Abuja. An eyewitness, who wishes to remain anonymous, told me on the phone that he saw Brigadier Sakara storming out of the presidential villa early this afternoon. And about two hours later all hell broke loose. Brigadier Sakara's present whereabouts are unknown," she announced.

"Which faction do you suppose will emerge victorious?"

"That's going to be a close call. As matters stand right now, General Hakabala and Brigadier Sakara are equally matched."

"Turn it off. Are we ready for plan C?" Sakara said.

"Yes, my pilots are ready to take off. You give the order and the presidential villa will be bombed out of existence," Air Commodore Ebutie replied with confidence.

"Good! The—" Sakara was interrupted by a knock at the door. "Come in," he snapped.

The major with the cherub face marched in and flashed a salute. "I have Lieutenant Colonel Achibong and Dr. Femi Adenekan at the bungalow, sir. A telephone call came in while we were in the interrogation room just before we escaped and I allowed Achibong to answer it—"

"I didn't call there," Sakara snapped.

"He told me the call must be either from you or the airport, sir, and that's why I allowed him to answer it." The major looked uncomfortable.

"Who called?" Sakara glared at the major.

"Achibong refused to tell me, sir. He said the information is for your ears only. But I heard him mention the name Ademola—"

"What? And did you say Femi Adenekan is with him?"

"Yes, sir. The two were on their way to DMI when—"

"Go and bring Achibong here right away. Keep Femi in the bungalow." Sakara dismissed the major. He then gave the order for the execution of plan C, authorizing the Nigerian Air Force to commence their aerial attack on Abuja. He received the news that all the major Yoruba-speaking cities were under his command. Two of his most loyal officers were presently negotiating with Ibo officers for their support. Sakara was optimistic. He intended to seize power from Hakabala, force all the generals into early retirement, release all political prisoners, and immediately hand over the government to a duly elected civilian leadership. He did not for a moment regret turning down Akin's offer of two million dollars. He smiled, realizing that he had never allowed himself to get too comfortable at the top. At forty-seven and unencumbered, he did not need more than his salary to survive.

Throughout Babasa's reign, when conspicuous consumption, ranging from fresh caviar to stretch Rolls Royces, was the vogue, Sakara treated such vulgarities with contempt. He refused to travel abroad, like other members of the military ruling class, who eventually became hostages to English and French luxury. He was easily bored but enraged whenever he found out that yet another general had paid double the market price for a house or flat in London, Paris, or New York. But he kept tabs on everyone, thus strengthening his power over them. He then used the information to blackmail his enemies into submission or support. Yes, they all hated him, but what mattered to Sakara was that they also feared him.

While he waited for Achibong's arrival, his mind wandered to the events of the past several years: the first nine months of Babasa's seven-year regime had been the best. He had delivered on his promise to carry out a national census, which pegged the population of the country at over ninety million, with the national birth rate rising faster than the death rate. He had gutted the ivory towers, mostly in the south, appointing intellectuals to key government positions and in the process silencing the opposition. He had moved the capital from Lagos to the northern city of Abuja.

Grandiose building projects were embarked upon, enabling a few well-connected civilian contractors to line their pockets with billions of dollars which they stashed away in secret bank accounts all over Europe. In 1991, while the United States and the rest of the world busied themselves fighting the so-called Mother of All Wars in the Gulf, Nigeria sold crude oil to America totaling twelve point four billion dollars. Babasa and a few of his cohorts found ways to divert twelve point two billion dollars to their personal accounts, leaving only two hundred million in the national treasury. The collective voices of the opposition and critics became a source of irritation to the government. To divert attention from his fraudulent activities, Babasa announced his intention to hand over the running of the country to a civilian government. The people became preoccupied with the election campaign. Millions in stolen money stashed in Swiss accounts found its way back to Nigeria. As the results of the June 12, 1993 election came in, it looked like the clear winner was going to be a southern businessman, who hitherto had been part of the status quo. There was celebration all over the country. Foreign observers, including a former U.S. president, concluded that the election was one of the fairest they had witnessed in any Third World country. The world waited for the winner to assume the presidency and wake up the land of the sleeping giant of Africa.

A couple of months later the world gasped in shock when Babasa announced his decision to annul the results of the election. Amidst the clamoring and condemnation from every corner of the globe he quietly exited the center stage, leaving behind a country in chaos, hemorrhaging in the hands of a powerless interim government headed by another southerner. On November 23, 1993, Hakabala snatched the reign of power in a *coup*, and a new era in the never-ending history of black-on-black pogrom began.

By every measure Hakabala proved to be the quintessential military dictator whose penchant for control was as bloody as it was absolute. The more tyrannical he became the larger his paranoia grew. Draconian decrees were promulgated in order to imprison or execute dissidents.

Sakara winced at the thought of Achibong, to whom he had confided years back his ambition to become president of Nigeria one day. Now the idiot had betrayed him. "Achibong knows the price for such treachery," he mused, "I must be careful how I handle him. He is nobody's fool."

There was a knock at the door.

"Come in," Sakara said with a smile.

Achibong entered, flashed a lethargic salute and stood at attention, looking ill-at-ease in his military uniform. Sakara waved the cherub major out of the room. "Sit down, Ben." He pointed to a chair.

"Thank you, sir," Achibong said nervously.

Sakara's hatred flared, conscious of Achibong's bleak stare. "Hakabala confirmed what Eniola told me about you!" The words slashed the silence like a sword.

Achibong's Adam's apple ascended, then dropped slowly. "I was compromised, sir."

Sakara nodded. "Aren't we all?" He said with feigned sympathy. "Soon Hakabala will be history." The black of his eyes focused on the tip of his nose, studying Achibong.

"I did not betray you, sir. I doctored the tapes before handing them over to General Hakabala. That's the truth, sir." He was crestfallen.

Sakara nodded again. He waved Achibong's apology aside. "What do you have for me?" He smiled at his *non sequitur*.

"Dr. Ademola is due to arrive at the airport in a few minutes, sir." Achibong looked hopeful.

"I have more important concerns at the moment. I am going to give you the responsibility of arresting Ademola. He is still a fugitive known to be armed and dangerous. You know what to do." He watched Achibong's reaction keenly.

"Yes, sir." Achibong jumped to his feet and then flashed a smart salute.

"Take Major Alao with you," Sakara said, dismissing Achibong. He waited for a couple of minutes before pressing the button on his desk.

The Hausa officer that offered to take care of Achibong marched in and stood rock-still.

"He's all yours—as soon as Dr. Ademola is arrested."

28

The two men sat on the wooden chairs facing each other. They seemed to be gathering themselves. Then in an angry tone Femi asked, "At whose order are we being detained?"

Achibong shifted in his chair. "Your brother-in-law, of course." He shuddered before leaning forward. "Brigadier Sakara discovered that your sister was passing information to me."

"What information?"

"Sshh!" Achibong pressed a finger against his lips, looking over Femi's shoulder at the door. "Believe me, it's not anything you need to know. Chances are, your sister is dead by now."

"What the hell are you talking about? She better not be." Femi did not care if he was heard. His heart began to race. He shut his eyes and boxed his anger. "Think! If Achibong is right about Eniola, my own death may be imminent. How many guards are out there?" With selective attention, he directed his senses toward the distant sound of a generator which was interrupted by the occasional chirping of birds. "Where is this place?"

"Until now, only Sakara knew of the existence of this building. It must be his private interrogation house. That's not good news," Achibong said.

Femi got on his feet as if he wanted to stretch his legs.

He scanned the windowless dark room. He tiptoed to the door, pressed his ear against it and listened. He came back to his chair after a few minutes. "I believe there's only one soldier outside the door. But tell me, what do you think happened to my sister?"

"I'm not certain. But something terrible must have—Listen, soon they will come for us. But just in case you manage to survive this somehow, there are two things you should know. First, as soon as you go back to Sakara's house—" Achibong described the location where he picked up the tapes from Eniola. He told Femi what to do with it. He told him that Sakara had ordered him to prepare a bomb that was to be planted in the cave atop the hills of Abeokuta. The bomb, he said, was in the trunk of his jeep parked here in the compound. "Femi, whatever you do, don't get anywhere near the jeep at 2010 hour—"

"What is that in human language?" Femi interrupted.

"Ten minutes after eight tonight. The bomb is the most powerful I've ever put together and—"

The door swung open and the officer with the cherub face marched into the room. The light from a powerful flashlight slashed the darkness like a luminous sword. "Come with me!" He pointed to Achibong.

Femi saw Achibong look over his shoulder, fright creasing his face, before he exited the room.

McFlarthey looked into Achibong's eyes and immediately beckoned Wayne toward him. "What's going on here?" He shifted his gaze from Achibong to the other officer whose cherub face failed to conceal his hostility.

"Who are you?" The major came closer.

McFlarthey scanned the faces of the crowd who were

beginning to gather. Their hatred and fear set off alarms in his head. And then he saw a white man running from the parking lot towards them. "Who's that?" he asked Wayne.

"Most likely someone from the embassy. I was able to speak with the ambassador before we landed, sir. " Wayne beckoned the man toward them.

"Howdy, Mr. McFlarthey?" the man said with a Texan drawl.

"Am I glad to see you," McFlarthey said. "Is the ambassador with you?"

"No, Mr. McFlarthey—I'm Tom Connally, First Secretary, U.S. Embassy," he said with a rigid smile.

McFlarthey noticed the change on Achibong's face. "This young fellow looks like he's about to do something drastic," he thought but asked, "Why is this man being arrested?"

"I'll handle this!" The major stepped forward. He grabbed Ademola's wrist and was about to handcuff him when Connally tapped him on the shoulder. He spun around. "This is not a diplomatic problem." He looked as though he would punch Connally in the mouth if he didn't get out of his way.

In a flash, Achibong's face became a mask of fury as he took a deep breath and with all his strength, smashed his knee against the major's lower back. The handcuffs slipped out of his hand as he grabbed the air in a futile effort to retain his balance. He fell down, rolling on his side. Achibong snatched the gun from the holster and pressed the nuzzle against the major's temple. Between breaths he said to Connally, "I have valuable information for your government in exchange for political asylum."

McFlarthey was perplexed. "What the hell is going on? I need to get my family and Dr. Ademola away from this madness to *Abeecootah*."

Connally shook his head. "The ambassador instructed

me to bring you straight to the embassy. You arrived in this tropical hell at the very worst of time, Mr. McFlarthey. All American citizens are advised to get out of Nigeria immediately. There's a—"

"I didn't fly halfway across the world with my ailing son to be instructed by the ambassador where I can or cannot go. Where are you parked?" McFlarthey flared.

The major got on his knees, bunched a fist and slammed it against Achibong's leg.

McFlarthey heard the gunshot as Achibong pulled the trigger and a red dot appeared on the side of the major's head. He slumped to the ground, dead.

McFlarthey's face and neck turned red with rage. He looked around. The crowd that had gathered a few minutes before had disappeared, returning to the safety of their cars around the airport. Brown dust and humidity combined to heighten the presence of death all around. McFlarthey saw the look of terror and desperation on Achibong's face a split second before the strange silence was permeated with the sound of marching boots on gravel.

Achibong's legs came alive. He sprinted toward the parking lot like a hunted rabbit in the middle of a concrete jungle.

"Bloody hell! Catch that bastard. I want him alive, Go!" the leader ordered two of his men, their semi-automatic rifles held high in the air. "Go back to the vehicle and bring the petrol and necklace. That fool will smell pepper today," he barked at one of his lieutenants. A shroud of fatalistic heroism cloaked his essence as he jabbed a finger toward Ademola. "Cuff him!"

McFlarthey quickly took Jason away from Wayne whose eyes turned indigo blue as he stepped forward, blocking the officer's path.

"Get out of my way!" The officer looked as though Wayne had just pricked his eye with a needle.

"Not on your life." Wayne glared at the officer.

"K—k—ill—" A morsel of anger lodged in the officer's throat, choking him, immobilizing him.

Connally seized the moment to step forward. "I'll handle this," he said. "I'm with the American Embassy. These people, including him—" he nodded at Ademola, "these people are the guests of the ambassador. I'm sure there's been a mistake."

"There's no mistake! This man is under arrest. I have my order to take him in. This is still Nigeria if I have to remind you, not America." The officer stopped as two of his lieutenants grabbed Ademola and commenced to drag him away.

McFlarthey felt a sudden chill. He shook his head as though wanting to get rid of a nightmare. He hastily compartmentalized his wealth, power, and above all, his anger, and rearranged his priorities . His main objective was getting his family the hell away from this place. "Come with me, Kathleen." He grabbed her wrist.

"We can't just walk away and leave Dr. Ademola with these people." McFlarthey's sudden decision alarmed her.

The officer looked satisfied and was about to walk away with Ademola when McFlarthey said, "We are going with you to wherever you intend to take this man." He turned to Connally. "Get the ambassador on the cell phone and ask him to contact the president of this country. He must tell him that my family and I have been abducted by these people and he must act immediately."

"You can't do that," the officer snapped.

"The hell I can't!" Connally proceeded to walk toward his vehicle when he bumped into Dr. Awoyinka. "Sorry."

Awoyinka's eyes rounded when he saw Ademola, sandwiched between two soldiers, hands cuffed behind his back. "There must be—" The rest of the word choked Awoyinka as a soldier's fist smashed against his face. He fell down.

"If anyone else tries to prevent me from doing my duty, that person will be shot on the spot." The officer's voice sliced the nervous silence as he glowered at Connally. "Move!" He shoved Ademola with a renewed force of hatred that could not be kept in check any longer.

McFlarthey stood his ground. "Nobody here is trying to prevent you from doing your job, however, this man has the right to defend himself." He was breathing hard but in control of his voice.

The soldier swung sidewise to face the parking lot.

McFlarthey also swung around to look at his wife.

"What's the matter, William?" Kathleen asked, alarmed.

"Don't look," McFlarthey whispered.

But Kathleen did anyway.

Achibong burst into view, exhausted, breathless, and bloodied. His army uniform hung in shreds from his broad shoulders. Four soldiers dragged him toward the officer who spat, then nodded. They pushed and shoved Achibong, taunting and yelling. Their sweat-drenched, dark faces were merciless. They pelted him with tree branches. A Land Rover pulled up and two soldiers got out. One of them rolled out an old car tire, laid it on the ground, and reached into the back of the vehicle to extract a jerrycan of gasoline.

McFlarthey's heart knocked dangerously against his chest. He couldn't look away despite the scream in his head to do so. He saw one of the soldiers knock Achibong to the ground, kicking him several times. The other, face set in a rigid scowl, snatched the tire and lowered it like a giant necklace over Achibong's head, locking both his arms to his sides and rendering him helpless.

The commander's command filled the air, "Lieutenant Colonel Achibong, you are hereby found guilty of treason under Decree Number 0012. By the authority conferred on me by the commander-in-chief and head of state of the Republic of Nigeria you are sentenced to death by *necklacing.* Your execution shall be carried out with immediate dispatch."

The soldier with the jerrycan uncapped it and doused Achibong with gasoline. The second soldier reached into his pocket and extracted a box of matches.

"Help!" Achibong choked, staggering forward. The weight of the tire brought him tumbling to the asphalt.

Kathleen screamed, "Oh my God! They're going to burn him alive!"

29

A s the afternoon neared sunset, the inside of the
bungalow was like a furnace. Femi was soaked in
perspiration, his breathing labored. He banged on
the door again as he had several times before. He heard the
same gruff voice ordering him to keep quiet if he knew
what was good for him. But unlike before, Femi sounded as
though he was on his last breath: "I can't breath. There's no
more air in this room. I'm scribbling a note on the wall to
inform Brigadier Sakara about what happened here. My
blood is on your hand if you let me die here." His voice
sounded deathly. He waited and listened intently.

An arrogant silence assaulted his ears. He got more frustrated by the second. And just when he was about to yell, he
heard the muffled sound of military boots on the concrete
floor. Sluggish at first, he held his breath and counted, holding the legs of the wooden chair high above his head as the
steps approached. He waited. The steps stopped at the door.
His lips trembled with anticipation and fear. Nothing but
the prolonged silence of caution assaulted his ears. His knees
began to shake. He put the chair on the floor and was about
to bang on the door when the horn of a car bleated like an
angry goat and the sound of boots outside the door hurried
away and faded.

Sakara scanned the faces of the ten officers in the room, satisfied that the men were unanimous in their choice. He turned to stare at the face of the reporter that filled the television screen. The middle-aged white man sounded rather disappointed that the carnage he was reporting had ended so soon. "This is the first time in the history of this nation that a *coup* took place without the airports, electrical power supply, television and radio stations being shut down." The correspondent smiled. "General Hakabala was killed when the presidential villa in Abuja was attacked by aerial bombardment late this afternoon. Top officers loyal to the slain leader have been rounded up and summarily executed. The nation, and for that matter the world, awaits the public appearance of Brigadier *Seegun* Sakara to assume the top post. I have been told by a top army officer that the announcement will take place within the hour—"

As Sakara listened to the latest report on CNN, the officers slapped each other on the back. There was applause in the room. Sakara smiled and nodded his approval. He beckoned Air Commodore Ebutie toward him. "Is the speech ready?"

"Yes, sir! Colonel Okpara sent out the invitation to all the media people to gather at Dodan Barracks at 2100 hours for the announcement." Ebutie extracted an envelope from his pocket and handed it to Sakara. "Here's the speech, sir, exactly as you dictated it. The common people of the nation are going to welcome you with open arms. This change is just what the country needs."

Sakara slit open the envelope, extracted a sheet of paper and nodded with satisfaction after reading the short announcement. "Good!" He added the paper to the sheaf of printouts in the green file in his hand. "Now I can rewrite the fable of Robin Hood," he thought, "a black warrior taking back stolen riches from the thieves to be returned to the needy." He intended to force those on the list to hand over

all the ill–gotten gains from their foreign bank accounts back
to the government. That would be his first order of business.
But before that, he needed to get someone else to produce a
bomb powerful enough to blow the cave atop Olumo Rock
to bits. He looked at his watch and wondered why he had
not received the report on Achibong and Ademola. The
thought of having Ademola finally trapped brought back the
vivid picture of the beating he had received from his father
after failing his exam at Mayfield. This time the bastard
would join his fornicating mother and father and the treacherous Eniola in hell. He intended to torture him with the
most agonizing device in his possession before burying him
in concrete. The thought of seeing Ademola's reaction after
being told of his mother's slaughter filled him with unimaginable joy. His anxiety peaked when he heard the familiar
knock on the door. With a profound effort he contained his
eagerness.

"Come in," Air Commodore Ebutie said.

The door creaked open and the officer charged with the
responsibility of killing Achibong came in smiling. He saluted and remained at attention.

"At ease," Sakara ordered.

The officer flashed another salute before spreading his
legs apart and clasping his hands behind his back.
"Congratulations, Your Excellency, sir! I pledge my absolute
loyalty to you and my fatherland. I am proud to inform you
that my assignment was completed with success. I have the
prisoner in place as you ordered, sir."

"Ola Ademola, I will repay you with compounded interest," he promised himself, but said, "Good," before returning
the officer's salute. He looked at his watch again and turned
his attention back to the officers in the room. "Gentlemen,
let's reconvene at Dodan Barracks thirty minutes before the
scheduled press conference. I have an urgent matter to
attend to. Good evening."

Everyone jumped to their feet, saluted in unison, and waited for Sakara to exit the room.

ᔫ

Ill at ease, Ademola squinted in an attempt to adjust his eyes to the darkness in the room. The air was weighted with stale perspiration. With a dwindling effort he controlled his breathing but his shoulders ached terribly. His frustration and anxiety crested at the thought of not being able to give the kolanut and kaolin to Dr. Awoyinka before his wrists were cuffed behind his back. Johnson's last words filled his mind: "Whatever you do, son, don't let the boy out of your sight until you enter the cave. Without the fetishes in your hand, Jason will die."

Now groping in the dark, he sensed the presence of someone else in the room. As much as he wanted to see or speak to the person, he dared not until the sound of the vehicle that brought him to the bungalow faded to silence. He jumped when he felt the touch of a hand on his chest. "Who are you?" he asked.

"Sshh! It's me, who else do you expect? Where did they take you?"

Ademola stiffened. The voice sounded vaguely familiar. His chagrin at being cuffed and thrown into darkness like an animal receded. "Who are you?" he whispered.

"Femi. Where—"

"Femi Adenekan—Eniola's brother?"

"Oh my God, is it you, Dr. Ademola?" Femi's voice cracked.

"Yes, what are you doing—where are we?" He wished he could free his hands to embrace Femi. He swallowed hard and felt a burning sensation as tears welled up in his eyes.

"How—when did you get back?" Femi wrapped his arms around Ademola's neck. "Who brought you here?"

"Soldiers. What are you doing here?"

"Sakara's hatchetmen! There was another soldier here with me, Sakara's assistant at DMI. That's who I thought you were. Achibong—"

"He's dead. Burnt alive," Ademola said coldly.

"Oh my God! We have to get away from here before they come back. Achibong told me that this is Sakara's personal torture chamber. He also said that it's likely my sister is dead by now."

Ademola froze. "Eniola dead? How?"

"That's what Achibong said. I hope it's not true. But if Achibong is dead as you said, Sakara must have ordered his execution. No one else would dare risk antagonizing him. He has become incredibly powerful and dangerous. I'm next, Dr. Ademola. We never liked each other. He—there must be a way for us to escape from here. How many guards are out there?"

"There were several when we came in. One of them let us into the compound. The rest were stationed outside the gate. But what difference does that make? My hands are cuffed and the door is locked from outside. We—wait a second." Ademola's mind became infused with a sudden thought. "Are you an *Abiku*?"

"A what?" Femi asked, confused at the irrelevance.

"An *Abiku*, you know, like me, a child that—"

"I know what an *Abiku* is, but I'm not. Even if I were, what's the connection?" Femi asked in a tone of voice suggesting that he thought Ademola might have lost his mind.

"There are two objects in my pocket that I need to make use of. If you are not an *Abiku*, you can't help me take them out. But you can help with my pants."

"How?"

"Take them off." Ademola sat down on the floor. "I don't know if this is going to work but it's worth a try. Be careful not to touch my pocket. Just pull the legs."

Femi got on his knees and was about to loosen Ademola's buckle when a tap at the door interrupted him.

"What's going on in there?" the voice of the guard filtered through the space between the door and the floor.

Ademola remained on his back, motionless. He heard the sound of shuffling feet, and then the jingling of keys. He looked away from the door and saw Femi stealing toward the door. Femi stopped to pick up the chair just when the click of a key signalled the intention of the guard to open the door. Femi raised the chair above his head and waited. The door eased open and the beam of a flashlight cut the darkness. Femi remained behind the door, ready to bring the chair crashing down on the guard's head. But the soldier remained at the doorway, maintaining a safe distance.

He scanned the room with the beam. It landed on the sprawled body of Ademola and stopped. "What are you doing there?"

Ademola's chest heaved and his knees began to shake. "I—I'm trying to sleep," he managed to say.

"Get up! You sleep when I say so. Where's the other prisoner?" the guard asked suspiciously, raising his other hand. Ademola's eyes widened when he saw the soldier's finger curl around the trigger of his revolver. "Get up!"

"I can't." Ademola measured the distance between the soldier and Femi, and realizing that the soldier was not yet within harm's way, he whimpered, "You have to help me, I can't move. Please!"

"Where's the other prisoner?" the soldier asked again, insistent. He took a couple of backward steps, and trained the beam at the space between the door and the jamb.

Ademola's heart leapt to his throat as Femi raised his leg and kicked the door with such force that the impact shook the building. The sound of metal on concrete filled the air only to be replaced by the scream of the guard whose hand was wedged between the door and the jamb. With the agility of a wrestler, Ademola vaulted to his feet just as Femi grabbed the revolver from the ground and yanked the door open. The incredulity on the soldier's face mirrored his shock and fear. His left hand went up in a futile attempt to use the flashlight as an offensive weapon.

At the same moment Femi's face transformed into a mask of fury as he kicked the soldier between the legs so hard it sounded like punting a football. The flashlight slipped out of the man's hand. He grabbed his crotch, eyes bulging, sucking the dank air as he fell to his knees, rolling onto his side. "Get up!" Femi kicked the soldier with a renewed force of hatred. "Where are the keys?" He was breathing hard as he pressed the muzzle of the gun against the soldier's temple.

Ademola got to his knees, twisting his body slightly in order to grab the flashlight from the ground. He got up, turned, and trained the beam of the flashlight on the soldier. He winced as Femi booted the soldier in the stomach again, knocking him unconscious, and was about to search the soldier's pocket when Ademola said, "Look, there, in the door."

Femi grabbed the soldier's neck, bent him double and wrapped the man's belt around his wrists and ankles. He dragged the still body into the room, locked the door, and extracted the bunch of keys. He tried all the keys, but none worked on the cuffs.

"Let's find a hammer or something else. There's got to be one around here." Ademola handed the flashlight to Femi.

The stench of pain and death hung in the air like *harmattan* dust as the two searched each of the five rooms filled with unimaginable torture contraptions.

"We must hurry up and get the hell out of here!" Ademola said, convinced that others would come for them soon.

Femi was about to exit the kitchen when the beam of the flashlight landed on an object that caught his attention. He froze. "What's that?"

Ademola also froze. Not at the sight of the object, but the sound of grief in Femi's voice. "What's the matter?" he asked.

"That!" Femi took a couple of steps toward the sink. "Oh my God!" His whisper was laden with foreboding and horror. "The pendant!" His hand shook as he clutched a piece of ceramic the size of a quarter with an inlay of Mickey Mouse wearing a French beret. Slowly, he turned it over in his hand. "I bought this pendant in France for my niece, Taiwo. She liked it so much she wouldn't take it off her neck, not even to let her brother or Eniola touch it. My niece was here in this building. God, what has that bastard done to my sister and her babies? What—" His lips began to quiver.

"Are you sure Sakara is involved in all this?" Ademola felt a sudden chill.

"My sister is somewhere in this place. And I'm not leaving until I find her. That bastard is going to have to kill me too." Femi banged the butt of the gun in his hand against the cabinet. "I can feel her presence deep in my bones. She's here." He ran out of the kitchen into another room, groping in the dark, touching the walls, the floor, and muttering hysterically, "She's here. They are here. I'm not leaving until I find her. I must find—"

"I think this is all one big mistake, Femi. Why would Sakara kill Eniola and his own children? It doesn't—"

Femi ran out of the room and grabbed the front of Ademola's shirt. "No, they are not," he snapped. "Eniola told me everything. She was forced to marry that cross-eyed fiend!"

"Get a grip, Femi. You are not making sense and we really need to get away from here fast." Ademola tried but failed to shake Femi off.

"You think I'm mad, don't you? Well, I've got news for you, Dr. Ademola. My sister was pregnant before she was forced to marry that maniac. The twins are yours."

"What?"

"God is my witness, doctor. Now you know."

"What's that?" Ademola cocked his head sideways.

Femi's eyes widened. "Soldiers! They're coming in."

❧

30

As the green Range Rover sped out the gate of Ebutie's house, Sakara looked over his shoulder and grunted in satisfaction upon seeing the six jeeps behind filled with soldiers in combat uniform. The two jeeps in front were equally manned. They drove for thirty minutes on the crowded streets around Ikeja. It was as though the people were oblivious of the *coup* that had just taken place. As the convoy crossed the northern boundary of the township, a phalanx of army vehicles loomed a couple of miles away, blocking the secondary road.

"Stop here," Sakara ordered. "Tell the others to wait at the checkpoint ahead until I return," he told his *aide de camp* who hurried out of the Range Rover. "Go!"

The driver drove onto the fork that turned into a narrow path, which fed into a dirt track. They continued for two miles and were stopped at a makeshift checkpoint by a soldier who looked like he wished he was elsewhere.

Sakara glared at the soldier, who reacted as though he realized that he was about to step on a land mine. He saluted and ran to remove the barricade from the track.

As soon as the headlight caught the gate of the bungalow, Sakara asked, "What the hell is that? Where are the guards?" He waited for the vehicle to enter the compound. "Lock that gate!" he ordered his driver. The compound was pitch dark. "Why is the generator off? Something has gone wrong!" He marched inside and found the guard, hands and feet bound, mouth gagged. "What happened?" Sakara hammered the soldier with more questions. And he was told about the incident leading to Ademola's and Femi's escape. Frustrated, he fumed, "Nothing else is more important than getting that bastard and destroying him." To the driver, he said, "I need a helicopter to fly me to Abeokuta. Go straight to the airport!"

⤳

Earlier, as Achibong's necklaced body became a roaring conflagration, Wayne had told McFlarthey that he was dead wrong about Nigeria being a safe place. He advised his boss that they should get the hell away from the country. McFlarthey was at a loss. He stood in front of the airport, watching as Ademola was driven away.

"William, what are we going to do?" Kathleen asked, nervously wringing her hands. "The fetishes that Dr. Johnson gave to Dr. Ademola for Jason's protection are—"

"What fetishes?" Awoyinka asked, instantly alert.

"The kolanut and kaolin Dr. Johnson gave to Ademola," McFlarthey said.

"If Ademola has them with him, there's not much we can do about that at the moment. We need to get your son to the cave. Hopefully the master diviner will know what to do."

"I don't think so," Wayne snapped. "Mr. McFlarthey, I suggest we get back on the plane."

McFlarthey turned to Connally. "Where's your car?"

Connally pointed to the white Bronco a few yards away. "I'll be glad to take you to the Embassy, Mr. McFlarthey."

"What I want you to do is get the ambassador on the phone and make sure he talks to the president of Nigeria right away. We have to rescue Dr. Ademola—he's Jason's pediatrician. He brought us here."

"Your son?" Connally looked uncomfortable. "Must be important for those two who arrested him to come out in the open without their usual army of bodyguards. Those two are some of the most dangerous men in this country." Connally's Texan accent was more pronounced.

"He is an American citizen," McFlarthey snapped.

"That isn't going to make any difference. By the time the ambassador gets State to intervene, chances are your man will be dead, Mr. McFlarthey. There's a breakdown of law and order here. A bloody *coup* just took place and the next man to head this country is top on the list of the most unpredictable and dangerous bastards here."

"It's your job to see to it that Dr. Ademola does not come to any harm—what?" McFlarthey snapped, turning to Wayne.

"It's Jason, sir. He doesn't look well."

Awoyinka stepped forward. "We need to get your boy to Abeokuta right away."

McFlarthey agreed. They all trooped into Awoyinka's Peugeot station wagon and sped toward their destination as if the devil were in hot pursuit. The closer they got to Abeokuta, the sicker Jason became. There was a contagious panic in the car. They made it to Abeokuta just as the sun touched the horizon. Awoyinka parked the station wagon at the entrance to the forest, waited for McFlarthey, who carried Jason on his shoulder, and followed the footpath toward the cave. The walk was difficult and laborious especially for Kathleen. At the precise moment they reached the top of the hill, something moved between the legs of the three-legged *akee* tree. And then disappeared just as suddenly.

"What the hell was that?" McFlarthey asked nervously, his voice muffled by the encroaching sound of owls and other night animals. The wind began to blow and the smell of moisture filled the air. He looked up to the black sky and his mind filled with images of white missionaries being led into a cave by a cannibal witchdoctor. He shook his head in an attempt to rid himself of the silly thought.

The figure re-emerged between the legs of the tree, the silhouette of a diviner with a slight stoop, now moving toward them. His bald head glistened in the semi-darkness. He was naked but for a leather loincloth.

"Who's that?" McFlarthey whispered.

"A diviner. He has to cleanse you and your family before you can enter the cave." Awoyinka bowed in greeting to the diviner. The two men spoke in Yoruba before Awoyinka told McFlarthey that Jason must be cleansed first.

Kathleen glanced at her husband nervously.

Awoyinka quickly took Jason from McFlarthey and lay him on the floor beside the diviner, who was on his knees. The diviner undressed Jason and commenced to chant. He stopped to bathe the boy with some slimy liquid from a clay pot. The putrid smell of the concoction was nauseating. Jason's cleansing ceremony took three minutes. When all were cleansed, the diviner and Awoyinka led the way into the dark and dank cave which smelled of decaying flesh, fruits, and forest vegetation.

"Where are we?" McFlarthey asked.

"This is the most sacred place in the Yoruba world. You are very lucky to be here," Awoyinka whispered.

"How's that?"

"This is the first time that anyone other than a few chosen diviners or a newly crowned king have entered this place. The term for coronation in Yoruba is *j'oba* which literally means to 'eat the king.' Upon the death of a reigning king, his successor is brought into this cave. And after various libations he eats the heart and lungs of the dead king," Awoyinka said matter-of-factly.

"Why would they do such a thing?" McFlarthey asked, shocked.

"That's the way of my people."

McFlarthey felt the sudden urge to vomit.

～

Racing toward Abeokuta in Achibong's jeep, Femi slammed his bunched fist against the steering wheel. "I'm going to kill that cross-eyed degenerate with my bare hands."

Ademola seemed nonchalant.

"How can you be so calm about this?" Femi accused.

"Listen to me. Haste is the Achilles heel of the most well-intentioned. Timing is everything. Sakara's time to face the music is not now. But it will be soon." Ademola shuddered. Seconds after they heard the sound of approaching soldiers, Femi had found an axe in the kitchen. He whacked the handcuff, barely missing Ademola's hands. Ademola reached into his pocket, extracted the kolanut and kaolin, and commenced to massage them. His hand became luminous and the fetishes pulsated, filling the room with the amplified sound of breathing. Femi covered his ears and then shut his eyes as the luminosity spread to the rest of the house. Just then the patrol of armed soldiers came goose-stepping toward them.

"What the hell is that?" one of the soldiers shouted, his eyes rounded with fright as he stared at the house. He dropped his gun, spun around and dashed out through the gate. The bungalow looked like an alien ship getting ready to ascend from the jungle. Its luminosity was dazzling, and the sound was ear-shattering. The rest of the soldiers dropped their guns, ran out of the gate, and took to the forest as fast they could.

Ademola pulled Femi by the hand to exit the building.

Outside, the compound looked like an illuminated island. In the surreal brightness, Femi discovered the four holes in the ground. And with the determination of the possessed, he dug out the holes and extracted the bodies of Eniola and the twins. Shocking and morbid as these circumstances were, Ademola knew they had to get away from the house immediately. He did not want to confront Sakara as yet regardless of the power of the fetishes. But Femi wanted to stay and wait for Sakara. It took a while before Ademola could convince the outraged Femi to leave the bungalow. Femi had gone back to the room, stripped the soldier naked, and reluctantly put on the soldier's uniform, while Ademola stood guard.

"When they brought me here, we passed two checkpoints. With you dressed like a soldier, chances are those idiots will not know who you are. You must tell them that you were ordered to take me to another location," Ademola suggested. And it had worked.

As Femi turned off the road and drove into the forest, Ademola stared out the window into blackness. He felt inside his pocket and commenced to massage the kolanut and kaolin again. Instantly his senses became magnified. The ache in his wrist reminded him of the near-miss when Femi whacked the handcuffs off with the axe.

In a moment his eyes adjusted to the darkness and he saw the forest change into a bright three-dimensional vista. The moonless night twinkled with millions of stars. Night animals traversed the moist path lit by the headlights of the vehicle, their yellow phosphorescent eyes flashed in the dark. Flowers were everywhere, colors of the rainbow, gloriously shaped, emitting their own luminosity. Ademola was not just mesmerized by the beauty that surrounded him, he was relieved to be free, hopeful that he still had enough time to get to the cave in order to save Jason. The thought of getting out of Nigeria and re-uniting with Simone filled his essence and he became homesick despite being back in his homeland.

Then, a lone teardrop landed on the windshield, and then another. And another. The windshield was awash in dribbles and soon the soft rain turned into a hurricane. The wind screamed and howled, shredding everything in its path. Leaves flew and strong branches bent to breaking point in acquiescence. The jeep drove into the screaming wind, which now sounded like the beating of wings. The wings whipped angrily as it came closer, accompanied by the rumbling sound of thunder and impending lightning.

The noise rose to an ear-shattering level. Hovering above the trees was a helicopter, its rotating blades dazzling. Femi slammed on the brakes and the jeep skidded, smashing into a fallen *iroko* tree, blowing the two front tires and blocking the muddied path.

Ademola jumped out. "We're almost there," he shouted, covering his face with both hands as the beam from the helicopter flooded the area. He knew instinctively that he had been seen by the sky stalker. "Come, Femi, let's get away from here. Now!" His chest heaved as he ran. He had never set foot on the ground of the forest so he had difficulty navigating the muddied path that led to the three-legged tree. The rain falling in torrents did not bother him, but the ear-shattering sound of the helicopter did. The closer he got to the cave, inexplicably guided by the fetish in his possession, the angrier he became, as his mind filled with the loneliness of his ten-year absence and the images of Eniola's and the babies' cement-encrusted bodies. All because of the degenerate Sakara who would do anything to destroy him. "But why?" he asked in an inner frenzy of ignorance and frustration.

Ademola's longing to see his father and mother so overwhelmed him he stopped to catch his breath. Then the soft and comforting voice of his mother filled his essence: "my husband, the sparkle in my eyes," the name of endearment she used only for him, "whenever the world rubs you wrong, always remember that my love for you is for eternity. Do not react in kind to the wickedness of man. It is the wise and the strong who take the longest breath when provoked. My heart will always be filled with your love as long as you remember that what one handles delicately is never destroyed, it is that which one handles with force and in haste that causes one grief."

                  ↬

The yellow flame of an *atupa* flickered in the darkness, creating irregular shadows on the wall as the blind master diviner sat cross-legged on the raffia mat. On the floor to his right was a clay dish, a calabash bowl filled with dark grey powdered herbs, a razor blade, a bottle of palm oil, and a clay bowl, containing several three-lobed kolanuts.

Awoyinka was on his knees to the left of the diviner. Next to Awoyinka was a wooden bench on which sat Kathleen and her husband. To the left of Kathleen was Jason who lay on his back, face ashen. Wayne was on his feet between Jason and the diviner thus completing the circle.

In the center was a carved ebony divination tray: thirty-one birds were carved around the edge of the tray. The inner circle depicted two human forms smoking long pipes. At the top was carved the face of *Esu*, the medium that transforms human sacrifices into food for the gods. On the bottom were carved a crab and a mudfish, creatures that move in marginal realms. The innermost circle of the tray, which measured seventeen inches in diameter, was smooth.

"We are ready, my venerable master," Awoyinka whispered in Yoruba.

The diviner cleared his throat. "The world of the Living has always been the mirror image of that other world. What the Living perceive as the right side of things are in actuality the left side of things for the Unborn. In this world, I am blind. The opposite is true in the world of the *Abikus*. There, my sight is sharper and brighter than could ever be imagined." The solemn voice echoed in the dark like that of a masquerader. He picked up the calabash bowl and poured some of the dark grey powder in the center of the tray. He then spread the powder evenly to cover the innermost circle. He took a deep breath, ran a bony hand over his face, closing his eyelids. His lips began to quiver. He cleared his throat again and then invoked each section of the tray as he spiritually "opened" it by inscribing lines and dots on the powdered face of the innermost circle. He accompanied every inscription with soft, throaty chanting in the old Yoruba spiritual language. He invoked the spirits of past diviners whose praise-names were "The-one-who-proposes-with-the-right" and "The-one-who-implements-with-the-left," a Yoruba belief about the use of the right hand in social and secular affairs and of the left in sacred and spiritual affairs. He praised his ancestors in flowery terms. And then he invoked the cool, gentle gods, including *Obatala/Orisanla*, the divine sculptor and big god; *Olosa*, god of the lagoon; *Olokun*, goddess of the sea; *Erinle/Osoosi*, water lord and hunter; *Oduduwa*, first king at Ile-Ife; *Osanyin*, lord of leaves; *Osun/Yemoja*, queens of their respective rivers. Finally, he appealed to *Orisa gbigbona*, the hot, violent gods that included *Ogun*, god of iron; *Sango*, lord of thunder; *Oya*, Sango's wife and queen of the whirlwind.

He stopped the incantation suddenly and snapped his fingers. The diviner with the loincloth hurried in and tapped Wayne's shoulder.

"What?" Wayne jumped instinctively.

"He wants you to step aside," Awoyinka said.

Wayne obeyed and thereby created a narrow opening in the circle.

The master diviner's forehead was beaded with sweat as he repeated the incantation several times. With each repetition his voice got louder and his chest and stomach heaved laboriously.

There was movement in the cave.

Simultaneously, the diviner fell to his knees, bent forward, his forehead almost touching that of Jason. The stirring became stronger and a gust swept through, perfusing the cave with the strong smell of forest vegetation, wet leaves and flowers, cassava, banana, mango, guava, orange, pineapple, kolanut, and cocoa. The wind became weighted with the distinct smell of the lagoon and the ocean, portending the arrival of the gentle gods and goddesses.

The diviner hastily covered Jason's ears with both palms as though he did not wish the boy to hear the encroaching thunder. He grunted and his sightless eyes stared at the inscription on the tray. His body began to shake as a soft, guttural incantation in old Yoruba drifted down from what was once the ceiling of the cave.

McFlarthey gazed upward, and to his amazement saw the dark sky above. A gentle wind sighed. The diviner's coppery-yellow eyes dimmed and then shut, lips trembling. He repeated the incantation several times, each time more forcefully than before. His face and neck were drenched in perspiration. A streak of lightning stabbed the darkness, followed a few seconds later by the roar of thunder.

The diviner, seemingly aided by the spirits of his ancestors, pleaded, praised, cajoled and flattered. With tears running down his cheeks, he got down on his stomach, head raised and angled as his blind eyes scanned the wide, dark sky. A streak of lightning lashed out and hurried behind a cloud shaped like a pregnant woman, and all the stars dimmed as the diviner said, "This child is a very special *Abiku*. Without the kolanut and kaolin, the key to his survival is far beyond my power. This child has been chosen by entities that are diametrically opposed, and they will destroy the world to have him. He has to be escorted back to the cosmos of *Abikus*. It's a treacherous and dangerous journey, but we cannot proceed without the key which Ademola holds in his hands. Without it the child will not last another hour in this world." He took a deep agonizing breath and his anguished sightless eyes glowed in the dark.

"Isn't there anything else you can do? Dr. Johnson told us that Jason's only hope of survival is here," McFlarthey said.

Awoyinka translated.

"I don't know why he told you that!"

"He did and—"

"Let me prepare the child for the journey, just in case Ademola makes it here on time," the diviner said with mysterious optimism.

"Thanks," Kathleen said nervously.

"Tell the boy's father and mother that what I am about to do to the child is not as painful as it may seem. They might want to leave the cave for a while."

He waited for Awoyinka to translate.

"Thanks, but we wish to stay!" Kathleen responded.

"Tell the old man we didn't travel halfway across the world with our son only to leave him in a dark cave with—"

"Sshh!" Awoyinka silenced McFlarthey.

"Tell him to start then," McFlarthey said stubbornly.

The diviner nodded, moved the divination tray aside and asked Awoyinka to move Jason to the middle of the circle. He reached into the bowl and extracted four fresh kolanuts which he placed around the boy's body, one on the floor by his head, one by his feet, and one by each hand. He dabbed Jason's ashen forehead with palm oil. Then he moved closer to the boy's body, razor blade in hand. He shut his eyes and said several incantations. He nodded to Awoyinka who swabbed Jason's cheeks with a wad of cotton. With the precision of an expert, the diviner made two small incisions on Jason's left cheek and placed the blade on the mat.

Jason's face creased with pain as he cried out, "Mommy, mommy—" Kathleen stroked her son's head.

The diviner rubbed the dark brown powdery herbs from the dish into the incision. He picked up the blade again and did the same on the boy's right cheek. He raised his head and locked his dead eyes with those of Kathleen's just as she flinched. He smiled as though he could see her reaction. He then moved to Jason's left wrist, made two incisions, rubbed in the powder, and repeated the procedure on the other wrist. Satisfied, he scooted back.

Jason's body stirred but his face did not regain color.

The diviner remained still for a while. He shook his head in resignation. "Without the kolanut and kaolin my power is—" He jerked his head sideways like a lizard sensing an approaching fly.

"Damn!" Sakara pressed his face against the window of the helicopter. He stared as Ademola dashed through the legs of the *akee* tree and disappeared into the cave. "Land there," he shouted, pointing to the top of the rock made visible by the powerful beam from the helicopter.

"I can't do that, sir," the pilot shouted back.

"Yes, you can!"

"The chopper will crash, sir. There's not enough clearance for the blades. We will crash!"

"Where else can you land this damn thing?" Sakara bellowed, unable to contain himself. "Where is the bomb package?"

"Your *aide-de-camp* has it with him in the Range Rover, sir. He should be nearing the entrance of the forest that leads to the top of the hill. I should be able to land on the road a few meters from here, sir."

"Go!" Sakara looked down again as the helicopter made

a U-turn in the air, barely missing the branches of the tree. As much as he wanted to kill Ademola, he knew that he would not be satisfied until he saw his illegitimate half-brother's face when he revealed to him how his mother died. To do that, he had to get Ademola out of the cave before blasting the place to hell. He turned to the pilot. "Get me as close to the entrance of the forest as you can. I will get off the chopper and walk to the top of the hill. As soon as the Range Rover arrives, tell my *ADC* to bring the package to me. Do you understand?" The pilot nodded and commenced his descent. The landing was dangerously bumpy.

Sakara jumped off the chopper like a commando. He dashed away and disappeared behind the edge of the forest. He was soaking wet when he reached the spot where Achibong's black jeep had been abandoned. He jumped over the trunk of the *iroko* tree that blocked the footpath. "My *ADC* will have to leave the Range Rover here and walk the rest of the way to the top of the hill," he thought with anger. He cursed in frustration when he couldn't read the dial on his wristwatch, needing to know how much time he had left before the scheduled announcement. The rain continued to pummel the ground.

He ran back to Achibong's jeep, opened the left front door, and reached in to look for the light switch. He flicked it on, flooding the forest path with light, and ran to the front of the jeep. It was five minutes before eight o'clock. "I have thirty-five minutes to finish the job here and be back at Dodan Barracks," he calculated. He pulled out his gun and ran the rest of the way to the foot of the tree.

⌒

"Who goes there?" the master diviner asked as the sound of footsteps approached the inner section of the cave.

"It's me." Ademola's voice echoed in the dark, bouncing off the rough surface of the cave.

Stifled relief filled the cave as the diviner commenced to chant, sightless eyes staring skyward in contained anticipation. He sighed, knowing Ademola had arrived. "Sit down, my son. Give me the kolanut and kaolin!" The diviner hastily placed the old kolanut and kaolin on Jason's chest. The kolanut became luminous and the kaolin, infected with the luminosity, lit up with equal radiance. Hair-thin rays shot out of the objects and connected to the other four kolanuts which shriveled and darkened upon contact.

The sound of Jason's heartbeat filled the inside of the cave. Then just as suddenly, a silence enlarged the gloom. Everyone looked up as though expecting a full moon to light up the sky. It didn't. The wind became quiet.

"What?" McFlarthey whispered in the dark upon hearing the voice of the diviner as it invaded his thought.

"Just listen to your hearts," the diviner said.

"I—I will," Kathleen said.

McFlarthey heard her voice. "What's going on?" he enquired, confused.

Kathleen also heard her husband's voice as though he spoke.

"Congratulations to all of you." The diviner's voice pierced the thoughts of everyone present. "We have all been privileged to experience the ultimate gift—the power of omniscience: the ability to read each other's mind. That which is the exclusive purview of the Creator is now ours for a short while. As we commence this journey to the land of the children yet unborn, we shall perceive the glory of creation, and hopefully appreciate the folly of mankind's obsession: the need to be on equal footing with God."

The sound of the jungle and the ubiquitous concert of insects filled the air. Birds cawed overhead, flying in circles, their flapping wings adding fluted rhythm to the symphony.

The music became a spirit vehicle transporting everyone from the floor of the cave. The luminous rays from the kolanut and kaolin made everything unreal as forms and shapes dissolved into a black cloud.

They were transported away only to emerge into the Other World. All around everything was darker. The music changed. Human voices, several thousands, *a cappella*, serenaded them as they passed through invisible doors of black clouds that opened to yet blacker doors at dizzying speed. They screeched to a stop in front of the blackest cloud, a solid wall.

The musical voices stopped as a speck, the size of a pinhead, glowed at the center of the wall. The speck grew, breathing, as it became a human male fetus. It spoke. The old Yoruba words were like the sound of ceremonial drums, rhythmical and captivating: "*E kaabo o.*"

A female fetus with a pair of slanted eyes joined the boy, smiling as her lips parted, "*Bo ku cai.*" Yet another boy, smooth black skin glistening, said, "*Uno abiala.*"

They were joined by a pair with dark, almond-shaped eyes and longer noses, "*Brukhum Habaem, Marhaba.*" Together, three more, "*Karibuni, Velkommen, Pasok.*"

Holding hands in a circular dance, four more emerged, "*Kalosorisette, Hosh Geldiniz, Hwan Young Hap Lea Da, Bienvenue!*"

"*Bienvenida, Wilkommen, Dobro Pojhalovat,*" added three more voices.

They came and greeted the visitors from the land of the Living, in all the languages that humans have ever spoken.

Finally, in a crescendo, all the voices erupted into a symphony: "*WELCOME!*"

Everything became still.

A lone voice, ageless, sexless, and divine, pierced the silence, "Welcome!"

"Oh, my—are we in the presence of—"

"NO!" the voice answered Kathleen's unfinished question.

Kathleen's eyes misted, "B—but—"

"Jason, come forward."

Jason got on his feet and seemed to levitate toward the center of the black wall. His fifteen-month old body changed into a fetus, umbilical cord in his hand. He then turned upside down, assuming a fetal position ready to be delivered. The pink skin was covered with *vernix caseosa* with almost all the lanugo hairs already shed. The umbilical cord stretched from the center of the abdomen with its tip glued to the left eye. A gentle humming sound ensued. Then the dark wall behind him exploded into a million snowflakes. He pressed harder and the screen cleared, sharp color images emerged:

Jason's tiny body was pulled from between Kathleen's legs, flat on her back in a hospital delivery room. Jason's cord was cut and a cry emerged from his tiny lips. The images on the screen scanned through Jason's development until the age of twenty-eight years. He was handsome, brilliant, reckless and self-destructive, deprived of nothing. He became the richest and the most powerful man in the world. His empire and network was universal. His wealth fueled his ambition and inflated his already fragile ego. He did not just threaten. He ordered. And out of fear was obeyed. His uncountable armies of employees scattered all over the world pillaging the earth. He added a sophisticated and most destructive weapon to his arsenal. The neutron bomb. A homolosine projection of planet Earth appeared on the screen. The light of many suns arose from the bowels of the earth, a gargantuan white mushroom-cloud towered over the entire globe and the screen turned black.

"Amazing." The voice reverberated. To the ears of the human visitors, it was the voice of the generic Man, sexless, ageless, and accentless in its crispness and resonance. "It is amazing that the planet that has existed for millions of years can be destroyed so easily? The richest and most beautiful planet bequeathed to mankind is destroyed by pressing a plastic button. That was the future that is also the past."

Jason's mission was to stop the madness! But en route to earth, his program was altered by the *entity* that controls the darker side of universal existence.

"Like the *dark force*, we need planet Earth. But for a different reason. *He* wants it devoid of humans, we need it for the life that exists there. Our survival is tied to the continued existence of humans on Earth. This is the world of the *Abikus*. The Yorubas know this cosmos is inhabited by the most intelligent children that visit your world. We do not create or destroy, only incubate and nourish. When our children are ready, we send them to Earth, the only planet that needs them. Once there, they share their specific message with humans who then use the intelligence to create, discover, or pioneer any of numerous inventions or ideas that make your world a better place. But they must return to the land of their nativity before their second birthday anniversary. Some are prevented from coming back by knowledgeable diviners. That we don't mind as long as the parents appreciate the fact that all children chose their parents before their births. And for that reason, the parents must show their appreciation by doing the right things in raising their offspring. Whenever they fail in their parental obligations, the children become easy targets, and they are thus recruited by *him*. Unfortunately, the worst atrocities on Earth are perpetuated by some of our children whose programmed assignments are altered by *him*."

Immediately the screen was filled with tiny snowflakes. The fetus that was Jason pulled the cord away from his left eye and a beautiful smile radiated from the face. Still clutching the cord in his hand, he turned and assumed a sitting position.

Fifteen-month-old Jason McFlarthey levitated back to the floor and everything became still again.

31

The cave lit up as though someone had switched on a hundred fluorescent lamps. The master diviner crinkled his nose as if wishing to rid himself of the overpowering smell of mildewed *iroko* tree bark, decaying leaves, and the sweet and pungent fragrances of jungle flowers. The distant sound of the rain splashing against the floor of the forest and the whipping of the wind against leaves and branches reaffirmed their return from the dark realm of *Abikus*.

Jason's body stirred, his ashen face regained color and a radiant smile appeared. He opened his eyes, stared at the ceiling, and was about to get up from the raffia mat when the diviner reached out a hand to cover the old kolanut on his chest. The luminosity disappeared.

"Your son is in good health and here to stay until he grows old." The diviner took the kolanut and kaolin off Jason's chest and handed them to Ademola. "You are now the custodian of the power that sustains life. Be careful with it, my son," he said as Awoyinka helped him to his wobbly legs. "You must all get out of here. There is no safe place in this country for you." He held onto Awoyinka. "Take me to my bed. I need to rest."

McFlarthey embraced Jason. His voice cracked when he said, "Is he going to be okay?"

"Yes, so is the other one soon to be born." The diviner's

voice smiled in the dark.

Ademola pocketed the kolanut and kaolin. He struck a match and guided the flame with the cup of his hand to light the *atupa* on the floor beside the diviner's raffia mat.

"Please tell the diviner that I am forever in his debt," McFlarthey said.

Ademola did.

The diviner dismissed him with a wave of his bony hand. "You must hurry!" He pointed to the rough wall. "That's your exit. Do not go out the same way you came in."

"That's a solid wall. How can we go through it?" Wayne asked.

Ademola glared at him.

"What!" Wayne's hands shot forward, palms up, looking like a kindergartner caught using a four-letter word in the presence of the principal.

"Don't mind him, my son. That's your only way out of here. *Dokito*, show them what to do," the diviner said.

Awoyinka stepped forward and deftly pried a rock the size of a football off the wall. Sultry air wafted through the hole. "Help me with this," he said over his shoulder to Ademola. The two men pried more rocks off the wall. They stopped when the hole became large enough for Kathleen to walk through. She was followed by Wayne.

"Thank you very much, my friend." McFlarthey's voice was thick with emotion.

"Give me the child for a second," the diviner said in Yoruba, his eyes staring at McFlarthey.

As though he understood the language, Jason thrashed his legs, unclasped his grip from around his father's neck in an attempt to jump to the ground.

"Easy!" McFlarthey cautioned, setting him on his feet.

Jason walked unsteadily into the outstretched hands of the diviner. The two engaged in a tight embrace that lasted a few seconds. "The world is a marketplace we visit, the other world is home," the diviner said in old Yoruba. He then let go. He reached under the mat and extracted a bundle which he handed to Jason. "You can't go out there into the world naked as you are." A gracious smile rimmed his eyes.

Jason smiled back, accepting the gift.

"Goodbye, my son." The diviner let go with reluctance.

Jason reached forward and kissed him on the forehead before returning to his father who unwrapped the bundle. He smiled. "Thank you very much," he said to the diviner and quickly helped his son to put on the hand-woven beige cotton dashiki which reached to Jason's ankles.

Ademola knelt beside the diviner. "Now that I've completed my assignment, I wish to visit my family before going back to America."

The diviner did not speak for a while. Staring into the darkness, he rubbed his palm over the back of his left hand. He turned to stare at Ademola as though he saw him. There was sadness in his voice when he finally said, "One whom a rabid dog is chasing does not tarry. You have a dangerous enemy that would stop at nothing until he kills you. You must leave with the boy and his family. Your father will— and your mother will be happy to hear that you are in good health."

A sudden chill went up Ademola's spine. "But—"

"There's no but, son, you must hurry."

Ademola held the diviner's hand and squeezed. He got up and was about to follow McFlarthey out through the opening when the diviner said, "It's a long walk through the secret passage to the other side of town, son. There's a stream at the foot of the hill. Follow it for half an hour and you will be twenty minutes away from the airport."

"Thank you." Ademola bent to pick up a rock then froze. Femi! He dropped the rock and dashed through the opening toward the entrance.

"Where are you going?" the diviner's voice trailed behind him, bouncing off the walls of the cave.

"I can't leave Femi behind!" Chest pounding, he prayed that Eniola's brother was still alive.

~

Sakara's unbelieving eyes rounded when he saw the silhouette of a man between the legs of the tree. He stared at him for a moment. "It's the bastard! This time you will not escape, son of a whore." He pulled out his revolver and calculated the distance between him and his target. He raised the gun, aiming it at Ademola's legs.

Ademola shifted suddenly and looked in Sakara's direction. "Femi." His was voice barely above the sound of the rain splashing against the leaves and the forest ground.

Sakara froze, a predator readying for the spring. "So Eniola's brother was nearby. Two birds caught with the fling of a stone," he mused, with heightened hatred.

"Femi, it's me, Ademola. Come over here!"

Nothing.

Ademola shook his head and stepped out of the legs of the tree. He tip-toed toward the shrubbery behind which Sakara was hiding. He stopped a couple of yards away and wiped the water off his face. His eyes darted left and right, searching the darkness in front of him.

Like a famished lion after a vulnerable waterhog, Sakara sprang from behind the shrubbery. Ademola turned but it was too late. Sakara's clenched left fist landed on the back of Ademola's neck, stunning him. He lurched forward but Sakara prevented him from falling to the ground by grabbing the collar of his shirt. "There's no escape for you," he hissed between breaths. The shock and fear on Ademola's face fed Sakara's hunger for vengeance. "There's no better time than now to even the score!"

"Why, Seg—"

"Shut up!" He pressed the muzzle of the revolver against Ademola's ribs. "This time, you are all mine."

"Please, just tell me, why are you doing this?"

"That's the most asinine question yet," Sakara spat.

"What are you talking about?"

"We all pay for our deeds."

"What deed?"

"Well, it is true that those who defecate on the footpath forget, but the one that steps on it does not. Your selective memory is further proof of my point."

"What point? Segun, I don't know what this is all about." Ademola failed to pry Sakara's choking grip from around his neck.

"I see now that you're not only a bastard, you are also a bloody liar."

"Okay, I give up, sometimes a liar does not only believe his lies, he often forgets them. So why don't you remind me?"

"I liked you, I trusted you, I even respected your intelligence. But you took all that away when you and that scumbag Crowder conspired to ruin my life in 1963." Sakara began to have difficulty breathing. Confronting Ademola finally was proving to be more taxing than he had imagined.

"Conspired?"

"Don't insult my intelligence with your amnesia, you bastard."

"You really have to believe me, Segun, I don't know what you're talking about."

"I failed the final exam at the end of our first year at Mayfield and you know why." Sakara tightened the grip on Ademola's neck.

"Be—because you didn't study," Ademola choked, gasping for breath.

"No, you bastard! It was because—"

413

"Stop calling me bastard!"

"But you are. Your mother *was* a whore!"

Ademola bunched a fist and with deadly force slammed it against Sakara's left temple. A shot rang out as Sakara pulled the trigger. The bullet missed Ademola's head, smashing against the trunk of the three-legged tree. Ademola grabbed Sakara's wrist, just as the second shot rang out. Sakara's choke-hold loosened, enabling Ademola to sink his teeth into his assailant's wrist. Sakara let go of the gun which fell to the wet ground. He extricated himself from Ademola and descended on him like a tornado, landing vicious blows to his face and neck, kicking his stomach, a feral animal with an insatiable thirst for blood. Ademola fell to his knees, his hands spread out like a blind spider in a futile attempt to parry the blows. Blood snaked down from his nose, and his left eye looked like an over-ripe, half-eaten guava. The right eye hadn't fared better. But he took the pounding without any attempt to run away. He remained pinned down on his knees as Sakara, now panting, delivered more punches.

"You will join your whoring mother and my fornicating father soon," Sakara said between labored breaths. "Do you know what I did to your mother? I buried a six-inch dagger between her breasts. The whore is dead and her charred body is buried in an unmarked grave. I wish I had the time to show you, but I must hurry back to Lagos. I have a country to run." He landed a bone-crushing fist on Ademola's shoulder blade, cracking it. Ademola groaned and fell face down to the ground. Sakara bent over, turned Ademola over on his back. "You and your stupid arrogance, always acting as though you are better than everyone. Get up, bastard! Yes, my fornicating father was right about the gun vanquishing the pen. And I hold the biggest gun in my hand, ready to destroy pseudo-intellectuals like you. I will use my power to help the poor masses of this great country—"

Ademola grunted. "Liar." He tried to get up.

Sakara booted him in the stomach.

"I will kill you." Ademola doubled up and used his arms to block Sakara's kick.

"I thought a good angel like you would never think of killing his fellow man," Sakara derided.

"I am good because I am bad, idiot!"

"Come again?" Sakara stopped.

"The reason I am good is because deep down inside me I've always known how bad I am. It is fools like you who think that they are so good inside they don't have to be nice to others. But you're wrong! With all your guns, you're nothing but a no-good weakling. Crowder was right about you. You're stupid. Dumb enough to fall for his antics at Mayfield. I knew about it after the fact. But you can believe whatever you choose." Ademola staggered to his knees and was about to get on his feet when Sakara landed a crushing blow to the side of his face, knocking him unconscious.

Consumed with a renewed rage, Sakara did not see Femi rushing out of hiding, fist clenched around the butt of a gun which he raised high above his head. But Sakara sensed something behind him. Like a seasoned stalker, he spun around and caught Femi's hand in midair. With the frenzy of a feasting lion intruded upon by a scavenging night marauder, Sakara charged at Femi, and with a mortal punch, knocked him unconscious. He pressed the gun against Femi's upturned forehead, started to pull the trigger, then stopped, shaking his head. "Not yet, I'll be back" he promised. Chest pounding, he raced down the hill to the fallen *iroko* tree blocking the footpath. "Why hasn't my foolish *ADC* gotten here yet with the bomb to blast the cannibals in the cave to bits," he fumed. "I must hurry before Ademola and Femi regain consciousness. Blasting bullets through their skulls would be compassionate. They must die slowly in excruciating pain."

He raced toward the headlights of Achibong's jeep that

lit the forest ground. He saw another pair of yellow lights darting behind the jeep. Using his hand as a visor to lessen the glare of the lights, he squinted and then took a deep breath when he recognized that the approaching vehicle was his Range Rover. His hands went up in the air, beckoning his *ADC* toward him. He waited, resting his foot on the trunk of the tree that had fallen in front of Achibong's jeep. He hastily looked at his Rolex watch; the dial read five seconds before 2010 hours.

"Come on!" he said between clenched teeth. His mental calculation warned him that he barely had enough time to plant the bomb in the cave and be back to Lagos for the press conference which would introduce him to the world as the commander-in-chief and military head of state of the Federal Republic of Nigeria.

Instantly, his instinct short-circuited his emotional desire for vengeance. Like an antelope catching the scent of a prowling predator in the air, he jerked his head up to stare at the jeep again. "Oh my God! That's Achibong's jeep." His mouth opened, eyes widened in horror as he remembered that he had instructed his dead assistant to prepare a bomb to be used to blow up the cave tonight. "The bomb can't—" He sprang from the tree, dashed to the jeep, and yanked the door open.

His crossed eyes burrowed into the bridge of his nose as his head filled with voices:

"Please let me touch my baby," his mother pleaded.

"One does not get so red in the eyes with anger that one is able to light a cigarette with the fire," his father warned him.

"Damn you to hell," Ademola's mother cursed.

"Segun, I was forced to betray you. We're both victims," Eniola cried.

"Daddy, please, don't hurt my mommy," Kehinde pleaded.

"The bomb is timed to detonate at 2010 hours, sir," Achibong said with a sharp salute.

"N—N—No—" Sakara stuttered, glaring at the shoebox in the back seat of Achibong's black jeep a split-second before what sounded like a volcanic eruption deafened the forest, and a conflagration flared.

↜

Inside the cave, the master diviner held his breath as the bomb blast reverberated, shaking the hills like a powerful earthquake. He sat cross-legged looking like a Buddha on a diet. Moments later, he started to chant. Then there were footsteps. His blind eyes which looked like the ripe fruits from the *akee* tree stared into the darkness. "Welcome, my children." His voice was full of life.

"Thank you, my venerable master." Ademola approached the diviner with Femi limping along.

"You know the way out of here through the secret exit, my son, God is with you." The diviner pointed at the gaping hole on the wall of the cave. "Don't forget to put the rocks back where they belong." As they made their way through the opening, the diviner whispered into the darkness:

"*Ohun ti o yi paari ki i tan…*
   Ipade wa bi oyin."

(What has not finished does not end…
   Our reunion will be sweet as honey…)

November, 1994
P.W.P.
U.S.C.
Los Angeles.

417

ACKNOWLEDGEMENT

My special thanks go to Dr. Ola Olambiwonnu and Dr. Hargurmeet Sandhu for lending their expertise in the field of pediatric critical care and pulmonology, Mr. Shelly Lowenkopf, who is ever-so-chagrined by "mediocrity when a best-seller is in the offing," and Dr. Diane de Avalle-Arce, my tireless editors and copy editor whose enthusiastic assistance helped make Abiku a pleasurable read. Mr. Abe Polsky, Ms. Tony Jaymes-Wayman, and Mrs. Ana Craven for editing.

My thanks also go to Dr. Ayo Akingbemi, Ms. Reena Singh, Lieutenant Colonel Olu Bamgbose, Dr. Dapo Popoola, Mrs. Delores Olambiwonnu, Ms. Serena Soltes, Ms. Adele Horwitz, Mr. Mat Pallamary, Mrs. Maria Rodriguez-Vargas, Mrs. Ruksana Mohammed, Ms. Catherine Ryan-Hyde, Ms. Bonnie Detweiler, Mr. Gary Tokunaga, Master Ali Ezzani-Kotun, Ms. Susie Wallenstein and Mrs. Linda Santora Noureldin for reviewing the manuscript and providing many valuable suggestions. And last but not least, Mrs. Miriam Ezzani-Kotun, who read, typed, re-read, edited, and retyped the original manuscript and the innumerable rewrites that followed.

ABOUT THE AUTHOR

Debo Kotun was born in Lagos, Nigeria in 1948 and according to Yoruba belief, he was expected to die before age two. But with the timely intervention of *babalawos*, spiritual diviners, he survived and emigrated to the United States in 1971. He studied at Johns Hopkins University, Yale, and the New School for Social Research. *Abiku*, his first book, won the 1995 Phi Kappa Phi Award at the University of Southern California. He is currently working on "Dada," the first sequel to *Abiku*, in Los Angeles.